DREAMING AGAIN

HOLLYWOOD LEGENDS BOOK FOUR

≈

MARY J. WILLIAMS

© 2016

ABOUT THE AUTHOR

Writing isn't easy. But I love every second. A blank screen isn't the enemy. It is the opportunity to create new friends and take them on amazing adventures and life-changing journeys. I feel blessed to spend my days weaving tales that are unique—because I made them.

Billionaires. Songwriters. Artists. Actors. Directors. Stuntmen. Football players. They fill the pages and become dear friends I hope you will want to revisit again and again.

Thank you for jumping into my books and coming along for the journey.

HOW TO GET IN TOUCH

Please visit me at these sites, sign up for my newsletter or leave a message.

http://www.maryjwilliams.net/home.html
https://www.facebook.com/maryjwilliamsauthor
https://twitter.com/maryjwilliams05
https://www.pinterest.com/maryj0675/
https://instagram.com/2015romance/
https://www.goodreads.com/author/show/5648619.Mary_J_Williams

MORE BOOKS BY MARY J. WILLIAMS

Harper Falls Series
If I Loved You
If Tomorrow Never Comes
If You Only Knew
If I Had You (Christmas in Harper Falls)

Hollywood Legends Series
Dreaming with a Broken Heart
Dreaming with My Eyes Wide Open
Dreaming Again
Dreaming of a White Christmas (Caleb and Callie's story)
(Coming in December)

One Pass Away Series
After the Rain
After All These Years
After the Fire

Hart of Rock and Roll
Flowers on the Wall (coming in August)

TABLE OF CONTENTS

PROLOGUE

WYATT LANDIS BREATHED in the fresh air through the open window of his Ford flatbed pickup truck. Every season had its own scent. He realized that the early days of fall with the warm days and crisp nights smelled different in the mountains than in the city. On the radio, the classic rock station provided him with the perfect musical accompaniment to an adventure he hadn't asked for but now embraced with surprising alacrity.

Push him and Wyatt pushed back. The only ones who could move him were his family. Love and guilt. They were a difficult combination to outmaneuver.

In Los Angeles, he kept his windows rolled up and the air conditioner blasting. Even if he had thought of taking the time for a leisurely drive, the air quality wasn't up to these standards.

The road ahead was empty. Nothing but mountains on both sides of him. Behind, he had left his job, his family, and the day-to-day pressures—most of which he put on himself. His demons weren't as easy to outrun, but with each mile that passed, he felt a weight lifting.

If he could find a way to leave his dreams in the dust, this trip would be a complete success.

Wyatt slowed for a curve. The bright afternoon sun bounced off the truck's hood, the shiny red paint intensifying the effect. His sunglasses were little help. Man could invent only so many tools to combat Mother Nature. In the end, when she wanted her way, there was nothing you could do. Wyatt couldn't see. And no amount of squinting or shading the glare with his hand helped.

The unfamiliar road made things worse. Wyatt knew there was only one solution, but before he could bring the vehicle to a stop, something appeared in front of him. He swerved to the right, the tires catching in the loose gravel on the side of the road. Try as he might,

1

there was no way to prevent disaster. His seatbelt kept him in place, but the truck was out of his control.

Wyatt's vision cleared just in time for him to see the tree he was about to hit. A huge, solid pine that looked like, in a battle of metal against wood, it would easily be the victor.

One last thought flashed through his mind just before impact. If this were karma? Punishment for letting himself relax and feel an optimism he hadn't felt in a long time? Then Wyatt agreed with the experts. Payback was one nasty bitch.

HOW MUCH TIME had passed, he didn't know. His head was killing him, and something wet ran down his face. He wanted to open his eyes, but it took too much effort.

Frowning, Wyatt thought he heard a voice. A woman. Not anyone he knew—he was certain of that. But there was something about it. Something that made him want... more.

When the voice faded away, Wyatt groaned. He tried to reach out and call her back. *Don't go. Stay with me.* But the words wouldn't come.

"Stay still. An ambulance is on the way."

It took a herculean effort, but Wyatt managed to open his eyes. Blinking once, then twice, he tried to focus on the shadowy figure leaning over him.

"There you are." The words were followed by a laugh—sweet and warm. "Don't move until the EMTs check you out. That was quite a crash. The tree won, by the way."

His vision was still blurry, but for a single moment, it cleared. He saw a halo of blond hair and the honey brown eyes—the kind a man could lose himself in.

"Are you an angel?" he slurred.

She laughed again. "Sorry, buddy. Not even close."

Wyatt would have argued. Her laugh alone sounded like it had been sent from heaven. But when he opened his mouth, no words came out. The world spun around, making him slightly nauseous.

The image of his angel blurred. Panicked that she would disappear, he tried to reach out to her. To his consternation, he couldn't raise his hand.

"Easy. You're going to be fine," she assured him.

Wyatt thought as she smoothed back his hair. Her touch calmed him and once more he tried to speak. But this time, it wasn't simply the words that wouldn't come. He couldn't stay awake. His eyes grew heavy and slowly, though he tried his damnedest to keep her in view, his angel slipped away.

CHAPTER ONE

"YOU NEED TO stop, Wyatt."

"Dad—"

Caleb Landis shook his head. This was his son—his first born. He loved him with all his heart. Unfortunately, he was too much like his father. Or at least the man he had been before he met and fell in love with Wyatt's mother.

Caleb knew what made Wyatt tick. That driving ambition to be one step ahead. It fueled his waking hours to the exclusion of everything else. Wyatt had the added impetus of a marriage that ended tragically. Though he denied it, Caleb suspected that Wyatt had kept a lot of the details to himself. No matter how his mother pushed, he remained silent.

Of all of his sons, Wyatt was the most reticent. His feelings were harder to decipher. His son ran from demons Caleb could only guess at. It hurt to watch his child suffer, knowing there was nothing he could do. Or rather, nothing he would let him do.

The endless hours Wyatt spent wheeling and dealing started to take their toll. A few hours a week spent with his parents and his brothers weren't enough of a break. Wyatt needed a prolonged respite. Convincing him wouldn't be easy, but Caleb held a trump card. One that was impossible to ignore.

"Your mother is worried."

Wyatt rolled his eyes. With a sigh, he met his father's gaze. Deep blue, like his own. There were other physical traits that left no doubt to his paternity. The tall, lean frame that Wyatt worked hard to keep that way. Unlike his brothers, he spent long hours behind a desk. His daily visit to the gym kept his muscles strong and his mind sharp. Sharp enough to know how to outmaneuver an old fox like his father.

"You can't pull that one, Dad. Mom doesn't need you delivering her messages. If she's worried, she'll tell me. What is this really about?"

Caleb's eyes grew serious.

"You want it straight?"

"When have I not?"

"Fine. Your mother has been too busy to notice, but as soon as Callie returns from Venice, she will. *I'm* worried. So are your brothers." Caleb didn't sit. He slapped his palms on Wyatt's desk, leaning forward. "Something has changed. You were getting better—relaxing. We thought you had finally put Stephanie behind you."

"I have," Wyatt insisted. Apart from the nightmares that popped up without warning. But he didn't share that with his father.

"Then what's going on? The last-minute family dinner cancellations are bad enough. According to Colt, he can't pin you down for a simple beer. Nate and Garrett tell the same story."

"My brothers have big mouths. I don't hang out with them, and their egos are bent out of shape? Well, boo hoo."

"This is exactly what I'm talking about." Caleb dropped into the chair opposite Wyatt's desk. "The four of you always hang out. The fact that my boys are friends is one of my greatest joys. Brothers don't always get along. You, Garrett, Nate, and Colt are tight. You always have been."

"You're reading too much into it, Dad. Movies don't get made on their own—you know that better than most. I'm not avoiding anyone. I'm busy. That's all. Sometimes a cigar is just a cigar."

"At my busiest, I have always found time for my family. And don't throw Freud at me. You know I hate that shit."

"What did you say?" Wyatt asked, tongue in cheek.

"Shit," Caleb said with emphatic glee. "When Callie is out of town, I cuss like a sailor. It's the only chance I get."

Wyatt's mother, the legendary screen beauty, Callie Flynn, did her best to keep the men in her life from cursing. She didn't always succeed, but around her, they made a concerted effort to tone down their language. PG only. Occasionally one of them slipped, but not often. The goal of every Landis man was to make Callie happy. Not because she demanded it. Because they adored her.

"Have I been a good father?"

"The best."

Wyatt meant it. Caleb had always been a hands-on father, taking pleasure in spending time with his children. He never acted as though it was an obligation or duty. The Landis household was filled with love and laughter. That had been true the day Wyatt was born, and it was still true—almost thirty-three years later.

"Then do as I ask. Step back for a week or two. This company won't fall apart if your nose isn't to the grindstone eighteen hours a day."

"But—"

"I started Landis Productions before I met your mother. God, what was that?" Shaking his head, Caleb let out a long breath. "Over forty years ago. I think I can keep things afloat until you get back."

I don't want to go, Wyatt wanted to shout. These days, work was the only thing keeping him sane. Down time meant an idle mind. His brain was filled with a labyrinth of bad memories and guilt. Sleep was bad enough. The thought of long, empty hours with nothing to do but *relax,* terrified him.

"I'm in the middle of negotiations to acquire the rights to J. L. Winter's newest bestseller. Every production company in Hollywood wants to get their hands on *Left of Mayfield*. It doesn't help that the author is a recluse. I don't even know if J. L. is a man or a woman. Getting a meeting is impossible. Everything has to be done by phone. With the agent."

"What will happen if we lose the bidding war?"

"What do you mean?" Lose? Wyatt tried to wrap his mind around the concept. When he wanted something, it became his. Caleb was the same. Or *had* been. Was his father getting soft?

"Will it be the end of the world if, one time, Landis Productions misses out?"

6

"Yes."

Caleb laughed. "Just checking. I agree. Besides, your mother wants to play the lead."

Wyatt knew that. It was a juicy part. Perfect for Callie Flynn. His mother wasn't only a pretty face. She could act. No. That was putting it mildly. She was one of the most respected actresses of her, or any, generation. She had two Academy Awards to prove it. Done right, by Landis Productions, *Left of Mayfield* would put her in the running for a third.

"Colt is pushing hard to play Callie's son," Wyatt smiled. "And I thought he wanted to avoid typecasting."

Mother and son playing mother and son. Superstars. The legend and the one in the making. The press—and the public—would eat it up.

"When the part is that juicy, I guess he's willing to risk it."

"There you go. If we want to keep Mom and baby brother happy, I should stay and finish securing our rights to the book. Do you want to tell her if it falls through?"

"Callie's done this long enough to understand. And Colton can withstand a little professional disappointment."

Wyatt didn't argue. About his mother, or Colt, or the vacation. He knew better. There were times when Caleb Landis could be persuaded to change his mind—he wasn't an unreasonable man. Wyatt was his son. Plus, he had worked beside his father long enough to know that this wasn't one of those times.

Sitting back in his chair, he met Caleb's gaze and sighed.

"When do I have to leave?"

"WHEN DAD SAID take a vacation, he meant for you to grab a week in Tahiti. Or Aspen. Not buy a used truck and drive God knows where."

"Tahiti isn't what it used to be. And I went to Aspen last fall. Hand me that blue sweater."

Frowning, Colt tossed it onto the bed. Silently, he watched while Wyatt packed one medium-sized bag. Not enough for several weeks away from home. Colt took more for an overnighter. It had him worried. No, that was too strong a word. Uneasy might be a better way of putting it. Why would a man pack for less than a week when the plan was for at least three—maybe more?

"I know what you're thinking." Wyatt zipped the bag. "Is he mentally stable enough to go off on his own? I'm not suicidal, asshole."

"I wasn't worried about your state of mind. I wondered if we really had the same genes. Three shirts and two pairs of jeans? It's the end of civilization as we know it."

"But Mom will be happy to know that I packed plenty of clean underwear."

"Who packs dirty underwear?"

He shoved the suitcase at Colt with more force than necessary. "You're lucky you've found a woman who puts up with your less than stellar sense of humor. And this isn't my only bag. There's a bigger one, already packed, in the closet."

"Sable's in love with my body," Colt said with a straight face, but his blue eyes sparkled with laughter—and relief. "The day I develop a paunch, she's out the door."

"Then you better hit the gym. You've found a gem; do whatever it takes to keep her happy."

"Wyatt—"

"No." Wyatt shook his head, taking the case from the closet. "We aren't going down that road. Not again. Bring my bag. I need to grab some water from the fridge."

"You know, if you had told me what kind of burr crawled up your ass the past few weeks, Dad wouldn't have kicked you out of your office."

"No burr."

Wyatt filled a cooler with bottles of water. His refrigerator didn't have much else in it. A couple of beers and what looked like a dried-up piece of cheese. He rarely ate at home so there was no need to stock up on groceries. If he wasn't ordering takeout at the office, he was having dinner at his parents' house. The state of the art appliance looked nice in his remodeled kitchen, but it didn't get a lot of use.

"Then what's wrong?"

"I love you, Colt. You're the best brother I could ask for. I feel the same about Garrett and Nate. So when I say this, I hope you won't be offended." He met Colt's gaze. "Back off."

"That's it?" Colt followed him out the front door. "I was expecting more. Hell, now I know there's something wrong. You can't even work up a good insult."

Colt was right. They were a close-knit family. It was impossible to keep a problem secret because someone he loved would nudge him, aka badger relentlessly, until he spilled his guts. If he didn't speak with his parents, Wyatt had three brothers willing to listen. More often than not, Wyatt turned to Colt, and vice versa.

Despite the five-year age difference, they were extremely close. Perhaps because Garrett and Nate were twins. Or maybe it was that deep down, in spite of the way it looked on the surface, Wyatt and Colt had similar personalities.

Colt came across as charming and carefree, but when it came to something he wanted, he was as ruthless as Wyatt.

However, the source of Wyatt's unrest was not something he could share with his brother. Or any of his family. It was the real reason he had agreed to take time off. His dilemma was one he had to come to terms with—on his own.

"Maybe when I get back." Wyatt waited while Colt loaded his suitcase onto the floor of the truck's passenger side before adding the larger one. "You don't need to worry. I need some time alone."

"Call me once a day." Colt gave him a hug, patting him hard on the back. He eyed the faded red truck, feeling another wave of unease. Wyatt drove a Bentley. Classy. Old school. The old Ford was not his usual style.

"Once a week," Wyatt countered.

"Every other day."

Wyatt laughed. The kid was used to getting his own way. Women swooned over his pretty face and men were charmed by his—well, his charm. Wyatt had fallen victim to it himself more often than he liked to admit. But not this time.

"Once a week." When Colt would have argued, Wyatt cut him off. "Be smart and let it go, or I won't call at all."

"Stubborn bastard."

"Takes one to know one."

"True," Colt grinned back. "It's a Landis family trait."

"I'll see you in a few weeks. A month at the most."

When Wyatt started the truck, Colt tapped on the opposite side window, motioning for him to roll it down.

"Drive safe and don't pick up hitchhikers."

"Yes, Mom."

"Hey."

Wyatt shot Colt an impatient look. Always the actor, his brother loved to draw out a scene.

"I love you, man."

Well, hell. How could he be pissed off at that?

"I love you, too. Take care. And give Sable a kiss for me."

Knowing Wyatt's affection for his fiancée, Colt tried one more time. "Will you call *Sable* every other day?"

"Goodbye."

Still laughing, Wyatt pulled the truck onto the highway and headed east. He let his family think his trip had no planned pattern or destination. But he knew exactly where he was going.

Agreeing to get out of his office was one thing. Leaving work behind completely was another. He would keep his promise and find time to relax. However, who said he couldn't mix a little business with his pleasure?

JOIE TRENT LIKED small town life. Most of the time.

She was a big-city girl who three years ago stumbled across a little piece of heaven and never left. The sign on the outskirts of town read: *Welcome to Monroe, Nevada. Population Eight Hundred and Sixty*. That number rarely fluctuated more than three or four in a given year. Death or birth. One taken away, one added.

Monroe was a tight-knit community. Privacy was respected. Though, as with any small town, gossip was a favorite pastime. Joie thought her days of being the subject of speculation were over. After three years, she had settled in nicely. She had a small circle of friends but held a nodding acquaintance with almost everyone. They accepted her as one of them. Today, she wondered if that was a good thing.

"Why are you making this difficult?"

"Me?" Joie looked from her best friend to the others gathered at the *Monarch Café—Queenie's* to the locals. "I left my home, believing I could stop in for a cup of coffee, and you ambush me with this? How does that make me difficult?"

"You said no," Carole Fletcher countered. "One little yes, and all will be good."

Carole had been the first person Joie met in Monroe. Bold, brash, and never shy to speak her mind, the curvy redhead was always ready for a good time. Since Joie tried to go through life with the same attitude, the women had hit it off immediately.

A flat tire had brought Joie to Monroe. Carole and the feeling that she had come home had kept her there.

"We are friends." Joie knew she was stating the obvious, but she was making a point.

"Since day one," Carole nodded.

Joie gave her a sweet smile—one a cobra would use just before it struck its prey. If a cobra could smile.

"Friends don't ask friends to prostitute themselves."

Joie saw the shock in Carole's eyes. The sentiment echoed throughout the café.

"Prostitute!" Waldo Strickland sputtered. "Prostitute?" He looked around, his voice rising with every word. "Did she say, prostitute? I… What…?" He threw up his hands, obviously at a loss for words. For Waldo, a man who could talk the ear off a corpse, that was saying something.

"See what you've done?" Slowly shaking her head, Carole patted Waldo's shoulder in what Joie could only call an overdone show of sympathy. "This poor old man asks so little of life. A warm place to lay his head. A good meal. And a place to watch his favorite band on Founder's Day. Waldo's time is waning. Are you so selfish that you would deny him this small comfort?"

"Waldo turned fifty last month. He's healthy as a horse and has more interests than all of us put together. Dial down the guilt trip, Carole. I'm immune."

They both knew that wasn't true. For all her carefree attitude, Joie's emotions ran deep. She cared about others. Not what they thought about her—those days were long gone. But she hated to see someone in pain, or in need. She would bend over backward—then go the extra mile—if it meant she could make someone's life a little better.

"Cut the crap, Carole." Dexter Brink, chef extraordinaire at the *Monarch Café*, served Joie a cup of coffee and a piece of his famous coffee cake. He was thirty-six years old. His dark hair liberally peppered with gray. Divorced with sole custody of his ten-year-old son, he was madly in love with Carole. Carole hadn't made up her mind if she felt the same. "You don't need to manipulate Joie. She wants what is best for Monroe. Don't you, honey?"

"Is this a piece of cake, or a bribe?" Joie inquired.

"Should I take it back?"

"No." Joie took a quick bite, marking it as hers. "I was just asking."

"The coffee cake comes without any strings," Dexter assured her. "That said, there's a whole one cooling in the back. You can take it home if…"

"Dexter Brink!"

"Sorry." Dexter had the good grace to look embarrassed. "We need that piece of land, Joie. Brad Makepeace is holding it for ransom. Ten thousand dollars? What the hell? He knows he might as well ask for a million."

"It's his land. If he doesn't want a bunch of tourists traipsing around, causing damage, that's his business."

"It's an empty field," Carole reminded her. "He purchased it five years ago and ever since, it has sat there—undeveloped. Why would he object to the town clearing away the weeds and building a temporary bandstand?"

"Did you ask *him*?

"We thought you could do that," Pearl Blaine smiled. The ninety-year-old woman did that much more often now that she had a new set of dentures.

"At dinner," a quiet voice chimed in.

Opal was the shy Blaine sister, having lived in Pearl's shadow most of her eighty-seven years. If she found the gumption to speak up, Joie knew she was fighting a losing battle. She had a soft spot for the Blaines—especially Opal.

"There has to be another way. Brad will expect more than a meal in return for this favor."

"No one expects you to sleep with Brad," Carole said.

"Unless you want to. What?" Nan Dimitri asked when her husband Ike jabbed her in the ribs. "Brad is an attractive man. Single. Charming. Why shouldn't Joie let nature take its course? I say it's a win-win situation. We get the field, and she gets—you know."

"Nan!"

Nan blinked, surprised by Carole's reprimand. "Didn't you say that Joie needed some male companionship? Why shouldn't it be Brad?"

"Did you say that?" Joie demanded.

"Maybe," Carole admitted. "But it was said with love. And was *not* for dissemination."

Joie gave Carole a disapproving look. Her lack of a sex life was an ongoing joke. One that Joie found less amusing the longer it continued. Sex was nice. Great, when done properly. But finding a partner was a bit of a challenge. Men were willing to help out—Brad Makepeace being one of them.

However, she refused to jump into bed, just to scratch an increasingly annoying itch. She wasn't attracted to any of the local men. Brad *was* attractive. And charming. But he didn't ring her bell. To Joie, there was nothing as sad as bad sex. It left her feeling more restless than when she started.

Even if Brad were her last resort, Joie would rather go it alone. She knew how to give herself an orgasm. Something told her that Brad was all about himself. He certainly was that way out of bed. More than once she caught him checking himself out in a plate-glass window on the main street. That was fine—everybody did that now and then. But he did it in the middle of a conversation. It was rude. And self-involved. Why should she believe he would be any different under the sheets?

"I know how much this means to the town." Joie heard herself and wished she had a roll of duct tape handy. But the look of hope in the eyes of her friends stopped her from sealing her mouth shut—in actuality or metaphorically.

"It's one meal." Carole circled Joie's shoulders with her arm, squeezing. "Brad has been asking you out for over two years. Consider this killing two birds with one stone. You are helping your fellow citizens, *and* you're throwing that poor guy a bone."

"Or a boner," Waldo snickered.

"Really?" Pearl punched him in the arm. For a woman who had lived more than nine decades, she packed quite a punch. Enough of one to have Waldo rubbing his arm and apologizing.

"Sorry, Joie."

"Keep that kind of talk for your boy's night poker games," Pearl admonished, not letting Joie get a word in.

"Yes, ma'am," Waldo mumbled, more like a ten-year-old boy than a man whose forties were behind him.

"Are you brokering this deal, or is getting Brad to ask me out up to me?" Joie asked Carole.

"You make it sound like that will be difficult. Brad asks you out every time he sees you. Make sure you cross paths in the next few days, and he will take care of the rest."

"I'll call you the next time he stops in," Dexter said.

"Dating by committee," Joie mumbled as she left the café. "And they say romance is dead."

"Romance is where you can find it." Carole walked with her across Percy Street. "Besides, you never know. Brad may have hidden depths." The women exchanged amused looks. "Okay, maybe not. But the date might be less sucky than you expect."

"Talk about damning something with faint praise." Joie laughed. "I will try to not hate it. That's all I will promise."

"Get Brad to lower his price. What happens after that is up to you."

The town's main thoroughfare didn't bustle with activity. At best, it could be called a trickling stream of traffic. That changed for one week a year during Monroe's Founder's Day celebration. Businesses counted on the influx of tourists. What they made during seven days would tide them over for the rest of the year.

"Where are you off to?" Carole asked as she unlocked the door to her shop.

She sold one-of-a-kind hand-knit items. Everything from oven mitts to baby blankets. Most of her business came from her online store. Her items had become so popular, some high-end department stores carried a line of her clothing. Carole thought it was hilarious when she found out the eye-popping amount of money she could make from one sweater. But after years of barely scraping by, she wasn't going to argue.

"I've been hired for Mikey Lofton's seventh birthday party." Joie took a curly blond wig from her purse, playfully waving it in Carole's face.

"Why?"

"Because I'm damn entertaining."

"I know that," Carole laughed. "I mean why did you agree? Mikey is a spoiled monster. His mother treats him as though he's the second coming. And all those kids hopped up on sugar? You, my friend, are a glutton for punishment."

"It's fun." Joie shrugged. "Besides, I adore birthday cake."

"And never gain an ounce. I think I hate you."

"No, you don't." Joie gave her a hug. "You're coming over for dinner, right?"

"It's binge-watch Wednesday. You couldn't keep me away."

Every Wednesday, Joie and Carole picked a show on Netflix to veg out on. Sometimes they were enthralled. Most of the time, not so much. But it wasn't about the show. It was about spending time together. For a small town, there was always something going on. Between their jobs and civic events, finding time for a best friend could be a challenge. Binge-watch Wednesday was set in stone. Nothing short of illness or a natural disaster kept them away.

Joie slid behind the steering wheel of her car. It had seen better days. Even when it was new, it was nothing fancy. But it got her from point A to point B, and that was all that mattered. She flipped down the sun visor, using the mirror to put on the wig. She didn't take the time to look at herself. Why would she? She saw her reflection every morning while she brushed her teeth.

However, if she could hear what other people thought when they met her, she might be surprised. Joie drew people in. She made friends feel special and strangers feel like friends. Her beauty came from within and shined brightly—through her smile and her personality.

Joie was twenty-eight years old. She stood a little over five feet six inches tall and as Carole had commented, could eat anything and not gain weight. She liked to think of herself as lean—not skinny. There was some hard-earned muscle tone under her button-up blouse and khaki cargo pants.

Several years ago, Joie had decided if she couldn't develop curves, she could at least make the most of what she had. She ran five miles every day and lifted weights three times a week. It hadn't increased the size of her breasts, but she was proud to say that her body was sleek and toned.

Joie had a nice face. Some might call it pretty. She thought her eyes were too big, but as a date once pointed out, why was that a bad thing? They were a nice shade of brown. Like rich honey—warm and expressive.

A man could get lost in those eyes. That compliment came from her last long-term boyfriend, Linc Pinter. He was the last man she had dated before moving to Monroe. If pushed, she would have admitted her move had a lot to do with the town—and a good amount to do with getting away from Linc.

Shaking her head, Joie grinned. She was who she was. Top to bottom, all the parts were in working order. Good teeth, good skin. Her dark hair was thick and shiny. Hell, even her periods were on time and were little more than an inconvenience.

She supposed it was normal to want what she didn't have. Long legs and curves were on her wish list. But it was unproductive, and ungrateful, to dwell on what couldn't be. Short of major plastic surgery, Joie Trent was who she was. And elective surgery was out of the question. Just the thought of going under the knife made her shudder. Weeks of painful recovery time. Hiding out so no one saw the bandages or the swelling or the bruises. And why? So you could emerge looking ten years younger—and no longer like yourself?

Joie had witnessed her mother go through it too many times to ever want it for herself. She liked knowing that she was born this way. Nothing nipped, tucked, or enhanced. Her only augmentations came from the pots and tubes that littered her bathroom counter.

Checking her watch, Joie wondered where the morning had gone. She started her car, thrilled when the motor turned over on the first try. She had thirty minutes until she was expected at Mickey

Lofton's birthday party. It was a fifteen-minute drive, which left her plenty of time to set up.

Why did she do it, Carole had asked. The salary wasn't much, but Joie never scoffed at money. Her real payment was the children's laughter. She couldn't put a price on that.

Joie pulled onto the street, heading south. She was a nurturer at heart, with the soul of a rebel. If she had followed the path laid out for her by her mother, she would be married—perhaps for the second or third time—living off a rich husband and gossiping about her neighbors.

Joie chuckled. The next time she spoke with her mother, she would tell her that at least she had the gossip part down pat. Or maybe she would keep that to herself. Kristen Lawrence Trent Fairchild Randall Lowenstein Majors did not have a sense of humor—especially where her only child's life decisions were concerned.

The road out of town wound into the Ruby Mountains. Another reason Joie loved living here. No matter where she turned, the view was breathtaking. It was a three-hundred-sixty-degree panoramic wonderland. It was the complete opposite of where she came from, where the best view was of her neighbor's security fence or the perfectly manicured backyard.

Monroe and the mountains that surrounded it were real—not manufactured. A place where she could breathe and be herself.

At the moment, being herself meant a crazy blond wig, a red clown's nose, and twenty screaming kids under the age of ten. Joie switched on the radio to her favorite classic rock station and sang along to CCR blasting out *Bad Moon Rising*.

This was the life she chose. And it was damn near perfect.

JOIE DIDN'T SEE the accident. But she did see the aftermath. That and the man who peeled away in a dilapidated Honda Civic.

It was impossible to get the license plate number. It was obliterated by multiple layers of rust with an overlay of mud. All she could do was call in a description of a heavyset man, average height, wearing jeans, work boots, and a red and blue plaid shirt. Along with the car, it described half the male population of Elko County.

Stopping her car, Joie parked it on the far side of the road, away from any potential traffic. Smoke rose from the crashed truck. Though from the road, she could only see the back bumper; she assumed it came from under the hood. She didn't need more than a rudimentary knowledge of cars to figure that out.

Her first instinct was to rush from her car, eager to help the possibly injured passengers. But common sense took over. She grabbed her phone, dialed 911, then approached the driver's side.

"Please state the nature of your emergency."

"Colleen?" Joie was relieved to hear a familiar voice. "This is Joie Trent. I'm about a mile out of town, south side. There has been an accident. A truck hit a tree."

"Is the truck the only vehicle involved?"

"There was a Honda Civic, but the driver took off when he saw my car come around the bend. There is a man in the truck. The driver. From what I can see, he isn't moving. It doesn't look like there are any passengers."

"Right. I've dispatched an ambulance and informed the police. Whatever you do, don't move him. If he regains conciseness before the ambulance arrives, try to keep him calm and assure him help is on the way."

"Right."

Joie moved closer to the truck, peering inside. He looked like a big man. Too big for her to move if she wanted to. Blood ran down his face from his forehead to his chin. She knew that head wounds were notorious for bleeding a lot, but in her book, no amount was a good amount.

"Hey. Are you awake?"

Silly question but this was a first for Joie. She didn't know what she was supposed to say to an unconscious man. When she heard him groan, she sighed. *Thank God*. Definitely among the living. She hadn't wanted to contemplate the alternative.

He blinked. Once, then once more. Joie found herself looking into the bluest eyes she had ever seen. True, they were a bit unfocused, but the color was spectacular.

"There you are." She was so relieved, she had to laugh when he tried to lift his head. "Don't move until the EMTs check you out. That was quite a crash. The tree won, by the way."

"Are you an angel?" he slurred the words.

An angel? Her? She had been called everything from stubborn to hilarious—and a few words not suitable for younger audiences. But an angel? That was a first.

She laughed again. "Sorry, buddy. Not even close."

THE NEXT TIME Wyatt became aware of his surroundings, his laughing angel was nowhere to be seen.

A hospital room.

There was no mistaking the look or the smell. Cold and antiseptic, Wyatt hated the very thought of it. He remembered too well the night his wife died. He stood in the room, soaking wet from the unexpected rainstorm. Stephanie's broken body lay on the bed, hooked up to the monitor, the steady beep the only proof that she was still alive.

The doctors had held little hope that she would regain consciousness. Her injuries were too severe. But Wyatt stood vigil, determined to be there in case the experts were wrong. She lasted another three hours before succumbing. As long as he lived, he would never forget the moment the beep of the machine stopped. Flatline. It was a thing and a sound. It, Stephanie, and their unborn child haunted his dreams.

"Look who decided to join the living?"

Wyatt groaned. His head hurt like a son of a bitch. The last thing he needed was an unnaturally cheery Florence Nightingale wanna-be.

"Where is my angel?"

The second he said the words, Wyatt realized how they must have sounded. It made sense for the nurse to rush from the room, calling for a doctor. It was clear that the patient had suffered brain damage. Why else would he be worried about an angel? No, Wyatt corrected himself. Not *an* angel. *His* angel. Maybe he *had* hit his head harder than he thought.

"Nurse Weller informs me that you've decided to wake up."

Wyatt watched as a middle-aged man in a white coat took a penlight from his pocket. Again with the cheery attitude. Maybe it was a prerequisite. Along with medical school, all employees must sound like a modern-day Pollyanna.

"How long have I been here?"

"Only a few hours." The doctor, Dr. Aldeen, according to his nametag, checked Wyatt's eyes. "Do you remember what happened?"

"The sun was in my eyes. Someone or something was in the middle of the road. I tried to avoid them and hit a tree."

"That would explain that nasty cut on your head." The nurse laughed at what had to be an old joke.

"When can I get out of here?"

Wyatt hated hospitals. More than that, he didn't want word of this getting back to his family. His mother would be on the first flight out of Los Angeles, accompanied by his father, his brothers, and all three fiancées. That was the last thing he needed.

"Why don't you relax and let me finish examining you. Can you tell us your name? There was no ID on you or in your truck."

Even with a splitting headache, Wyatt was a quick thinker. The Landis name was too famous for this to go unreported. News of his accident would be splashed across every social media site before he could blink. That meant reporters hounding him and his family. There had been too much of that lately. The only way to avoid it was for no one to find out. And the only way that would happen was if the hospital thought he was somebody besides Wyatt Landis.

"Wyatt." No need to change his first name. "Wyatt Rogers."

"Well, Mr. Rogers, I would say you were a very lucky man. The tree prevented you from falling into a very deep gorge. And someone found you immediately."

"Someone?"

Wyatt was thinking clearer. He wouldn't ask about *his angel* again, but he couldn't help thinking of her that way.

"The young woman who called in the accident."

"How is he, Doc?"

A uniformed police officer had entered the room. Short and squat, Wyatt thought he looked like something from central casting. Needed: one prototypical cop. Military buzz cut, shaggy mustache, round, protruding stomach. The only thing missing was the southern accent and a toothpick clenched between his teeth.

"Hey, Tolliver. I was just telling Mr. Rogers that one or two feet either way and he might not be here."

"Ya, the trees around here have hard bark and deep roots. Give it a year or two and you won't be able to tell anything happened." Tolliver leaned closer to Wyatt. "Your head might not be as lucky. Is that going to scar, Doc?"

"Hard to tell." Patiently, Wyatt waited while they discussed his injury. "Most of the laceration is above the hairline. Once it heals, I doubt it will be noticeable."

"That's good." Tolliver pulled up a chair. "It wouldn't matter to me, but a handsome guy like you, well, it would be a shame."

Wyatt wasn't sure how to respond so he simply nodded.

Tolliver pulled out a notepad and pen. "Want to tell me what happened?"

Repeating what he had told the doctor, Wyatt realized there wasn't much to tell. The officer probably knew more than he did.

"I wish I could be more help, but it happened so fast."

"Understandable. We don't know if the guy who stole your wallet—"

"Wait," Wyatt interrupted. "Someone stole my wallet?"

"You did have a wallet?" When Wyatt nodded, Tolliver continued. "Theft is the most logical explanation. A witness saw a man fleeing your vehicle. We did find your cell phone.

Wyatt took the phone, grateful that only he had access. Unless the police had figured out his password, his identity was still a secret.

"Don't worry," Tolliver assured him with a grin. "Your secrets are still your own. Not that we didn't try to look. We didn't know when you were going to come around, and it seemed the best way to identify you."

"I understand why you want to catch the man, officer. But I'm more interested in getting out of here. When do you think that will be, Dr. Aldeen?"

"There are no obvious signs of a concussion, but I would like to keep you here overnight for observation."

"Unless that's imperative, I would rather check out." And be on his way. He had someplace he wanted to be, and an overnighter in a hospital was not part of the plan.

"It's up to you," Dr. Aldeen said, but it was apparent that he didn't agree. "I'll have your release papers drawn up along with something to sign stating that you are going against my suggestion."

"Put it in front of me and I'll sign." *ASAP*.

"You've become a bit of a celebrity."

"Excuse me?" Wyatt heard the word celebrity and his heart sank.

"Take a look."

Tolliver handed him a newspaper. The headline in the *Monroe Cryer* read *Local Woman Saves Stranger's Life*. Wyatt relaxed. *Stranger* meant his identity was still unknown. He knew the smartest thing to do was sign the papers and get out of town. He told himself not to read about his savior—angel. But curiosity, and something stronger that he wasn't willing to explore made him look.

"Joie Trent? Is that the woman who found me?"

"You know Joie?" Tolliver asked with a frown.

"No."

"That's interesting. Most folks don't pronounce her name correctly. I know I didn't. But you had it right the first time."

Wyatt looked at the name again. Joie. He supposed some people might have a problem with the name. Joy was a reasonable alternative. However, from his first glance, he saw Joey—he didn't hesitate.

Joey. Silently, Wyatt said again. He liked it. It was unusual. And memorable. Like the woman herself.

"I've always been good with pronunciations," he said by way of explanation. Which was true. "Is she a resident of…" Wyatt glanced at the paper's masthead. Monroe? What were the chances?

"You're in Monroe, Nevada," Tolliver explained. "Smack dab in the middle of the Ruby Mountains."

Monroe had been Wyatt's destination. Before the accident, he knew that he was close, but not this close. Now he was faced with a dilemma. If he stayed in Monroe, he was stuck with a false identity. There was always the option of telling the truth. Right now, before it went any farther, he could speak up. I'm Wyatt Landis, not Wyatt Rogers. A few words to help Tolliver and Dr. Aldeen understand why he lied and all would be set right.

However, Wyatt's reasons for inventing an alias were still viable. He didn't want to worry his family. And he didn't want the press descending on Monroe. Not before he had finished his business.

He hated to do it, but for the foreseeable future, he was Wyatt Rogers.

"That truck of yours is going to require a major overhaul," Tolliver shook his head, sympathy in his voice. "Plus, you need to cancel all your credit cards. Looks like you're stuck in Monroe until tomorrow."

Longer, if Wyatt had anything to do with it. He would call Colt. He wouldn't mention the accident, explaining that he had lost his wallet, and he needed some cash—ASAP. Colt would have questions, but putting his brother off was easier over the phone. It would give him the time he needed. The time to find the elusive author, J. L. Winter, and acquire the rights to *Left of Mayfield*.

CHAPTER TWO

JOIE AND CAROLE decided to binge on an oldie but goodie. They loved *Sex and the City*. Always had. Always would. Tonight, they hadn't felt like venturing into the unknown. They wanted something that they knew they would enjoy. If they wanted a guaranteed good time, revisiting Carrie and her pals were a no-brainer of a choice.

Tonight, they were at Carole's apartment. It wasn't spacious, but the place was perfect for her. One bedroom. A decent kitchen. The bathroom sported a bathtub big enough for a woman to stretch out and ease away the stress of the day and a shower with plenty of water pressure for those days when she was in a hurry and couldn't indulge in a long soak.

The living room space allowed Carole to entertain a few friends when she was in the mood, or feel cozy and comfy when she wanted to be alone. Like the woman who decorated the apartment, the colors were bright and vibrant. Orange, red, yellow. Splashes of magenta and cerulean. It shouldn't have worked. But with her eye for design, Carole was able to arrange things just so. The result could have hurt the eyes. Instead, it was a welcoming pop of energy. Just like Carole.

"How did they get this into the paper so quickly?"

A glass of wine in hand, Joie sat on the secondhand sofa that Carole had personally reupholstered in a soft material the shade of an evergreen forest.

The story in the *Monroe Monitor* contained few details about the accident. Then again, there were few to be had. "And why didn't Cyrus call me for my side? Or at least ask me for a quote?"

"Everything moves fast these days. As for getting your side?" Carole lifted a piece of pizza from her plate, pausing before taking a bite. "I'm sure he'll get around to that. It doesn't matter. Tell me about the hunk with the killer blue eyes."

Small towns, Joie sighed with a shake of her head. Who needed a newspaper when word of mouth worked so well?

"You know as much as I do. He looked like he was in good shape. Flat stomach, strong arms. I would say he's thirty or a little older. Great chin."

"Chin?" Carole almost choked on her pizza. "I want sexy details, and you concentrate on the guy's chin? Next, you'll be telling me he had nice wrists."

"Don't discount the lesser-used erogenous zones. Have you ever had a man start at your fingertips and kiss your palm, then linger at your wrist?"

"No," Carole's eyes were filled with regret—and envy. "What's it like?"

Joie shrugged, then grinned. "I have no idea. But I'd like to find out."

"Okay. I will give you his wrist if you tell me something else. Jan Weller, my friend who works as a nurse at Monroe Emergency, swooned over his eyes. Are they as spectacular as she claims?"

"Yes."

For some reason, Joie didn't know how to elaborate. She was a woman of words. Ask her about the weather, and she could go on for ten minutes, expounding on the breeze, or the quality of light. If she wanted to expound on a painting or a piece of sculpture, she didn't have to think twice. Her descriptive powers never failed her. Until now.

No. That wasn't entirely true. Joie knew how she felt. If pushed, she could have told Carole about that first moment he opened his eyes. The second they focused—on her. The flare of admiration. The spark of interest. And her reaction.

It puzzled Joie. She wasn't a stranger to a man's admiring glances. *Before* she moved to Monroe and after.

Brad Makepeace was a perfect example. He made no secret of how he felt. He wanted her. For what, Joie wasn't certain. She wasn't naïve—far from it. Sex was on his mind. But beyond that? Who knew. She wasn't interested so she had never bothered to find out.

However, something had happened when she looked into the cab of that crashed truck. She had felt an odd zing in the pit of her stomach. It made no sense—considering the situation—that in a split second, he had made her feel... sexy. Sexier than she had felt in a long time.

The man identified by the paper as Wyatt Rogers had sparked more of her interest in one glance than Brad Makepeace had managed in almost three years.

It was unsettling—and reinforced her resolve. If one glance from a barely conscious stranger could get her juices flowing, why should she have sex for sex sake, when potentially, her next great bed partner was just around the corner?

Joie knew that Wyatt Rogers was *not* that man. He would leave town as soon as his health, and his truck, allowed. But he gave her hope. A great big, stomach-clenching, juices-flowing truckload of hope.

"What are you smiling about?" Carole handed her a napkin.

"Anticipation."

"For your dinner with Brad?"

There was so much excitement in Carole's eyes, Joie didn't want to disappoint her. She hadn't seen Brad yet. There was no date. But because she promised, Joie planned on making it happen—soon. If Carole wanted to believe some spark would miraculously appear, let her. What harm was there in that?

"Why not?" Joie stretched out her legs. She picked up the remote, hitting play. The familiar theme music filled the room, signaling the start of their marathon *Sex and the City* session. "Carrie and company never gave up on men. Neither will I."

"There you go. Brad might not turn out to be Mr. Right. But what is wrong with Mr. Right Now?"

Joie didn't answer. There was no way in hell that she would end up in bed with Brad. However, it had been awhile since she had gone out on a date. Maybe she would get lucky, and Brad wouldn't bore her to tears. Or, if she were really lucky, *she* would bore *Brad*.

Joie hit the pause button. "Carole?"

"Hmm?" Carole asked as she gobbled up a long, gooey string of mozzarella.

"What if my charms aren't enough to sway Brad? Will it be the end of the world?"

"I have every faith that you have it in you to sway any man. But," Carole rushed on when Joie frowned, "if Brad doesn't budge, we will find an alternative."

"I love this town." Joie fiddled with the edge of her plate. "It's home. I hate to let everyone down."

"The only way you could let us down would be by blaming yourself for the failings of Brad Makepeace. All you can do is ask him to change his mind. I know we teased you, but I would be horrified if you actually slept with Brad. He's a pompous dick who spends most of the time with his head up his ass." Carole giggled, her eyes sparkling. "Maybe he likes the view."

Carole was the best friend anyone could ask for. With a few words, she lifted Joie's burden and put things into perspective. After all, it was only a field. If the town had to find an alternative, then that is what they would do. And to hell with Brad.

Happy and relaxed, Joie settled back, sipped at her wine, and resumed the show. Carrie Bradshaw knew how good it was to have friends. And thanks to Carole and the good people of Monroe, so did she.

FINDING A PLACE to stay in Monroe, Nevada was not a problem. Finding a place to stay when you had no money and no identification wasn't as easy. Or it shouldn't have been. Wyatt learned quickly that small towns were different. Or maybe it was Monroe. Either way, to his surprise Dr. Aldeen offered to call the *Heritage Inn* and secure a room for him.

"It's not a problem," the doctor told him. "My sister owns the place. She's happy to put you up for the night."

"I will pay her back as soon as I can."

"Don't worry about it," Dr. Aldeen assured him. "Margie understands your situation. Besides, there's always something that needs doing around her place. If you don't mind a little physical labor, you can pull some weeds, or clean out the gutters." The doctor gave him a warning look. "After I check you out again. Stop by tomorrow morning. I want to make sure there aren't any lingering problems from the crash."

An hour later, Wyatt waved goodbye to the orderly who had been kind enough to give him and his luggage a lift, and walked through the front gate of the *Heritage Inn*. It was the kind of place his mother would have loved. Charming. That was the word.

To his left, the long front porch sported a wicker swing perfect for two. On his right, there was a small table and chairs. He imagined the guests sitting out here after dinner, enjoying the view of a small park where a stream ran lazily through the center. Hanging baskets lined the porch, and the walkway was awash with colorful blooms. Wyatt couldn't name the flowers, but they were plentiful and well-tended.

At first glance, things looked immaculate. But with closer inspection, Wyatt could see what the doctor meant about there always being something that needed doing. Little things like the flaking paint along the porch rails and the slightly overgrown hedges along the lawn's border. The inn was neat as a pin. Immaculately clean from the glossy windows to the dirt-free boards under his feet. It was clear that the owner took pride in her business. It was just as clear that she didn't have the time, or perhaps the resources, to keep up with general maintenance.

Wyatt's first instinct was to make a few calls and have the jobs professionally done. A snap of his fingers, in addition to a few bucks from his bank account, and the *Heritage Inn* would shine like new.

Then he remembered where he was and what he wanted to accomplish while in Monroe. Wyatt Rogers didn't have access to the money of Wyatt Landis. His influence and power were locked away with his real identity. Which meant if the porch were going to get painted, he would have to do it himself.

The idea wasn't objectionable. Wyatt had done his share of manual labor. When it became clear that he wanted to follow in his producer father's footsteps, Caleb Landis was thrilled. However, he wasn't willing to hand Wyatt the keys to the kingdom—his son had to earn it.

Wyatt had been expected to learn the business from the ground up. Part of that education included spending one memorable summer building sets in a little village in Romania. By the beginning of September, Wyatt had thick calluses on his hands and appreciation for the hard work that went into something he had previously taken for granted. Sets didn't build themselves. It took sweat and hard work. From that summer on, he treated every aspect of the movie-making process with equal respect.

Wyatt smiled when he thought about that summer. At seventeen, he hadn't a care in the word beyond the blisters on his palms, making his father proud, and talking a local barmaid into sharing her bed. God, it had seemed so easy then. That was the wonderful thing about youth. Everything was possible. He had been fearless because he had no idea what life was going to bring. If he had, he would have been scared shitless.

Allowing himself a moment to savor the memory of that summer, Wyatt jumped with surprise when the front door unexpectedly opened.

"There you are." A pretty woman with short dark hair and a bright smile greeted Wyatt like an old friend. "You must be Wyatt. I'm Margie Kincaid. Welcome to my home."

Genuine. That was the first word that popped into Wyatt's head. Margie Kincaid put out her hand, taking his, and shaking it with a firm grip. She appeared to be in her mid-fifties. Slender, with dark eyes, she was dressed in blue jeans and a dark blue sweater. Tied around her waist was an apron that sported a splash of something red. Margie seemed to be a woman comfortable in her own skin. She didn't wear a ton of makeup in an attempt to conceal her age. A bit of mascara and a touch of color on her lips. That was it. In Wyatt's opinion, less was more.

Again, it brought to mind his mother. Callie Flynn didn't shy away from her age. When your birth certificate claimed you were fifty-five, but you looked twenty years younger, why would you? True, Hollywood was not kind to women of a certain age. But his mother's stature and the blessing of damn good genes meant she had as much work as she wanted. Quality projects. Like the one that had brought Wyatt to Monroe, Nevada.

But finding the elusive J. L. Winter would have to wait. Right now, Wyatt had more immediate matters to deal with. For instance, lying to a woman whose smile made him want to confess all. Quite an admission for a man who prided himself on never letting emotion get in the way of a deal. Maybe that knock on the head had done more damage than he thought.

"Thank you for helping me out, Ms. Kincaid. I'm not used to relying on the kindness of strangers."

Wyatt winced. Paraphrasing *A Street Car Named Desire*? God, he was the product of his upbringing.

Margie gave his hand another friendly squeeze before letting go. "Blanche Dubois," she nodded as though everyone she met quoted Tennessee Williams. "One of the all-time great parts. I saw the Broadway revival a few years ago."

If Wyatt had ever doubted that it was a small world, he never would again. The revival that Margie mentioned had been produced by his father. The part of Blanche Dubois? It won his mother a Tony. When he was back in Los Angeles, he would tell Callie. Knowing her, she would insist on dropping by the *Heritage Inn* the next time she could get away for a few days. Margie and the town of Monroe would never be the same.

"I'm sorry if your brother put you on the spot." Wyatt gave Margie his most charming smile. He wanted to get off any subject related to his family. "I hate to put you out."

"Barry knows I never would have forgiven him if he hadn't sent you my way. What's the point of having all this room if I can't help out someone in need?" Margie picked up the small bag. "Come along. Let's get you settled. Dinner will be ready in twenty minutes."

Wyatt followed her into the house. "You've given me a roof over my head. Please don't think I expect you to feed me." Though the mere mention of food had his mouth watering. When the scent of spicy tomato sauce hit his nose, Wyatt realized how long it had been since his last meal.

"At the moment, I have four other guests. Dinner is optional, but they have opted to eat here. There's plenty," she smiled over her shoulder as she started up the stairs, "so don't worry."

Wyatt wouldn't argue. He realized that it was a bit of an effort to lift his feet. Steps that shouldn't have been a problem made him feel winded. On top of that, his head felt like someone was using it as a conga drum. A hot meal and a good night's sleep. That was what he needed. Tomorrow he would worry about Margie and his unprecedented bout of conscience.

"If you feel like taking a shower, it's at the end of the hall. I hope you don't mind sharing. First come, first serve."

"No problem."

Wyatt wasn't going to tell Margie that he had never shared a bathroom in his life. The closest he came was camping with his father and brothers. But he doubted that peeing on the side of a tree while Garrett, Nate and Colt gathered wood, was the same thing. He didn't like the idea, but it was only for one night.

"Take your time." Margie made a concerned noise when she took a good look at his forehead. "If that bruise is any indication, your poor head took quite a thump."

"It's not that bad."

"So you're one of those. All stoic and long-suffering. I thought you might be." She reached into the pocket of her apron, taking out a bottle of aspirin. "Here. There's a water glass on the bureau."

Wyatt didn't know whether to weep or drop at Margie's feet in gratitude. Deciding neither was appropriate in front of a virtual stranger, he accepted the pills with a simple word of thanks.

A few minutes later, the aspirin in his system, Wyatt put his priorities in order. A shower sounded like heaven, but instead, he picked up his phone and called his assistant. After some internal debate, he decided it would be easier than dealing with his brother. If he had Colt send him money, there would be questions that he wasn't ready to answer.

Derrick was vain, self-important, and had a superior attitude that made him one of the least popular people Wyatt had ever known. Derrick was also efficient and bone-deep loyal.

When Wyatt asked Derrick to arrange to have money and a new credit card sent to him by personal messenger, his assistant didn't ask a single question. When he told him not to tell anyone—especially if they were named Landis—he knew that Derrick would keep his mouth shut.

Wyatt sat on the bed. It was tempting to lie down. Knowing he would fall asleep the second his head hit the pillow kept him upright. He needed a shower. He needed food. And, though he would have liked to put it off, he needed to call Colt.

The second he heard his brother's voice, Wyatt felt better. Family. In his universe, there was nothing better. Even if he planned on keeping the accident from them. He was fine so why cause them unnecessary worry? That would be his justification when he finally told them what had happened. Wyatt expected his father to ream him out. His mother would kiss his cheek and hold him close. Wyatt swallowed. Was it wrong for a grown man to suddenly want his mommy? No, he decided. As long as he kept it to himself.

"How's the vacation?" Colt asked.

In the background, Wyatt heard laughter.

"Did I interrupt your weekly orgy?" he teased.

"Hey, you are speaking to the reformed. I'm a one-woman man."

It wasn't long ago that a statement like that would have sounded ridiculous. Because Wyatt knew Sable. Because he had seen the way Colt looked at her—the way they looked at each other, he didn't doubt his brother for a second.

"Sable deserves better. I hope you never forget how lucky you are."

"I know." For once, Colt was dead serious.

"I wanted to check in—as promised."

"Mom is out on the patio. Hold on a second while I get her."

"Tell her I'll call her in a day or two." Wyatt was in no condition to hold out against his mother. One word and he would spill his guts.

"Wyatt—"

"Take care. And say hi to everyone."

Before Colt could finish his protest, Wyatt ended the conversation. He had done his duty and called his brother. If things went his way, the next time they spoke, his business would be concluded. Monroe and his accident would be in his rearview mirror along with any lingering guilt over not letting them know about his brief trip to the hospital.

Wyatt grabbed a change of clothes from his suitcase and headed down the hall. He wouldn't change his family for anything in the world. But sometimes without doing a thing, they could be a pain in the ass.

CHAPTER THREE

JOIE SLOWLY ROTATED her head to the right. Then repeated the motion to the left. Eyes closed, she concentrated on the movement, clearing her mind of everything but this. Breathe in. Breathe out.

The room was silent. No music to distract her as she rolled her shoulders forward. There was time for noise. When she wanted to sweat, she would crank up the volume and literally dance her ass off. But this morning was about finding her inner peace, not working off last night's pizza.

"Are we finished?" Carole asked, lifting one eyelid.

Holding up her hand, Joie silently counted down from ten, releasing the air from her lungs. She let her body slump forward. As she rose, she nodded.

"We're finished."

"Thank God." Carole collapsed onto her yoga mat, her shirt damp and clinging to her body. "I'm a mess, and you look as fresh as when we started."

"That's because I do this on a regular basis," Joie reminded her. "Not just when I feel guilty over a few extra calories."

"Well, I burned them off this morning," Carole said. "Next time I'll call Dex. No offense, but a few rounds of mattress tag with him is a lot more fun. Not to mention better for my disposition."

"If you would give the guy a break and finally agree to marry him, you could pep up your disposition whenever you wanted."

Carole sighed. "He's pushing hard for me to commit."

Joie knew why Carole hesitated. And she sympathized even if she didn't agree.

"When are you going to stop punishing Dex, and yourself, for another man's mistakes? You married your high school sweetheart. He turned out to be a major dud."

"A major cheater," Carole corrected. She grabbed a towel, scrubbing the sweat from her face with more force than necessary. "I know that Dex loves me. He's a good man. A… kind man. He's dynamite between the sheets. And in the shower. And on the kitchen table. And—"

"I get it." Joie tossed Carole a bottle of water. "Dex is a sex god. However important that is, you have to admit his other qualities are why you love him."

"Did I say anything about love?"

"Nope."

Joie rolled up her mat, placing it on the shelf. The room was small for a second bedroom but perfect for yoga and meditation. Well, she didn't exactly meditate. When she wanted to think, she would plug in something mellow, lie on her back, and stare at the small crack in the ceiling. Between Lou Rawls and trying to decide if the imperfection in her otherwise perfect house was getting bigger, after twenty minutes or so, she was refreshed and ready to go.

Yoga had the same effect. Joie wasn't going to ruin the effect by getting into a debate over Carole's love life. Been there, done that. Her friend was a smart, capable woman. But she couldn't let go of her pain. Until she did, neither she nor Dex would be happy.

"I need to get moving." Carole tossed her towel into the nearby hamper. "There is a delivery of Irish yarn due at nine o'clock."

An hour later, fresh from a shower and a breakfast of toast and berries, Joie left her house and headed for the post office. She had known the moment she saw the blue and white cottage that barring leaking pipes and moldy walls, she had to have it. Even the street name was perfect. Poplar Lane.

She didn't need a psychiatrist to tell her why it was love at first sight. The street. The house. The slightly messy yard with an inconveniently large tree that blocked out the light. This was her minor rebellion against her childhood. She grew up in a household where everything had to be just right. As an adult, she insisted on chaos. Not a lot. A little here and there. It was good for her soul. And her sanity.

"Morning, Joie." Lonnie Birch called out from where he was pruning his prized rose bushes. "I read about you in the paper. Quite the adventure."

"I'm glad I was there to help out."

With a wave, Joie picked up her pace, before he could say anything more. Lonnie was a sweet man, but if she gave him the slightest encouragement, he would talk her ear off. She checked both ways before crossing the street. She stepped onto the sidewalk just as Wyatt Rogers exited the coffee shop in the company of a woman she didn't recognize.

Joie considered her instincts on such matters to be above the norm. Wyatt and the petite redhead didn't give off a romantic vibe. If she were to guess, they seemed more businesslike than friendly—the manila envelope that he carried in his right hand added fuel to that assumption. *Interesting.* Another mini-mystery to the already mysterious Mr. Rogers.

"Thank you." She heard Wyatt say as she got closer. The redhead nodded. They didn't hug or exchange handshakes before she turned and walked away. *Yes*, Joie thought, *definitely business.*

"Good morning," she said, smiling brightly. Technically, she saved this man's life—or at the very least expedited his rescue. Shouldn't she give him a warm greeting?

"Good morning," he answered absently.

Joie didn't know how to take that. It was obvious that he didn't recognize her. However, there was a brief flash of appreciation in his blue eyes, sending another zing straight to her stomach. It wouldn't go beyond that. He was passing through, and she didn't sleep with strangers. But his interest was nice, and she was glad to know she hadn't imagined that feeling.

Let him go, Joie's good girl voice told her. But the devil that sat on the other shoulder wouldn't let the moment pass.

"After everything we've been through, I can't believe you don't recognize me."

Wyatt frowned, his gaze sharpening. Joie could almost hear the wheels turning as he tried to remember. The decent thing to do would be to tell him. After all, the man barely got a glimpse of her. *He thought you were an angel*, the troublemaker's voice whispered. *He had to be out of his head.*

"I'm sorry?" Wyatt leaned closer. "Do I know you?"

Joie stared into his eyes. *Say the word and you can know anything you want.*

"Oh, shut up," she mumbled, then groaned when she realized Wyatt had heard her.

"I'm confused." His gaze narrowed. "You act as though you know me. Engage me in conversation. Now you want me to shut up? I thought I was the one with the head injury."

"How are you?" Instead of explaining, Joie concentrated on the bandage on Wyatt's forehead. "There was a lot of blood."

"How do you—" Joie could tell the moment the light dawned. "Angel?"

Oh, boy. Angel, indeed. She needed to set him straight—immediately.

"I'm nobody's angel, Mr. Rogers." When she heard herself say his name, Joie couldn't control her snort of laughter.

"Has anyone told you that you are a confusing woman?" Wyatt shook his head. "What's so funny?"

"Mr. Rogers. Like the children's television host?" When Wyatt continued to give her a confused stare, Joie laughed again. "It's just the way my mind works. You share a name, but that's where it ends."

That was putting it mildly. The original Mr. Rogers had been calm. Soothing. Wyatt stirred her up. His body alone made her think of things that would have shocked his television counterpart. Those arms. Wow! It made her glad the day was warm.

Without the need of a jacket, Wyatt was dressed in a t-shirt that showed off his toned biceps to perfection. Joie didn't consider herself a shallow woman, but when faced with a body like his, who could blame her for mentally drooling down her chin?

"Okay." Wyatt's tone told her that he wasn't sure what to make of her. Should he stay or run for the hills, hoping the crazy lady didn't follow? "You are the woman who helped me yesterday?"

"Smart," Joie nodded. "Change the subject. I don't blame you. I have the habit of veering off on odd flights of fancy. It's always best to steer me back to center as quickly as possible. And yes," she held out her hand. "I'm her. Joie Trent."

"I'm glad to get the chance to thank you."

Wyatt's grip was firm, his palm warm but not damp or clammy. Another plus in his favor.

"No thanks necessary. Anyone would have done the same thing."

"Not anyone," he reminded her.

"Right. The idiot who robbed you. I would apologize for the citizens of Monroe, but I'm ninety-nine percent certain he wasn't from here. I don't suppose there's much hope of catching him?"

Wyatt shrugged with a philosophical air. "I canceled my credit cards. Even if he's stupid enough to use one, chances are he'll get away with it."

"Did you have much cash on you?" Realizing that could be construed as prying, Joie backtracked. "Forget I asked."

To her surprise, Wyatt took her arm, gently guiding her from the center of the sidewalk so that pedestrians weren't required to dodge around them. *Handsome, sexy, and considerate.* Joie sighed. He looked more and more like someone she would like to get to know.

Just her luck that he was only passing through. Or was he? It occurred to her that Monroe might have been his destination. If that were true, Joie's day just got a lot brighter.

"I don't mind answering. No, I wasn't carrying a lot of cash. A couple of twenties and a few ones. My accident didn't make him rich."

"Good."

"Weren't you blond?"

The question came out of nowhere, causing Joie to lift her hand to her dark hair. She thought for a second then smiled.

"Big? Poofy? With lots of corkscrew curls? It was a wig."

"Fashion statement?" he asked.

"Birthday party. I was the entertainment for a bunch of eight and nine-year-olds."

"Is that your profession?"

Normally, Joie would have shrugged the question off with a joke. But Wyatt seemed genuinely interested in her answer so she elaborated.

"It's more of an avocation than a vocation."

Wyatt nodded. "I get that. Making kids happy. And then there's the cake. Though I go for the frosting first."

"Exactly," she exclaimed, amazed that he got it. "Do you have children?"

A shadow passed across Wyatt's face. It was brief, and he did a good job of recovering, but Joie saw the raw emotion in his eyes. Children—his children—was obviously a sore subject. Was he estranged from them? An ugly divorce, perhaps? In the next instant, Wyatt answered her question—leaving her with more unanswered ones.

"No children."

Another shadow entered his eyes. Pain. Joie understood about loss and how devastating it could be. She recognized the signs. It was hard to shake, sometimes lingering for a long time. Raw—like an open wound. If she thought it would help, Joie would have taken his hand. But something told her that Wyatt wouldn't welcome comfort from a stranger. Or anyone else.

"I'm on the way to the post office."

The non-sequitur and her artificially bright tone seemed to startle Wyatt. Smiling, he shook his head.

"I'm not certain how to respond to that."

"Your reaction was perfect," Joie smiled back. "Confused and bemused. I'm used to it. It was my way of saying, I've kept you long enough. I hope you are feeling better. How long until your truck is fixed? And are you passing through or will you be in Monroe for more than a few days?"

Wyatt laughed. It was a good sound, Joie thought. Deep and engaging. It made her want to join in—so she did.

"I had no idea there could be so much subtext in one little sentence."

"If you were sticking around Monroe, I could teach you a course in parsing my sentences."

If she were alone, Joie would have slapped herself upside the head. In one awkward phrase, she had almost invited him to stay in Monroe and practically guaranteed that she would be available if he did. Hardly subtle. The only easy way out would be if the ground opened up and swallowed her whole. Since the odds of that happening were not in her favor, she decided to make as smooth an exit as possible.

"Post office. Good luck."

Smooth as glass. If that glass were broken into a million jagged pieces. Joie turned to leave, then stopped. Damn it. This wasn't her. Yes, she could be a little goofy and say odd things at inappropriate times. But never in her life had she played the tongue-tied twit to such perfection. This might be the last time she saw Wyatt. She wouldn't let this be his last—and only—impression of her.

"Just to clarify? I can string words together that form a coherent sentence. For some reason, you make me babble."

"Why?"

A man of few words—speaking to a woman of too many. In an alternate universe—far, far away—they would make a perfect match.

"I may never know." Joie thought that was a great exit line. With a smile—and a touch of regret—she left him without a backward glance.

WYATT FOUND HIMSELF thinking of Joie as he went about getting his affairs in order. She fluttered around his brain—popping up at odd moments. *Fluttering and odd.* They were appropriate words for a woman who was unlike anyone he had ever met. The more he thought about it—thought of *her*—the more he came to the conclusion that he liked her.

Liked. It was a singular word with many interpretations. In this case, it meant she made him laugh. Joie Trent brightened his mood, something that wasn't easy to do. He didn't walk around with a gray cloud constantly threatening a downpour. On the other hand, it was harder and harder for him to remember the last time he was truly happy. He had gotten so good at faking it that he wasn't sure he knew what the real thing felt like.

Until this morning. His smile had come without effort. His laugh as easy as it was unexpected. Joie wasn't the angel he had thought her to be. She was something better. A woman who knew nothing of his past. When she looked at him, she saw a man. Not a Landis. Not a tragic widower. Simply Wyatt. He didn't have to be a genius to figure out the appeal in that.

"The drive shaft is broken."

The mechanic, Dave of *Dave's Automotive Repair*, wiped his greasy hands on an equally stained cloth. If it accomplished anything except passing back and forth the same black sludge, Wyatt would have been surprised.

"Sounds serious."

"Nah. The problem is I don't have the part. That truck is over twenty years old. I'll do a search for the shaft, but we're talking at least a week. Maybe more."

Perfect. He wouldn't have planned a knock on the head, but the truck gave him the perfect excuse to hang around Monroe without looking suspicious. He could nose around until he found J. L. Winter. It might be easier than he imagined. Either way, his access to the town and by association, the author, made a little blood and a few stitches a small price to pay.

And if he happened to run into Joie while he was here, all the better.

"Great." Wyatt scribbled on a piece of scrap paper near the cash register. "Here is my phone number. Call me when the truck is ready."

Dave frowned. "Don't you want me to quote you a price? Labor and parts might set you back a bit."

Right. He kept forgetting that Wyatt Rogers didn't have the resources of Wyatt Landis. A man in his situation wouldn't blithely approve repairs without finding out the final cost. It was an old truck. Chances were it would cost less to buy a new one—or at least one that was pre-owned—rather than fork out his hard-earned cash on what amounted to sticking his finger in a leaking dike.

"I guess that accident scrambled my brains more than I thought," Wyatt said with a good-natured shrug. "How much are we looking at?"

When Dave gave him the estimate, Wyatt tried not to show his surprise. That was all? Hell, he spent more in a month detailing his Bentley. Wyatt was trying to decide if he felt a touch of rich man's guilt—something he had never experienced with his Beverly Hills upbringing. No, it wasn't his money that made him uncomfortable; it was the lies. He tried to live a straightforward life. Not easy in the movie industry. But he had always prided himself on making the best deal without cheating or subterfuge.

It was the height of irony that he had married a woman who thrived on duplicity. It warmed her blood and fueled her waking hours. She had wrapped him in a tangled web that two years later, he hadn't completely escaped and wasn't sure he ever would.

"I get that it's a lot of money, son," Dave said, misinterpreting Wyatt's silence. "Tell you what. If you don't mind a little hard work, there is always some grunt work to do around here. No offense."

"None taken." Wyatt looked around the garage. "I see you have a car up on the hoist ready for an oil change. Mind if I give it a go?"

"You done this before?" Dave motioned him toward the car.

"Yes."

It had been awhile, but Wyatt was certain he still knew one end of a wrench from the other. The six months he spent on the maintenance side of a movie crew was about to come in handy.

CHAPTER FOUR

FINDING TIME TO nose around about a certain author was harder than Wyatt had envisioned. Between his work at the garage and the odd jobs he had taken on around the inn, he was damn busy for a man who was supposedly on vacation.

Wyatt stood under the showerhead, a sigh of pleasure escaping his lips as the hot water rushed over his tired body, loosening his muscles. Lifting weights hadn't prepared him for hours of physical labor. If he kept this up, his physique would soon rival his brother Nate's.

Monroe was an interesting town. After three days, he realized the residents weren't as nosey as he would have expected. No one casually dropped by the garage to shoot the breeze with the new guy. He wasn't stopped on the street or approached at the coffee shop. Not that people weren't friendly. There were plenty of greetings. He must have said hello, good morning, and afternoon over a dozen times. However, the personal questions he expected hadn't materialized.

Normally, Wyatt would have been fine with that. After a lifetime watching his mother dodge reporters and paparazzi, he should have appreciated that he had found a town that respected his privacy.

Unfortunately, this was not a normal situation. How could he snoop when snooping was frowned upon? What he thought would be a fairly simple task was turning out to be harder than he expected.

"Hey. Are you almost through?"

The pounding on the door reminded Wyatt that he shared the bathroom with five other people. He tried to take his showers at what should have been non-peak hours. But it never failed, ten minutes at the most and someone interrupted. If he stayed in Monroe much longer, he would have to consider finding other accommodations.

"Hold your horses." Wyatt shut off the water, reaching around the shower curtain to grab a dry towel. He knew who was outside the door. If he didn't know better, he would swear that Mrs. Blake, the middle-aged lady who was staying at the inn with her husband, was deliberately stalking him. She always seemed to be around. In the garden. On the porch. Outside of the bathroom. If Wyatt were there, she soon followed. He had tried engaging her in conversation, but the lady had little to say. She seemed more interested in… looking.

Fine, he thought. *If she hoped to see something, he would give her what she wanted.*

Without bothering to dry off, Wyatt wrapped the towel around his waist. Without warning, he pulled open the bathroom door, eliciting a gasp from Mrs. Blake. She didn't move, her eyes wide as she stared at his bare chest.

"It's all yours."

Wyatt slipped past the gaping woman. Frankly, this kind of blatant admiration was new to him. He wondered how Colt put up with it every day of his life. Feeling the woman's eyes follow him down the hall, Wyatt picked up his pace, happy to reach the safety of his bedroom. As soon as the door was shut, he turned the lock and relaxed. It was crazy, but the woman gave him the willies.

Putting Mrs. Blake out of his mind, Wyatt quickly dressed in a pair of jeans and a dark green button-down shirt. According to Margie, the monthly town meeting was scheduled for tonight. She informed him that it was always entertaining. Residents used the gathering as a chance to air their grievances. Invariably, a heated argument broke out. In Monroe, the third Thursday of the month was considered a must-see event.

It seemed like the perfect place to find out about J. L. Winter. Perhaps, if he were lucky, the reclusive author might be there in the flesh. Of course, luck hadn't exactly been on his side lately, but things were bound to break his way eventually. Tonight might be the night.

With that thought in mind, Wyatt grabbed his jacket and headed downstairs.

"Aren't you staying for dinner?" Margie asked as he entered the kitchen. She stood by the open oven basting a browning piece of meat.

"No thanks, Margie."

Wyatt loved pot roast, but he didn't feel like sitting across from Mrs. Blake. The lady and her husband would be on their way in the morning. Tonight, he would grab a burger at the diner.

"There will be plenty of leftovers. How about a roast beef sandwich to take with you for your lunch tomorrow?"

"It sounds like heaven."

"Good." Margie wiped her hands on a towel. "Will I see you later at the town meeting?"

Wyatt nodded, a smile on his lips. "I wouldn't miss it for the world."

THE PATTY MELT was hopping with activity. Wyatt looked around the diner for a place to sit, but to his surprise, there wasn't an open table or free seat at the counter.

"Sorry," the waitress told him. "Town meeting night is always like this. Patty always brings in some extra help, but tonight two of our usual servers called in sick." She fluffed her frizzy, ink-black hair. It was teased into a massive beehive and hair sprayed within an inch of its life.

"Any chance I can get something to go?"

"Sure." She took a pad out of her uniform pocket. As she raised her pencil, she gave him a speculative look. "Say, aren't you that fella who was in the accident?"

Wyatt chuckled ruefully. As nicknames went, it wasn't very catchy, but around Monroe, that fella who was in the accident had quickly become his go-to moniker. He supposed that simply calling him Wyatt would be too much to ask. He didn't see the point in arguing. Besides, as a movie producer, he had been called a lot worse.

"That's me." Because he couldn't resist, he added, "My name is Wyatt, by the way."

"Sure, honey," she said with a wave of her hand. "I hear you have money problems. Nothing to be ashamed of. Would you like to pick up a few bucks? It's minimum wage, but the tips are good."

Wyatt opened his mouth to respond, but nothing came out. Was she offering him a job at the diner? Starting immediately? Amazing. All over the country people were out of work, but in Monroe everywhere he went, someone had something to offer him. Nothing permanent, but Wyatt imagined if he stuck around long enough, he would make a pretty good living as a jack of all trades.

"Sorry, Candy. Wyatt doesn't have time tonight." Joie Trent put her hand on his arm. "Come on, our table is over here."

Wyatt could tell that Candy wasn't happy about having her potential workmate whisked away, but he was fine with it. Waiting tables was a fine, upstanding profession, one he would be happy to live his entire life without undertaking.

Then there was Joie. Who in his right mind would object to having a beautiful woman rescue you? She had been in his thoughts, off and on, since their encounter outside the coffee shop. He hadn't planned on seeking her out. He hadn't the time. It wouldn't be fair to her to start something then disappear a week or two later.

Wyatt laughed. And he called Colt arrogant. He assumed Joie was interested. As though his good looks and charm were irresistible. Not all women were like Mrs. Blake back at the inn. Some—most— were more discerning. He wanted to believe that Joie was one of them.

"Want to share the joke?" Joie smiled as he took the seat opposite her.

"Do you ever find yourself—your thoughts—utterly ridiculous? So much so that you have to laugh?"

"Frequently."

"Really?"

Wyatt hadn't expected such an emphatic answer. Funny, sharp-witted, and self-aware. Joie Trent was the most fascinating woman he had met in a long time.

"Things slip out of my mouth—as you know." Joie shrugged good-naturedly. "However, as hard as it may be to believe, I do have a filter. The things that I don't say would shock the average Monroe resident. I have to laugh at myself. It's either that or a straitjacket."

Wyatt understood. At his lowest, his thoughts had been so dark he wondered if he were destined to walk around without light. It wasn't as bad anymore, but he had his moments. Perhaps Joie had the solution. He was a fan of black comedy—finding humor in the macabre had always appealed to him. He needed to start thinking of his past as an exercise in the outrageous.

"Is laughter the answer?" Wyatt hadn't meant his question to have such a serious tone, but Joie didn't seem to think it odd.

"Isn't it preferable to the alternative?" She took a deep breath, her honey-colored eyes drawing him in. He wanted the warmth he saw in them. "My father died when I was twelve."

"I'm sorry."

"It destroyed me. I didn't want to get out of bed."

"What got you through?"

"He did," Joie nodded. "I know, it sounds crazy. How could a dead man give me comfort? Memories. It took a few days, but I started to think about all the times we had together and the things he used to tell me. I know he wasn't thinking about dying, but in his way, he prepared me for it. Life, he used to say, is a beautiful gift. Laugh as often as possible, Joie, even when you feel like crying. Why be sad when there is a joyous alternative?"

"It can't be that simple." Wyatt wanted it to be, but he knew better.

"It isn't. I'm not always happy, Wyatt. I have blue moods. But I refuse to get bogged down in them. Laughter. Dad called it nature's mood enhancer. Way better than any drug."

"So the answer is as simple as *be happy*?"

"Wouldn't that be nice?" Wyatt was surprised when Joie took his hand between hers. "Think happy, Wyatt. When the dark begins to descend, chase it away. Call a friend. Go for a run. Watch *I Love*

Lucy. Whatever it takes. It doesn't always work, but more often than not you will be amazed at the results."

"We aren't talking about me." Uncomfortable with where the conversation had led, Wyatt pulled his hand back.

"You're right." Joie picked up a menu and perused the selection. "I've eaten here dozens of times. You would think I would have this thing memorized by now."

"Joie." Wyatt felt like he should apologize though he wasn't certain why. "I didn't mean to be so abrupt."

"And I didn't mean to make an uncalled-for assumption." Her eyes twinkled at him over the edge of the menu. "Let's start over. First, thank me."

"Thank you?" Wyatt had no idea what she was talking about.

"You're welcome." Joie gave him a satisfied nod.

"No," he laughed. "I meant, why should I thank you?"

"For saving you from Candy. She would have had you bussing tables before you could blink. She's a sweetheart most of the time, but she runs this restaurant like a drill sergeant."

"I would have said no."

"If you say so." Joie went back to reading the menu.

"You don't know me, but trust me when I say that no one talks me into anything."

"Ha!"

"What does that mean?"

Joie set the menu aside. Folding her hands on the table, she looked him directly in the eye. "How long have you been in Monroe?"

"Three days."

"And how many people have asked you to do chores for them?" She put air quotes around the word chores.

"Not that many." Wyatt mentally ran through the list. Six. Ten if you counted the ones he hadn't gotten to. "They pay me," he said defensively. Wyatt Landis was *not* a pushover.

"Mrs. Wade paid you with peanut butter cookies."

"On the open market, those things would be gold."

"No argument here." Joie patted his hand. "Don't look so upset. You're a nice man. Live with it."

Nice? Wasn't that how she would think of a favorite uncle? Or a pal? This was only their second extended conversation. How had he already entered the friend zone? Wyatt was in Monroe on business. He wasn't looking to pick up a sex partner. But damn it, he was only human. Wyatt felt his alpha male surge to the surface. His ego demanded at least a cursory interest on Joie's part.

"The other day I had the impression you found me attractive."

"I did," Joie nodded. "I have found you attractive every time I've seen you. Even with blood running down your face. What's your point?"

"You think I'm nice *and* attractive?"

Laughing, Joie dropped her chin to her chest. "Why do men have a problem with nice? The world is filled with bad boys, Wyatt. Nice is much harder to come by."

"So you do think I'm sexy?" He felt a surge of satisfaction.

"I said attractive. Sexy is something else altogether."

Before Wyatt could ask her to clarify what the hell that meant, Candy stopped to take their order.

"Thank goodness Marlene was able to make it." She plucked the pencil from where it was pushed into the front of her massive hairdo. "What can I get for you?"

"Is there any of the special left?"

Candy chuckled. "Cal put a helping aside as soon as he saw you arrive.

Happily rubbing her hands together, Joie shimmied in her seat. "I love that man."

"What's the special?" Wyatt inquired.

"Steak sandwich and home fries. A slice of huckleberry pie is included."

"That sounds good. I'll have the same."

"Sorry, hon. Pie's gone, and there won't be any more steak until tomorrow."

"Don't worry," Joie said, taking pity on him. "I'll share."

"Thanks." Wyatt ordered a bacon cheeseburger before passing Candy his menu. "I haven't had huckleberry pie since I was a kid. My family used to go camping in Oregon. There was a local place that fixed the berries every way you can imagine. But that pie." Wyatt sighed at the memory. "Heaven."

Joie scooted her chair closer, genuine interest in her gaze. "Tell me about your family."

Wyatt smiled. That was easy. There was so much to say that had nothing to do with the movie industry.

"I have three younger brothers. Pains in my ass, each and every one."

"You love them."

"I do," he nodded. "And I like them—most of the time. My dad raised us to respect each other."

"That's an interesting way to put it."

"How do you mean?"

Joie thought for a second, a small frown forming between her brows. "I've heard someone say they were taught to respect their elders. Or other people. I've never heard anyone say their father taught them to respect their siblings."

"Dad believes everything starts at home. Respect. Compassion. Love. If you treat your family right, chances are you'll do the same to the rest of the world."

"That is one of loveliest things I've ever heard." Wyatt saw her swallow, blinking her eyes. "Your father sounds like a man worth knowing."

"I think so."

Wyatt didn't mention that there were plenty of people in Hollywood who thought his father was a hard-assed son of a bitch. But that was business. No one—not even his competitors—would dispute that Caleb Landis was honest to the bone.

"What about your mother? Ah," Joie sighed. "She must be quite a woman."

"What makes you say that?"

"The look in your eyes when I mentioned her. Every woman should have a son who worships her. At least, that is *my* mother's opinion."

Joie hit the nail straight on the head. He believed his mother could do no wrong. All the Landis men felt that way. Callie Flynn was the center of their universe—the sun around which they orbited. No matter where their lives took them, they would always return home. Because of her and the loving environment she provided.

"Does she?" he asked

"Does she what?"

"Have a son who worships her?"

"Nope. There is only me. I love the woman to bits. But worship? She's a little too... self-involved to inspire that kind of devotion."

Their conversation was interrupted by the arrival of their food. Not that Wyatt was disappointed. He had learned a few things about Joie, and he couldn't remember the last time he had shared so much.

"I'll give you a bite of my sandwich if you return the favor."

"Deal."

They spent the rest of the meal talking around mouthfuls of food. There was no particular subject matter. Likes and dislikes. Wyatt found out that Joie loved corn on the cob—but only freshly picked. He told her about his love for one-of-a-kind items. There was something to be said for mass production, but he preferred something that was made with care and time.

One of a kind. Wyatt rolled the words over in his head. Like Joie. She was like no one else. An original through and through. A woman like Joie was rare. No wonder she fascinated him.

"Are you going to the town hall meeting?"

Their main courses finished, Joie placed the piece of pie between them and handed him a fork.

"Margie made it sound irresistible." Wyatt savored the first bite. Tart and sweet all at once. Delicious. "The threat of a fight breaking out has to be a big draw."

"Tears, yelling, wild punches thrown in the heat of the moment. The fact that we know the players makes it better than *Game of Thrones* and *Scandal* put together."

"*I* don't know the players," Wyatt said, licking his fork. "But it sounds too good to miss."

"Then let's get going. The seats fill up fast. I like to be on the aisle, toward the back. You get the best view from there."

Wyatt automatically reached for the check. He couldn't remember having dinner with a woman and not paying for their meal. Whether it was a date or business, he didn't think twice. However, Joie had different ideas.

"I invited you." She snatched the bill from his fingers.

"You rescued me," he reminded her. "That means I owe you."

"Nope. My treat."

"But—"

"Think like a modern man, Wyatt. It's the twenty-first century. Women are allowed to treat a man to a meal." She gave him a warning look, anticipating an argument. "Tell you what. Next time you can pay."

"Will there be a next time?"

"That depends on how long you're planning on gracing Monroe with your presence. If you stick around long enough, I would say the chances are pretty good."

Wyatt waited for Joie outside, breathing in the crisp fall air. How long would he stay? The part for his truck was on back order. The body work would be finished by the time it arrived and after that, it would take less than a day for Dave to finish the repairs.

The decision was his. He could stay on after his truck was in running condition or he could continue his vacation on the road, occasionally stopping when the mood hit him. That had been his plan. He would track down J. L. Winter, make his pitch, and be on his way.

However, the longer he stayed, the less appealing the idea of leaving became. Where was it written that he couldn't change his mind? A few weeks in Monroe? With the promise of Joie's company for dinner? Why not?

Because she thinks your name is Rogers. Lying to Joie and everyone else for a few days was one thing. Maintaining the lie for close to a month was another matter altogether. If he stayed, he would have to come clean. That opened a whole can of worms he wasn't sure he wanted to deal with. Wyatt would have to think about it before he made up his mind.

Joie exited the diner, a warm, friendly smile on her face. She made it tempting. To see her every day? To let go of the past and allow himself a glimpse of happiness? It tipped the scales heavily in Monroe's favor.

"Are you ready?"

Was he ready? Wyatt didn't know. But perhaps it was time to find out.

CHAPTER FIVE

MORE OFTEN THAN not an event rarely lived up to the hype. The more it was built up, the bigger the disappointment. Wyatt went into the one-story building with tempered expectations. How entertaining could a monthly meeting be?

To his surprise and delight, the Monroe town hall meeting turned out to be one of those rare exceptions that proved the rule.

Joie was right. The folding chairs that lined wooden floors filled up quickly. They were able to get the last two seats, five rows from the back and on the end. Next to him, a large man wearing overalls and a dusty, grease-stained, jean jacket offered him a swig from a bottle of homemade dandelion wine.

"No," Wyatt shook his head when the man would have handed him a bottle cloaked in a wrinkled paper sack. "But thank you."

"Joie?" The man waggled the bottle.

"Another time, Sammy."

"Okay," Sammy took a swig. "But you get more bang for your buck at these things when you start out with a little buzz."

"Having a good time yet?" Joie whispered.

"The start is fantastic," he told her with a grin. "I'm afraid the rest will be a letdown compared to Sammy and his home brew. Like going to a concert where the opening act steals the show."

"Sammy is good," she admitted. "But nothing upstages the main attraction. Gum?"

Wyatt accepted a piece. Sugar-free cinnamon. Not his usual flavor—he was a spearmint man—but he had to admit, he liked Joie's taste in chewing gum.

"Here we go. I love this part," she said, taking his hand. Wyatt didn't know if it was deliberate or if she were caught up in the moment. Either way, he was fine with it.

An air of anticipation filled the room as the crowd gradually quieted. A woman in an elaborately embroidered hooded robe entered and walked onto the raised dais. Her steps measured as though she moved to the beat of a silent tune. When she reached the center of the stage, she turned. Pausing, she lifted her hands to slowly lower the hood.

"Wow!" Wyatt breathed, his tone hushed.

"I know." Joie leaned close. "Every month she does something different. What do you think? Is she a leopard or a cheetah?"

Wyatt stared at the elaborate makeup. Swirls of yellow and black covered the woman's face, her headdress a long series of interlocking braids—also in yellow and black. It must have taken hours to achieve the overall effect. All Wyatt could think was that whoever was responsible would be in high demand back in Hollywood. He made a mental note to seek out the artist.

"It's a cheetah. See the teardrop markings under her eyes?"

"Yes!" Joie sent him an impressed look. "How do you know that?"

"My mind is filled with useless information."

"It wasn't useless today."

Was it strange that her comment made his chest swell—just a bit? Wyatt felt like an awkward teenager who had impressed the prettiest girl in school. Except he had never been awkward. Or worried about impressing anyone. According to Colt, he came out of the womb ready to take charge. He ruled his brothers before moving on to ruling Hollywood.

Suddenly, Wyatt felt as though he had entered unstable territory. Instead of feeling rock solid, the ground under his feet wobbled, sending him right, then left. For the first time in his life, he was off center. And to his amazement, it wasn't a bad feeling.

"Why?" Wyatt nodded to the woman who held the room's attention.

"Why not?"

Wyatt understood showmanship. But it seemed a bit much for a town hall meeting. "There's no significance or historical tradition?"

"It's called fun, Wyatt." Joie's smile teased. Then she winked. "You must have heard of it."

"I have a passing acquaintance." Though it had been a while.

"Then enjoy. Sheila spends a lot of time planning her look. After the meeting, I'll show you what she's done in the past."

"Citizens of Monroe. Welcome. We gather to discuss old and new business. Please respect your neighbor's right to be heard."

Sheila's voice carried to each person. There was a microphone only a few feet away, but she had no need of it. Wyatt heard training in her clear tones. At some time, this woman had formal training. Her presence and her ability to project to the back seats told him she had spent a fair amount of time on stage.

She clapped her hands three times before spreading her arms wide.

"Let the meeting commence."

The rest of the evening didn't quite live up to the opening, but it still entertained. There was a dispute between neighbors over whose dog impregnated a third man's purebred Chihuahua.

Considering that one of the dogs was a Great Dane and the other a St. Bernard, Wyatt voted for option number three. The mechanics alone made him wince. But everyone involved seemed convinced the culprit was either *Tinder* or *Baby*. Short of prenatal DNA testing, it was decided they would have to wait until little *Misty* gave birth.

"What if half the puppies look like *Tinder* and half look like *Baby*?" Wyatt whispered.

Joie did her best to keep a straight face. It seemed like bad taste to laugh considering *Misty's* owner was just across the aisle.

"Then, in *Misty's* case. That would be a big, fat ouch."

Wyatt snorted, garnering him a squinty-eyed stare from the man holding *Misty*. She seemed unconcerned, sleeping through the proceedings.

An hour later, the gavel fell, and the meeting was adjourned. Coffee and cookies were available in the back, which meant no one was in a hurry to leave. Wyatt had figured out that tonight was as much a social gathering as anything. Some considered the milling around, visiting with neighbors, and snacking on assorted homemade baked goods the best part of the evening.

"That brownie looks good."

Wyatt couldn't believe he was hungry. Between his bacon cheeseburger and half of a generously sized piece of pie, he hadn't expected to want anything until morning.

"Better grab one while you can," Joie gave him a gentle nudge. "They are usually the first to go."

"Can I get you one?"

Joie's attention seemed to have strayed to something across the room. Wyatt scanned the crowd, but couldn't tell where she was looking.

"Sure." She sighed, her expression pensive. "You go ahead. I have something I need to take care of."

Joie didn't wait for his response. She weaved her way through the sea of bodies, stopping in front of a man Wyatt guessed to be close to his age. Average height, average build, he was dressed in a blue polo shirt and pressed dark brown Chinos. The guy's expression turned from bored to interested the second he saw Joie.

"Hey, Wyatt." Dave slapped him on the back with his free hand. In the other, he carried a cup of black coffee. "Did you enjoy the show?"

"Yes." Wyatt frowned. "Who's the guy talking to Joie?"

"Brad Makepeace." Dave snorted. "He tried to get people to call him Bradley, but after a couple of years, he gave up."

"He lives in Monroe?"

"Mostly. He has a place at the edge of town. Big house. He bought up some other property—God knows why. Likes to spend money, I guess." Dave chuckled when he saw Wyatt's expression. "Don't worry, son. Joie isn't for sale."

Wyatt didn't respond. It wasn't any of his business. But he did think Joie could do better. It was obvious that Dave didn't think

58

much of Brad Makepeace. That lack of endorsement was good enough for him.

Whatever Joie said to him seemed to make Brad happy. His smile grew to predatory proportions. When the man put his hand on Joie's arm, Wyatt had to control the growl that formed at the back of his throat.

Shit. What the hell was he doing? Joie was a friend. A new one at that. He was attracted—who wouldn't be. But that was all. Wyatt forced himself to turn away. If she were dating the blandest man in America, so what? In his brain, he clicked on a big neon sign that read *NONE OF MY BUSINESS.*

Business. Forcing himself to turn away, Wyatt reminded himself of his reason for being in Monroe. He had a specific purpose—to track down the elusive J. L. Winter.

He looked around, his gaze stopping on Margie. She was surrounded by five women. They seemed like the perfect place to begin his quest in earnest.

Seeing him approach, Margie took his arm, drawing him into the circle. "Here's the perfect person to help. A man's point of view is exactly what we need."

An attractive woman about Margie's age snorted, causing the other women to laugh.

"Don't mind Nan. At the moment, she's not a big fan of the male half of the human race."

"Do you blame me?" Nan rounded on Wyatt. "I loved a man for over twenty years. I shared his bed. Made his meals. Carried and delivered his children. What do I get for all my years of devotion? Betrayal, that's what. He decided he would rather spend the rest of his life with a twenty-year-old cocktail waitress from Reno."

"Bastard."

If he weren't in mixed company, Wyatt would have added cock-sucking asshole. He viewed cheating as deplorable and inexcusable. If Nan's husband had wanted out, he should have asked her for a divorce before starting up with another woman. Until they had talked things through and were legally separated, he should have kept his dick in his pants.

Nan blinked several times as though surprised by his support. "You don't think it was unreasonable of me to lock him out of the house?"

"I think it was unreasonable of him to expect you to let him in. *He* cheated. *He* left. Let his tootsie in Reno put a roof over his head and take care of his dirty laundry."

"I…" Nan's expression turned from belligerence to distress just before she burst into tears and ran toward the exit. One of her friends raced after her.

"I didn't mean to upset her."

Wyatt's stomach clenched. He hated to see a woman cry. Knowing he was responsible made it worse. His father told him and his brothers that if he ever found out that they had deliberately hurt a woman's feelings, he would send a boot up their asses. When Caleb Landis spoke, his word was a promise, not a threat.

It had made such an impression on Wyatt that he was tempted to look over his shoulder, half-expecting to see his father—and his boot—bearing down on him.

"Don't let it bother you," Margie patted his arm. "Nan has let anger carry her through for the last few weeks. A good cry will do her good. You gave her what she needed to let the tears loose. If I know Nan, you can expect to receive a batch of her famous fudge in the next few days. Sort of an apology/thank you."

"She has no reason to apologize. And I didn't do anything worthy of a thank you." Wyatt found the idea appalling.

"You don't have to understand. Simply take the candy." Margie laughed "Trust me and my hips. It is irresistible."

There were times when Wyatt swore that women spoke a different language. He wished his mother was here. He could take her aside and ask her to translate. But since that wasn't possible, for his own sanity, he let the subject drop.

"I vote we read *Night Turns to Day*. It's been on our list the longest."

Wyatt looked from woman to woman, wondering what he had missed. It felt as though he had walked in on the middle of a conversation.

"The reason *Night Turns to Day* is still on the list, Kayla, is because none of us wants to read eight hundred pages of whiny, existential crap. Just thinking about it makes my head hurt."

"Then why did you agree to add it?" Kayla asked Margie.

"Because you wouldn't rest until we agreed," a dark-haired woman answered for Margie.

"Diane is right, Kayla," Margie shook her head. "I don't know why you're obsessed with that book."

"It looks interesting."

"We belong to a book club," Margie explained to Wyatt, ignoring the whining Kayla. "It's time to pick a title before our next meeting, and we can't agree which one it will be."

Wondering if this were his lucky day, Wyatt felt like pumping his fist into the air. This was the opening he had been looking for.

"How about J. L. Winter?"

The women exchanged looks. Wyatt held his breath, wondering what they were thinking.

After a few moments, Diane inquired, "Which one?"

Wyatt didn't see any reason to specifically mention *Left of Mayfield*. He was interested in the author, not a specific book.

"Take your pick."

"I've read them all," Margie said. "But I wouldn't mind if we chose one to discuss."

Seizing the opportunity, Wyatt pushed a little harder. "I heard that J. L. Winter lives in this area."

It seemed like the perfect starting point. But no one jumped on board with him.

"That's interesting," Margie shrugged.

Wyatt frowned. Had his source gotten things wrong? Perhaps J. L. Winter *didn't* live around Monroe. The problem was finding out one way or the other before he wasted any more of his time.

"So what will it be, girls? Do we go with a book we know or do we delve into the unknown?"

With that, Wyatt realized he wasn't going to find out anything else tonight. Not from these ladies.

"Let me make a note to remind myself." Diane took her phone from her purse. "I'll send out an email first thing in the morning. If a majority of our members agree, I say we go with *Left of Mayfield*. That's the last one I read."

"Hi, Margie. Diane. Kayla." Joie joined the group. She turned to Wyatt. "Are you ready to go?"

"Sure," Wyatt smiled. "It was nice meeting all of you."

"Oh, believe me, the pleasure was all ours."

The sound of three grown women giggling followed Wyatt across the room and out the door.

"Did I miss something?" he asked.

"Probably. There is always something that happens during and after one of those meetings that I don't catch. I figure if I catch ninety percent, I'm doing well." Joie lifted her face to the cool evening breeze. "Isn't mountain air divine? There's nothing like it."

It would have been easy to forget his train of thought and concentrate on Joie. Her smile alone was worthy of contemplation. As they passed the post office, Wyatt had the urge to pull her behind the building. It would be the perfect place to find out if her lips were as sweet as they looked.

As ideas went, it was one of his better ones. It was also impossible. One kiss wouldn't be enough. And two would be too many. Wyatt gave himself a mental shake, reset his brain waves, and backtracked five or six thoughts.

"I meant, did I miss something concerning Margie and her friends? They giggled when we left."

"So?" Joie swung around the lamp post until she was in his path.

Wyatt stepped around temptation. "So. Giggles are for adolescents and flighty teenagers. Not grown women."

"I do. I'll bet your mother does too." Catching up, Joie slid her arm through his.

"She does not." *Did she?*

"Pay closer attention next time she's around. Especially if your father is close by."

Wyatt liked walking with Joie like this. Arm in arm. It was sweet and a bit old fashioned. And sexy as hell. "Name the last time you giggled."

"That's not fair. I don't know the last time I sneezed, but I can guarantee it happened," she rubbed her cheek on the sleeve of his jacket. "And it will happen again."

"Joie?"

"Hmm?"

Wyatt sighed. Nope, he wasn't going to ask her if she would like him to kiss her? Why torture himself with the answer? Yes or no, it wasn't going to happen.

"Never mind."

"Okay." They walked a few steps in silence. "Wyatt?"

"Hmm?"

"Would you like to kiss me?"

"Yes." Why lie? "But I won't."

Joie stopped, her hand tugging on his arm to ensure he did the same.

"Won't? Not can't?" Her eyes met his. "No girlfriend? Or boyfriend? A deserted wife or a fiancée patiently waiting for your return?"

"None of the above. Can you say the same?"

"Me?" Joie sounded genuinely surprised—and amused. "I'm as free as a bird."

"What about the pasty-skinned guy? The one with starched Chinos?"

"Brad." It wasn't a question. Joie took her hand away and sighed. "How could I forget? You're right. Kissing you would be in bad form."

"That's an interesting way of putting it."

"It is, isn't it? *Bad form*. I've read too many Regency romances."

"And Brad?" He should be annoyed. But for some reason, Wyatt found her circuitous verbal routes charming.

"I can't kiss you when I have a date with Brad. It's a long story, but I promised some friends I would go out with him. Tonight was the first chance I've had to follow through."

She made a date with another man while he was across the room? Watching? *None of your business, remember?* Wyatt chanted the words again and again. *None of your business. None of your business.* It didn't help. He was pissed off. At her for making the date. And at himself for his unreasonable attitude.

"I don't want to go out with him." She looked so downhearted, Wyatt decided it was impossible to stay mad.

"I know you said it's a long story, but I don't have any place to be."

"Me neither. Come on." She took his hand and led him into the coffee shop. Because of the town meeting and the refreshments served after, there were plenty of empty seats. Joie picked a table near the window.

"Can we have two coffees, Agnes?"

"Sure thing, Joie."

"Sorry," Joie began to remove her jacket. "Did you want something else?"

Wyatt helped her, hanging it behind her chair. He didn't notice Joie's surprised reaction to his gesture, or the pleased smile that flitted across her mouth.

"Coffee is fine."

Joie waited until Agnes served their drinks. She wrapped her hands around the hot mug, taking a sip.

"First. And I have to get this out of the way. Your eyes kill me. They are so blue. But not that cold, creepy blue you sometimes see. Yours are warm. Like a clear summer sky."

Since a discussion of his eye color was the last thing he expected, Wyatt wasn't sure how to respond.

"Thank you?"

"I know. What do your eyes have to do with the time of day in Beijing?"

Or the price of tea in China? But Wyatt liked Joie's turn of phrase better.

"Like I said, I wanted to get that out of the way. About Brad."

Wyatt listened as Joie explained. The Founder's Day celebration. The plot of land and the exorbitant rent Brad Makepeace demanded. It made perfect sense. Until she got to her part in it.

"Is this a barter proposition? The piece of land for your body?"

"That's what I wanted to know." Joie's eyes sparkled.

"What was the answer?"

"Don't worry, my honor is not in danger." Joie laughed, but he didn't see the humor. "They *are* my friends, Wyatt. No one suggested that I should sleep with Brad—unless I want to."

"Jesus."

"Which I don't."

"It's none of my business." If he said it often enough, eventually he might believe it.

"I would have agreed. But I made it your business when I asked if you wanted to kiss me. It was wrong of me because I knew I couldn't let you. So I had to explain."

"Making it my business." *Well, shit. What mantra could he recite now?*

"Do you understand?"

"Yes."

"Good." Joie settled into her seat with a little bounce. She smiled. It was contagious. Wyatt smiled back. "Here's my proposal. I go out with Brad. A week from tomorrow because he wasn't free any sooner. The next day I look you up and—"

"And what?" Wyatt didn't like the way her smile turned into a frown.

"Will you be here in a week?"

"Yes." That was a promise he knew he would keep.

Joie nodded. When her smile returned, it seemed brighter. "The next day I look you up and finish what we haven't started."

"In other words…"

"Kiss."

One week. He could get a lot done in seven days. There was his truck to help repair. He needed to paint Margie's front porch. Mrs. Lister, a few blocks down, was having problems with the lock on her front door. And J. L. Winter. By then, he will have found out if the author lived in the area and if so, where.

Yes, Wyatt could get a lot done in one week. And his reward would be a kiss. Only one. After which he would say his goodbyes and head down the road.

"One week." Joie sipped her coffee.

Wyatt took a drink. It was nice to have something to look forward to. *One week followed by one kiss.* His eyes lingered on Joie's mouth. *He couldn't wait.*

CHAPTER SIX

MORNINGS WERE THE best. Crisp and clear, Joie loved to take a walk just as the sun began to peek over the Ruby Mountains. Today, a perfect example of what early fall should feel like, she bundled up in a sweater and scarf. In the spring, her outfit was much the same. Summer meant warmer temperatures. However, the mountain climate meant it remained cool until midday. The sweater turned into a jacket—with the scarf in place. In the winter? It depended on the snowfall—and how soon the sidewalks were shoveled.

"Watching you is a study in exhaustion," Carole called from the window of her apartment.

Joie was at the end of the block and across the street. She knew from experience that she and Carole could exchange quite a few words before she disappeared around the corner at the end of the block. She turned her head but didn't break stride.

"Start walking instead of watching. Your heart will thank you."

"My heart is just fine, thank you."

Joie saw a flash of movement behind Carole. It looked like Dex had talked her into letting him spend the night.

"I guess you've already had your early morning exercise."

"How did you...?" Carole looked over her shoulder. "Hey. Joie saw you. Sneak out the back before the whole town finds out. I have a reputation to protect."

"Too late. Your voice carried all over town and into the next county." Dex joined Carole at the window. "Morning, Joie. Want to stop for breakfast? I'm making omelets."

"Another time. I have an early appointment."

"See you later," Carole called out.

Joie watched Carole slap away Dex's hand, then laugh when he picked her up and carried her out of sight.

With a sigh, Joie took a right and cut through the alley behind the grocery store. She loved her friends. Their happiness made her happy. However, there were times when she couldn't stop a wave of envy from washing over her. She wanted someone to wake up with. Someone to playfully tease. A man of her own who would carry her to bed and make love to her as the morning slipped away.

Unbidden, an image of Wyatt popped into her head. Lately, the man had a way of slipping into her thoughts without warning. Luckily, she didn't mind the intrusion. He was so damn pretty she would be crazy not to enjoy the view.

"Morning," Wyatt called as he ran past her. "Long time no see."

Joie didn't turn. "Three days."

There was no need for Joie to look over her shoulder to see where he was headed. She clearly heard him slow his pace and change direction until he was headed toward her.

Think of the devil, and he will appear. Or something like that. Though Joie didn't consider Wyatt Rogers to be the devil any more than she was the angel he once mistook her for. They each were something in between.

"Like I said. Long time no see."

Joie knew it was silly, but she felt a little thrill run down her spine. "Don't let me interrupt your routine."

Wyatt, his dark hair covered by a knit cap, looked like your typical jogger. If the jogger had a long, lean body that even a baggy hoody and sweatpants couldn't disguise—and killer blue eyes that had her suppressing a sigh. The man made her want… She couldn't say exactly. It was easier to say he made her want and leave it at that.

"I was almost done. Instead of circling around the bank, I'll circle around you instead."

Joie laughed when Wyatt zipped around her once, then one more time for good measure. He had quick feet, she would give him that. She kept up a steady pace while Wyatt slowed to more of a shuffle than a run.

"Do you do this every morning?" she asked. If this were his usual route, it seemed strange that she hadn't seen him before.

"I mix it up. When the weather is cool, I like to run in the afternoon. This morning, I felt like getting an early start. When I saw you chugging along like the little engine that could, I was glad I did."

"Is that an insult?"

"Not at all," Wyatt assured her. "I love that story. It's about determination."

"I am a determined woman. I'm also going to have full use of my knees when I'm seventy. Haven't you heard? Walking is better for the joints."

"My joints are just fine." But he matched her stride. "I will admit, there's something to be said for your way. It's hard to do this when you jog."

This was taking hold of her hand. It took Joie by surprise—in a good way. She didn't know if the gesture were deliberately romantic, but Joie wanted to think so. It was nice. Sweet. The perfect end to her perfect morning walk.

"I've been thinking." Joie came to a stop outside the gate to her house. "This kiss thing."

"I've thought about it quite a bit myself."

"That's nice." *Nice? Really, Joie?* "Better than nice." Still holding his hand, she raised her eyes to his. "What are we waiting for? Brad isn't my… boyfriend? When do we get too old for that term? Never mind. My point is, I want to kiss you. You want to kiss me. Why am I letting a man who isn't even a thing get in the way?"

"After a few sleepless hours thinking about that, I—"

"I kept you awake?" The tingle zipped from her spine—lower—to a region that as of late she had woefully neglected.

"I have a lot on my mind." He grinned. "However, you've taken up a lot of my thoughts. Especially when I'm alone." Wyatt squeezed her hand. "In bed."

"There you go." Joie smile widened. She appreciated a man who got to the point. "I've found myself tossing and turning."

"Thinking of me?" Wyatt turned her words around on her.

"I've liked it. Thinking of you," she clarified. "I can't remember the last time a man made me restless."

"Restless. Good word."

"And accurate. So? To kiss or not to kiss? What is the answer?"

"Oh, honey. We will kiss." Wyatt tugged on her hand, pulling her closer until she was certain she could feel the heat radiating from his body. One more inch and they would touch. But Wyatt kept their clasped hands between them. "I've never been a fan of anticipation. If I want something, I go after it."

"I would ask if you succeed, but something tells me that would be a silly question."

Joie was a strong-willed woman. She never caved—unless she wanted to. However, Wyatt's eyes. And his smile. And the feel of his hand in hers. It would be hard to say no. No matter the question.

"No is not a word I'm accustomed to hearing."

"I'm not saying no, Wyatt."

"You didn't let me finish. I like thinking about you. I like wondering how your lips will feel on mine and if you could possibly taste as sweet as I've imagined."

"This isn't a Carly Simon song, Wyatt." Joie tried to pull away, but Wyatt held tight. "Sometimes anticipation is painful. I need a good night's sleep. See? Dark circles. Bags. I'm no longer twenty years old. My skin doesn't bounce back like it used to."

Wyatt narrowed his eyes, taking the time to carefully study her face. "What are you talking about? Your skin is beautiful. How old are you? Twenty-five? Twenty-six? With that bone structure? You won't ever look your age."

"Really?" Joie couldn't help it. Wyatt's compliment made her a little giddy. Crap. It had been too long since she had one-on-one time with a man. One compliment and her brain was halfway to mush.

"Thank you." She was annoyed, but there was no excuse for bad manners. "Let's forget about it." This time, she put more force behind her tug. Wyatt let go of her hand immediately. "Right from the start, I made too much of a silly kiss. Even if it happens, it can't live up to the hype. Let's do us both a favor. No kiss. Deal?"

"No."

"No? That's it?" Joie had had enough. She put her front gate between them and headed for the house. "Have a nice day, Wyatt."

"A verbal agreement is legally binding, Joie."

Joie kept walking. "What are you? A lawyer?" she called out.

"We have a deal. One kiss. Mutually given on the day after your date with the whitest man in America."

"Fine." Joie huffed, hoping she sounded resigned. It was difficult when her insides were jumping with joy. She paused on the steps and turned. "Answer one question. What is your problem with Brad? You don't even know the man."

Wyatt started to jog away. "You're a smart woman. Figure it out."

"HE'S JEALOUS," CAROLE told her later that afternoon.

They were in Joie's living room. It was like the rest of the house, small but perfect for her. Hardwood floors gleamed, the sunlight showing off the natural maple finish.

"Why? No, seriously," Joie said when Carole snorted. "This isn't one of those insta-love romance novels that you like to read late at night. Wyatt is a mature, rational man," Joie rolled her eyes. "Again with the snorting?"

"Sorry." Not looking the least bit contrite, Carole took a bite of her chocolate chip cookie. "I love the fact that you, my levelheaded, world-wise best friend still owns a pair of rose-colored glasses."

"I don't," Joie informed her with conviction. Then she added, "Would that be such a bad thing?"

"Didn't I say that I love it?"

"Yes. But you know how I feel about putting my head in the sand. Naivety is fine up to a point. My mother has proven—over and over—that blind trust leads to heartache and an empty bank account."

Between husbands, Joie's mother spent her time in search of her next true love. Blind trust could be an expensive proposition. A lesson something Kristen Majors refused to learn. A kind word. A hard body. Some outrageous flattery. It didn't take much for Kristen to lay herself open. As she told Joie on more than one occasion, *what is the point of living if you do it behind a wall of mistrust?*

Joie had no answer. If her father were alive, the point would be moot. He loved his wife, indulging her every whim. But without him to hold her close, Kristen bobbed around—a ship at sea without hope of a permanent tether. The men she married enjoyed her flightiness up to a point, soon losing patience.

Kristen had her sights on number six. The Texas oilman liked shiny things, and no one sparkled like Joie's mother. The chances of it lasting were slim to none. But one never knew. Kristen had been blessed with eternal optimism. At some point, the law of averages had to be on her side.

"You are nothing like your mother, Joie."

Carole had met Kristen on several occasions and liked her. Everyone liked her mother. But prolonged exposure tended to breed contempt. Perhaps that was a bit harsh. There wasn't a mean bone in Kristen's body. However, she didn't have an ounce of self-awareness. Sarcasm was lost on her, and direct criticism led to nothing but tears. She was exhausting. That was why Joie lived in the Nevada mountains, and her mother lived any place but here.

"My father taught me to laugh my troubles away. Laughing at Mom isn't easy."

"Because she doesn't have a sense of humor. You can't laugh with someone when they don't get the joke," Carole pointed out. "Kristen is an airy confection. You, my friend, have substance. If you didn't, we wouldn't be friends."

"I don't know what I'm worried about." Joie handed Carole a cup of hot tea before joining her on the sofa. "Wyatt is passing through. We've flirted. A kiss. How much trouble can that cause?"

"If done right? A hell of a lot."

"Not with Wyatt." Joie heard herself and laughed. Unlike her mother, she knew when she sounded like an idiot. "Listen to me. I barely know the man, and I've decided our future. One kiss. How arrogant was that? I know where a kiss can lead."

"If done right?" Carole repeated with a wink. "All kinds of fun places."

With a sigh, Joie plopped back onto the sofa. "That's the problem, isn't it? I want more. Not necessarily forever, but I want a lover, Carole. How can I expect Wyatt to be that man when in all likelihood he won't be around beyond next week? I'm stuck between a rock and—"

"Wyatt's *hard* place?"

Joie almost spewed tea across her prized, handmade, Persian rug. Grinning, she wiped the escaped liquid from her chin.

"I'm sure Wyatt's hard place is brag-worthy. If fact, from what I've seen, all of him is. It doesn't change the facts."

"Right. You don't do temporary." Carole's look spoke volumes. "Then again, you don't do long term, either."

"That's not true. I just said I wanted exactly that. Finding someone is another matter."

"Honey. Listen to the voice of experience. The perfect someone doesn't exist. And if he did, you would be bored in no time."

"In other words, I should jump Wyatt the first chance I get?"

"About that," Carole hesitated.

"Uh oh." Joie knew that look. She set her teacup on the glass living room table. "What have you found out? Is he married? Damn it. I asked, and he said he wasn't."

"Not married. He's a widower."

"Someone looked him up, didn't they?" Joie scrubbed a hand over her face. "For a town that claims to value a neighbor's privacy, that seems counterproductive."

"We don't pry," Carole corrected. "However, checking a man who has no history with anyone in Monroe is smart. The information is for our eyes only."

"Sometimes I hate the internet." Joie shot Carole a frown. "Should I hate the internet?"

"Let me start by saying he isn't a criminal or suspected of being one. From all accounts, Wyatt has lived a good, clean life without as much as a traffic ticket. That's saying something. I received three just last year."

"Are you dragging this out for dramatic effect?" The longer Carole stalled, the more Joie was tempted to break her personal code and google Wyatt herself.

"Are you familiar with the Landis family? The Hollywood Landises?"

"I don't live in a cave."

"I had to explain who Kim Kardashian is."

"Tell me what possible good will come from that information? Thanks to you, I have knowledge of a quasi-celebrity who makes a living by being a quasi-celebrity. Thank you very much."

"You're welcome."

"Carole—" Exasperated, Joie's head fell onto the sofa's back cushion. "I assume Wyatt is a Landis?"

"Right the first time. Wyatt Landis. The oldest son of Caleb Landis and Callie Flynn. He has three brothers. As I said, he was married, but his wife died two years ago in a car accident. They were separated at the time."

Joie felt a wave of sympathy. "Children?"

Carole shook her head. "There are plenty of pictures—if you're interested in what his wife looked like. Nothing like you, by the way."

"Why should that matter?"

"Because you're human? Come on, Joie. You like this guy. His last name. His dead wife. None of that should matter. But because he's a Landis, everything changes. They are one of the most high-profile families in this country. Perhaps the world."

"It goes with the territory, I suppose."

Callie Flynn was Hollywood royalty. So was Caleb Landis. That made their sons the movie industry equivalent of princes. The spotlight would have been on them from birth. Growing up with that kind of attention had to affect you. However, Wyatt seemed natural. Down to Earth. Joie didn't believe his demeanor was an affectation. If it were, he should consider joining his mother and brother. His acting rivaled theirs.

"What do you think he's up to?" Carole asked with a frown. "From all accounts, the man is stinking rich. Why play handyman to a bunch of small town hicks?"

"Hicks?"

"Bumpkins? Rubes? The unwashed masses?"

"I get it."

Joie laughed at Carole's silliness, but her mind raced a mile a minute. Wyatt Landis. Did a different name change the way she thought of him? She wanted to say no. But information always mattered. Good, bad, or indifferent. There was no putting the genie back in the bottle.

"What do you think?" Carole pulled up her legs, tucking her bare feet under them. "Does Wyatt enjoy slumming it? That's Brenda Mayhue's guess. She believes he does this periodically."

Brenda Mayhue had an opinion on everything. If she didn't have a theory about Wyatt, Joie would have been surprised. As the owner and operator of Monroe's only beauty parlor, the woman considered it her obligation to know all the gossip and expound on the subject. Gossip was not king in Monroe. Until you stepped across the threshold of *Le Haire Boutique.* Inside Brenda's domain, all bets were off.

"He does what periodically? Run his truck into a tree? And besides, why would I listen to anyone who spells hair with an e." Joie was all for giving a business name a clever twist, but that was just wrong.

"It's French." Carole snickered. "Okay. The woman has sniffed too much hairspray. It doesn't change the facts. Wyatt wants us to believe his name is Rogers. Why?"

"I know."

Carole's eyes widened. "Dish, girl."

"This stays between us." Joie walked to her desk. She opened the top drawer and took out a piece of paper. "Don't tell Dex. And stay away from the beauty parlor."

"I won't need my roots done for another four weeks." Carole took the paper. Reading, she let out a slow whistle. "This is dated almost a month ago."

"I haven't decided."

"Fair enough."

Joie waited. *Two words? Carole never ended with only two words.*

"Come on," she urged. "You must be busting a gut. Spit it out."

Carole waved the paper at Joie. "This is the equivalent of putting a multi-million dollar check in your desk drawer instead of the bank. What are you thinking?"

"I have enough money."

"Aw. That's sweet." Carole patted her sofa. When Joie took a seat, she slung an arm over her shoulders. "Honey. Take it from your best friend. When it comes to money, there is no such thing as enough. This?" She waved the paper in front of Joie's face. "You could start a home for wayward girls. Or make it your life's work to get harlots off the street."

"Wayward girls? Harlots? What is this, Victorian England?" Leave it to Carole to make a joke. Was it any wonder Joie loved her?

"I sometimes wonder. My mother is under the impression that I'm living the life of a nun. She thought I was a virgin when I got married and that I haven't had sex since the divorce. How Victorian is that?"

"Maybe I should start a home for the re-education of clueless mothers."

"There you go." Carole squeezed, pulling Joie closer. "I don't care what you do about the money. But I'm dying to know what you are going to do about Wyatt Landis."

Joie sighed. "I haven't the slightest idea."

76

CHAPTER SEVEN

WYATT STARED AT the ceiling. There was no point in looking at the clock. If five minutes had passed since the last time he checked, it would be a surprise. He had gone to bed at eleven thirty, and now it wasn't quite three. If he were lucky, he had dozed for five or ten minutes.

Back in Los Angeles, the solution would be a simple one. He would either use his home gym for a few hours or head to work. In Monroe, there was no place to work out. As for work? It was hard to head for his downtown office when downtown was over five hundred miles away.

Lately, he spent his days in Dave's garage fixing cars or playing Mr. Fixit. He couldn't do either until the sun came up in another… Wyatt gave in and looked at the clock. In another four hours. Even then, Dave didn't open until eight. And Mrs. Birch wouldn't appreciate him fixing her garage door before she had her first cup of coffee.

Wyatt pounded the pillow, trying to relax. How had it come to this? For as long as he could remember, he wanted one thing. To work at a job where he was the boss and allowed him to dress each morning in an expensive, perfectly tailored Italian suit.

To be honest, the suit part came later. But Wyatt knew early on that he wanted to be like his father. He was five years old when he had his epiphany. People respected his father. They looked up to him. And his word was law. For a little boy with three younger brothers whom he loved to boss around and a stubborn streak a mile wide, it was a no-brainer.

Caleb Landis was one of the most powerful producers in Hollywood. Wyatt decided that when he was all grown up, he would follow in his father's footsteps. To a five-year-old, grown up meant ten or eleven. Wyatt eventually achieved his goal, but it took a little longer.

His father didn't hand him a thing. Caleb Landis started at the bottom. He expected his son to do the same. And Wyatt wouldn't have had it any other way. There was no pleasure in winning the race if his father carried him most of the way then set him down three feet in front of the finish line. Wyatt found his own projects. Fought to get them financed. And worked his ass off to make sure they were quality productions brought in under budget.

Before he turned twenty-five, Wyatt's reputation in the movie industry was set. He could be a hard-nosed son of a bitch. But he was a fair one. Do the job the right way and Wyatt was your friend for life. Screw him over—or make the attempt—and you found yourself with an enemy. One that never forgot. He wasn't averse to handing out the occasional second chance. But they were rare. And the leash was short.

Wyatt's Hollywood had little to do with glitz and glamour. He dealt with bottom lines. A producer who didn't make his investors money wasn't in the business for long. His father taught him that. And Wyatt learned the lesson well.

Landis Productions was a true partnership. When Caleb asked his son to become his partner, the position was earned. Equals. At least in the office. At home, Caleb ruled. He always had. And if Wyatt had his way, he always would.

In Wyatt's world, there was order. He preferred it that way. Since coming to Monroe, that order had been disrupted. Jeans and t-shirts had replaced designer suits and ties. Instead of a neatly ordered office, he spent his days surrounded by grease and a chaos of tools and auto parts.

Yet that wasn't the reason he couldn't sleep. Wyatt was oddly Zen with his new, but blessedly temporary, lifestyle. He hated to admit it, but his family had been right. He had needed to get away. A change was doing him good.

He wasn't terribly concerned with his inability to locate J. L. Winter. He knew that the author hadn't signed with anyone else, and while he was away, his father worked on securing the rights to *Left of Mayfield*. One of them would succeed. They always did.

Which brought him back to his sleeplessness. It didn't take Steven Hawking's brain to figure it out. Guilt and desire. Neither emotion was new to him. However, this was the first time they came as a package deal. The population of Monroe thought he was Wyatt Rogers. These people had welcomed him. Opened their homes. Given him jobs. All without asking a single question about his past. He didn't like lying to them, but he could have lived with it. Lying to Joie was another matter altogether.

His conscience was giving him fits. It reminded him that a man—one with an ounce of honor—would tell her the truth before things progressed beyond the handholding stage. Even a kiss was crossing the line. Honor might be an old-fashioned concept, but it was one that Wyatt took seriously. In his work—and his personal life.

The solution was simple. Wyatt should tell her who he was. Then leave town. They had no future. Nothing beyond a mild flirtation. He couldn't offer her anything beyond an affair. And even if that were fine with Joie, it wasn't fine with him.

With a growl of frustration, Wyatt turned on the bedside lamp. Grabbing his phone, he scrolled through his contacts until he came across the name he was looking for. He knew it wasn't fair to wake a friend. Then again, what were friends for?

Feeling like some human interaction, he bypassed the usual phone call and decided on a little face time.

"What the hell, Landis? Do you have any idea what time it is?"

"To the second. You didn't have to answer."

Drew Harper snorted. "Normally I wouldn't have. But with all the trouble your family has gotten into lately, I figured it had to be an emergency."

Drew had a point. The Landises had used H&W Security quite a bit in the past year. Between the need for bodyguards, security details, and high-tech electronics, Wyatt's family had kept the company on speed dial. It helped that the men who lent their names to the company were also good friends.

"No emergency. But I do need your services."

"Keep your voice down," Drew cautioned. "It's okay, sweetheart. It's only Uncle Wyatt. You'll soon learn that he's a bigger pain in my ass than all your other uncles put together."

"Is that…?" Before he could finish, Drew lifted a tiny, gurgling bundle, positioning her in front of the camera.

"Meet Adele Rose Harper. The second love of my life."

Wrapped in a soft yellow blanket, the baby was a beauty. She had her mother's eyes. And nose. And chin. Then she smiled, and she was all Drew.

"You lucky S.O.B." Wyatt felt a tug of sadness and a deep sense of longing. "How is Tyler doing?"

"Are you kidding?" Drew laughed. He lightly kissed the baby's cheek and was rewarded with a happy sound that made Wyatt's heart clench. "My wife didn't let a little thing like childbirth slow her down. She's already working on her latest masterpiece. Which is why Addie and I are having some daddy/daughter time."

"Tyler is working now?"

"She an artist. When inspiration hits, there's no stopping her. During the day, she takes Addie to the studio. But she's at the polishing stage, and there's too much crap flying around for this one's little lungs. Just a second while I put Addie in her crib."

Drew disappeared, but Wyatt could hear him as he settled his daughter. The cooing and off-tune humming followed by a few words spoken too low to decipher. However, there was no mistaking the tone. Drew Harper, badass businessman, was a bundle of mush in his daughter's tiny hands. Just as it should be.

"She's out like a light." Drew's expression was slightly bemused, as though he hadn't gotten used to the emotions his little girl stirred inside of him.

"Sorry about this. If I'd been thinking, I would have waited until later to call."

"No harm done. Addie's tummy is full, and she'll be out until dawn. Hopefully." Drew yawned. He stretched his long arms over his head. A few seconds later, he looked into the camera, his eyes sharp and focused. It was a look Wyatt knew well. "What's up?"

"I need you to do a background check."

"Well, well, well."

"What?"

"Who is she?"

Wyatt frowned. "What makes you think it's a she?"

"Because you never learn. You had me do a check on your brothers' women."

"I stand by my decision. It made sense to know as much as possible about my potential sisters-in-law."

"You're lucky no one found out. Though I would have enjoyed watching Nate kick your ass."

Wyatt didn't try to deny what his brother's reaction would have been. "You wouldn't have been invited. The fact remains, I did what I thought was best, and I would do it again. The ladies checked out. My brothers are happy. That's all that matters."

"Arrogant as always." Drew shook his head. "Now, back to you. It's about time you took the leap. What's her name and how much can you tell me about her?"

"It isn't a woman."

"Ah." Drew raised an eyebrow, but he didn't miss a beat. "Good for you, man. Love is love, no matter the gender. What's *his* name?"

Wyatt sighed. Aware of the baby sleeping only a few feet away, he lowered his voice. "Fuck you, Harper. I'm not gay."

"Hey, I don't judge. This is the twenty-first century. There's no reason to be embarrassed."

He could see Drew's lips twitch.

"Funny." Wyatt wasn't laughing. "Remind me to kick *your* ass the next time we're in the same room."

"Sarcasm and threats at this time of the morning? What's going on?" Drew moved closer to the screen, peering at Wyatt. "You look different."

"I know. It's the bags under my eyes."

"No. I've seen you with those before. Your eyes look tired, but your face is relaxed. Those tight lines around your mouth have smoothed out. And there's at least a three-day growth of beard on your face. The man I know shaves every day. Sometimes twice. Now I'm worried. Who are you and what have you done with Wyatt Landis?"

"I'm on vacation," Wyatt mumbled. Friends, no matter how good, could be major pains in the ass.

"What?" Worried, Drew looked at the sleeping baby. With a sigh of relief, he lowered his voice. "Did you say vacation? As in away from work? You?"

"I've been known to take time off."

"True," Drew nodded. His expression grew serious. "But not since Stephanie's death."

Leave it to Drew not to mince words. It was one of the reasons he liked the man. Even his family hesitated before saying his wife's name as though any reminder would send him into a downward spiral. Wyatt waited for a beat, expecting the usual jolt. When it didn't come, he felt something else. Surprise and… relief. It had taken two years, but it seemed the clouds might have finally cleared for good.

"I will admit I was pressured into taking time off."

"There's a shocker."

"However," he continued, laughing in spite of himself. "I'm enjoying myself."

"There *is* a woman." Drew's smug expression grated on Wyatt's good mood. Mostly because his friend had hit the nail on the head. "Is this guy you want me to check out causing her trouble?"

"Not that I know of. I don't expect you to find anything. But after Nate's problems in Montana, I don't want to take any chances."

"Smart." Drew picked up a pen and paper. "What do you know about him?"

"Not much. His name is Brad Makepeace and he lives in Monroe, Nevada."

"And?"

"That's it. He has some money. Maybe."

"Okay." Drew yawned. "I need to catch a few hours of sleep. I suggest you do the same, my friend." The teasing sparkle re-entered his eyes. "You sure you don't want me to check out the woman? I'll make it a two-fer special."

Wyatt shook his head. "No," he said emphatically.

"Now I know she's had a good influence on you. I'd like to meet this miracle worker sometime."

"Drew. Not a word to my family. I…"

"You are officially a client," Drew told him. "H&W Security tells no tales out of school."

"Thanks."

"Take care. I'll call you as soon as I know anything."

Wyatt hung up. With that taken care of, he suddenly felt tired. Crawling into bed, he rested his head on the pillow and began to drift off as soon as he closed his eyes. However, it took his brain a little while to quiet.

He had been right to have Brad Makepeace investigated. As he told Drew, there was no reason to take any chances. Even more, he was happy with his decision to leave Joie out of it. Everyone had a past. She was entitled to keep hers to herself.

You could stick around and give Joie a chance to tell you her story—in her own time. Wyatt's last thought before sleep claimed him was that just a week ago the thought would have surprised him. Right now all he felt was tempted.

CHAPTER EIGHT

ONE OF THE things that Joie liked about her life was its lack of drama. She got up when she wanted. Ate when she was hungry. Visited with friends when she felt like human companionship. At night, she went to bed when her body told her it was time. She had no one to answer to. She made the rules. Then broke them whenever the mood hit her.

Because she chose to live in a small town where she knew her neighbors, and they knew her, Joie was able to control the level of chaos in which she became involved.

Brad Makepeace was a perfect example. He had never hidden his interest. And she had never led him on. The game, if you could call it that, was a simple one. He asked her out—with respect. And she said no—with kindness. She *chose* to change the dynamic. For the good of the town, but mostly because her friends asked. If she had refused, they would have accepted her decision.

As she dressed for her date, Joie took special care. It didn't matter that she didn't consider this a romantic occasion. Brad deserved to be treated the same as any man with whom she shared a meal. That meant she took time with her makeup. She dried and styled her hair. And she picked a flattering dress from her closet with a pair of heels that gave her legs the illusion that they belonged to a woman several inches taller.

She had explained the situation to Brad, giving him the option of turning down her invitation. He hadn't hesitated to say yes. Something told Joie that Brad believed that once he had her alone, he could win her over. Maybe he could—if their date had occurred before she met Wyatt Rogers.

No. Joie frowned at her reflection. Wyatt *Landis*. She was still coming to terms with that revelation. However, in the tradition of Scarlett O'Hara, she would think about it tomorrow. Tonight, Brad deserved her undivided attention.

Brad, with his boy-next-door, Midwest, Mom and apple pie looks, couldn't compete with Wyatt. It wasn't his fault. Chemistry. Or desire. Or whatever you wanted to call it, had a mind of its own. Until she dealt with Wyatt, no man, especially one she had never been attracted to, would stand a chance.

Joie held up a pair of ruby earrings. They had belonged to her grandmother and came to her last year when the dear lady passed away at the grand old age of ninety-eight. Deciding the color nicely complemented the winter-white sheath, she put them on. A touch of lipstick and one last twirl in front of the full-length mirror, and Joie decided she was ready to go.

She reached for her purse just as the doorbell rang. The clock on the wall read seven thirty exactly. Joie had to hand it to him. Brad was punctual.

"Great timing," she laughed as she opened the door. "I'm ready—Mom?"

"Hello, my darling girl." In a swirl of expensive perfume and designer clothing, Kristen Majors breezed past Joie. "Close the door, Joie. You don't want to let the cold in."

How many times had she heard that phrase when her father was alive? He would always end it by hugging himself close and shivering. Then he would wink. The memory made Joie smile—and her heart ache.

"Joie! Did you hear me?"

Shutting the door, Joie turned and was enveloped in her mother's warm, loving arms.

To look at them, you might not think they were mother and daughter. Kristen had more curves and softer features. Joie had her father's eyes and his dark hair. Kristen's eyes were grey and her hair whichever color suited her at the moment.

"Hi, Mom." Joie happily held on. "It's good to see you."

It was always a surprise when her mother visited, though Joie had no problem with her dropping in. Kristen brought with her an energetic vibe that was hard to resist. And because she never stayed long, there was no chance of their personalities clashing.

They had learned long ago that though they loved each other, their personalities were not suited to long mutual exposure. In a day or so, her mother would be on to her next adventure, leaving Joie to settle back into her quiet life. It was a well-oiled routine that suited them.

"Look at you." Kristen held Joie at arm's length, checking her from head to toe. "A dress, high heels, and Mama's earrings?" She peered closer. "Is that mascara? Who is he?"

"No one special." Which was true. Joie said a silent thank you that her date was with Brad, not Wyatt. Her mother was a whiz at sniffing out the slightest bit of genuine interest in the opposite sex. Kristen called it her superpower. Joie called it annoying as hell.

"Hmm." Kristen gave her one last look before nodding. "Too bad. However, not every man has to be *the one*?"

"Since when?" Joie asked with affection.

"I have dated just for fun."

Joie didn't dispute her mother's claim. Though she doubted it. When she wasn't married, Kristen treated dating as a competitive sport. The objective? True love followed by matrimony and a happily-ever-after ending. So far she was zero for five. No, that wasn't fair, Joie conceded. Her parents had a wonderful marriage. If her father were alive, Joie had no doubt they would still be married—happily and forever.

But that wasn't the case. Since her husband's death, Kristen was determined to find happiness. Joie didn't fault her objective. It was her method that was suspect.

She and her mother never argued. But it was easy to hurt Kristen's feelings. Joie knew they were headed down a slippery slope. The best solution was to change the subject.

"I'm happy to see you, Mom."

"But why am I here?"

Every now and then, her mother could get straight to the point. Since those moments were few and far between, Joie never took them for granted.

"Yes."

"I have news, my love." Kristen waved her left hand in front of Joie's face. "Congratulate me. As of yesterday, you are looking at Mrs. Edwin Poindexter."

So her mother had gotten her man. Joie wasn't surprised. Getting a husband was never her problem. Keeping one was another matter.

The diamond on Kristen's finger was eye-popping. Either Edwin was as rich as her mother had claimed, or he was a business man by day, jewel thief by night. Joie hoped for the best—concerning Edwin and her marriage.

Joie hugged her mother close, saying a silent prayer. Then whispered with complete sincerity, "I love you. Be happy."

"I *am* happy, darling." Kristen twirled away, laughing. "Edwin is in Las Vegas waiting for me. We're going to Paris for our honeymoon. *Paris*, Joie. From there, the sky's the limit."

The knock on the door signaled Brad's arrival.

"Why don't I move my date to another night? Brad isn't going anywhere."

Joie had known before she made the suggestion what her mother's answer would be. Almost to the word.

"Put off a date for your mother? I wouldn't hear of it. We can talk anytime. Besides, you look beautiful. You shouldn't waste all the effort on me."

Kristen, a firm believer in making a man wait, sauntered to the door. She paused for a few beats, then swung it open, her smile welcoming.

"Come in."

Brad hesitated. Kristen was a lot to take when one knew what to expect. A stranger—especially a man—was smart not to jump right in before deciding if it was safe.

"It's all right, Brad." Joie walked into his line of sight, suppressing her urge to laugh. "Kristen doesn't bite."

"Not unless you ask me to."

"Down, girl," Joie cautioned with a shake of her head. The woman was incorrigible. "Remember, you're a newlywed."

"Newlywed, but not dead." Thrilled with her impromptu rhyme, Kristen's tinkling laugh filled the room. "I'll have to tell that one to Edwin. He'll bust a gut."

"I…" Brad didn't know what to say, and Joie didn't blame him. Taking pity, she grabbed her jacket. "Kristen Poindexter, meet Brad Makepeace. Brad, this is my mother."

"Your mother?"

Joie couldn't tell if Brad were surprised or horrified. The look in his wide-eyed stare could have passed for either.

"Don't you dare say that we look more like sisters than mother and daughter."

Joie sighed. Her mother was having way too much fun at Brad's expense.

"She's right," Joie jumped in when Brad opened his mouth. "Don't. You. Dare."

Whatever he had been about to say, Brad was smart enough to keep to himself. He paused. Regrouped. Then sighed.

"Shall we go?"

Joie had never seen anyone look quite so relieved. Staying silent, Brad nodded.

"Don't worry about me," Kristen said, waving from the doorway. "Stay out as late as you like."

"Your mother is—"

"An original?" Joie smiled as he helped her into his car.

"Okay."

Joie laughed while Brad walked to the driver's side. *An original.* Her mother would like that. And most of the time so did Joie.

IT WAS CRAZY. Check that. *He* was crazy. Wyatt couldn't remember a time when jealousy ruled his thoughts. Yet here he was worrying about a woman he barely knew and her date with a man who seemed to be exactly what he appeared. A fairly successful businessman who lived an uneventful, unexciting life.

If Wyatt could believe the report Drew sent him that afternoon, Brad Makepeace's only crime was that he wanted the same woman as Wyatt. Not that it was a crime. More of an annoyance.

The idiocy of the situation wasn't lost on him. His nerves were in a knot over what? A kiss that hadn't happened? Jesus. What was he? Twelve? That was the age he had his first kiss. At the time, it had been an epic event. A rite of passage with Paula Drake, the prettiest girl in the neighborhood.

In truth, it had been awkward. They had bumped noses, their teeth hitting with so much force, he was surprised one of them hadn't walked away with a chip. It might have lasted five seconds. But for a week, Wyatt had floated on a cloud of prepubescent wonder. The rest of the summer, he and Paula practiced every chance they could find.

In September, Paula moved on to a boy three years older, and Wyatt simply moved on.

Wyatt had polished his technique considerably since then. He had enough experience to know that kissing Joie would be memorable. Epic? That was to be seen. But he knew his restlessness—his worry that Brad Makepeace might possess some hidden charms that Joie wouldn't be able to resist—was beyond crazy.

As he entered the *Monarch Café*, Wyatt breathed in the heady aroma. He stopped just inside the door and looked around. This was what he needed. A good meal and the distraction of the other customers.

"They aren't here."

"Who isn't here?" Wyatt blinked in surprise.

Dexter Brink walked up to him, a grin covering his face. The man was tall. Tall enough to look Wyatt straight in the eyes—an unusual occurrence since he had been in Monroe. The Landis men were above average in height, the men of Monroe, not so much.

"Weren't you looking for Joie and Brad?"

Was he? God, he hoped not. Wyatt didn't think he was that far gone. It was bad enough to wonder what Joie was doing on her date. Seeking her out would be over the edge. *Way* over.

"I'm here for dinner. That's all." Wyatt wanted to groan when he heard the defensive tone of his voice. Unfortunately, there was no taking it back.

"Right." Dex let it pass, but his lips twitched. "There's an empty table by the window. In case you want to watch the door across the street."

"Why would I want to do that?" Wyatt was afraid he already knew the answer.

"Joie and Brad went into *The Bonnie Lass* about twenty minutes ago. If you're patient, you'll have a perfect view when they exit."

"I'll sit at the counter." Where his back would be to the window—and *The Bonnie Lass.*

"Suit yourself."

"How can a town this size support so many restaurants?" Wyatt asked as he followed Dex across the room.

"We Monroeites like to eat out. Thank the Lord. Otherwise, I would be out of a job."

"Does the chef always seat his customers?"

"I saw you come in. I thought you might like to commiserate." Dex poured him a glass of water. "Carole is on a date. In Las Vegas."

"That's quite a way to go for dinner."

"Dinner and tickets to see Celine Dion," Dex ground out the words. "I hate Teddy Street."

"I assume he is Carole's date?" Dex nodded. "I know I haven't been in Monroe for long, but I thought you and Carole were together."

"We are." Dex tore pieces from the paper napkin he had been about to place in front of Wyatt. "When it suits Carole. She gets an itch, and I'm supposed to scratch it. But if I ask for anything, I'm pushing her. What the hell. We've been doing this dance for over a year. Is it wrong that I'm tired? I want to slow down and appreciate what we have."

"It isn't wrong. But..." Wyatt hesitated, even though Dex had asked.

"Go on. I could use an impartial opinion."

"If Carole doesn't want to settle down, you should respect her wishes."

"That's all I've done." Dex balled up the napkin and threw it onto the floor. "She loves me. I know it, the town knows it." Several people within earshot nodded. "Carole knows it. This date tonight is typical. Every time I get too close, she runs. A sleepover in Las Vegas is her way of pushing me away."

In Wyatt's opinion, going away with another man seemed like more than a push.

"What are you going to do about it?"

The question came from an elderly gentleman two stools down. He kept his head down, taking a mouthful of soup.

"The ball is in Carole's court, Larry."

The man snorted. He turned his head, his mouth curled in contempt. "If you were a man, you would get in your car, drive to Vegas, and stop whatever shenanigans Carole is up to."

"I don't know—"

"Exactly." Revving up, Larry set down his spoon. "What is wrong with your generation? You let your woman go off with another man. And you!"

"Me?" Startled, Wyatt looked from Dex to Larry. "What do I have to do with it?"

"Joie is a woman worth fighting for. So is Carole. But what are you wimps doing? Crying. Whining. Well, boo hoo."

"I wasn't crying," Wyatt mumbled.

Why did he suddenly feel like he was talking to his father? Larry sounded too much like Caleb Landis for his comfort. He may have been twenty-five years older and so frail he looked like a puff of wind would blow him over, but Larry had a strength of conviction that was pure Caleb.

Which reminded him. He needed to call his parents. One thing Callie Flynn did not put up with was wayward children. No matter where in the world Wyatt and his brothers traveled, they stayed in touch. Because their mother insisted. But mostly because they wanted to. Wyatt had learned long ago that he needed his family for his sanity. That meant keeping them close—even when he was hundreds of miles away.

"A woman likes to know she's wanted," Larry continued, breaking up a handful of saltines into his soup. "

"How did I get dragged into this?" Wyatt demanded. "Joie is on a date. It has nothing to do with me. In fact, it's your fault."

"Me?" Dex stepped back before Wyatt could jab him in the chest with his finger. "I don't run Joie's social life."

"Did you or did you not pressure her into going out with Brad Makepeace?"

"Well," Dex sputtered. "I…"

"Ha!" Wyatt raised his finger triumphantly. "Do you or do you not expect her to charm him using her feminine wiles?

"Now wait a minute." Dex rose to his full height. "I resent that implication. No one suggested she sleep with Makepeace."

"Unless she wanted to," Larry added with a chuckle.

"You think this is funny?" Respecting his elders was one thing. However, Wyatt believed that only went so far.

"I think *you* are funny." Larry waved his spoon at Wyatt. "You have been in Monroe how long?"

"A little over a week."

"You've made yourself pretty handy, haven't you?"

"I help out where I can." There it was again. Larry gave him the *dad stare*. Wyatt had felt it many times. Caleb Landis was a master.

"Helping out is fine, but it doesn't give you the right to judge us. The people of Monroe are loyal. Joie is one of us. That means when we need her help, she steps in. It's a date, son. One meal. Brad Makepeace might bore her to death, but her virtue isn't in danger."

"You're right." Wyatt came to get some dinner and calm down. Instead, he worked himself up into a state worse than when he arrived. "I apologize."

"No need. I can't say I blame you." Larry turned his gaze toward Dex. "You, on the other hand, are another matter. Are you going after her or not?"

"I'm not chasing Carole to Las Vegas." Dex removed his apron. He walked to the kitchen door, then yelled, "Clancy? I'm taking the rest of the night off."

"I thought you weren't chasing after her?" Larry sent Dex a self-satisfied look.

Dex said something under his breath.

"Speak up, son. I'm an old man."

"With ears like a bat." Dex sighed. "I said, a man is entitled to change his mind. You nosey old so and so."

Larry laughed so hard Wyatt was afraid the old man would tumble from his stool. Just in case, he prepared himself to catch him on the way down.

"Kids. You think you know everything. But all it takes is a push in the right direction for you to figure out you still have a few things to learn."

"Yes, sir."

"Order the beef stew," Larry told him. "And if you buy me a piece of cherry pie, I'll keep you company."

Wyatt gave the waitress the order. He spent the next hour listening to Larry's stories about Monroe. The man had a natural gift as a storyteller.

"Have you ever thought about writing a book?"

"Why?" Larry looked genuinely puzzled. "I like to talk. Telling tales is the best way to keep them alive. Are you going to forget?"

"I'll remember," Wyatt assured him.

"There you go." Larry put his money on the counter. "You done?"

Wyatt had polished off his stew and his own piece of pie.

"Yes, sir."

"Call me Larry. Why don't we walk off our meal? On the way to my place, I'll tell you about my septic tank."

Wyatt shook his head. He didn't know if Larry really needed a handy man or if he simply wanted the company. It didn't matter. Wyatt was happy to spend more time with the old man.

However, if the septic tank needed fixing, Larry was out of luck. Plumbing was out of his wheelhouse. Thank goodness.

As he and Larry made their way down the street, Wyatt couldn't help taking one look over his shoulder toward *The Bonnie Lass*. His evening had turned out to be much better than he had anticipated. He knew it was petty, but he couldn't help hoping that Joie didn't feel the same.

"WHY?" JOIE FELL onto the sofa in a limp heap. "Why couldn't Brad surprise me? I expected him to bore me to tears, and he did. Two hours of the most inane conversation possible."

"You're exaggerating." Kristen handed Joie a cup of tea.

Catching a whiff, Joie lifted it closer to her nose. "Herbal? Honestly? You know how I feel about this stuff."

"It's raspberry. Your favorite."

"No," Joie corrected. "The fruit is my favorite. The problem with herbal tea is that it makes a promise then doesn't deliver. This." She set the cup on the table, "tastes like dishwater. As does every herbal tea ever concocted. The closest it gets to raspberries is the picture on the packet."

"You drink too much caffeine."

"According to my doctor, I am in perfect health. For a woman pushing thirty."

"Please. Don't remind me."

Joie hid her smile. She knew one mention of age, and her mother would forget whether her tea was caffeinated or not.

"I don't look old enough to have a daughter who...." Kristen swallowed, not able to say the number. "You don't look that old. Why must you remind me?"

"Relax. You can pass for my sister." Thanks to a few strategically placed nips and tucks. But Joie kept that observation to herself.

"Edwin thinks I'm twenty-eight."

Either Edwin was a liar, or he needed a pair of glasses. Again, Joie kept quiet.

"Are you happy, Mom?"

"I told you I was." Kristen took a bright red compact from her purse, checking her already impeccably applied makeup.

"Mom." When she didn't look up, Joie covered her mother's hand and lowered the mirror. "Look at me. Are you happy?"

Kristen sighed. Her smile reached her eyes, but she wasn't as jubilant as she had earlier tried to make Joie believe.

"Edwin is not your father."

"No man is."

"I'm going to tell you something, Joie. But promise me it won't go any further than the two of us."

"I promise," Joie said it automatically. However, she knew that if her mother's secret had anything to with Edwin treating her as anything less than a queen, Joie wouldn't think twice. Some promises shouldn't be kept.

"I have come to the conclusion that your father was my only true love."

"Oh, Mom." Joie rested her head on her Mother's shoulder. "Isn't it nice that you found him? I know your time together was too short, but you were lucky. Some people *never* get what you had."

"Are we still talking about me?"

Surprised, Joie paused before answering. Something had changed. Since the last time they were together, her mother had acquired a touch of self-awareness and a good dose of empathy. In the past, she wouldn't have grasped the subtext of Joie's words. Tonight, she seemed genuinely in tune with her daughter's emotions.

"I remember what it was like with you and Dad."

"I'm glad." Kristen ran a hand down her hair. "My parents were not happy people. I think that was the first thing that drew me to your father. After his nice ass."

Joie laughed. This *was* different. They rarely spoke about her father. And in such a light, intimate way. She knew how much it hurt her mother to think about what she had lost. Perhaps she was finally moving on. For the first time, Joie felt a genuine desire to meet Edwin Poindexter. If this were his influence, the man deserved her respect and gratitude.

"He could make you laugh."

"Always," Kristen nodded. "No matter how upset I was, your father knew exactly how to lighten my mood. When you were a baby, simply hearing his voice would calm you. We lost a good man, Joie."

Joie felt her throat tighten, and tears gather in her eyes. It had been a long time since she had cried over her father. However, it was the first time she had cried with her mother. They had dealt with their grief in different ways. Joie drawing into herself. Kristen throwing herself into the world—and other men. Finding a way to grieve together, no matter how many years had passed, felt good. And somehow right. A final tribute to her father.

"I *am* happy, Joie." Kristen handed her a tissue from her purse as she used one to wipe her cheeks. "Edwin is exactly what I need. Kind. Patient. Generous to a fault. For the first time since your father, I've found a man who understands me. He accepts me as I am. You have no idea what it is like to try to be what you think someone wants."

"I imagine it's exhausting. And impossible to maintain."

"My bright girl. You *do* understand." Joie relaxed into her mother's hug. "Thank goodness you have your father's brains. I used to wonder what you got from me."

Joie kissed her mother's cheek. Breathing in, she made a memory so that she would always remember this moment.

"What did I get from you? That's easy. I got you."

"I love you, baby."

They saturated several more tissues before they finished. But the tears were cleansing. When she said goodbye to her mother the next morning, Joie was sorry to see her go. Another first. She promised to take a week or two next spring and visit her mother in Texas.

Joie waved goodbye wondering at life's sudden twists and turns. One never knew what was coming. Sometimes it was bad. Or in this case, it was beautiful. But if she kept her head up and her heart open, it was never dull.

CHAPTER NINE

"HOW WAS YOUR trip?"

When Carole didn't answer, Joie pulled her head out of the refrigerator. Her friend had dropped by for breakfast. Joie tried to decide if she could stretch one egg and a tiny chunk of cheese into a passable omelet. A trip to the grocery store was definitely in her future.

"Carole?"

"I'm trying to decide how to answer. How was my trip?" Carole picked up her coffee. She took a long, thoughtful sip, her eyes narrowing. "Right now, I should be soaking in a huge jetted tub while waiting for room service to deliver my fresh strawberries and lightly buttered toast."

"Sorry. All I have to offer is a skimpy omelet and the ends from a loaf of whole wheat."

"You're a doll. It's Dexter Brink who is at the top of my shit list."

Joie turned toward the stove, hiding her smile. Inside, she cheered Dex. It took a lot of balls to drive through the night to Las Vegas when he had no idea what his reception would be once he got there.

"No one forced you to come back with him."

"He did."

"What?" Joie dropped her spatula. Carole had left that fact out in her first telling. "He physically forced you? Dex?"

"He forced me with his big puppy dog eyes."

"Jesus, Carole. I was prepared to kick his balls up to his throat."

"Be my guest." Carole sighed, her eyes showing her lack of sleep. "I was happy to see the idiot. What does that say about me?"

"Do you really want me to answer that?" Joie wanted to sympathize. But a lot of women would gladly trade places with Carole. A good man who loved her that much? Boo hoo.

"I know. It was a mistake to go to Las Vegas with Teddy."

"But." When it came to Carole and Dex, there was always a but.

"I felt my walls crumbling. Teddy seemed like the perfect way to shore my foundation."

"You know that I'm a big fan of metaphors. But let's get down to it. You want to marry Dex. You're scared. You used Teddy hoping Dex would break it off with you. He would be the villain, and you could say, '*See. I knew he was too good to be true.*'"

"I hate you."

"No, you don't." Joie handed Carole a plate. As impromptu breakfasts went, it wasn't bad. "You hate that I'm right."

"On top of everything else, Teddy didn't argue. Another man shows up—blessedly after we had seen Celine Dion—and takes his sure-thing date away. What did Teddy do? He shrugged and left to play poker. Not the most flattering reaction."

"I wonder if he ran into Edwin," Joie mused.

"Who?"

"My mother's— Never mind."

"Then, the huge cherry on top of my crappy sundae? Dex insists that we drive back to Monroe. Immediately."

"He has a job." Honestly, Joie was getting tired of defending Dex. She knew this game. Carole wanted her to point out why Dex was right. That stopped right here. She felt like a third wheel on a dysfunctional bicycle.

"I—"

"Nope." Joie slapped her hand onto the table. "I'm out. You and Dex have to solve your problems without me as your buffer."

"Fine." Carole sulked for about thirty seconds. "Did I mention my kitchen is flooded?"

"When did that happen?" Joie demanded. Carole was a master at giving out information bit by bit.

"While I was in Vegas. One of the pipes broke under the sink. It ran into the living room."

"What about your shop?"

"Thank God for small miracles. Dex thinks there's some damage to the ceiling, but it hadn't leaked through."

"What a pain in the butt." Joie never stayed annoyed with Carole for long. Finding out her best friend's home was underwater cleared the air quicker than usual. "You'll move in here until everything is repaired."

"I was hoping you'd say that." Carole squeezed Joie's hand. "You should have seen Dex. Mr. Take-charge. He's called a plumber. And a carpenter. And didn't mention that if he hadn't come to get me, the entire inventory in my store would have been ruined."

"He's a keeper."

"I know," Carole sighed. "Looks like I'll have to marry the big jerk."

"What!" Joie leaped from her chair, pulling a laughing Carole into her arms. "When did you decide this?"

"About five minutes ago. Once I tell Dex, there will be no living with him."

"We have a wedding to plan." Joie twirled Carole in a circle.

"God." Caught up in Joie's enthusiasm, Carole hugged her friend. "I swore I would never do this again. What if it's a disaster?"

"What if it's the best thing that ever happened to you?"

"What if after five minutes in my mother's company, Dex hightails it for the hills?"

"We keep them apart until after the ceremony." Joie wasn't about to let Carole *what if* herself into changing her mind. "He's the love of your life."

"He is." Carole's eyes widened. "Dexter Banks is the love of my life. Holy crap."

"How does it feel?"

"I might throw up." Carole swallowed, taking a deep breath. "Nope. Your breakfast is staying where it is. Crap. Now I want to cry."

"Go ahead." Joie patted her back. "I might join you."

"I refuse to tell Dex that we're getting married with red, swollen eyes."

"He won't care."

"I will." Carole rushed to the downstairs bathroom. "Great. The bags under my eyes have bags. Ideally, I would awake from nine hours of uninterrupted sleep. Head to a spa for a few hours of pampering before flying in the top makeup artist in the country to give me that natural look that only the best cosmetics can achieve."

"When have you ever cared about all that crap?"

"The thought's run through my head on occasion." Carole fluffed her hair. "However, Dex has seen me at my worst."

Joie enjoyed seeing her friend with a case of nerves. Carole was only calm when she didn't care. "He loves you. What else matters?"

Carole turned from the mirror. Her expression made Joie gasp. Joy. It was in her eyes. It made her skin glow. And it made Joie's heart soar with happiness.

"Nothing else matters," Carole said. In spite of herself, tears filled her eyes. "Nothing but Dex."

THE SUN BEAT down on Wyatt's bare skin. He could feel the sheen of perspiration. It felt strangely good. Right.

He had started the day in a t-shirt, long-sleeved pullover, and jacket. Each piece was discarded as the hours wore on. It was fall, but the combination of his exertion and an unseasonably warm day, made it feel more like early summer.

For a man who was used to working behind a desk, his little vacation as a handyman turned into a full-time job. At least that was how it felt today. His brothers would bust a gut laughing if they could see the button-down Wyatt ass deep in physical labor.

Wyatt had some skills learned when he was much younger. He could wield a hammer without taking out his fingers. But there were some things beyond his abilities. Thank God for YouTube and his iPhone.

He still wasn't sure how he had come to work the entire day on Larry's roof. *It's only a few loose shingles,* the old man assured him. It shouldn't take more than an hour. Ninety minutes tops.

Three hours later, Wyatt was sweating his way through a job that would extend into tomorrow and possibly the day after that. Larry was a charming manipulator from way back. Since it was a trait that Wyatt used to his advantage on more than one occasion, he appreciated it in someone else. Theoretically. Having it used on him was another matter.

However, Wyatt's new friend provided him with an endless supply of water and a damn fine lunch. It had been a long time since he had feasted on tuna fish sandwiches and Ruffles potato chips. An added bonus was the crispy, tart, dill pickle, courtesy of the widow down the lane. And a thick piece of chocolate cake. Baked that morning by his neighbor. It seemed Larry had an unending supply of lady friends. To look at him, the old man didn't look like a Casanova. However, as Larry put it, it was all about supply and demand. There weren't many men his age. Ones that were mobile and had their own teeth? Forget about it. All he had to do was sit back and let the ladies come to him.

Thinking about that conversation, Wyatt chuckled as he lined up the new shingles that had been conveniently delivered that morning to Larry's garage.

"How's it going?"

Speak of the devil. Larry stood in the middle of his lawn looking up at Wyatt. He made no effort to hide his grin.

"Slowly." Wyatt adjusted his sunglasses. "It's amazing how a few little shingles turned into most of the roof."

"Huh." Larry scratched his head. "Must have been that big windstorm we had about a month ago."

"Must have been."

Deciding this was as good a time as any to take a break, Wyatt left what he was doing and descended the sturdy ladder that he had found hanging neatly in Larry's tool shed that morning.

"Here's some of that fancy bottled water I know your generation likes."

Grinning, Wyatt took the bottle. Larry used that line every time. Usually, while drinking the water himself.

"Thanks."

Unscrewing the cap, Wyatt sighed with pleasure as the first trickle of water hit the back of his throat. Three gulps and the bottle was empty.

"Need another?" Larry sipped at his can of Coke. "There's plenty in the fridge. Lots of variety if you want something stronger."

"For instance?" Wyatt didn't drink more than the occasional beer—and never when he was working. But he was curious what Larry considered *something stronger*.

"Root beer. Orange soda. Some lemon lime crud my grand-nephews like."

"Oh," Wyatt hid his smile. "The *hard* stuff. No, thanks. But I will take advantage of your garden hose. I'm sweating like a pig, and a cool down sounds good."

"Help yourself." Larry waved him toward the side of the house. "I'll be inside if you need me."

The hose was conveniently wound around a storage contraption Wyatt recognized from his mother's garden. As he unwound the length, he thought about his own house that sat in the Hollywood hills. He kept it neat—inside and out. Or rather, the crew he paid kept it that way. But unlike Larry's, it wasn't a home. It was a place for him to crash for a few hours between work and visiting his family.

It hadn't bothered him before now. Wyatt had bought the place a year and a half ago—six months after his wife's death. The condo he and Stephanie shared while they were together—the one she continued to live in after they had separated—sold quickly. Wyatt would have been content to continue as he was. The hotel he had moved into when he left Stephanie suited him. Room service at any hour. His bed was made every day with fresh sheets. Clean towels were always hanging in the bathroom, but if he needed more, they were only a phone call away.

It was a bachelor's paradise. Unfortunately, his family—led by his mother—didn't see it that way. Hotel rooms were depressing, she insisted. Not that she used that word. Speaking of the big D was a no-no. It was true he hadn't been in the best shape after Stephanie's death. It was one more shovel of guilt on an ever-growing pile that had started a month after their wedding and never let up.

At one point, Wyatt wondered if he would ever pull himself out. He had watched as his wife suffered bouts of untreated manic depression. He would make Stephanie see a doctor. However, getting her to stay on the prescribed medicine was another matter. He would watch her take the pills, making sure she swallowed. Then, as he later found out, the second he turned his back, she would stick a finger down her throat and vomit them up. Short of watching her every second of every day, Wyatt had no recourse.

Wyatt knew what depression looked like. And though he had never hit the soul-crushing lows he watched Stephanie experience, he came close. The difference? The reason he didn't fall into that gaping black pit and never crawl out again? The answer was simple. His family.

Stephanie had suffered from a chemical imbalance. But she also grew up with indifferent parents. As an only child, she wasn't blessed with three brothers who would figuratively kick his ass when they saw him drifting away from them.

The Landis clan stuck together. Someone was always there to listen. Though not even Colt—Wyatt's most frequent sounding board—knew everything. There was one secret he had kept to himself. It haunted him. His dreams were filled with images that tore him from his sleep.

But he was better. This trip. This unplanned respite in Monroe, Nevada had done him a world of good. Perspective was something one could preach, but it was hard to achieve behind a desk in Los Angeles. Seeing the same old things. Speaking with the same old people. For the first time in over five years, Wyatt felt like he could breathe without the familiar weight of failure pressing down on his chest.

Reaching down, Wyatt turned on the water. Bracing himself, he lifted the nozzle and let the cold water wash away the film of drying sweat. It cleansed his body, just as Monroe had started to cleanse his spirit.

"Oh. My. Goodness."

Joie heard the voice before she could see the speaker. It was accompanied by a breathless sigh and two distinct giggles. As she peeked around the corner, she recognized three of the town's most upstanding citizens. Mayor Barbara Osweiler. The deputy mayor, Lana Fielder. And Lana's sister, Pat Crandall. Joie knew them from various town events and get-togethers. Upstanding was the way she would have described all three women. Certainly not the type to stand in the middle of the sidewalk tittering like adolescent girls.

"What do you think that is about?" Carole asked.

Intrigued, Joie shrugged.

They had come from Carole's apartment. The water damage wasn't disastrous. However, it made staying there an inconvenience. Carole packed enough clothing and necessities for a few nights, and they were headed to Joie's house when they heard the three women. Curious, they had changed direction, following the sounds.

"Afternoon, Mayor Osweiler."

"Yes," the mayor nodded. "It certainly is."

This sent the other women into another fit of giggles. Exchanging puzzled expressions with Carole, Joie turned to see what had them so enraptured.

"Wow!" Carole licked her lips. "I thought Wyatt looked good with his clothes on. Half-naked Wyatt is… Wow!"

"Don't forget the water," Lana Fielder said, bouncing from foot to foot.

"How could I?'

Joie didn't comment. Whatever she might have said dissolved on her tongue the second she spied Wyatt. *Holy Hotness, Batman.* She didn't know why he was standing shirtless in Larry Mahoney's yard. Or what had prompted him to tip his head back to let the water from a running hose cascade across his face and down his body. Nor did she care. He looked like a bronze sculpture come to life. Impossibly chiseled. Improbably perfect.

"I want to lick every drop from his body." The mayor fanned herself with her purse. "I didn't think real people had arms like that. Or abs. And his back. Lord have mercy."

"What do you think, Joie?" Carole had recovered enough from the spectacle to send her a teasing look. "Since you're the only one of us with a snowball's chance in hell of fulfilling the mayor's fantasy, do you think Wyatt tastes as good as he looks?"

Joie wanted to kick Carole in the butt. Wyatt's free show was winding down, which meant the ladies were eager for something new but related, to gawk at. Luckily, Wyatt picked that moment to notice his audience.

"He's looking this way."

To say her words had their desired effect was putting it mildly. Barbara, Lana, and Pat gasped. Collectively, they did a comical Bugs Bunny head swivel toward Wyatt then back at her before hightailing it around the corner.

Carole played it cool. With a wink, she waved at Wyatt. Joie couldn't imagine what he was thinking, but she had to hand it to him. As though this sort of thing happened every day, he winked back.

"The man has style." Carole sighed. "If you want to throw him back, the women will be lining up to catch him."

"He isn't mine. To keep or throw or anything else."

Nor was Joie sure she wanted him to be. The big lug was lying about his identity. It didn't matter that she and everyone else in town knew. So he wasn't a serial murderer on the run or a deadbeat dad hiding from his baby momma.

Carole was right. A man who looked like that could have any woman he wanted. And probably did. On the other hand, Joie was more selective. It took more than a mouth-watering body, killer blue eyes, and a slightly crooked smile to get her panties in a twist.

"You're kidding yourself. You want him."

"I know." Wyatt still looked her way. She couldn't see the color of his eyes from here, but she knew. Damn him. "One kiss."

"Right," Carole scoffed. "Good luck maintaining that fantasy. Wyatt is a man, not a twelve-year-old boy."

"I'm aware." Joie licked her suddenly dry lips.

"He hasn't taken his eyes off you. Can you feel the heat?" Carole fanned herself with her hand. "Another few seconds and *I'm* going to start sweating."

"What should I do?"

Carole sent her a surprised look. Joie didn't ask that question. Ever. She knew what she wanted. When she didn't, she figured it out. Whether it was moving to Monroe or picking the perfect color to paint her house. Joie had a clear picture of her life.

"Oh, honey. Welcome to the club."

"What club?"

"The *That Man Has Scrambled My Brains* club. Membership isn't exclusive. But the perks, if you're willing, are outstanding."

Joie didn't like the sound of that. Scrambled brains? No, thank you.

"Can I revoke my membership?"

Carole laughed, wrapping an arm around her waist. "It isn't easy. My advice? Confront him. Ask Wyatt why he lied about his identity. It might not be what you think."

"And if it is?"

"That will be up to you. But you know what?"

"When it comes to Wyatt?" Joie shook her head. "Enlighten me. Please."

"When the air is clear, and there aren't any more secrets? I don't think you'll care about the whys. Kiss him. Take him to bed. Let yourself enjoy what he has to offer."

"It's tempting." Joie watched as Wyatt dried himself off with his t-shirt. "What if sex is all he's offering?"

"What did Oliver Twist say? *Please, sir. I want some more*?"

"Oliver Twist was starving."

"So are you." Carole gave her one last squeeze before letting go and picking up her suitcase. "Gorge yourself, Joie. A feast like Wyatt Landis may never come along again."

There was no denying that Wyatt was a feast for the eyes. As Carole walked toward her house, Joie started across the street— toward Wyatt. What she would say when she got there, she didn't know.

"Hi." *Brilliant, Joie. Scintillating.*

"Hello."

Wyatt's slow smile sent a shot of heat through her body. It was a little crooked. Just as she remembered.

"You look… Hot?" Joie groaned. Silently, thank God.

"Was that a question?"

"Maybe." Carole had called it. Her brains were scrambled.

"Larry conned me into fixing his roof."

Wyatt pulled his t-shirt over his head. No, Joie almost screamed. It was a shame to cover perfection. At least his sculpted biceps were still on display.

"Hey," Wyatt waved his hand in front of her face. "Are you still with me?"

"You have a beautiful body."

Joie's eyes slowly widened. She felt a blush spread over her cheeks. *Well, hell.* She expected Wyatt to laugh. Or tease. To her amazement, she could have sworn he looked embarrassed. Not as embarrassed as she was. But he was definitely uncomfortable.

"Beautiful? Not rugged? Or manly?"

"Definitely beautiful." Wyatt's discomfort lessened hers. She felt as though they were on equal footing again.

"Wrong. That would be my brother."

His brother? As in Colton Landis? The mention of his movie-star brother was the perfect opening for Wyatt to confess his true identity. Joie held her breath, waiting for him to step through. To help, Joie gave him a small push.

"How many siblings do you have?" As if she didn't already know.

"Three. I'm the oldest."

For a second, Joie thought he would say more. But when Wyatt turned to pick up his jacket, she realized the moment had passed. If it had ever existed. Perhaps he never planned on coming clean. Chances were he would leave town without revealing to her who he was.

"I'm an only child."

"I was eight when I asked my parents if we could give my brothers back." Wyatt laughed. "I was informed that it didn't work that way. I was stuck—an older brother for life."

"From the sound of your voice, I would say you got used to them."

"Garrett, Nate, and Colt are a continual pain in my ass. They are also my best friends."

Joie had never worried about being an only child. She had friends. And if she were lonely, she made up stories in her head to keep her company. Still, it must be nice to have siblings. The shared memories. The closeness that came from growing up together. Wyatt was fortunate. And she loved that he knew it.

"You love them."

"I do." Wyatt's grin widened. "Mom insists."

"Your mother. What is she like?"

Joie was fascinated to hear what it was like to grow up as the son of a bona fide screen goddess. Callie Flynn was a legend. A few of her films ranked among Joie's all-time favorites.

"My mom." Wyatt seemed to think about it. Then he shrugged. "She is the most beautiful woman I have ever known. Inside and out."

There was such simple sincerity in his words. Callie Flynn was a lucky woman.

"About—"

"Tell me," Wyatt interrupted, leaning down until the blue of his eyes were all she could focus on. "How was your date?"

"Fine." She didn't want to trash Brad. However, she refused to embellish. The date had been a bore. Brad was a bore. "I owe you a kiss."

"I remember."

Joie didn't step back when Wyatt moved closer. She wanted to erase the few inches between them until her body was pressed against his. She breathed deeply, taking in his scent. Sweat—clean and musky. Plus, something else. Elusive. Unique. If she could market it as a fragrance, the label would read Wyatt. She filled her lungs and sighed. She would make a fortune.

"Wyatt."

"Joie."

They spoke at the same time, stopping to let the other continue.

"You first," she said.

"Come with me." Wyatt took her arm, leading her to the side of the house and away from prying eyes. "I have a confession to make."

"Go on." Joie took his hand, chanting silently. Tell me your name. Tell me your name. The voice in her head was so loud she almost missed it when Wyatt said the words.

"My name isn't Wyatt Rogers. It's Wyatt Landis."

Relieved, Joie let the air out of her lungs, unaware until that moment that she had been holding her breath.

"I know."

"You— What? When did you find out?"

She couldn't tell what he was thinking. Perplexed? Exasperated? *Join the club, fella.*

"I found out yesterday."

"Okay." Wyatt seemed to relax. "How?"

"Carole told me. Most of the town has known from day one."

He began to pace, running a hand through his damp hair. Joie didn't know what he was thinking, but she could practically hear the wheels turning. Wyatt was a ponderer. She hadn't known him long, but that aspect of his personality was obvious. It was something they had in common.

"All this time. The job at the garage. Fixing things around town. Everyone knew I didn't need the money?"

Joie nodded. She could figure out where he was going with this. She decided to stop him before he drew the wrong conclusions.

"It wasn't done out of spite or mean-spiritedness."

"Right," Wyatt snorted.

"You think this was an elaborate joke at your expense?" She wanted him to understand that the people of Monroe—her friends—didn't play those games. "Dave at the garage? Margie? Larry? They aren't mean-spirited people, Wyatt. You've been in Hollywood too long. Not everyone has ulterior motives."

"Then tell me. Why? What did they get out of it? Besides cheap labor."

"Idiot," she muttered.

"Excuse me?" Wyatt crossed his strong arms over his chest. Joie knew damn well that he had heard her.

"I called you an idiot." To emphasize her point, she spelled out the word with her finger on his forearm. "For over a week, you have been shown kindness."

"Tell that to my aching muscles."

"No one forced you to do the work." Joie jabbed his arm—hard—for good measure. "Margie and the rest decided you had to have a good reason for keeping your identity hidden. Since they knew you weren't a desperate criminal, they did what they would do for anyone. They respected your privacy."

Joie turned to leave so Wyatt could mull that over. But before she had taken a step, he stopped her.

"What about you?" Slowly, he backed her up—step by step—until she bumped into the house.

"Me?"

Joie had to tip her head to look at him. Wyatt had her trapped between his muscled arms. His palms were flat against the wooden siding, making escape difficult. She could have tried to duck and run, but he would have caught her before she had traveled three feet. Besides, she wasn't afraid. Just the opposite. She couldn't wait to see what he would do. She *did* owe him a kiss.

"Were you going to tell me you knew?" Wyatt bent until his nose was only inches from hers. She could hear his breathing, the uneven sound made the rhythm of her heart stutter in an interesting way.

"I hadn't decided."

"You would have let me kiss you?" His lips moved close enough for her to feel the heat of his breath against hers. She was tempted to close the gap between them but found the anticipation too delicious.

"Maybe." When she sensed he was about to move back, she grabbed his t-shirt and whispered, "Maybe not. It *is* only a kiss."

"I suppose you're right. Or are you?" Wyatt's blue eyes grew impossibly dark. "Let's find out."

This wasn't a first kiss. Joie knew what one of those felt like. Where was the uncertainty? Or the hesitation while trying to figure out which way to turn their heads? She waited for his lips to feel too soft. Or too hard.

No, this wasn't a first kiss. This was a full onslaught delivered by a man who had supreme confidence in what he was doing.

"You taste like butterscotch."

"I—"

Was she supposed to respond? Apparently not. Wyatt had barely whispered the words against her lips when his mouth covered hers again. His tongue lightly touched hers—teasing. Joie sighed, wrapping her arms around his waist. She gave into her desire. She wanted—needed—to be closer. Arching her body, she rubbed her breasts against him.

"You're entering dangerous territory."

Wyatt paused for a moment to nuzzle her cheek. His beard scratched her tender skin, and all she wanted was to scream *more*. Make me feel… everything.

"It doesn't feel dangerous," she breathed, tipping her head to give him better access.

"Tell me. How does it feel?'

"Right." Joie sighed the word. "Perfect."

"Shit."

Not the word she had expected. Blinking, Joie's eyes focused on Wyatt's face.

"I admit it's been awhile, but was the kiss that bad?"

"It was…"

Joie waited as though Wyatt's next words were the most important ones ever spoken. At least to her.

"Yes?" she urged.

"Nice."

"Excuse me?" Joie heard him clearly. When he pulled away, she wanted to sink to the ground. But pride kept her upright, her knees solidly locked in place.

"It was nice. Thank you."

Wyatt pulled on his jacket. His face wasn't devoid of emotion. It was… calm. She supposed that was the best way of putting it. Was it possible for a kiss to rock your world while your partner was unaffected? Wyatt would have her believe it was. And she might have believed him. If she hadn't heard the harshness of his breath. Felt the heavy beat of his heart. Seen the passion in his eyes.

Wyatt might look as cool as a cucumber. But when he was in her arms, there had been heat. Enough to burn if he hadn't put on the brakes.

"Nice, my ass."

He looked her up and down. "That's nice too. Now, if you'll excuse me. I promised Margie I would unclog her bathroom sink."

"That's it?"

Joie couldn't believe he was walking away. If she were the violent type, she would have picked up a rock and hurled it at him. On second thought. She spied the perfect projectile when he turned. His cool blue eyes froze her in place.

"Turns out you were right. It *was* only a kiss."

CHAPTER TEN

ONLY A KISS.

The words mocked Wyatt, echoing in his head as he stood in the shower stall, water beating over his tired body. He could still see the hurt in Joie's eyes as he said it. From the moment they met, she had been nothing but kind. And how did he repay her? By giving her a verbal slap in the face.

What the hell was wrong with him?

Talk about redundant questions. Wyatt knew the answer as well as he knew the back of his hand. He had married a manic depressive sociopath who screwed with his head and left him questioning his judgment.

Professionally? He never wavered. His decisions were sharp and to the point. Last year had been Landis Productions' best. Next year promised to be even better. When it came to business, Wyatt had nerves of steel.

Personally? He was a mess. Go left? Stay the course? Jump? Sit? Wyatt had let his dead wife get in his head. Stephanie haunted him. Two years after her death, he couldn't let go of his mistakes. He didn't think he ever would.

What he should be asking himself was why had he dragged Joie into his shit? He knew better. He was damaged. Not broken. However, the scar tissue around his heart was thick. Impenetrable. Or so he had thought.

Joie. Bright, vibrant, joyous Joie. He was drawn to her warmth like a plant that had been stuck under the ice and snow. She was the sun. So tempting. That one kiss told him everything. Her passion would be addictive. He already craved more. Another taste. Another touch.

What if he gave in? Would it be so bad? So what if he couldn't give Joie more than a week or two? The memories would be good. He would make certain of that. Didn't he deserve a little happiness, no matter how brief? Wasn't he allowed—just this once—to take what he wanted and damn the consequences? Everyone did it. Why shouldn't he?

Because his conscience reminded him, *you aren't that guy*. The thought of dimming the light that beamed from Joie—even the slightest bit—made his stomach roil. If she were the sun, he was a black hole. He would greedily suck up her warmth giving nothing in return.

Not because he didn't want to. Because he had nothing to give.

Closing his eyes, Wyatt rested his forehead against the cool tile. God, he was fucking pathetic. Until he could pull his head out of his ass. Until the thought of Stephanie and his myriad of mistakes didn't mentally bring him to his knees, he knew he should leave Joie alone.

Easier said than done when he could hear her sighing with pleasure. He could feel the brush of her breasts against his chest. He could taste her. *Butterscotch*. Just the thought made him lick his lips.

Go. Stay. He couldn't decide. Was Joie the answer? His personal life was stuck in neutral. Could she help him get it in gear? Would it be fair to ask that of her?

Pounding his fist on the wall, Wyatt turned off the water. So much for a relaxing shower. He grabbed a towel and quickly dried off.

Business was easy. His personal life was hard. But for the first time in a long time, he knew what he wanted. Joie. Why couldn't it be easy? He had watched his brothers do it. They were able to maneuver through the obstacles and come out on the other side with the perfect woman by their sides. Love. Marriage. Forever. He knew it hadn't been easy—but they made it look that way.

The crazy part was, Wyatt wasn't looking for all of that. All he wanted was a little taste of normal. No drama. No histrionics. A woman who wanted to be with him just because. Not for his name or his money. Or because she had become fixated on systematically destroying his life.

Wyatt laughed, but it wasn't a happy sound. His rivals would find this hysterical. Indecision and moral dilemmas were not traits that were associated with him. He went after what he wanted. Period. And damn it, he wanted Joie.

He would be upfront. Explain his limitations. Lower Joie's expectations—if she had any. *Here is what I have to offer. Take it or leave it.* What could be easier than that?

With that settled, Wyatt headed to his room. Joie was his treat. A reward. Though he had no intention of telling her that. If she wanted to play, he would play. If not... He didn't want to consider that possibility.

Pulling on a clean pair of jeans, Wyatt began to plot out his strategy. Another few weeks in Monroe was an appealing idea. He liked the people. They knew who he was—always had. He was surprised how little that revelation bothered him. As Joie pointed out, Margie and the rest of the townsfolk's motives were innocent—a lot more innocent than his. If they wanted, he would continue to do odd jobs. He liked the work. He was in the best shape of his life. And it gave him the opportunity to nose around.

Wyatt hadn't forgotten his original goal. The ever-elusive J. L. Winter. He would track down the author. Someone would give him a lead; he was sure of it. In the meantime, there was Joie.

Heading down to dinner, there was a lightness to his step. He always felt better when he had a clear plan. He had spent too long in the shadows. It was time to step out into the light. Joie's light.

ONLY A KISS.

Joie punched her pillow, pretending it had killer blue eyes and a slightly crooked smile. Jerk. For good measure, and her satisfaction, she hit it once more.

It wasn't fair. Wyatt got her all worked up. But was he happy to just walk away? No! He had to leave her with a verbal slap in the face. *Nice?* She had been panting, her bones on the verge of melting from the heat. One word from him and she would have thrown her virtue to the wind. If she had any virtue left to throw.

Normally she loved this time of night. Just after midnight, she could hear the house settling. Every creak and groan—they belonged to her. She found comfort in the thought. But at the moment, she couldn't settle. For the first time, her little cottage felt lonely.

There was no comfort in knowing Carole was down the hall. Because she wasn't. Dex showed up at dinner time with enough food to feed half of Monroe. The newly engaged couple billed and cooed until Joie felt as though a sugary coating had settled over her. She was relieved when he talked Carole into spending the night with him—something she had never done before.

Joie wondered how long Carole would keep up the pretext of staying with her. Dex had a house on the edge of town. Big enough for two. He began asking her to move in a month after their first date. It had taken him a couple of years, some heated arguments, a lot of make-up sex, and the patience of Job. But now that he had his woman, Joie doubted that Carole would continue to hold out. Why should they wait until after the wedding when they wanted to be together?

With a sigh, she decided to give up. Her body was tired, but her mind wouldn't shut off. She had but one choice. Show up at Wyatt's door and demand that he take her to bed. Sex was on her mind. Sex with Wyatt. If he would cooperate, she could get her good night's sleep.

Unfortunately, there were too many pitfalls involved. Not the least of which was that she would have to wake Margie—and probably her guests. Nope. Too embarrassing. And hardly a sure thing. She was better off waiting until there was no one around to witness him shooting her down. Or screwing her brains out.

Damn, Wyatt Landis. Joie rolled out of bed. She liked to sleep in a silky nighty. It felt cool against her skin and didn't bind. How did people sleep in clothing? Pajamas? Socks. And panties? Come on. Her pussy was confined all day. At night, she had to let it breathe.

Laughing at the hilarious direction her thoughts had taken, Joie grabbed her robe and headed down the hall. Her office wasn't a sanctuary. It was where she took care of business. The furniture consisted of a desk, some file cabinets, and a comfortable, wing-backed chair that she had found at an estate sale several years ago. The décor wasn't luxurious, but it did the job.

However, when it came to her choice of electronics, everything was top of the line. From her printer to her three-line telephone, she spared no expense. These were important to her job. And she took her job seriously.

Waiting on her desk right between a notepad and her backup drive, sat her baby. Her friend and confidant. She told it everything and it never judged. It kept her secrets and never complained if she went days without visiting. Joie ran a loving hand over the surface.

"Hello, sweetheart. Have you missed me?"

So she talked to her computer? Didn't everybody? It didn't talk back—more than your average laptop. When it did, then she would worry.

Joie rolled her shoulders, settling in for a long session. She went through her usual routine. First, she checked her email. Nothing there that couldn't wait. Just as she was about to log out, she changed her mind. Quickly, before she could talk herself out of it, she wrote a quick and to the point message.

Her finger hovered over the send button. Taking a deep breath, she released it across cyberspace. Or however email traveled. She didn't know exactly how it worked. Nor did she want to. Her words were able to get from point A to point B and back again. That was all that mattered.

With that taken care of, Joie opened her most-used program and pulled up the most recent file.

"Where were we?"

Closing her eyes, she ran through the story. As though she were watching a television show, scenes played out like a *Previously On* montage. After several minutes, she looked at the computer screen, put her fingers on the keys, and began to type. The words were slow to come. That was natural. It took a little while for her to get her rhythm.

Then it happened. Joie stopped thinking and let the story flow. She was no longer a woman sitting in an office. She was transported to the south of France—ten years ago. Her name was Belle, and her hair was short—the color of ripe strawberries. It was a new look. An act of rebellion. No one would ever again tell her what to do. Gone were the stodgy shoes and boring skirts with their matching jackets. She dressed for herself, and she was ready to throw off the weight of her past life. At thirty-three, she was ready for her life to begin.

Joie didn't work on a timetable. She wrote until the words stopped coming. Sometimes that meant thirty minutes. Sometimes she looked up and an entire day had passed. This session was somewhere in between. When the scene cleared, her heroine was well on her way to the adventure of a lifetime and the sun was peeking through the window blinds.

Joie saved her work then sat back with a satisfied sigh. She had a deadline to keep. The book was due the first week of November, and she was never late. At this rate, she would send the manuscript off to her publisher with plenty of time to spare.

It seemed there *was* an upside to sexual frustration.

"I THOUGHT YOU would be bored out of your mind by now."

"You thought wrong."

Wyatt sat on the porch, an opened gallon of sunshine yellow paint by his side. He had been about to freshen up the inn's shutters when Colt called. It wasn't unexpected. His brother hadn't hounded him, but he did like to check in.

He gave Colt credit. This was only the fifth time they had spoken since the day Wyatt left Los Angles. The texts had been more frequent. But Wyatt didn't mind. It was a reminder that his family cared.

"It's been two weeks, Wyatt. You refuse to tell me where you are. Give. Is it a nudist colony? An orgy seminar. An S and M retreat?"

Wyatt had to laugh. Leave it to his brother.

"Why does your mind automatically run toward sex?"

"It's the way I'm hardwired." Wyatt could picture Colt's grin. "I'm almost twenty-eight years old, and no one has complained yet."

Nor were they likely to start. Women fell at Colton's feet before he could walk. His good looks and charm had made him a movie star before he turned nineteen. His talent had kept him one.

"I'm enjoying my vacation."

"Doing what?" Colt sounded skeptical.

Wyatt's gaze landed on the can of paint. "The usual things. Relaxing. Whiling away the hours."

"I hope you're telling me the truth, but somehow I can't picture it."

If Wyatt told Colt the truth, his brother would definitely think he was lying. Playing handyman in a small town was not Wyatt's style. Nor was a steady fashion diet of blue jeans and flannel shirts. But sometimes truth was stranger than fiction.

"As long as you're doing okay, I don't care where you are." Colt paused. "You are okay, aren't you?"

"Better than okay. I'm..." Wyatt searched for the right words. "Finding peace."

"That's great, Wyatt. I almost hate to tell you the news."

Wyatt tensed. "Why? Has something happened? Is it Mom? Dad?"

"Jump back from the ledge, big brother. The Landis clan is hearty and hale. I was talking about work. If I tell you what happened, I'm afraid you'll hightail it out of nirvana."

"I wouldn't call it nirvana." Though for him, Monroe was a nice equivalent. A little shop talk wasn't going to change that. "Tell me what's up."

"Dad received an email early this morning. From the elusive J. L. Winter."

"No shit." Up until now, what little contact they had was through the author's agent. "What did it say?"

"She wants to sign with Landis Productions."

"Just like that?"

"Hardly." Colt chuckled. "You put in a lot of work wooing her. I guess it finally paid off."

"I know but—Wait. Did you say *she*? J. L. Winter is a woman?"

"Definitely. I read her email. For a woman of mystery, she was quite forthcoming. Your research was spot on. She lives in Nevada. A little town called… What was it?"

"Monroe."

"That's right."

Wyatt didn't know how he felt. All this time he had been close to his target. It was frustrating and laughable all at once. She had to have known he was here. Everyone else in Monroe did. Why not come to him directly instead of emailing his father? It made no sense.

"J. L. Winter is a pseudonym, by the way."

"We already figured that out."

"But now we know her real name," Colt said smugly. "Joy Trent. I wonder if she's as pretty as her name?"

"Joy?" Wyatt felt his temper start to heat. *No fucking way.* "Spell it."

"I don't have the email in front of me. But now that you mention it, the spelling was unusual."

"J. O. I. E?"

"That's right," Colt exclaimed. "Hey. How did you know?"

"Lucky guess. I have to go."

"Wait. Don't you want to know the details?"

Wyatt understood Colt's confusion. He always wanted the details. The more, the better. But right now, he had more important things on his mind. Like ringing the neck of a certain woman whose memorable kiss filled his thoughts for the last twenty-four hours.

"Have Dad send me the information. And Colt? Her name is pronounced Joey."

"How the hell do you know—"

Wyatt cut Colt off. Forgetting the paint and the shutters, he rushed into the house and up the stairs to his room.

"What's your hurry?" Margie asked as he ran past her.

"I'll finish painting tomorrow," he called out as he descended the stairs two at a time.

"Will you be back for dinner?"

When Margie heard the front door slam, she took that as a no. Wherever Wyatt was headed, she didn't envy whoever had gotten him riled up. This was the first time she had seen this side of him. Not that she was surprised to find out he had a temper. Most people did. But Wyatt was riled—no doubt about it.

Margie went back to dusting. She trusted her instincts and they told her that Wyatt was not a violent man. He was angry about something, but she didn't think he was out for blood. She began to whistle. Word would get around as it always did in Monroe. In a few hours—the next morning at the latest—she would find out what happened. A neighbor would call. Or stop by if the gossip was particularly juicy.

This was Wyatt Landis. Naturally the news would rate as juicy. That meant visitors. Margie did a mental inventory of her kitchen. She picked up her dust cloth and can of Pledge, putting them away in the hall closet.

If she were correct, she should expect visitors. Around here, gossip traveled in a pack, she thought as she took eggs and butter from the refrigerator. And the pack always expected cookies.

CHAPTER ELEVEN

JOIE POKED HER head out of the bathroom. She had just gotten out of the shower when she thought she heard a loud thump. She listened. There it was again. More of a pounding than a thump. Whoever was at the front door was impatient—and didn't believe in doorbells.

"Go away!" she yelled.

Her hair was wet and so was she. Meaning she was in no condition for visitors. Besides, this one had a rude knock.

"Open the door, Joie."

Wyatt? Joie wrapped her hair in a towel and grabbed her robe from the hook behind the bathroom door. The man was impatient—which was annoying. However, it didn't occur to her to keep him waiting—or not go at all. She had a few things to say to Mr. Wyatt Landis, and though she would have picked a more convenient time, this would do.

"Damn it, Joie!"

The rhythm of the pounding increased as did the noise. Or perhaps it had to do with her getting closer. Either way, she had had enough. If he kept that up, he would pound a hole through her door.

"What is your problem?"

Joie was eager to see him, but she wasn't a fool. This scene had played out in too many movies. Scantily clad woman stupidly opens her door to a serial killer. She wasn't putting Wyatt into that category, but better safe than sorry. Until she knew what was going on, the solid oak would act as a barrier. Him on that side. She on this one.

"Let me in."

Wyatt's voice had an edge to it. For all her *I'm not an idiot* thoughts, Joie couldn't control the shiver that ran across her skin. Nature had a nasty habit of playing havoc with a woman's good sense. An alpha male had come knocking, and it sent fissures of awareness through her body. Was the wolf at her door? The big, bad variety? She didn't know. But damn, her juices were flowing. It wouldn't take much persuasion to get her to throw caution to the wind.

"I'm not dressed for company."

Like that would keep him out. But it was the only excuse she could think of.

"Joie. Please. Let me in?"

There it was. That silky smooth hint of persuasion that women had fallen for since Adam figured out how to talk Eve out of her fig leaf. Joie had never bought the old *Eve as a temptress* line. Adam knew the score. When they fell out of Eden, there was plenty of guilt on both sides.

"What do you want, Wyatt?"

"To talk."

Joie leaned against the door. Was she imagining the heat radiating from the surface? Was Wyatt's hand inches from her face? Her finger traced the outline of the doorknob. She was about to turn the lock when his lowered voice made her freeze.

"J. L. Winter? Really? Now who's the liar?"

She should have known. Joie sighed then whispered, "I didn't lie."

"Did you say something?"

"I didn't lie." As she spoke, she whipped open the door. "If you had asked, I would have told you."

"Same here."

Wyatt didn't wait for an invitation. With surprising care, he used one hand to push her out of the way, then strode into the house.

"I couldn't ask because you lied."

Determined to come out the winner of this argument, Joie slammed the door. He hadn't reached the living room before she was hot on his heels.

Wyatt rounded on her. "You lied by omission."

When his eyes met hers, the blue matched the color of the sea during a raging storm. Her stride stuttered, but she recovered quickly. He could throw his well-honed intimidation methods at her all day. Joie was not easily intimidated. If anything, her resolve strengthened at every challenge.

"You flat out lied. Ha!" She crowed when she saw a slight flicker of guilt. "Try and wiggle out of that one, buddy."

"I don't wiggle." His shield of arrogance may have slipped, but Wyatt recovered quickly. "Are you or are you not the writer known as J. L. Winter?"

"What are you, a lawyer?"

"Yes."

"Oh." Why didn't she know that? "I thought you were a movie producer."

"Movies. Plays. The occasional TV mini-series."

Wyatt circled her. Had she called him the Big Bad Wolf? Wrong analogy. He was a caged tiger. Powerful. Lithe. Stalking his prey with lethal grace. Joie felt a tingle that started at the base of her neck, quickly spread to her breasts. When it reached the apex of her thighs, all she could do was sigh.

"And law?" Joie asked, desperate to distract him.

"It interests me. Plus, knowing the rules, and how to bend them to my will, is an advantage in the business world."

Bend them to his will. That sounded like a challenge. Joie straightened her shoulders and hardened her resolve. Flowing juices were one thing. But no one—not even sex on a stick Wyatt Landis—controlled her will.

"Step back." When had he gotten so close? She crossed her arms. "I mean it, Wyatt. Step back."

Joie stood her ground. She knew that physically she was vulnerable. But this was her house. Her territory. He was invading her personal space. She met his gaze head on and waited.

"Are you afraid of me?" Wyatt took two steps back. Then for good measure, one more. "I would never hurt you."

"I wouldn't have let you into my house if I thought you would. But I won't let you intimidate me, Wyatt. I didn't do anything wrong." Her eyes narrowed when he would have argued. "And you know it."

"You emailed my father." Crossing his arms over his chest, Wyatt matched her stance—and narrowed *his* eyes. "Why not come to me?"

"Well, crap." Joie hadn't seen this coming. It was disappointing—to say the least. "I hurt your ego? I thought you were better than that. I guess I misjudged you. Instead of a strong, grounded man comfortable in his own skin, you're a big fake with daddy issues."

"Daddy issues? Did you say daddy issues?"

Wyatt looked surprised. No. He looked flabbergasted. Then to her amazement, he threw his head back and laughed. Deep and full-on, it continued until tears ran from his eyes.

Joie put her hands on her hips, shaking her head. "I don't get the joke."

"Joie. Honey. I respect my father. I love him. My loyalty is absolute. But in no way, at no time, can you accuse me of issues. Daddy or otherwise."

She watched as he let out one more chuckle before wiping his eyes. She was willing to admit she might have read him wrong. It brought a renewed burst of awareness. Wyatt was intense and sexy. Gorgeous in an anti-pretty boy way. He was smart and kind. Add to that a wicked sense of humor. All she could think was *oh my*.

"Good to know. What are your problems with me emailing him?"

"It means you don't trust me."

"That wasn't the reason, Wyatt."

"Then you do trust me?" He retraced one of his steps—just one.

The look in Wyatt's killer blue eyes made her smile. Hope. Heat. And a mysterious twinkle she wanted to investigate. But not yet. There were a few things they needed to clear up.

"I had decided to sign with Landis Productions before we met."

That brought him up short. "Why did you take so long to tell us?"

"Let me qualify what I said. I hadn't decided if I wanted my book made into a movie. But if it happened, your company had always been my first choice."

Wyatt sighed, his eyes closing as his head fell back. Joie didn't know what else to say. She could sympathize with his frustration. But she had no obligation to explain herself—or make excuses. It had been her decision. Made in her own time.

"I overreacted."

"Yes." Surprised and pleased, Joie smiled.

His deep blue eyes met hers. What she saw made her heart race. Swallowing, Joie licked her lips.

"But I won't apologize."

Have you ever? Wyatt Landis did not strike her as a man who made mistakes. Or rather, a man who believed his behavior required justification. An apology was the equivalent of admitting he was in the wrong. Good luck getting that admission from him.

"I didn't ask," Joie said. Then she muttered, "But it would be a nice touch."

"You knew who I was."

In a blink, Wyatt had closed the distance between them. Stubbornly, Joie held her ground. She tilted her head, hoping her expression didn't give away her thoughts. It was difficult to hold onto her tough girl persona when she was dressed in nothing but a bathrobe and he smelled like... Joie took a deep breath. God, he smelled like Wyatt—her new favorite fragrance.

"I found out who you were a few days ago. So what?"

"You knew before you sent that email to my father. Why not come to me?"

Wyatt didn't touch her. However, she could feel the heat from his body as his breath lightly caressed her face.

"You're standing too close." With one finger, she pushed at his chest. Moving a two-ton boulder would have been easier. Wyatt's body had all the give of solid steel.

"I would like to get closer." His eyes dropped to the opening of her robe. There wasn't much to see—only a few inches of skin. However, it was obvious that she had nothing on underneath. Her nipples were hard, and the thin red satin did nothing to conceal the fact. "Much closer."

"We were talking about your father."

Weren't they? Somehow the conversation had veered in a different direction. Joie wasn't certain how she felt about that. Wanting Wyatt was one thing. Acting on it? Hell, why kid herself? If he asked, her answer would be a big *yes, please*.

"I was pissed off when I got here," Wyatt whispered, his gaze moving to her mouth.

"And now?"

"Borderline pissed." His hands moved to her waist. That one touch made Joie sigh. "The reason has shifted."

Joie licked her lips again. She hadn't meant to be provocative— they were dry. But the flare of heat in Wyatt's eyes let her know it affected him. Intrigued, she did it again—with deliberation. Slowly, she used her tongue to trace her upper lip. When he groaned, she couldn't contain her smile.

"Witch." Wyatt's fingers dug into her flesh. He moved his hand to the length of cloth that held her robe together. Slowly, he pulled on the end of the belt. "You know what's about to happen."

It was a statement, not a question. Joie had a choice. Wyatt wasn't going to proceed unless she gave him permission. There was no way in hell she would turn him down. But knowing with one word he would back away? That was a whole different layer of sexy.

Keeping her gaze steady, Joie covered Wyatt's hand with hers.

"Let me help you."

Together, they made the final tug.

Wyatt didn't need any more encouragement. His lips closed over hers. She loved how he took the kiss from zero to a hundred miles an hour. There was a time for gentle exploration—this wasn't it. She wanted it hard and fast. Play time could come later.

Joie threaded her fingers through his hair, pulling him closer. When she felt the touch of his hands on her bare skin, she moaned. He skimmed her waist, moving to her back. His hands were slightly roughened from the work he had done around town. Hard and soft running up and down her spine, her nerve endings coming to life.

"Last time it was butterscotch. Now you taste like wild cherries." Wyatt breathed the words as he lightly bit her earlobe.

"Which do you prefer?" Joie gasped.

"It's all good, sweetheart. How does the rest of you taste?"

"I have no idea."

"Sweet." He licked the sensitive skin of her neck. "Addictive. I can't get enough. I need to sample every inch of you."

Joie tugged at his jacket until Wyatt shrugged it off. Thrilled that she didn't have to ask, she watched as his t-shirt hit the floor. Oh, sweet heaven, his body was glorious. Slightly tanned, his skin was taut. The muscles well defined. She reached out, tracing the ridges on his rippling abs.

"I want to kiss you. From here," Joie touched his lower lip. "To here." Slowly, her touch moved down his neck, over his chest and stomach, and ended at the bulge between his legs.

"You're playing with fire." Wyatt's chest rose and fell with increasing urgency.

"Good."

Wyatt pushed her robe from her shoulders. It was slipping down her arms when Joie heard the front door open.

"I don't know if Joie is home. I'll just—Whoops."

"What the fuck?" Thinking fast, Wyatt tugged her robe into place.

"I have a roommate." Joie peeked around Wyatt. She didn't know if she were blushing, but if there were ever a time, this would be it. "And she brought her fiancé with her."

"Bad timing," Carole said, making the understatement of the year. "We'll go. Dex. Stop staring. Out! Now!"

The door slammed. Joie didn't know whether to laugh or… No, laughter was her only option.

"That was—" She snickered. "Awkward."

"That's one way of putting it." Wyatt bent to retrieve the belt to her robe.

He seemed so calm. So put together. She was a hormonal mess and Wyatt, with his amazing abs and rock-hard arms, looked like he had stepped off the pages of a magazine. No photoshopping required.

"I guess Carole and Dex killed the mood." Joie saw another shower in her future. This one ice cold. "Maybe another time."

Wyatt calmly tucked her belt into his back pocket. Then with one smooth motion, he swept her into his arms.

"The hell with that." He didn't run up the stairs. His pace was measured. Deliberate. "I always finish what I've started." His voice was calm, but his eyes blazed with blue fire.

Joie grinned, wrapping her arms around his neck. Delighted, she nuzzled his firm, stubbled jaw. "I like a man with conviction."

"Conviction. Determination. Is this your room?"

Busy nibbling his neck, Joie nodded.

"Where was I?" Wyatt paused by her bed. "Right. Conviction. Determination." He tossed her onto the mattress. With three quick movements, he unsnapped his jeans, dropped them to the floor, and pushed them out of his way "Plus stamina. The Energizer Bunny has nothing on me."

Joie was ready with a pithy quip, but the words died on her tongue the second she stopped bouncing and got a look at Wyatt. If she hadn't been flat on her back, she would have dropped to her knees in thanks. And while she was down there, she would have taken a closer look at what appeared to be mouthwatering perfection.

"The condoms are in the bathroom."

Not exactly the sexiest thing she could have said. But when Wyatt grinned and headed toward the direction she pointed, Joie reconsidered. After all, sexy was subjective.

"Were you a Girl Scout?" Wyatt asked as he returned with not one condom, but the entire unopened box. "Your cupboard is ruthlessly organized and you are prepared."

Joie bought the condoms three days ago. As soon as she knew she wanted to sleep with him. It had been awhile since it was necessary to have them around. "I was never one for organized group activities."

Her eyes followed his every move. He tore into the box, removed a packet, then carefully set the rest on the nightstand—within easy reach.

"I prefer one on one myself."

"Wait." She held up a hand when he would have joined her. "I want to take a picture for posterity."

"I trust you, Joie. But nude pictures have a way getting into the wrong hands."

"Not to worry. This is what I meant." She held up an imaginary camera. "Snap. My brain is the best storage space I own. And it never runs out of space."

Laughing, Wyatt crawled across the bed. "I forgot to pose." He disposed of her robe.

"Next time." Joie was delighted. She could be her silly, goofy self with Wyatt. In the past—with other men—that wasn't always the case.

He arranged her body until she lay on her back and his knees straddling her thighs.

"My turn."

Wyatt lifted his own camera. Joie liked that his eye wasn't hidden behind a viewfinder. She lifted her arms above her head, making her breasts jut out.

"How is this?"

"Screw the camera. I won't need help remembering this."

Later, Joie would think it one of the sweetest things anyone had ever said to her. She didn't have time to think of anything but Wyatt's gorgeous body as it hovered over hers. She watched in anticipation as he bent to kiss the underside of her breast. His tongue caressed her skin, causing shivers of pleasure to shoot through her body.

"Sweet. Just as a thought."

"Wyatt."

"Hmm?" She could hear the smile in his voice—feel the curve of his lips.

"I need you. Now."

"You'll have me." His eyes met hers. "When I'm ready."

"That isn't nice."

"Nice?" He lightly bit her nipple. "No one has ever accused me of that."

What he proceeded to do to her fell so far beyond the boundaries of nice, Joie decided to retire that word from her vocabulary. Who needed it when there was wild? Mind-blowing? Soul-scorching? The words were never ending. But when she moaned, the only one she needed—the only *thing* she needed—was Wyatt.

"You'll tell me if I do something you don't like?"

Joie laughed.

"What?" Wyatt looked up from between her legs. His fingers were busy doing things that should have been illegal, but luckily, weren't. Not that she cared. The law be damned. This felt too good. "Does that tickle?"

The brush of his thumb made her gasp. The slide of his finger made her moan. The look on his face? Self-satisfied arrogance.

"If that didn't feel so good, I would tell you to go to hell."

"You think that feels good?" He added a second finger. "Just wait."

Wyatt's lips trailed a path of kisses across her stomach. Joie watched, fascinated. She didn't want to miss a second, but when his mouth replaced his fingers, she only saw stars. A bright burst of light blinded her. Her chest rose and fell until she had no breath at all.

"Breathe, Joie."

It was so simple. *Breathe*. Why hadn't *she* thought of that? Because she couldn't think. She could only feel. The second she took air into her lungs, she came. Long and hard. It hit her with a withering blast, leaving her limp. A pool of utterly satisfied flesh. Where she found the energy to smile, she didn't know. But she must have because it was the first thing Wyatt commented on when he pulled her into his arms.

"You're happy."

"I'm…" Finding the right word was impossible. For a woman who made a living using her descriptive powers, she had nothing. So she grabbed hold of his. "Happy works."

"That was quite a scream."

"I did not scream." Or had she? Did it matter? Nope.

"My ears are ringing." With a chuckle, Wyatt kissed her cheek. Then lingered on her mouth.

"Aren't you forgetting something?"

"What's that?"

"This."

Joie wrapped her fingers around his erection. It was so hard she could have used it to pound a nail. The heat almost burned her hand.

"We'll get to it."

"*I'll* get to it."

A woman with a mission, Joie felt rejuvenated. Keeping hold of him, she moved into position, her legs firmly gripping his hips.

"Ready?" she asked.

"You think I'm going to protest?"

Joie felt the grip of Wyatt's fingers on her thighs. Borderline painful, it oddly added to her pleasure. Perhaps she had a touch of the masochist running through her veins. The thought didn't bother her. She believed in doing what felt good. If it were consensual, it was nobody else's business.

"What's holding you up?" The tension in Wyatt's voice was palpable. "Please tell me you haven't changed your mind?"

Without a word, Joie lowered herself. The fit was tight. She hadn't had sex in a while, and Wyatt was a very big boy—thank you very much. However, with a little patience, and the help of gravity, she had soon taken all of him.

Resting her hands on his chest, Joie lifted her hips. Up felt fantastic. Down was better. Wyatt seemed to agree. His hips found her rhythm with ease and before long, they were moving as one. Their breathing matched. He sat up, brushing his chest against hers. Their kisses were wild and abandoned. Their hands seeking out and finding each other's most sensitive places.

It didn't take long. Soon Joie was rushing toward another orgasm with Wyatt right beside her. Up. Up. Higher. When she thought she couldn't take any more, Wyatt pushed her a little further.

"Now," he urged, biting down on her nipple.

The burst of pain didn't send her over the top. It shot her into the stratosphere. It was a rocket ride—fast and exhilarating. She held onto Wyatt, knowing she wasn't flying solo. He was with her all the way. At the apex of her pleasure, and on the way down. Floating down and landing safely in his arms.

"I—" Joie wanted to thank him but didn't have the energy.

Wyatt settled them under the covers, pulling her close. "Shh," he whispered, brushing his lips across her forehead. Knowing Wyatt was there, next to her, was all she needed. With a sigh, her body relaxed, her mind shut down, and she closed her eyes. Feeling the beat of his heart under her cheek, she drifted off to sleep.

CHAPTER TWELVE

"MY FAMILY THINKS that I pay for sex."

As a conversation starter went, that was a doozy. Wyatt didn't know why it came out of his mouth, but now that it had, he was curious what Joie's reaction would be.

"What's the going rate?"

He hadn't expected that. She looked at him over a slice of pizza, waiting for an answer.

"Hell if I know. Does it matter?"

"I don't want to get short changed."

Wyatt sent a mouthful of water spewing. Luckily, he had the wherewithal to turn his head. The floor was wet, but he missed their dinner.

"Now, look what you've done." As he wiped his mouth, Wyatt hid his grin behind his napkin.

"Me?" Joie handed him a towel for the floor. "You're the one who brought up prostitution. I simply ran with it. You can't blame a girl for wanting to get paid what she's worth."

"Since I've never in my life doled out money for sex, I can't help you there. But if you want to know what I think *you're* worth? You would beggar a billionaire."

"I know we're talking about me selling my body. But I can't help it. I feel like you gave me a compliment."

"I did." Laughing, Wyatt shook his head. "*I* feel like I should apologize."

"Never mind. Tell me why your family is convinced you associate with call girls."

"No hookers?"

"Too low rent." Joie pushed her salad around on her plate. When they decided to order a pizza, they agreed to be good and get something good for them to go with it. It turned out neither of them wanted to be good. "In a pinch, I can see you ordering up one of those impossibly beautiful women that only exist in books or Julia Roberts movies. But a pickup off the street? I don't think so."

"Was *that* a compliment?"

He waited while she pondered the question. "As close as I can get given the topic."

"I'll take it." He finished wiping up the floor, then joined her at the table. "As for my family. I should be more exact. My brothers speculate. I don't think my parents go there. At least I hope they don't."

"Feel like telling me where they came up with the idea?"

"It's complicated." And no, he didn't want to talk about it. However, he brought it up. It wasn't fair to drop the subject without some explanation. "I work long hours. It makes a social life... difficult.

"So they assume you have rent-a-sex on speed dial?"

"Something like that."

It was a fraction of the truth but far from the whole story. To his relief, Joie seemed willing to let it go.

"Want to spend the night?"

Great. He avoided one landmine only to be plopped down in an entire field of them. He had his reasons why he didn't sleep with women. He liked sex. But he never stayed after.

"It isn't an essay question, Wyatt. A simple yes or no will suffice."

"I don't want you to get the wrong idea." She had given him an out. But it felt like it would be a cop out to take it. "This," he motioned between them. "It can't go anywhere."

Joie's eyes grew wide. "Are you saying that now that you've compromised my virtue, I can't expect you to rush out and buy me a ring? Boo hoo."

"Some women—"

"Let me stop you right there." Joie pushed back from the table. She retrieved a bottle of water from the refrigerator and unscrewed the cap. "I am not now, nor will I ever be *some women*. I don't expect anything because there is nothing I want. As long as you are in Monroe, consider me your lover. If you want to stay the night—now or in the future—you're welcome. But the decision is yours."

"And when I leave? Because I *will* leave, Joie."

"I hope we'll part as friends. Again. Your choice."

Wyatt had found little in life was ever that easy. There was always a catch. A hidden clause buried in the fine print. But for the life of him, he couldn't believe that was Joie's game.

"Relax." Joie slid onto his lap. "You know all of my secrets. As for yours? I'm a good listener. But I'm not a snoop."

"My choice," he said, his arms going around her waist.

"Now you're catching on." She wiggled her butt. "It's early. Relatively speaking. Want to take a quick trip around the world before you leave?"

Wyatt grinned. He was tired of looking for trouble before it started. He was going to take what Joie offered. If things changed, he could always leave. His truck was fixed, and there was nothing but open road in both directions.

However, for the next hour, he wasn't going anywhere. Except to bed with Joie.

THE HIGH SCHOOL auditorium buzzed with activity. Rehearsals for the annual Christmas pageant were in full swing. It was still two months away, but Tracy Finnegan wanted it to be perfect. She had started planning the program last summer.

That was around the time she recruited Joie to write a short play for the occasion. It had seemed like an easy enough task at the time. Watching a bunch of inexperienced, unmotivated teenagers butcher her words had Joie wondering if she had made a huge mistake.

"I can't get them into the spirit of the production," Tracy told her as they watched the actors listlessly run their lines.

This was the pretty redhead's second year teaching at Monroe High. They didn't have the budget for a full-time drama department, so she had stepped in. Her day job was teaching science. But she had a passion for theater and had hoped to pass it along to her students.

It was proving easier said than done. There were barely enough bodies to fill the parts. The ones that *were* here had volunteered because it fulfilled their extra-curricular requirement. Love of plays and the written word had nothing to do with it.

"They care more about checking their iPhones every thirty seconds than interacting with each other." Tracy wasn't much older than her students, but she felt the gap grew by the second. "See the boy on the far side of the stage? Yesterday, I asked him to tell his friends that we were meeting a half hour later on Thursday. He grunted, then sent out a mass text."

"What's wrong with that?" Joie asked. "He did what you asked."

"His friends were standing five feet away. What happened to this generation? They don't talk. They text."

Joie hid her smile. Tracy was the youngest old lady she had ever met. Not that she disagreed. But kids weren't the only ones who had lost the ability to carry on a conversation. Maybe it was because she spent so much time alone creating her stories, but Joie rarely used her phone for anything but making calls—and not that if it were possible to talk in person. She liked the face-to-face contact.

"I wish I could help you."

"That's just it," Tracy smiled for the first time since Joie arrived. "You *can* help."

Where had she heard that before? Oh, right. When her friends had forced her into a date with Brad Makepeace. It hadn't been a disaster. However, she had been bored to tears, and her mission had been a bust. Brad held firm. If Monroe wanted to rent his piece of property, they would have to pay through the nose. It was money they didn't have.

"I have to warn you, my track record in the help department isn't good. Calling it abysmal would be kind."

"Does that mean you'll try?"

Never jump without knowing your destination. Stepfather number two had shared that bit of unoriginal wisdom with Joie the day she graduated from high school. She had been sorry when her mother had filed for divorce three months later. But she remembered him, and his advice, fondly.

"I can't make any promises until you let me in on your request."

"Word around town is that you're seeing Wyatt Landis."

Oh, boy, Joie sighed. *Why hadn't she seen that coming?*

"Wyatt is a producer, Tracy. Your problem is teenagers, not raising money."

Tracy frowned. "Surely he does more than that. A producer is a leader of men—and women, right? I need a motivational speech. Wyatt looks like someone who can figuratively kick some butts into gear."

Joie looked at the group of kids milling about the stage. Uninspired was putting it mildly. If she put Wyatt in a room with this bunch, she was afraid he might kick few butts—literally. And she wouldn't blame him.

"I will ask." When Tracy squealed with excitement, Joie quickly tried to lower the other woman's expectations. "Even if he agrees, these are kids, Tracy. Wyatt hasn't been one of those in a long time. I don't think he relates to them or their interests."

"He's a Landis. That holds a lot of weight."

Joie laughed. "*Colton* Landis holds a lot of weight. Wyatt is strictly a behind the scenes guy."

"Colton Landis," Tracy fanned herself with her clipboard. Suddenly, her eyes widened. "Joie, you don't think—"

"No, Tracy. Absolutely not. Asking Wyatt to help is bad enough. I will not bring the rest of his family into the mix."

"Not the whole family," Tracy's voice practically quivered. "Though can you imagine if Callie Flynn and Colton Landis were to show up? OMG!"

"Keep your voice down." Joie looked around. Thank God for self-involved teenagers. They had no interest in what their teacher and her friend were up to. "Dial it back, Tracy. You'll be lucky to get Wyatt—and that is no guarantee. Do not mention Colton or Callie again. Understand?"

Tracy nodded, but there was a sparkle in her eyes that made Joie slightly uncomfortable. As she drove away from the high school, she hoped that she had gotten through to Tracy. Enthusiasm sometimes got in the way of common sense. If Tracy expected miracles, she was in for a big letdown. If she expected an influx of Hollywood superstars for the Monroe High School Christmas Pageant, her dreams would be dashed with several buckets of ice-cold water—personally administered by Joie.

There was only one Landis in Monroe. In Joie's opinion, he was the sexiest member of the family. If Wyatt weren't enough for Tracy, that was tough.

JOIE PULLED INTO the grocery store parking lot, grabbing a handy spot near the entrance. As usual, her cupboards were bare. However, with Wyatt dropping by on a regular basis, she had some incentive to rectify the situation.

Joie Trent had a lover. A big, sexy, enthusiastically creative man with stamina to spare. She didn't know how long Wyatt would be in her life. He could pack up and leave tomorrow. But while he was here, she planned on enjoying him.

Whistling, she made her way down the aisles. Joie had meant what she told him. Forever was not in her plans. At least not with Wyatt. Perhaps if he *were* Wyatt Rogers, it would be different. A man with no roots who decided that Monroe was the perfect place to settle down. They would have time to find out if they were suited.

However, Wyatt was not a man without roots. His ran deep in the Hollywood soil. Joie's were just starting to take hold. Here. In Monroe. She had promised herself long ago that she would never change her life to accommodate a man. That was her mother's M.O., not hers.

If the day came that she wanted to marry and start a family, it would be with a man who wanted a life here in Monroe.

Until then, she was more than happy to enjoy what Wyatt had to offer. His body, but not his heart. No sleepovers. No expectations beyond some fun. And great sex.

"You look like the cat that swallowed the cream." Joining her in the frozen food section, Carole snickered. "Maybe I should rephrase that. I don't know how much cream you swallowed."

Since there were no other shoppers within eavesdropping distance, Joie went along with her friend. "Was that a blowjob joke? Seriously? Carole Boudicca Fletcher. What would your mother say?"

"I seriously doubt that my mother knows what a blowjob is. She barely understands how I got here."

"You might be underestimating her. Odd and wonderful things can happen behind a closed bedroom door."

Carole shuddered. "Are you trying to make me lose my appetite for the next month? Parents are allowed to have a sex life—but their children shouldn't know about it. If that isn't a law, it should be."

"Contact your congresswoman." Joie debated between the frozen peas or corn. With a shrug, she tossed both into her cart.

"I know you aren't shopping for me. I take it Wyatt has a *large* appetite?"

"I don't shop for you because you are always with Dex." Joie had no comment about the size of Wyatt's anything.

"Speaking of which. I have decided to move in with Dex."

"Hallelujah." Joie raised her arms in praise. "So he finally wore you down."

"I'm letting him think that's the reason," Carole chuckled. "You should have seen him, Joie. When I told him, he was so cute. And grateful. There is something about a man's gratitude. Breakfast in bed after a night of lovemaking is the best way to start a day."

"I'll take your word for it." Joie had never been able to understand the appeal of eating in bed. Especially first thing in the morning. When she woke up, she wanted three things. To take a pee.

Brush her teeth. And a hot shower. In that order. The idea of food was utterly unappealing. "Why *are* you moving in with Dex?"

"After last night, that should be obvious. I didn't have time to apologize for breaking in like that. I hope we didn't put a damper on the mood."

"Nope. All's good."

"Come on," Carole cajoled. "That was the perfect opening. Tell me what happened."

"It was fine." Joie waited for a bolt of lightning to strike her down. *Fine*? It wasn't a lie, but it was such a gross understatement.

"Dex made croissants. How about some coffee and a roll?"

"Do you think that the lure of French pastry will make me spill my guts?"

"They have chocolate inside."

Joie was a sucker for chocolate. Besides, she had always planned to share. Not all the details. Some things were too personal. Wyatt had made her feel things she hadn't known possible. He had technique—something one didn't find every day. But it was more than that. When he kissed her, she felt as though nothing else mattered. For those moments, she was the center of his universe. His time. His effort. All on her. His focus didn't waver. That was a heady feeling.

In bed, Wyatt concentrated on her pleasure. He wanted her to enjoy every moment. He told her that her happiness intensified his own. In her experience, a man like that was a rare find.

"I need to finish shopping."

"I'll meet you at your place in an hour."

"Make it two. I have a few errands to run."

Carole bounced away like a little girl anticipating a treat. Joie knew how she felt. It had been four hours since her last Wyatt fix. She did a quick calculation in her head.

She knew that Wyatt was finishing up Larry's roof today. If she hurried, she could get her groceries put away and stop over there before she was due to meet Carole.

Was she pushing the boundaries that Wyatt had set? As she waited while the cashier checked her out, Joie answered the question with a resounding *hell no*. She wasn't asking for more than he said he could give. She wanted a quickie. A little early afternoon delight.

Wyatt had the right to say no. Loading her bags into the car, Joie grinned. The chances of that were slim to none. She knew that he wanted her. He had proved that the night before. Over and over and over again. She didn't think it would take much to persuade him.

She looked down at her figure-hugging leggings. Good choice. They did a nice job of showing off her butt. Undo a few buttons on her shirt. There. Joie checked her image in her rearview mirror. Not bad. Not bad at all.

Giving her hair a fluff, she dabbed on a bit of lip gloss. Passionfruit. A new flavor for Wyatt's enjoyment. He already liked the way she tasted. Why not give him a little surprise?

Before she left the parking lot, Joie picked up her phone. This was one of those times when she was grateful for the convenience. She wanted to give him a head's up that she was dropping by. He didn't have to know why until after she arrived.

One ring and he picked up.

"I was just thinking about you."

"Good thoughts, I hope?"

"X-rated." Wyatt's chuckle sent shivers down her spine. "So yes. I would say they were good."

"Are you busy?"

"No more than usual. Larry tells me he has a few more things for me to do after I wrap up the roof." Wyatt laughed again. "I think the old codger likes the company."

"*You* like *him*," Joie said as she pulled to a stop across the street.

"I do. He reminds me of my grandfather. Grandpa Landis always keeps us busy when we visit. It's easier for him to talk when we're in the middle of a project."

"That's nice." Joie hadn't known her grandparents on either side. She always felt like she had missed out. Listening to Wyatt, she felt a pang of envy.

"I haven't visited in a while. I'll have to round up my brothers and head to Ohio as soon as we can."

"Sounds like a plan." Joie stopped in the middle of the yard and looked up. To her disappointment, and no doubt Larry's neighbors, he had his shirt on. But his strong arms were on full display. As a consolation prize, it wasn't bad at all.

"Hello." Wyatt put aside his hammer. "What brings you here?"

"Not Larry."

Without another word, Wyatt made his way down the ladder.

"You are the perfect excuse for a break." He reached for her, then hesitated. "I'm sweaty."

"I like you that way." Joie took his hand and led him around the house. "That's a nice-sized shed. Big enough for two?"

Wyatt nodded, his eyes lighting with interest. He caught on fast.

"You would be surprised. Want to see?"

Joie gave a casual shrug. "Why not? As long as I'm here."

The door wasn't locked. Wyatt motioned her to precede him. She hadn't taken two steps inside when he pulled her around, his lips finding hers.

"I don't have a condom with me," he said a few minutes later, his breath heavy with desire.

"Not a problem." Joie took a full box from her purse. "I visited the drug store this morning."

CHAPTER THIRTEEN

"MEN NEED TIME to ourselves now and then. An evening out with our friends. We need time away from our women to do…"

"Yes?" Wyatt asked.

"Hell if I know." Dex drained the last of the beer from the bottle. "Carole said I should take a boy's night. I don't think I was supposed to ask any questions."

"You have an interesting circle of friends."

They consisted of two men Dex worked with at the restaurant and a quiet guy who had been introduced as T-bone. That was it. Just T-bone. Short and round, he looked nothing like his name, but Wyatt didn't care enough to ask. At the moment, the three were playing pool.

Wyatt was still trying to figure out how he had gotten dragged along with this motley crew. He could have said no.

He had thought he was going to spend a quiet evening alone with Joie. As he already knew, there was a big difference between hope and reality. Instead of a warm, willing woman, his current reality consisted of beer, peanuts, and pool. Not a bad night any other time. But Dex, T-bone, and the gang were a poor substitute.

After a day of replacing shingles—not to mention unclogging a bathroom sink—Wyatt had relished the idea of a hot shower, a good meal, and an old-fashioned make-out session on Joie's couch. Her *visit* that afternoon had only served to whet his appetite.

Wyatt chuckled to himself. He was worse than a randy teenager after his first taste of sex. He thought about Joie all the time. It was amazing the fantasies he could concoct when he was caulking around a plate-glass window or mowing a lawn. He wondered what the good people of Monroe would say if they knew what went on in his head while he played handyman.

It turned out that play time with Joie would have to wait. He had no sooner lifted his hand to knock on her door when Dex appeared with Carole right behind him.

"I'm sorry that you were forced into this."

Dex sounded so forlorn, Wyatt decided to forget about himself and cheer up his new friend.

"I was a little perplexed until Joie called me. She explained that Carole had decided on an impromptu wedding planning session." Wyatt had learned quite recently that there was no getting in the way of that. "My brothers are engaged. This kind of thing happens."

"It's new to me. Not that I'm complaining," Dex assured him. "It's taken me a long time to get Carole to say yes. Whatever she wants is fine with me."

"Can I give you a piece of advice passed on from my father?"

"I can use anything you've got."

"Marriage is a partnership. But never think that you are the majority shareholder. That belongs to your wife. It may be trite, but it's true. Happy wife, happy life."

A big reason why Wyatt's marriage was doomed before it began. Stephanie was an unhappy person. Nothing he did could change that. Unfortunately, that knowledge didn't keep the guilt at bay.

However, Wyatt knew what a good marriage looked like. His parents were the shining beacon to which he and his brothers aspired. Garrett, Nate, and Colt were on the right path. They had fallen in love with strong, stable, independent women.

Wyatt's mistakes had been too numerous to count. Starting with an unplanned pregnancy. Marrying Stephanie because she carried his child had seemed like the right choice—the only choice. It turned out to be a disaster. A hellish nightmare that should have ended with her death. Instead, it morphed into a different kind of hell—one he couldn't find a way to shake.

"Carole can have the upper hand," Dex ordered another round. "It's worked so far."

Wyatt pulled himself back to the present. He was getting better at shaking off his dark thoughts. Another reason to thank his father for this forced vacation. Maybe it was the mountain air. Or the physical activity. Or sex with the lovely Joie. Whatever the reason, Wyatt felt a spark of hope for the first time in years. Maybe he could outrun the past. Or bury it. Or? Pick your cliché.

A little more time in Monroe might turn out to be just what the doctor ordered.

"Yo, Dex. Long time no see."

"Donny? Well, where have you been keeping yourself?"

Left alone while Dex went to greet his friend, Wyatt sipped his beer, letting himself enjoy the unique sounds and rhythm of a bar in the middle of the week.

It was different than the weekend when the crowd tended to be rowdier and out for fun. Nor was it the same as a Monday. The first day of a workweek had its own laidback feel. You could never tell what you would get on a Wednesday. It could be deader than dead, or like tonight, surprisingly lively.

Wyatt had discovered this the summer he worked at a cantina in Greece. Different country, different language, different customs. But a bar was a bar, no matter the location.

He had been twenty years old and feeling his oats. It would be the last time he took off on his own for any length of time. The next year he began working with his father and from there, he had never looked back.

The few times he and his brothers ventured out for a few drinks were never relaxing for long. There was nothing Colt could do to hide his famously pretty face. Whether it took five minutes or an hour, someone always recognized him. That meant pictures and autographs—all graciously given. Wyatt didn't know how his little brother did it. No matter how many years passed, he never grew tired of his fans. He got that from their mother. She understood that she would be nowhere without the people who bought tickets to movies, and she treated them accordingly.

Callie Flynn and Colton Landis were universally loved and respected. By the people in the industry. But more importantly, by their fans.

Wyatt was proud of them for that. He knew that he had neither the talent nor the temperament to do what they did. His talents lay elsewhere. Their names meant big box office. He made sure there was plenty of money to get the movies made. It was the perfect combination.

"Mind if I sit here?"

Wyatt glanced to his right, surprised to see Brad Makepeace. Dressed in his usual pressed pants and polo shirt, he was sporting a hangdog expression. Since there were plenty of barstools open that were not next to Wyatt, he had to assume the man wanted to talk.

What the hell.

"Help yourself." Wyatt sipped his beer. "Peanut?"

"No thanks. I brushed my teeth before leaving home." Brad sat, posture perfect, and ordered a club soda—no lime.

"How's it going?" Wyatt could make small talk with almost anyone. The secret was to throw out one neutral subject after another until he found something that stuck.

"Good." Brad paid for his drink with three crisp one-dollar bills.

"Nice weather. Unseasonably warm. Or so I understand."

"Yes."

"Watched any good porn lately?"

"No." His glass halfway to his mouth, Brad gave Wyatt a wide-eyed stare. "Excuse me?"

"I'm trying here, man. For this to work, you have to meet me halfway."

For a second, Wyatt didn't think Brad was going to answer. No skin off his ass. If Joie's admirer wanted to sit in silence, that was fine with him.

"I've been in love with Joie since the first day I saw her."

"Okay." The man obviously didn't believe in polite conversation. "I don't know how to respond to that."

"I wanted you to know that I have officially taken my hat out of the ring. My love for Joie has withered and died before reaching its full, blooming potential."

"Again, I'm without words." Who the hell was this guy? No one outside of an overwritten play spoke like that.

"I discovered that we are not compatible."

Taking another drink, Wyatt nodded sagely. "Better to find that out now rather than after the kids are off at college."

"Joie and I have no children," Brad said with a confused frown.

And you have no sense of humor, you poor schmuck.

"What happened?" Wyatt found himself inexplicably curious. "Your *love* withered quickly."

"First, there was her mother." Brad gave a delicate shudder. "Have you met Joie's mother?"

"I can't say I've had the pleasure."

"She's… How do I put this delicately?"

Wyatt tried not to roll his eyes. "Don't worry. It's just us guys."

"She's brassy. Bold. I'm not comfortable with overly demonstrative people."

"Probably the reason you and Joie didn't have children," Wyatt muttered.

"I'm sorry. What did you say?"

"I have no idea." Wyatt brushed it off. "Please. Continue."

"Her mother I could have accepted. After all, she doesn't live in Monroe." Brad took a white cloth handkerchief from his pocket, dabbing his upper lip. "It was something Joie told me over dinner that I can't abide."

The possibilities were limitless. What would Brad consider a deal breaker? Love of dairy products? Maybe Joie insisted on filling her car with unleaded instead of premium. Wyatt was at a loss, but he had to know the answer.

"Go on."

Brad looked around, turning right then left, before leaning closer. With a lowered voice, he whispered, "She's a *Democrat*."

Wyatt waited for the punch line, but he soon realized Brad was serious. The idiot had stopped jonesing for Joie because of her politics? Jesus, it really did take all kinds.

"That's tough, Brad." Wyatt patted his shoulder. "Do you think it's contagious?"

"Why, no." Brad actually contemplated the possibility. "I don't think so."

"You're probably right. Though I have to admit. Last night? When it was dark and quiet? I had the sudden urge to vote for Hillary." Wyatt's parents were staunch Democrats. Something they had passed onto their sons. He didn't share this news with Brad for fear that the poor guy would spontaneously combust.

"If it happens again, feel free to give me a call. I can talk you down." Brad stood, smoothing the wrinkles from his pants. "But I would suggest staying as far away from Joie as possible. She appears to be a bad influence."

With a nod, Brad exited the bar.

Brad reminded him of someone. Racking his brain, Wyatt suddenly had a flash. *Tony Randall. That was it.* As a boy, he had met the comedy legend. He was Brad to a T. Perhaps a little more Felix Unger than the man himself but in Wyatt's mind, they were close enough to be a match. He wished he had a recording of that conversation. If he tried to describe it, no one would believe him.

"Wyatt," Dex called to him. "Want to shoot a game?"

"I'll be right there." He went to pick up his beer when his phone rang. Seeing it was Joie, he waved at Dex, pointing at his phone.

Dex nodded. "Take your time."

"Would you believe me if I told you I was just talking about you?"

"That's nice."

Wyatt didn't like the tone of her voice. "What's wrong?"

"I wasn't sure if I should call you." Joie spoke faster than usual, and that was saying something. She took a deep breath, but her words poured out in rapid succession. "Does this go beyond our agreement? I mean, you aren't my boyfriend. Friend, yes, I hope. But are we at the point where I call you in a semi-emergency?"

"Fuck the agreement, Joie." Wyatt pulled on his jacket. Wherever she was, he was on his way. "What happened? And spit it out fast, I'm getting nervous."

"I'm fine. Conscious, at least. A few bumps and bruises. The doctor is almost positive I don't have a concussion. Probably."

"You're at the hospital?" Wyatt headed for the exit. It was obvious he wasn't getting any details over the phone.

"The emergency room. You know the way." Joie tried to laugh, but it came out as more of moan. "Damn it, Petal. That hurts. Sorry, my nurse is new at giving shots."

"I'm on my way." Wyatt was halfway out the door.

"Grab Dex. Carole is here. Her arm is broken, and she's getting it set. I told her I would contact him."

What the hell? A potential concussion? Broken bones? They were supposed to spend the evening at Joie's picking out wedding dresses and flower arrangements. When had that become a dangerous activity?

"You're really okay?" Wyatt needed the words.

"Other than a headache and stiff muscles, I'm fine."

Wyatt took a deep breath, saying a silent thank you. "We'll be there in ten minutes."

Dex grinned when he saw Wyatt's approach. "We started the game without you, but T-bone only has a few more shots. You can play me next."

"We have to go." Wyatt tossed Dex his jacket. "They are going to be fine, but Joie and Carole are at the hospital."

Wyatt had to admire Dex. He didn't waste time with questions, rushing across the bar and out the door. If Wyatt hadn't caught up with him, steering him toward the truck, it was likely the guy would have run all the way to the hospital.

"This is faster," Wyatt said as he pushed Dex into the passenger side.

"Right." Dex gripped the dashboard, his knuckles turning white. "You're certain Carole is okay?"

"Joie wouldn't have lied, Dex." Wyatt ran around the truck. He was in the cab and had the motor started in a flash. "Carole has a broken arm. Buckle up."

"Fuck." Dex fumbled with his seatbelt. "When did looking at lace and doodads become a contact sport?"

"Joie didn't give me any details." Wyatt pulled onto the main road. "I didn't want to push her over the phone."

Wyatt wanted to know two things. Was it an accident? And if not, whose ass did he need to kick?

In Wyatt's experience, nothing good happened in hospitals. All his memories were of injury or death. When necessary, he forced himself to visit friends or colleagues. But if he could put it off, he avoided them like the plague.

Wyatt wasn't a betting man, but he would have laid down good money that he was never going to see this place again after his accident. Yet, less than two weeks later, here he was.

"What do you think that smell is?" Dex asked as they waited in the reception area.

"Death," Wyatt said without thinking.

"That's a cheery thought. I thought it smelled like bleach and every men's room I've ever been in."

"I guess it's a matter of perspective." For the fifth time, Wyatt hit the bell. Frustrated, he looked around for someone who worked there. "What if one of us were bleeding to death?"

"You have some gruesome thoughts, don't you?" Dex shook his head. "Not what I would have expected."

"I hate hospitals."

"No shit."

"Stop ringing that bell!"

The nurse looked tired and overworked. Under different circumstances, Wyatt would have sympathized. Tonight, he wanted her to do her job. Which meant telling him where to find Joie.

"We've been waiting for over ten minutes."

"I don't care." Her steely gaze landed on Wyatt. "Are either of you sick or injured?"

"No, but—"

"*Then stop ringing the bell!*"

Wyatt looked at the woman's nametag and smiled. Time to lay on a little Landis charm. "Nurse Lovett. I apologize for making so much noise. My friend is looking for his fiancée. Carole Fletcher?"

"Dexter," Nurse Lovett nodded. "Carole is down the hall. Fourth door on the right."

"Thank you, Deena."

"If you knew her, why didn't you say so?" Wyatt called after Dex. He widened his smile when the nurse crossed her arms over her chest. If anything, her gaze grew colder. "Small towns. I guess everyone knows everyone."

"I know who you are, Mr. Hollywood."

"Actually, the name is Landis."

Nothing. The woman's expression didn't change. Had he offended her in another life? Because sure as hell, he hadn't done anything in this one. So much for charm.

"I would like to see Joie Trent."

"Are you a relative?"

"No." It was obvious where this was going. Normally, Wyatt would have lied and said he was Joie's brother. Nobody ever checked. But he doubted it would fly with Nurse Lovett.

"Fiancée?"

"No, ma'am. Just a friend."

"That will do. Second door on your left."

"Really?" Wyatt took a step down the hall, expecting the nurse to change her mind.

"Are you hard of hearing? Second door on the left. Get going. I have better things to do than deal with you, pretty boy."

Pretty boy? She had the wrong Landis. But he wasn't going to argue. Wyatt wasn't certain, but as he passed by, he thought her lips twitched. Maybe Nurse Lovett wasn't such a hardass after all.

The door to Joie's room was open. The design was standard—nothing special. Not that he expected anything else. The goal was to get patients in and out as quickly as possible, which meant other than a bed and a bathroom, comfort was at a minimum.

Wyatt took the opportunity to look her over. She was pale. But other than a darkening bruise on her forehead, he couldn't see any other injuries.

Propped up against a pile of pillows, her eyes were closed. Joie looked so fragile. Nothing like the vibrant woman he was used to. Wyatt had the sudden urge to smooth back her dark hair, pick her up into his arms, and swear he would keep her safe until his last breath.

Whoa. Where had that come from? Wyatt ran a hand over his face. He was not the knight in shining armor type. He left that up to his brothers. The one and only time he tried to save a woman it had ended in disaster. Never again.

"Wyatt?"

If he had expected Joie's voice to sound feeble and forlorn, he should have known better. This woman was made of sterner stuff than that. She didn't wallow. She hadn't called him to save the day. She was more than capable of doing that all by herself.

Wyatt had to admit, it was an appealing quality. Who was he kidding? Joie was self-sufficient. Smart. Funny. Beautiful. In other words? The sexiest woman he had ever known. He felt a tug in the region of his heart. If she hadn't chosen that moment to smile, he would have run in the opposite direction—not stopping until he saw the outskirts of Los Angeles.

It was a foolish and cowardly thought. His heart wasn't in danger. Not from Joie. Not from anyone. It had been damaged beyond repair. And as long as he was around her, he planned on reminding himself of that—often.

"You look better than I expected."

"I had the nurse bring me a mirror." Joie's laugh was followed by a small groan. "You're either trying to be kind, or you were expecting a train wreck."

The closer Wyatt got, it became clear that she was in pain. Obviously, she had more injuries than were visible to the naked eye.

"Has the doctor prescribed pain medication?"

Joie shook her head. "They are waiting to make sure my non-concussion doesn't turn into the real thing."

"There must be something they can give you."

Wyatt hated to see anyone in pain. But watching Joie made him itch to grab the nearest staff member and force him to at least bring her an aspirin.

"It only hurts when I laugh. So save the jokes for another time, Shecky." Joie held out her hand. When he hesitated, she balled it into a fist, dropping onto the bed. "I'm sorry I interrupted your evening."

"You know better than that. I'm glad you called." Feeling like a jerk, Wyatt took her hand, straightening her fingers. Lightly, he kissed each one. "Will I hurt you if I sit on the edge of the bed?"

"They are bruises, Wyatt. Nothing more." Joie scooted over a few inches.

"I hate hospitals," he explained when he was settled. "I..." Wyatt took a deep breath. "Before my accident, the last time I was in one was the night my wife died."

"Wyatt." Joie's eyes filled with sympathy and concern. "I don't blame you. You can see that I'm going to be all right. Go home."

"No."

"But—"

"Joie." Keeping hold of her hand, he leaned close. "Look at me."

"That's no hardship."

"Flirt." Carefully, he brushed her lips with his. "I'm fine. You couldn't get me out of here with a truckload of dynamite."

"That might be a little extreme." Joie sighed when he kissed her again. "But I appreciate the sentiment."

"Do you want to tell me what happened?"

"It's crazy. Something out of a movie. Hey," Joie brightened. "You might want to get the rights to this one. It had blockbuster written all over it."

"Joie—" Wyatt couldn't decide if she were the most entertaining or most frustrating person he had ever dealt with.

"Sorry. When I'm stressed, I start to make everything into a story. It helps calm me."

"Want to know what calms me?"

"What?"

"Details."

Joie met his gaze, her eyes sparkling. "I'll remember that the next time I have you naked. The things I could tell you. The size of your—"

"I'm not a violent man, Joie. But—"

It seemed that Joie decided she had pushed her luck far enough. "Carole wanted some ice cream," she began. "Naturally that was the one thing I forgot to buy at the store. It was such a nice night we decided to walk. Preemptive calorie burning."

"Makes sense."

"We thought so. Monroe is a safe town, Wyatt. The whole time I've lived here, violent crime has been practically nonexistent. I walk those sidewalks by myself every day."

"Okay." Joie was working herself up. Though he felt *his* blood pressure rising, he maintained a smooth façade. "Breathe, sweetheart. In and out. That's right."

Joie let out a long stream of air, then continued. "We were a block from my house when it happened. A man in a ski mask jumped from behind a parked car. I was startled, but I lived in big cities most of my life. I assumed he wanted our money. Without hesitation, I handed him my purse and told Carole to do the same."

"Smart."

"I thought so. Unfortunately, he wasn't looking for a quick buck."

"Mother fucker," Wyatt growled. "Did he—?"

"He hit Carole." Joie's fingers tightened on his. "He had a bat, Wyatt. We handed him our purses, but he threw them aside. Before I knew what was happening, he swung, connecting with her arm. God, I will never forget that sound. I heard the bone snap. And Carole's scream."

Tears filled Joie's eyes, falling onto her cheeks.

"Shh." Gently, Wyatt slid his arms around her. "I'm sorry. But Carole is going to be all right."

"I know that now. At the time, I thought he was going to kill her."

"What happened to you?"

"I jumped on the bastard's back. From there I was able to dig my fingers into his eyes."

Wyatt felt his chest expand. Partly with fear. But mostly, he felt an overwhelming sense of pride. On top of everything else, Joie was a fighter. With care, he ran a finger over the bump on her forehead.

"I take it he didn't like that."

"You could say that. His scream was louder than Carole's." She smiled when Wyatt chuckled. "But he was strong. He shook me off. That's when I hit my head. The side of a car doesn't have a lot of give. Neither does the sidewalk."

Wyatt felt his stomach clench. "I don't like this movie."

"Nice beginning. Nasty middle. But it had a semi-happy ending."

"You and Carole are alive. I'd give that a standing ovation."

"He got away." Joie frowned. "I grabbed my purse. I always carry pepper spray. The son of a bitch wasn't satisfied to break

Carole's arm. He was going to hit her again. I sprayed him in the eyes just before he took his swing."

"You're a freaking superhero."

"My hands were shaking." Joie swallowed. "Hitting him was nothing but luck."

"I doubt Carole sees it that way." Wyatt didn't.

"He ran off. I can't be certain, but I thought I heard a car backfire, then head south. All I could think about was calling nine-one-one."

"Have you spoken to the police?"

"They left just before you arrived. They scraped under my fingernails. I had good samples of scumbag DNA." Wyatt could tell that Joie was running on fumes. He lowered her onto the pillows, making certain she was comfortable. "We need to go into the station as soon as we're up to it and give a more detailed statement."

"Give it a day or two. You need time to recover."

"Wyatt," she whispered.

"Hmm?"

"I know it was dark. And my head was spinning. But…"

Frowning, Wyatt rubbed her arm. "What is it, Joie?"

"He was going to hit Carole in the head. Maybe I'm wrong, but I don't think so. The angle of the bat. The direction of his gaze was easy to read. If I hadn't stopped him—" She shuddered.

"But you did." Wyatt believed her. What the hell was going on? "Did you tell that to the police?"

"Yes. But how do I tell Carole?"

"She has to be warned," Wyatt admitted.

"Carole is the most practical woman I know. It's scary as hell, but she'll handle it."

Wyatt nodded. "Who would want to hurt her?"

"I can't imagine. No one here in Monroe." Joie yawned. "We'll put our heads together and figure it out."

"Tomorrow." Wyatt pulled the covers over Joie's shoulders. "Rest until the nurse comes back."

"Will you stay?"

"Yes."

Joie closed her eyes, a smile on her lips. The smart thing was for her to stay the night in the hospital. It was already after ten. Wyatt looked around the room for a chair, frowning when he saw the only option. Standard issue. Not much padding and not made for comfort. But it would do.

Keeping an eye on Joie, Wyatt stepped outside her room. If she were right—and he had no reason to think she wasn't—the attack had nothing to do with her. Carole was the target. However, Joie's injuries were not to be taken lightly. Things could have gone terribly wrong—for both women. With a sigh, he took out his phone.

"You can't use that in here."

"Nurse Lovett." Wyatt should have known she would have the eyes of an eagle.

"If it's that important take it outside, Hollywood."

"I don't want to leave Joie alone."

"She won't be. The doctor prescribed some pain medication. I'll make sure she knows you're coming back." The nurse looked him up and down. "You *are* coming back?"

"Yes, Nurse Lovett. I am."

"Then there's no problem."

Wyatt turned to go, then hesitated. "Nurse?"

"Yes?"

"Do you have a problem with me?"

She raised an imperious eyebrow. "Why would I?"

"That's what I was wondering. When you speak to me, your tone is a bit… harsh. Not to mention the pretty boy and Hollywood digs."

"Good Lord. Go make your phone call," she scoffed, shutting the door in his face.

"Don't worry about it," an orderly told him. The man stood by the elevator. "Deena is like that with everyone she likes."

Wyatt sent the man a surprised look. "She likes me? What would she be like if she hated me?"

The doors to the elevator opened. Stepping on, the orderly winked. "Trust me, you don't want to know."

Mulling that over, Wyatt walked through the emergency room sliding doors. He hit a few buttons on his phone and waited.

"Who is on your shit list this time?" Drew Harper asked.

"Hello to you too." What was with the attitude tonight? First Nurse Lovett? Now Drew? Was he putting out a vibe he wasn't aware of?

"Are you calling just to say hello?" Drew challenged.

"No," Wyatt mumbled. He could almost see Drew's smug smile.

"Then I reiterate. Who did what? And how can I help?"

"Two of my friends were attacked. All signs point to it being personal."

That was all it took. The next time he spoke, Wyatt could hear the strictly business tone in Drew's voice.

"How much can you tell me?"

"Not much. But here's what I know."

CHAPTER FOURTEEN

THE STREET WAS littered with fallen leaves, their edges coated with a light frost.

In deference to the sudden change in the weather, Wyatt dressed accordingly for his morning run. Layers were in order. A t-shirt topped by a long-sleeved pullover. A sweater came next, then his usual hoodie. He didn't worry about his hands—it wasn't that cold. In a pinch, he could put them in his pockets. His knit cap kept his body heat from escaping through the top of his head. Wyatt chuckled. He assumed that was really a thing, but when he thought about it, the idea sounded ridiculous.

Around his second mile, his muscles began to loosen up. Wyatt rotated his head, hearing the popping in his neck. When he woke, his entire body ached. That's what a night in a hospital chair will do for you.

However, every little pain had been worth it when Joie opened her eyes and saw that he was still there. The spark of recognition followed by her slow smile. Wyatt would have slept on a bed of rocks for that moment.

Careful, Landis. Don't get too attached, the little voice in his head whispered. *You have no future with this woman. With any woman. Back away before you get any deeper.*

For the first time in a long time, Wyatt tuned out that annoying little voice. Joie wasn't asking for anything. She had made it clear that she felt the same as he did. Fun and games. Friendship was a nice bonus. *That* was what last night had been about. One friend looking out for another.

The little voice tried to sneak in a sarcastic *yeah, right.* Increasing his pace, Wyatt blocked out the unwelcome message. He didn't know if an epiphany had hit him sometime during the night or he was simply starting to get a grasp on his life. Either way, he realized that he had fallen into a rut. Work. Family. Work. Followed by more work. Everything had become insular, centering around the Hollywood community.

His brothers had other interests. For weeks on end, his parents would leave the movie industry behind. What they found to do with their time didn't matter. The important thing was that they did it away from Los Angeles, Hollywood, and their public personas.

Wyatt, on the other hand, used work as his recreation. When that had started, he wasn't sure. Long before he met Stephanie. He couldn't use his marriage as an excuse. He had dug this hole without anyone's help. And he wouldn't have discovered what he was doing if it weren't for Monroe, its people, and Joie.

The key was finding someone else to focus some of his energy on. Not the business or his past. The more he took on other people's burdens, the less important his seemed. Helping around town felt right. It made him feel good. Not completely whole. But a lot less empty.

Joie's doctor had discharged her first thing this morning. Carole needed a few more x-rays. Dex would take her home later.

Wyatt was prepared to coddle Joie for a few days. Tuck her in bed. Bring her hot soup. Help her in and out of the shower. He supposed he should have known better. Joie refused to play the invalid. Once she was clear of the hospital walls, she let him know that she had a schedule to keep.

"You need to rest," Wyatt had argued as he pulled up to her house. "What could be so important that you can't take a day or two to recover?"

"I rested all night. That pain pill knocked me out." Before he could protest, Joie hopped out of his truck. "My book is due in less than a month. I've never missed a deadline, Wyatt. It's a point of pride."

Wyatt wanted to argue, but he didn't see the point. Joie knew her limitations better than he did. He would have to trust her to take a break if she felt the need.

For his own peace of mind, Wyatt insisted on going from room to room. He hadn't expected to find anything. But there was always the chance, however small, that Joie and Carole's attacker had broken into the house and was waiting for them to return.

Joie pointed out that the police had already thought of that. Continuing, Wyatt hadn't replied.

"Keep the door locked," he told her before he left.

"I always do."

Wyatt appreciated that Joie tried to hide her smile. He didn't like the fact that she wasn't taking this as seriously as he thought necessary.

"Do you know who attacked you?"

"No."

"Are you certain he left town?"

"No."

"Is it possible—"

Joie put her hand over his mouth. Wyatt could see the impatience in her eyes.

"I am not a child, Wyatt." Instead of taking her hand away, she traced the outline of his lips with her finger. "Your concern is lovely. It's been a long time since anyone cared enough to annoy me this much."

Wyatt kissed each one, lightly nipping her index finger with his teeth. He grinned when she yelped—with surprise, not pain. "Glad I could be of service."

"If you want to do me a favor?"

"Name it."

"Go back to the inn. Change your clothes and take a nice, long run." She stood on her toes, her lips replacing her hand. For what the kiss lacked in longevity, it made up for in intensity. "Then come back here to take your shower. By then, I'll be ready for a break."

"Are you sure you're up for it?" Wyatt asked with a concerned frown.

"Are you?" Joie cupped him between the legs. "No. But you're on the way."

"That is cruel, Joie," Wyatt protested, but he didn't move away. "Running with an erection can be hazardous to a man's health."

"You have two choices. Strap it down."

"Or?"

"Think of England. And run fast."

Wyatt checked his watch. That had been a little over on hour ago. He liked to go at a fast clip, but this morning had to be a personal record. He would have gotten here sooner if Margie hadn't insisted on a rundown of what had happened the night before. Wyatt gave her the Reader's Digest version, promising more details at a later date.

As he rounded Joie's block, he gave one last burst of speed, zipping down the walk and up the front steps. He was hot, sweaty, and couldn't wait to get his hands on Joie. Thinking of the first time he came knocking, Wyatt politely rang the bell instead of announcing his arrival by pounding his fist on the door.

When Joie answered wearing the same robe as the last time, Wyatt grinned.

"Do you always answer the door half naked?"

Joie stepped aside to let him enter. "Only when it's you. Or the UPS guy. I'm a sucker for men bearing boxes."

"I'll keep that in mind." Wyatt breathed in her scent. Fresh. Joie with a hint of green apples. "Don't get me wrong. I love that look on you. But I'm a little disappointed that you already showered. You promised to wash my back."

"I couldn't wait." Joie leaned against the door, her eyes taking him in. "I swear the smell of hospital had seeped into my pores. Since I know how you feel about it, I didn't want to turn you off."

"Not possible." Wyatt lowered his gaze. "Lose the robe, Joie."

"But I'm all clean, and you're so sweaty." Slowly, Joie licked her lips. "If you touch me, I'll get dirty."

Wyatt knew it was deliberate—the way her tongue traced the line of her mouth. With a hungry growl, his eyes narrowed. "So you wanna play?"

"Maybe." She swallowed. "What are the rules?"

"Anything goes." Not taking his eyes from hers, Wyatt began to strip. "I'll give you thirty seconds head start."

"That isn't very long," Joie protested, but she was already headed for the stairs.

"You better be naked when I catch you."

Laughing, Joie called over her shoulder. "Or what?"

"I know you have a vivid imagination. Use it."

Joie stood just outside her bedroom, toying with the cloth tied around her waist.

"In my imagination, I let you take it off."

Wyatt kicked off his shoes. Down to nothing but his dark blue track pants, he strode to the base of the staircase. His smile predatory, he pinned her with his gaze. "I was hoping you'd say that."

Joie's eyes grew round. Not with fear, but anticipation. When he took the first step, she let out a yelp and rushed into her room.

"There's no place to hide, honey. You might as well stand and take your medicine."

Wyatt was up the stairs in a few strides, then paused outside her door. Surprised she wasn't waiting, he checked out the room. Maybe there *was* a place to hide.

"Always check behind the door." Before he could turn, Joie launched herself onto his back. "If this were an action movie, you would be toast."

"If this were an action movie, I would have anticipated your position." Wyatt flipped her over his shoulder onto the bed. Not waiting for her to stop bouncing, he quickly covered her body with his. "Now who's toast?"

"I prefer a romantic storyline. In which case, *I* anticipated *your* move." She stretched, rubbing her silk-covered body against his. "I am exactly where I wanted to be."

"A woman with a plan. My favorite kind."

With one hand, Wyatt grabbed Joie's wrists, pinning them above her head.

"This robe is in my way," he said, his tone menacing.

"So it is." Joie's lips twitched, but to her credit, she looked reasonably concerned.

"That means some form of punishment must be doled out. I could spank you."

"You could try," she snorted. When Wyatt simply raised his brow, she shrugged. "Fine. You could spank me, but you won't."

"Because…?"

"I wouldn't like it."

It was as simple as that. Pain wasn't his thing. Not getting it or giving it. It was good to find out that Joie felt the same. It was even better that she understood that he would never do anything she wasn't comfortable with. In or out of bed.

Bending close, Wyatt's lips kissed the base of her throat. "Tell me what you *do* like."

"That's a winner." She raised her chin, giving him full access. "You have magic lips."

Wyatt smiled against her soft skin. "That's a new one. Magic lips. I'll add it to my resume."

"Do that." Joie sucked in a deep breath, then sighed. "You can put me down as a reference."

"God, you smell sweet." He nuzzled her hair. Her scent was intoxicating. "At the moment, I can't say the same."

"You'll do." To Wyatt's surprise, Joie ran the tip of her tongue across his shoulder. "On the right man, there is nothing like clean, salty sweat."

"On how many men have you tested this theory?"

Joie licked him again. "Just you. I told you. It has to be the right man."

Holy fuck. That had to be the sexiest thing a woman had ever said to him. Playtime was over. He kicked off his pants. Slipping his arm around Joie's waist, he rolled them toward the end table.

"Now that you're on top, take off the robe." He grabbed a condom from the drawer. "This is going to be fast and hard. I don't want anything but this thin layer of latex between us."

"Be still my heart. There's nothing as romantic as latex."

As Joie disposed of the robe, Wyatt tore open the packet.

"Is that sarcasm?"

"I'm a single woman in her twenties. Have no doubt. That is the truth—pure and simple."

"Want to help?" He held out the condom.

Taking it without hesitation, Joie eagerly sat up. "And it isn't even my birthday."

"When *is* your birthday?" Wyatt sighed as Joie made quick work of wrapping her present. The touch of her nimble fingers was torture at its best.

"May twenty-third."

Months from now. Wyatt would be long gone by then. But he was allowed to send a friend a remembrance. Wasn't he? There had to be a book of etiquette that dealt with this subject. Ex-lovers. To gift or not to gift. How the hell should he know?

Wyatt groaned. Life could be hard enough. Why was he making it worse?

"Is that a *holy shit that feels good* moan? Or a *get your hands off my dick* groan?"

Mentally, he thanked Joie for dragging him back into the moment. With a smile, he smoothed back her hair before caressing her cheek. "Straight men never ask a woman to take her hands off his dick, Joie."

"Unless she's Lorena Bobbitt."

"That's it." Wyatt took Joie under the arms and tossed her on the middle of the bed. He quickly followed. "No more talk."

"I went too far, didn't I?" Joie's eyes clouded. "I talk too much. Jesus. Penis mutilation? Men don't want to hear that. *Especially* in bed. My brain goes in bizarre, inappropriate directions."

Wyatt covered her mouth with his, drawing out the kiss until Joie relaxed once more. If she could string a sentence together after that, he was losing his touch.

"You don't talk too much." Wyatt brushed his lips over the tip of her nose. "I love the way your mind works. It's fast and quirky and thoroughly entertaining. You keep me on my toes."

"But…?"

"My dick is hard." To emphasize the point, he rubbed the tip between her legs. When she gasped, Wyatt nodded. "See? You're right there with me. Hot. Slick. I can feel your body reaching for mine."

"Yes," Joie breathed.

All traces of worry had left Joie's eyes, replaced with growing desire. Wyatt could see her need, and it fueled his own. He didn't ask if she were ready for him. He already knew the answer. With one thrust, he entered her. Her body arched to meet him—slick, open, and gloriously eager.

"I said this would be fast and hard. Are you okay with that?"

"Yes," she gasped when he increased his rhythm. Joie wrapped her legs around him, her hands clutching his shoulders. "Please."

"So polite." Wyatt kissed Joie again, his tongue plunging into her mouth. "Scream for me, honey." He changed the angle of his penetration, smiling wickedly when Joie let out a high-pitched wail. Not exactly a scream but close enough.

"Did I hit a sweet spot?" He repeated the move. Joie shuddered, the breath leaving her lungs in a desperate gasp. "I'll take that as a yes."

"Yes! Yes! Yes!"

Joie grabbed his head, pulling his mouth to hers. No more words. Only the rising tide that swept them closer and closer to the edge. Knowing it wouldn't take much more, Wyatt took Joie's leg, pushing it to her chest. He held her gaze, unconsciously matching her breathing. One last thrust and they fell. Over and over. Together.

There were no words. Nothing could express what had just happened. It wasn't sex. Wyatt knew what that felt like. This was different. New. And so fucking frightening, he didn't want to know what it was. Not now. Maybe not ever.

Wyatt didn't know how much time had passed. Five minutes? Ten? Long enough for Joie to recover. She caressed his back with slow, soothing strokes while her lips nuzzled his neck.

"Let's take a bath," she whispered.

Still a little shaky, Wyatt nodded.

"Don't move," he said as he left the bed. "I'll get the water going."

"Wyatt?"

"Hmm?" He looked over his shoulder to see Joie stretch like a contented cat.

"Thank you. That was amazing."

Wyatt returned her smile, but he couldn't shake the feeling that something had changed. He twisted the taps to full blast, the water quickly filling the huge claw-footed tub.

With a sigh, Wyatt gripped the edge of the sink, looking at himself in the mirror. Nothing seemed awry. It was the same face he saw every morning when he brushed his teeth. Same eyes. Same nose. His mother's cheekbones. His father's chin. He was a Landis. Strong genes on both ends of the pool.

"What the hell is happening to you?"

When his reflection didn't answer, Wyatt shook his head. If it had, *that* would have been a problem. He was looking for trouble where there was none. *Enjoy the moment, asshole*, Colt's voice mocked. Great. Just what he needed. His brother was mocking him from hundreds of miles away.

He pulled his shoulders back. *Enough*. Nothing had changed. He was the same man he had been before he crashed his truck into that tree. A little more relaxed. But deep down, he was still Wyatt

Landis. When he left Monroe, all he would take were some memories. The rest—including Joie—he would leave behind without regret.

Wyatt walked to the bed and scooped Joie into his arms. She wound her arms around his neck. With a happy sigh, she rested her head on his shoulder. Okay, he was willing to admit, perhaps he would take a bit of regret back to Los Angeles. As he lowered her into the steaming water, his gaze dropped to her mouth. That smile. He would miss it. And her eyes. And her laugh.

Hell. As long as he was honest? Wyatt would miss *her*. Joie. Every inch. Every day. For the rest of his life. *Son of a bitch.*

"Are you joining me?" Joie took his hand and tugged. "Come on in, the water's fine."

Joie's expression, all at once teasing, sexy, and hopeful, did Wyatt in. How was he supposed to resist? *Was* he supposed to resist? Maybe tomorrow. Or next week. But not today.

"Scoot over."

There was plenty of room in the old-fashioned tub. Wide and deep with the faucets wisely out of the way. It meant Joie could rest her back on one side while he was comfortable on the other. His legs were stretched out on either side of hers.

"This is nice." Joie rubbed her foot along his upper thigh.

"Yes, it is." Wyatt didn't let enough *nice* into his life. He leaned his head back and relaxed. "Talk to me."

"Any particular subject?"

He raised one eyelid long enough to see that Joie, like him, had her eyes closed. The water covered her shoulders, but when he felt like taking a peek, her lovely breasts were in clear view. Happy with the knowledge, he let darkness close over him.

"When did you start writing?"

"Informally, I can't remember a time when I didn't write. My father would make up stories. Crazy, nonsensical tales. As I grew older, I started adding my ideas, much to Dad's delight. Eventually, we switched roles. I became the narrator. He the audience."

"Did he suggest that you start writing them down?"

"No. I was six years old. I could manage my name and a few simple words, but my vocabulary far outdistanced my spelling skills." She laughed. "It still does. Thank God for spell check and a fantastic editor."

"Spelling was always one of my strengths."

Joie lightly poked him in the chest with her toe. "Why am I not surprised? I bet you also excelled at algebra."

"I did all right." Straight As. Wyatt breezed through math and science. But there was no need to brag.

"*I* did all right. What's your IQ?"

"I have no idea." Which was the truth. He was never tested and had no desire to find out.

"Bet it's high."

"Bet yours is too."

"Mmm."

Wyatt didn't look, he could hear the smile in her voice.

"About your writing?"

"Dad began recording my stories—though I didn't know it at the time. I have a box full of cassette tapes that Mom found after he died."

Wyatt whistled. "They would be worth a fortune."

"Maybe. I'm keeping them for my children. If I have any."

The tension that entered his body must have relayed itself to Joie.

"I'm not hinting," she assured him. "Children are a concept I haven't fully grasped. Maybe yes, maybe no. I haven't set my sights on making you my baby daddy."

"I didn't think you had." Wyatt opened his eyes. This wasn't a subject he was comfortable with. Even with his family. But he wanted to tell Joie the truth. At least part of it. "My wife was pregnant before we married. It wasn't exactly a shotgun wedding, but if it weren't for the baby...?" He shrugged.

"Things happen. You wouldn't walk away from your child."

"No. My relationship with Stephanie prior to our marriage was short. A few weeks." It wouldn't have been that long if she hadn't been so beautiful. Wyatt could admit it. He let her physical appearance seduce him. The sex was good. He had seen through her façade. But not soon enough.

"The condom broke?"

"Something like that." The truth was horrifically complicated. Two words that perfectly described his three-year marriage. "I insisted on a DNA test. I was the father. No doubt."

"It isn't the best start. Couples have made it work."

Joie brought his foot to her chest. Wyatt didn't know why, but he found the gesture was oddly comforting.

"Our marriage was doomed before it started."

"And the baby?"

Wyatt looked into Joie's eyes. He hated to lie to her. But he had never told a living soul. Not even Colt. The world knew part of the story. His family knew a bit more. However, no one except him and a dead woman knew the whole truth.

"Stephanie lost our child." Wyatt choked out the words.

"I'm sorry."

Wyatt was used to the words of sympathy. His parents had grieved the loss of their first grandchild. His brothers rallied around him. The press and public left him alone—for the most part. Surprisingly, the loss of a child turned out to be the line they wouldn't cross.

His friends and colleagues felt compelled to say something. How could they not? With his barely contained anger and grief bubbling just below his calm exterior, Wyatt hadn't known how to react. In the end, he chose to nod and reply with a brief *thank you*. It was all anyone expected—thank the Lord.

Over time, Wyatt's anger didn't fade. But the world moved on. Dealing with other people's sympathy became a thing of the past. Dealing with the burden of guilt and regret never did.

Joie tugged on his hand. "Turn around."

With Wyatt's help, she maneuvered him until her breasts pillowed his back. She kissed his temple, her fingers threading through his hair until they found his scalp.

"Relax," she whispered.

At that moment, it was what he wanted more than anything. Closing his eyes, he let himself drift along with her gentle touch.

"Tell me a story."

"My specialty." Joie let out a laugh. The bright, happy sound soothed him as much as her touch. "The forest called to her with tantalizing promises. 'Come,' it would say. 'Lose yourself in my cool, pine-scented depths. With me, you will know only beauty and joy.'"

"I sense that the forest has a darker side."

"Shh," Joie put a finger against his lips.

It wasn't a long story. But it was filled with twists and turns. Villains and heroes. Heartache and a happily ever after. By the time the water in their bath had cooled, Wyatt's equilibrium had returned.

"Did you make that up on the spot?" he asked as he dried her with a soft, fluffy towel.

Joie nodded. "It wasn't bad."

"It was amazing." When Joie reached for a jar of cream, Wyatt took it from her, leading her to the bed. "Let me."

The scent was subtle. A little spicy, but not overwhelming. Wyatt smoothed it over Joie's skin, enjoying her sighs. He had meant it as a thank you for her story, but he found the act was as pleasurable for him as for her.

"You've done this before."

Joie was stretched out on her stomach. Wonderfully relaxed—stunningly naked. Wyatt messaged her foot, concentrating on the base of her instep.

"Nope." He kissed the back of her knee, his tongue taking a quick taste. "You're my first."

Joie snorted. "When was the last time you said that to a woman?"

"Is that your way of asking me how old I was when I lost my virginity?"

"Maybe."

Wyatt's fingers dug into Joie's calf, eliciting a moan.

"If I tell you, you'll have to reciprocate."

Waiting for a humorous quip, Wyatt was surprised when it didn't come.

"Never mind," she mumbled into the sheet.

"Did he hurt you? Give me his name. I'll track him down." Wyatt meant every word.

"*He* is a respected doctor. And no, he didn't hurt me."

Satisfied that no one needed his ass kicked, Wyatt moved to her thigh. "What's the mystery?"

"It's embarrassing."

"Now I have to know. What happened?"

Joie sighed. "Fine." Wyatt heard a note of resignation in her voice. "Let me preface this by saying I was young, stupid, and hooked on romance novels. Trust me, a hayloft is not as romantic as it's made out to be. Especially when the boy has allergies and his mother a keen sense of hearing."

Running his hands over her butt and lower back, Wyatt grinned. He had to hand it to her, Joie knew how to set a scene.

CHAPTER FIFTEEN

"DREW HARPER CALLED me last night."

After a morning of online wedding dress shopping, Joie and Carole stopped in at the *Monarch Café* for coffee and cheesecake. They were making progress on most aspects of the event, but Joie was convinced that a trip beyond the Monroe city limits was in order if they planned on finding Carole's dream gown. It had been awhile since they had been to New York. Maybe Vera Wang was the solution.

"Drew Harper?" Absently, Joie tapped her spoon on her plate, racking her brain for any reference to that name. "Should I know who that is?"

"He's a friend of Wyatt's." Carole handed Joie her phone. "I looked him up. Hubba hubba. That man almost puts your guy to shame."

"Wyatt isn't my guy." Joie looked at the pictures Carole had saved. There was quite a variety. But Carole called one thing right. Drew Harper was a good-looking man. "He's married."

"And I'm engaged. There's no harm in looking. And if Wyatt isn't your guy, what is he?"

Good question. Since she wasn't close to having an answer, Joie skirted around it.

"Are you going to tell me why he called?"

Carole sent her a look that said, *I know what you're doing*, then thankfully let it drop.

"Drew Harper and his partner run a security firm. Mostly high-tech stuff. Occasionally, they dip their toes into investigative work. Wyatt asked him to find out what he could about the man who attacked us."

"What can this guy do from...?" Joie checked the phone. "Harper Falls? I've never heard of it."

"It's in Washington State," Carole informed her with a superior smile—as though knowing that was a big deal. "As for what he can do? It's the twenty-first century. You can find out almost anything online—if you know what you're doing."

"If you have a place to start." Wyatt had plenty of time to tell her about this. She wondered why he hadn't. "We didn't see the guy. Or his car. You have no idea why you were targeted."

"*If*—not *why*. I know that you're convinced it was personal, Joie. But I'm not."

"What did Drew Harper say?" Joie might not have convinced Carole, but at least someone was taking her seriously.

"Mostly, he asked a lot of questions." Carole frowned. "To be honest, he freaked me out a little. I don't have any abusive ex-boyfriends. No one is obsessed with me. And there certainly isn't anyone who would benefit financially if something happened to me."

"You told him everything?" Joie thought they sounded like good questions.

"Yes. He told me to take some time and think about it. Sometimes a little push can open a big door." Carole's smile didn't quite reach her eyes. "His words, not mine."

"I suppose he's right." Joie had no idea what Drew Harper could or couldn't do. It certainly wouldn't hurt to have his resources behind the investigation. She had no control over any of that. It was Carole she worried about. "Promise me you'll take care."

"I always do."

Joie looked at her friend. The cast on her arm. The bruises hiding under her clothing. Bruises Joie knew existed because she had more than a few herself. It was frightening to think of how close she had come to watching Carole die. More than ever, Joie was certain that had been their attacker's goal. The problem was convincing Carole.

"I'll drop the subject. For now," Joie sighed when Carole raised her hands in victory.

"I would rather concentrate on happy things," Carole said. "Like a spring wedding. Dex has family back East. I wonder if I should make reservations at the *Heritage Inn* this far in advance?"

Realizing the subject of Carole's safety was closed, Joie nodded. "It wouldn't hurt. But as long as you don't pick the same week as the Founder's Day celebration, you should be safe."

"Oh, crap." Carole clapped a hand over her mouth. "Can you believe I forgot all about that?"

"You had a few other things on your mind."

"I'm on the planning committee. I know that schedule like the back of my hand. Damn it. I need to speak with Dex. If we move our wedding ahead two weeks, it will give everyone time to recover from Founder's Day. Or should we forget about early spring and go super traditional. The flowers around town are beautiful in June."

Joie was about to suggest Carole take a deep breath. But before she could do it, her friend jumped up, running toward the kitchen and Dex.

"Weddings." Larry took Carole's seat. "Why do they make women crazy?"

Joie smiled indulgently when she saw the direction of Larry's gaze. Without comment, she slid her uneaten cheesecake in front of him.

"It's a day most women have dreamed of since they were little girls."

"Not you." Larry motioned for the waitress to bring him a cup of coffee. Taking a bite of the creamy dessert, he sighed with pleasure.

Surprised, Joie asked, "What makes you say that?"

Always the flirt, Larry winked at the waitress as she delivered his coffee. "You have an independent streak in you a mile wide, young lady. Something like that doesn't suddenly pop up."

What Larry said was true. Her father had always encouraged her independence. When he died, she crawled into her imagination to cope. When her mother began her search for her next true love, Joie ended up in boarding school.

It hadn't been an easy transition, but in retrospect, it was the best thing that could have happened to her. Not only did it broaden that independent streak that Larry mentioned, but it also gave her a wider view of the world. Her classmates came from every walk of life. Some were scholarship students who had grown up with little or no money. Others had been born with every advantage.

Joie discovered that a person's background had little to do with who they were deep down. Nature or nurture. Or to paraphrase Shakespeare, a rose by any other name is still a bitch, no matter how much money is in her bank account.

Finding a way to successfully make it from girl to adolescent to woman hadn't been easy. But the journey had made her stronger. And added fuel to her already fertile imagination. From mean girls to kindred spirits, Joie had met them all during her time at Claymore Academy. And though the names had been changed to protect the less than innocent, each had made their way into her books.

"I used to concoct elaborate adventures in my head. It would have been hard to save the day with a mythical husband taking up space in my dreams."

"And now?" Larry's tone was casual, but Joie saw the twinkle in his eyes.

"Some of us aren't the marrying kind, Larry. You know that better than I do."

"Me?" Larry snorted. "I'm an old coot who turned his back on the only woman I ever loved. Did it cripple me? No. But I've regretted the decision more than once."

It just went to show, Joie thought. Everyone had something in his past that would surprise the rest of the world.

"I'm sorry, Larry."

"I wasn't looking for sympathy," Larry said, waving off her words. "I was making a point. Independence is fine and dandy. But it won't keep you warm on a cold winter's night."

"True. That's why they invented electric blankets."

"Clever." Larry pinned her with his gaze. "But again, not the point."

"How about sparing us both time and frustration, Larry. Tell me what you're getting at."

"Wyatt Landis."

Confused, Joie shook her head. "You've gotten more specific, but still not clear."

"Are you in love with him, girl?" Larry waved his fork in front of her face. "How clear is that?"

"Clear as mud." Joie felt like she had walked into the third act of a play. Without acts one and two, she was lost. "Why would you ask me that?"

"You think I'm blind?" Larry cackled. "I know what went on in my tool shed the other day."

Joie felt her cheeks heat.

"I'm glad to see you have the good grace to blush."

"Grace has nothing to do with it. Plus, sex is not love, Larry." At this point, there was no need to beat around the bush. "Wyatt and I are enjoying each other's company. That's all. Just like you and your neighbor ladies."

"I'm an old man. They are a bunch of old women. We've lived most of our lives, and we're taking a little comfort in our waning days. It's different for you and Wyatt. If you can't see that, I wonder if you're as smart as I thought." He pushed his chair back. Taking out his wallet, he dropped a couple of ones on the table. "I like that boy. He's one of the good ones. Thanks for the cheesecake."

"What did Larry want?" Carole asked as she returned. "Besides your dessert?"

"To be honest? I'm not sure."

Joie shook her head. It had been a perplexing conversation. Was Larry suggesting she was in love with Wyatt? Or had his goal been to plant the seed hoping it would grow? Either way, he was way off base.

Liking Wyatt and enjoying his body was a long way from love. She wasn't looking for a long-term relationship, but if she were, it would be crazy to look at Wyatt.

On the day he drove out of town and out of her life, Joie would send him on his way without an ounce of regret. And an intact heart. Falling in love with Wyatt Landis would be a huge mistake. But since there was no chance of it happening, Joie wasn't worried.

"Did you and Dex figure out a date?"

"June fifteenth," Carole said, her face practically glowing.

A twinge of something that felt a lot like envy zipped through Joie. *Where had that come from?* Silently, Joie cursed Larry. She did not want to get married. Eventually? Sure. Maybe. But not now. And not to Wyatt Landis.

"What's wrong?" Carole queried. "You look like you swallowed something sour. Is a June wedding too much of a cliché?"

"Don't be ridiculous. It will be perfect."

Joie was determined to make certain her best friend's special day turned out to be exactly that. Perfect. She ignored the second twinge. So what? She was only human. She could envy what Carole and Dex had without wanting it for herself. Couldn't she?

With a sigh, Joie sipped her coffee. *Damn, Larry.*

NEVER AGREE TO anything when you are five minutes removed from a mind-blowing orgasm.

Words of wisdom that Wyatt planned on having embroidered on a pillow as soon as he was back in Los Angeles. The problem was, it was too late to help him now.

"You didn't play fair," he groused—not for the first time.

"There are rules for such a situation? Show me a copy." Joie held open the auditorium door. "After you."

"The rules are implied, smartass." Wyatt waited for her before starting down the hall. "I wouldn't have let you take my dick into your mouth if I had known you were luring me into a quid pro quo situation."

Joie stopped, her eyes narrowing. With deliberation, she put a hand in the middle of his chest and backed him up against the wall.

"Do you know what you're suggesting?"

"I—"

"I do not perform sexual acts in anticipation of favors. Didn't we already have this conversation?"

"I wasn't calling you a whore, Joie. I merely suggested that under less euphoric conditions, I might have declined your request."

"Watch it, Landis. The lawyer in you is showing." Grabbing the front of his shirt, Joie tugged until his face was even with hers. "The timing of my request was coincidental. I liked giving you a blowjob. If you're lucky, I will do it again. And again."

Wyatt couldn't help it. Feeling like one of Pavlov's dogs, he began to salivate. "Yes, please."

Joie's lips twitched. "Isn't that what you said just before I took you into my mouth?"

Cupping her face with his hand, Wyatt ran his thumb over her lips. "Followed by a hearty and sincere thank you."

"In retrospect, my timing could have been better. If you want to back out, I'll understand."

"We're already here. I might as well find out what I've agreed to."

Smiling, Joie gave him a quick kiss. Which turned into something longer.

"Way to go, Ms. Trent."

The shout was followed by a wolf whistle. Joie laughed. Wyatt groaned.

"Teenagers," he grumbled. "Why must they be so obnoxious?"

"Were you any better when you were their age?"

"Probably not," he admitted reluctantly.

"Consider this payback."

Joie took his hand. She made him feel younger. Not *that* young. Wyatt had no desire to revisit his teenage years. But she put a spring in his step that had been missing for some time.

"Joie. Thank God."

"Wyatt, I would like you to meet Tracy Finnegan. Tracy, this is—"

"There is no need for an introduction." Tracy took Wyatt's outstretched hand. With a move that could only be described as slick, she insinuated herself so she was by his side, pushing Joie out of the way. "Wyatt Landis is a legend."

"No. That would be my parents. I'm just a humble producer." Just as slick, Wyatt took back his hand.

Tracy laughed. And laughed. Wyatt looked at Joie, who shrugged. *You have a fan*, she mouthed, obviously holding back a smile.

He groaned. *Teenagers and their giggly teacher? Could it get any worse?* As it turned out, the answer was no. But it didn't get much better.

Wyatt considered himself a reasonable man. Then again, he was used to getting his own way because he was smart and made certain he was the one with the leverage. How could he gain the upper hand when they had nothing he wanted? And honestly, he couldn't care less.

However, he had promised Joie that he would try.

"Where are you in the production?" he asked Tracy. He thought it was a reasonable question. Yet, Tracy seemed confused

"I've asked them to learn their parts. Is that what you mean?"

Wyatt shot Joie another look, which she returned with wide-eyed innocence. She knew what she had gotten him into, damn it. His only consolation was that he hadn't promised more than a few hours of his time. This group didn't need him. They needed a miracle.

"Why don't you run through the first scene?"

"Well..." Tracy kept her eyes on the floor.

"Is there a problem?"

"No one listens to me."

Tracy sounded close to tears. *Oh, no*, Wyatt thought. No, fucking way. What had Tom Hanks said? *There's no crying in baseball?* Wyatt felt the same way about the theater. At least the production end of it. Actors were temperamental and emotional. He left it up to the director and their agents to deal with them. There was a good reason Wyatt stayed behind the scenes. He didn't have the patience for crap like this.

A wicked smile lit up his face. Luckily he knew someone who did.

"Call it a day."

"What?" Tracy's head popped up. There was nothing like a panic attack to stem the flow of tears. "But we just got here."

"You're wasting everyone's time, Ms. Finnegan."

"Call me Tracy."

Panicked or not, it didn't stop Tracy from batting her eyes. Or flipping her hair. Lord save him from women who flipped their hair. The last time that got his attention he was about the age of these kids. And just as dumb. Hormones had a way of making idiots of us all.

"We'll reconvene the day after tomorrow." Wyatt took Joie's hand and headed for the door.

"But—"

"I'll let you know if there's a change of plans."

"What's going on?" Joie asked as they exited the building.

He appreciated that she hadn't questioned him while they were in the auditorium. Wyatt opened the passenger side door of his truck.

"I can't help them." He gave her a lingering kiss. "But I know someone who can."

"Who?"

With a wink, Wyatt jumped in the cab, scooting far enough across the seat to make room for Joie. He helped her in, reaching across her body to close the door.

"Who are you talking about, Wyatt?"

With a laugh, Wyatt started the engine.

"Ever hear of an actor by the name of Colton Landis?"

"I APPRECIATE YOU doing this, Colt."

184

"Not a problem. I like the idea of helping these kids. And if it means my big brother owes me a favor? All the better."

When Wyatt had called, he hadn't worried about Colt turning him down. The only thing bigger than his brother's ego was his heart. If his schedule had allowed, Colt would have spent every waking moment donating his time to charity.

Wyatt sometimes thought the world had missed out on another Mother Theresa—with a dick. But the truth was, Colt used his celebrity to do more good than he ever could have as an ordinary citizen. Few people outside of his family had any idea *how much* good.

"You want to know how I ended up helping a ragtag bunch of high school thespians?"

Absently, Wyatt watched as a group of tech-expert teenagers plugged a mind-boggling amount of cables into the back of a big screen television.

"You know I do."

"I'll tell you after you speak with them. And Colt?"

"Shit. I know what you're going to say. The story—all of it—will make us even." Resigned, Colt sighed. "You never give an inch, do you? Why not owe me a favor and let your mystery adventure be a bonus."

"Producers are all about the bottom line. We don't believe in bonuses."

Colt chuckled. "Don't I know it. You sound good, Wyatt."

"I feel good. Better. This time away has been good for me."

"That's great." He heard Colt whisper something. "Sable wants to ask you a question."

"I do not." Wyatt heard Sable Ford, Colt's fiancée, shout. "Your brother is the nosey one, Wyatt."

"Tell the lovely Sable that I'm well aware."

"When a woman loves you, isn't she supposed to be on your side?" Colt grumbled. "No matter what?"

"Hell if I know."

Wyatt meant it as a joke, but he should have known that Colt would read it as darker.

"Shit, Wyatt. Stephanie never loved anyone. Maybe herself, but I doubt it. Give yourself a break. There's a woman out there with a generous heart, and you'll find her if you give it a chance."

At that very second, the sound of Joie's laughter reached him. Was there anyone whose heart was more generous? Shit. Wyatt's thoughts were filled with her too often these days. If it were only the sex, that would be one thing. But it was more. Too much more. He couldn't keep her out of his head, and though he didn't know it, Colt wasn't helping.

"Falling in love isn't on my to-do list."

"Do you think it was on mine? Or Garrett's. Or Nate's? All I ask is that you keep an open mind. And an open heart."

"Haven't you heard? I don't have a heart."

"That's Wyatt, the ruthless producer. My brother's heart has never been in doubt. Which brings me to my question."

"You mean *Sable's* question?"

"Fuck you, Wyatt." Colt's words were laced with good-humored snark. "Or should I put it like this. Are you getting fucked?"

"None of your business, asshole."

"I knew it! There *is* a woman involved."

"I didn't say that." Damn Colt and his sex radar. He could always tell. It wasn't exactly a superpower, but it was close enough.

"Who is she?" Wyatt waited, knowing what was coming. "The author. You are in Monroe, Nevada. The town J. L. Winter calls home. You're sleeping with her, aren't you?"

"I don't sleep with women."

"And you're missing out on one of life's true pleasures. But forget that for now. The hell with the technicality. Am I right?"

"What if I told you that J. L. Winter is a seventy-two-year-old grandmother with dentures and a hump?"

"Whatever turns you on. I'm just glad you've found someone."

Wyatt suppressed his desire to laugh. He wasn't giving his brother the satisfaction. "You need help, Colton. Serious, professional help."

"I've seen her picture, Wyatt."

"How?" Wyatt knew for a fact that there were no pictures of J. L. Winter to be found. His best people had spent weeks looking.

"I googled Joie Trent. Boom. Instant success. She's a beauty, Wyatt. Those big, brown eyes alone are drool-worthy. And the rest of her? Yum. Yum."

Wyatt looked across the room to where Joie was speaking with Carole. He had asked her not to tell anyone about what he had planned. Even a hint that Colton Landis would make an appearance—even if it was only via Skype—would have triggered a stampede, bottlenecking Monroe with overeager fans.

Joie had kept her word. She had invited her best friend but hadn't mentioned that anything special was taking place. As she told Wyatt, Carole never would have forgiven her if she had missed this.

He could trust her, Wyatt realized. It wouldn't have occurred to her that she was in possession of a juicy piece of gossip. But even if it had, her promise would have stopped her from spreading the news. Joie's word was gold. Wyatt knew it—to his core.

"She's all right."

Talk about the understatement of the year. While he waited for lightning to strike him down for what could only be construed as a bald-faced lie, Colt laughed his ass off.

"And the sun is an inconsequential orb in the sky. Now I know something is going on. I want details, Wyatt. Big, juicy, no-holds-barred details."

"You don't share anything about your romps with Sable."

"That's because she's special. A man doesn't give out deets when it concerns the woman he loves. Holy shit! Wyatt, are you saying…?"

Holy shit, indeed. What the hell was wrong with him?

"Rein in the assumptions, Colton. I like her. Do me a favor and leave it at that." Wyatt felt a surge of panic. "And for Christ's sake, don't mention Joie to Mom."

"I won't. But, oh, brother, the fact that you don't want Mom to know makes me very happy."

Wyatt could almost see Colt rubbing his hands together in glee. Their mother liked to think she had a part in getting Colt, Garrett, and Nate together with their future wives. If she had the slightest hint that Wyatt was involved with someone, it wouldn't be long before she paid him a *casual* visit.

"I will say one thing, Colt. Joie and I are on the same page. We are enjoying each other's company. When I leave for home, it ends. Period."

"For your sake, I hope you're wrong. But, at least you're making progress. A casual affair might be just what you need."

"Maybe." Wyatt nodded when he got the signal that the broadcast was a go. "Looks like we're ready. Do you need a few minutes to do whatever it is you actors do before a performance?"

"The disdain in your voice is not lost on me, dickhead. But to answer your question. No. This is not a performance. I plan on speaking from my heart."

"Hambone," Wyatt muttered with a grin.

"Did you read my last reviews?"

"Yes, and so did you. Over and over again."

"Up yours."

Wyatt laughed. "And on that brotherly note. I will make your introduction."

It didn't take long to gather the small group of students together. They took their seats with all the enthusiasm he would have expected. Little did they know that he was about to make their day. Hell, he would bet the profits from his next movie that he was about to make their week, month, and year.

"I know that you're wondering what this is about. From the expressions on your faces, you must be anticipating a boring documentary filmed before *I* was born. You know, the Stone Age?"

That got him a few laughs. Knowing it was better to go out on a high note, Wyatt didn't delay.

"Sorry to disappoint you. I have invited someone to speak to you this afternoon. Since I'm almost positive you will recognize him, I will leave the introductions up to him."

The lights went out just as the screen lit up. Wyatt was off stage, but he didn't have to see the teenagers' reaction. Their screams almost deafened him.

"You're a hit." Joie raised her voice, over the din.

Wyatt shrugged. "Colt is. He's in his element."

She put her arms around his waist. "Those kids might think Colt is the hero, but I know the truth. You made this happen, Wyatt."

"So am I your hero?"

"Absolutely."

Wyatt lowered his mouth to hers. Joie's hero? He could live with that.

CHAPTER SIXTEEN

NOT SLEEPING WITH Joie was turning out to be harder than he had expected.

Wyatt imagined that all over the world there were men who would cut off their right nut to have a warm, willing, beautiful woman curled up next to them in the dark hours of the night. If not their nut, at least a vital organ. Hell, your body could function just fine with only one kidney. Finding someone like Joie was a one in a billion proposition. Make that a trillion.

As he slid from her bed for the fourth night in a row, Wyatt stopped to consider what would happen if he stayed. He didn't have the dreams every night. In fact, since landing in Monroe, they had almost stopped.

It was the *almost* that had him hesitating.

When Wyatt had been in Los Angeles, waking up in a cold sweat had become commonplace. He could count on it happening once or twice a week. The last time it happened here? He had to stop and think. Ten days ago? No eleven. But it had been intense. Crazier than usual. Tossing and turning through a jumbled mess of rain, blood, and the sound of a baby—his baby—crying for him. It always ended the same way. Desperately searching to no avail. And Stephanie laughing, calling him a fool.

"It's dead, Wyatt," Stephanie would taunt. "It. Not he or she. It. You'll never know who our baby might have been."

"Why?" he always demanded.

"Because you didn't love me."

Wyatt walked from Joie's bedroom, down the stairs, and out of the house, stopping by his old truck to unlock the door. He pulled himself into the driver's seat. With a sigh, he rested his forehead on the steering wheel.

That was why he couldn't stay with Joie. Because when he woke from the dream, he would lash out. Once or twice, he broke his bedside lamp until he wised up and moved all fragile items far from potential harm.

What if he hurt Joie? In his frustration. His rage. What if he hit her? Wyatt would never be able to live with himself if he caused her the slightest injury. Or upset. Just the thought of seeing fear in her eyes, fear he put there, made him sick to his stomach.

Starting his truck, he put it in gear and eased from his parking spot. Joie's safety had to come first.

Which meant, no matter how tempting, he would never wake up with her in his arms.

HALF-ASLEEP, JOIE rolled to her side, reaching for Wyatt. All she found was an empty bed and warm sheets. Taking his pillow, she breathed in his scent. Why did it make her want to cry?

Wyatt had made it clear from the beginning that he wouldn't stay. She would never wake up in his arms. And when she told him that it was fine with her, she had meant every word.

It seemed her words were coming back to bite her in the ass.

The clock read half past two. That was about right. Wyatt never stayed much later. Not that he jumped out of bed the second he orgasmed. One of the things she liked best about him was the way he would hold her while they talked.

She learned about his family. How tight-knit a unit they were. Joie would have expected stories about movie sets and celebrity-filled parties. But except for the Landis name, Wyatt's childhood had been relatively normal.

Sure, most kids didn't call famous movie stars Uncle this or Aunt that. Nor did they watch while their parents were awarded Oscars. But what intrigued Joie were Wyatt's tales of camping trips and family dinners. He didn't speak of Callie Flynn; he spoke of his mother. Caleb Landis was a loving, caring father first. A Hollywood legend second.

Wyatt didn't just talk about himself. He asked Joie about how she grew up. It was so easy to tell him about watching helplessly as her mother uprooted her life over and over again in hopes of finding a man who lived up to the unattainable standards left by Joie's father.

"I will never do that," Joie had told Wyatt. "My mother never thought that her life was as important as the current man in her life. In a snap, she would pack up her belongings. Leave her friends. Her job. All on the chance that this man would be the one. Spoiler alert. He never was."

"That had to be rough." They were lying on their sides, facing each other. Wyatt had taken her hand, bringing it to his lips. "You were in boarding school?

"Thank God. I will always be grateful for that. My father's life insurance allowed me to stay in one school until I graduated."

"Your mother must have understood how important that would be to you."

"Yes." It had taken Joie a long time to realize that her mother hadn't abandoned her. Instead of dragging her from town to town, marriage to marriage, Kristen had given Joie a gift. The gift of a stable life.

"On one level, Mom's decision was selfish. It was easier to find romance without a child to chase off men who weren't looking for a ready-made family. But I think she knew that I wanted to stay in one place."

Sighing, Joie moved to her back, taking Wyatt's pillow with her. Without thinking, she wrapped her arms around it as though he was still with her.

Talking with Wyatt was so easy. And it seemed he felt the same way. But there was one subject he almost never spoke of. His wife, their troubled marriage, and the child they had lost were off limits. Joie was fine with that. However, she sensed there were things that he needed to get off his chest. She wished he trusted her enough to let her be his sounding board.

Joie realized that sleep wasn't going to come. Though her body was tired, her brain wouldn't stop revolving in a never ending circle. If she stayed where she was, she was going to drive herself nuts.

Grabbing her robe from a nearby chair, Joie left the bedroom. She wasn't in the mood to write. Her current book was with her publisher, ahead of schedule, getting a once over. It was amazing how much she could get done after her lover left her bed and she couldn't sleep because her arms felt empty. A few weeks of that and she had finished her book in no time.

There were new stories to be told. Thank goodness for that. But not tonight. Instead, she took an envelope from the top drawer of her desk. It was filled with something she had kept to herself. Not even Carole knew what she had been working on in private.

Brewing herself a cup of tea, Joie debated whether she wanted that last donut with the yummy cream center. She had never been one to obsess over calories. But she did try to watch what she ate. According to her mother, the women on her side of the family had no problem with their weight. Until the age of fifty. Then *boom*! Blubber butts and thunder thighs.

Rather than worry about it, Joie viewed it as a challenge. If she ate properly now, she wouldn't fall into the trap of thinking she could always stuff her face with deep-fried everything and never pay the price.

Oh, what the hell. She would do an extra lap or two around town as soon as the sun came up. Right now, she needed a sugar fix. And if her butt started to grow in twenty years or so, she would pin the blame on Wyatt. He was the reason she sat at her dining room table with donut crumbs in the corner of her mouth. If he would get over his hang-up about spending the night, she could be in her bed, with him, burning fat instead of packing it on.

"I made the mistake of falling in love with you, Wyatt Landis."

Though she said it to an empty room, she was talking to him. It was his fault. Right? Just like the late-night donut, losing her heart to a commitment-phobic sex god wasn't her fault; it was his.

Damn Wyatt.

She had known it for some time. Admitting it was another thing. The final blow—or perhaps revelation was a better word—had come the day he stood on that auditorium stage. It hadn't been the words he spoke. Or the gesture of bringing in his superstar brother to inspire a group of kids who, let's face it, hadn't done anything to deserve that kind of gesture.

It had been a culmination of moments.

How could Joie have known he would turn out to be perfect. Or at least, perfect for her. He made her laugh. Made her moan. Made her day. And though he vociferously denied it, he *was* one of the good guys. Nice without a boring bone in his luscious body.

Joie hadn't been looking for love. Just the opposite. Who would have guessed it would come in the form of a man who was less inclined to embrace it than she was? If she had known this would happen, she would have left him in his crashed truck for the next passerby to find.

The cup of hot tea felt good in her hands. The weather had finally decided to catch up with the calendar, making the days cold and the nights colder. Warm when she came down here, Joie shivered, realizing she wasn't dressed properly for this time of year. Remembering that she had put some clothes in the dryer before going to bed, Joie hurried to the washroom.

Yes. She pumped her fist. Still warm. Removing a pair of mismatched fuzzy socks and a thick pullover, Joie left the bulk of the clothing where it was. She would take care of it later; right now she needed warmth. The days of running around in a thin robe and nothing else were a thing of the past. At least until late spring.

Joie sat at the table. She tapped the manila envelope with her finger. Once. Then a second time. She hadn't looked at it for almost six months. It was strange to doubt her talent. When she wrote her first book, she was certain it was a masterpiece. It hadn't been. However, it had sold a lot of copies.

All these years later, she was a better writer. Confident without that early cockiness. But this was different. Something new and unfamiliar. If it weren't good, her world wouldn't come to an end.

The sun would continue to rise. She would stay the course as a bestselling novelist.

But damn it, she wanted it to be good. No. More than that. She wanted it to be right.

One thing was certain; she wouldn't find out unless she opened the envelope. Joie took another bracing sip of tea before straightening the metal clasp. She pulled out the stack of papers and began to read.

The first page didn't suck. So far so good.

"IS THAT YOU, Wyatt?"

Wyatt stopped halfway up the stairs. He had run like a crazy man this morning. He wasn't certain how far he had gone, but considering his pace the brief hour he was out there, it had to be a personal best.

As a result, he was hot, sweaty, and ready for a long shower. When Margie called out, he wanted to yell that, no, it wasn't him. But she knew his voice. And at the moment, he was her only guest. With a resigned sigh, he retraced his steps and headed toward the kitchen.

"There you are," Margie said. When she got a look at him, her eyes widened. "You are soaking wet. Did somebody douse you with a hose?"

"It's only sweat." He shook his head when she offered him a cup of coffee. "I need water. A couple of gallons should do for a start."

"Help yourself. That water filter you installed the other day works like a dream. I hadn't realized my water had so many impurities. I swear, it suddenly tastes like it comes from a spring."

Wyatt gulped down a glass of water, quickly refilling the glass. He turned to Margie.

"Was there something I can help you with?"

"No. I can't believe it, but I think I've run out of things that need doing. That has to be a first." She stirred the pot of soup that would feed the guests that were arriving that afternoon. "Joie dropped that off for you while you were out running. I asked her to stay for breakfast, but she had errands to run."

Picking up the large envelope, Wyatt tested the weight. It was too heavy to be the contract. He knew that his father had sent the papers to Joie's agent. Since they hadn't heard anything yet, he assumed the agent or Joie was still mulling over the details that would give Landis Productions the right to turn her book into a film.

Normally, Wyatt would be chomping at the bit. When a deal was this close to closing, he lost his usual patience. There was so much that could go wrong at the last second. Sometimes the deal wasn't considered sweet enough. Or a last-minute bid was submitted. Once, the writer decided to opt out for no particular reason. Until the papers were signed and notarized, Wyatt took nothing for granted.

Strangely, he hadn't given the contract a lot of thought. He had spoken with his father a couple of times since Joie agreed to their terms. The wording was standard. The only things that changed were a few minor details and the amount of money. This would be a pay upfront and a back-end deal. They would pay a set fee for the book rights. Then depending on how the movie performed at the box office, Joie would receive a share of the profits.

With a bestselling book and two big stars, the potential payoff was huge for everyone involved.

Curious, Wyatt opened the envelope. At first glance, it looked like a manuscript. He felt a surge of pleasure thinking Joie had trusted him to read her latest masterpiece. But on closer inspection, it turned out to be something entirely different.

"Did Joie say anything about this?" Wyatt asked after reading the title page.

"Only that it was for you." Margie moved to the refrigerator. "Why? Is there a problem?"

"No problem."

Joie had written a screenplay for her book. That wasn't a problem. Unless it was terrible.

Heading to his room, Wyatt set the envelope on his bed. As he stripped off his clothing, his gaze kept wandering back to the pile of papers. So what if she had never written this kind of treatment before now? Knowing how to edit the longer work into a two-hour movie was a skill few people understood. There was a delicate line between creating a compelling narrative that was true to the source material and destroying what had made the book special in the first place.

Wyatt forgot his dream of a long shower. He jumped in, washed off the sweat, and jumped back out. Not bothering to do more than wrap a towel around his waist, he was back in his room in under five minutes.

Good or bad, he couldn't wait to read the screenplay. Good or bad, it called to him. Quickly, Wyatt pulled on a pair of jeans and a warm sweater, then settled on the bed. Fingers crossed, he turned to page one.

"WHAT IS WRONG with you this morning? You're as jumpy as a cat."

"I don't know what you're talking about." Joie handed Carole a bag of yarn.

"If you aren't fidgeting, you're looking at your watch."

Joie had stopped by Carole's shop, hoping for a diversion. Helping inventory supplies had sounded like a good idea, but it didn't keep her mind busy. All she could think about was what Wyatt's reaction would be.

Dropping off that envelope hadn't been an easy decision. Joie was proud of her work, but this was a new, unexplored territory and it made her feel vulnerable and exposed. Sending off her first manuscript had been nerve-racking, but any critique or rejection came from a distance. They were sent anonymously from faceless publishers and agents.

Putting her work in the hands of someone she knew—someone she loved—was a different kettle of fish. Carole was right, she was jumpy. Her nerves were on tenterhooks.

Joie didn't know how long it would take Wyatt to read the screenplay. It wasn't like a book—less detailed and fewer pages. Even so, he couldn't zip through it in an hour. Could he? No. Maybe two?

And what if Wyatt hated it? Would he try to be kind or was he a rip the Band-Aid off in one quick motion kind of guy? Joie wanted the truth. Without a sugar coating. She was a big girl. She could take it. Probably.

"The plumber thinks I was sabotaged."

That brought Joie's self-involved musings to a screeching halt.

"What does that mean? Sabotaged? As in someone deliberately flooded your apartment?"

"He can't be certain." Carole continued checking her stock, but Joie could tell her mind wasn't on it.

"Stop. I might be jumpy, but you're trembling." Joie took the pad and pen from Carole's hands.

There was a nice sitting area in the corner of the storeroom. The small window provided plenty of natural light. Between customers, Carole often sat in here, knitting and listening to music. Joie led her friend to the cushioned chair then took the one that sat opposite her.

"I'm a bit of a mess," Carole admitted. "Jerry, the plumber, didn't tell me his suspicions until this morning."

"Why the hell not?" Joie demanded. "He must have heard about the attack. That cast on your arm didn't happen by magic."

"Jerry isn't a big talker. I know," Carole rushed on when Joie would have protested. "He claims that he meant to tell me sooner, but his wife just had a baby and his hours have been erratic. This was the first time he's seen me since he started on the job."

As excuses went, it was pretty lame, but there was nothing to be done about it.

"What did he say?"

"It didn't look like the pipe had broken on its own. He thought someone might have hit it."

"Please tell me he still has the original pipe." Mentally, Joie crossed her fingers.

"No such luck. Jerry took it to the dump on Saturday."

"Jerry is an idiot." Joie jumped to her feet and began to pace. "Doesn't he watch television? Every other show is a procedural. Save the evidence, Jerry."

"I'm freaking out a little, Joie." Carole rubbed the part of her arm that wasn't encased in a cast. "I didn't want to believe that someone was out to get me. But now I wonder if you were right."

"I want to be wrong." Joie picked up Carole's phone. "Call the police. Then call Drew Harper. I don't care what happened to the evidence; you have to keep them up to date."

Taking her phone, Carole nodded. "I don't want to sound like a nervous Nelly," she said as she dialed.

"They can think what they want. It is their job to find out what is going on. This isn't a big piece of the puzzle, but it might turn out to be an important one."

Two hours later, after holding Carole's hand through her interview with the Monroe police and a call to Drew Harper, Joie had discovered two things. Officer Lon Petry was a condescending twit who didn't know the first thing about conducting any kind of investigation. And thank God for Drew Harper.

The policeman who had taken their original statements was out sick with the flu. Which left them in the less than capable hands of Officer Petry. Joie hated to make snap judgments about a man's character, but he appeared to be a clueless, mouth-breathing, knuckle-dragging misogynist. He made it clear that he thought they were overreacting. At any second, Joie expected him to ask if it were *that time of the month*. There was little to no chance that he would follow up on the broken pipes. First chance she found, Joie planned on reporting the man to Mayor Osweiler.

The exact opposite of Officer Petry, Drew Harper was courteous, sympathetic, and best of all, took what Carole said seriously.

"I can't help it," Carole said after she hung up. "I have a bit of a crush on that man."

"I don't blame you." Joie completely understood the appeal. A man with brains, looks, and treated them with respect. What wasn't to like?

"Dex is the love of my life." Carole sighed. "But Wyatt and Drew would tempt a saint. Luckily, they aren't interested. Or available."

"What does Wyatt have to do with it?"

"He made the call that put Drew on the case."

That was true. One more reason to love him—damn him.

"Did I say something funny?" Carole handed her a glass of juice. "Share. I could use a laugh."

"I don't know if it's laughable or pathetic."

They had moved upstairs to Carole's newly repaired kitchen. Since she had plans to rent the space, the renovations had gone beyond fixing the plumbing. There was a new coat of paint on the walls, and the old carpeting had been replaced with laminate flooring. Since her things were still at Joie's and she had practically moved in with Dex, Carole had already started spreading the word that the space was available.

"Tell me and let me be the judge."

"I'm in love with Wyatt."

"Okay." Carole joined her on the sofa. "Now tell me something I don't know."

"You knew?" Joie asked. "Why didn't you let me in on the news?"

"And have you bite my head off?" Carole gave Joie a sympathetic smile. "I know what it's like to bury myself in denial."

"At least you knew Dex was waiting for you to get your act together. You said earlier that it was too bad Wyatt was taken? That isn't true."

Carole shook her head. "I've seen the way he looks at you. If he hasn't said anything, it's because he hasn't realized how he feels. Give him time, he will."

"I don't have time. Wyatt could decide to leave tomorrow, Carole. Or this afternoon. Nothing is keeping him in Monroe. I'm surprised he hasn't left already."

"*You're* keeping him here." Carole looked so earnest, Joie was back to wondering if she should laugh or cry.

"Just for the sake of argument, let's say you're right. Wyatt is in love with me." Joie had to swallow after saying the words. They sounded so right. So perfect. "His life is in Los Angeles. That's where he works. Where his family lives."

"So?"

"So?" Wasn't it obvious? "Wyatt is not going to give that up to become a full-time handyman in Monroe, Nevada."

"And you won't go with him to Los Angeles?"

Joie didn't appreciate Carole's accusatory tone.

"I can't."

"Joie. It is one thing to follow a man on a whim. But this is different. You don't fall in love every day. And Monroe isn't going anywhere. I expect you to visit. Often."

"Back up. You make it sound like this is a done deal." Carole had jumped way too many steps. "First. Wyatt is not in love with me. Second, if he were, his first marriage was so awful, he isn't looking to do it again. Third—"

"Third," Carole jumped in, "you would rather live with a broken heart than take a chance on happiness."

"My heart is fine. And it is going to stay that way."

"But—"

Joie pushed on, not wanting to hear Carole's objection. "Why is it a given that unrequited love equals a broken heart? Dinged? Maybe. But I refuse to give anyone that kind of power over me. Wyatt can't hurt me unless I allow him to. End of story."

Carole scooted closer, hugging Joie with her good arm.

"What is this about?" Joie asked, hugging her back.

"Call it preemptive comfort. Not even you and your will of iron can prevent a broken heart, Joie. If Wyatt returns to Los Angeles and you stay in Monroe, the loss will hit you like a ton of bricks."

"You don't have to sound so happy about it."

"I will be happy."

Shocked, Joie pulled away. "Thanks a lot."

"I hope it will give you the kick in the ass you need. It isn't about uprooting your life. Or giving in. It means you want to share your life. Share, Joie. Equals. Together. What difference does it make where you live? The important thing is that you are together."

Joie didn't see the point in arguing. Carole was in that blissful, all is perfect with the world stage in her relationship with Dex. No one knew what that looked like better than Joie. She had seen it with her mother over and over again. She couldn't reason with a woman when she was blinded by that first burst of love everlasting.

"Stay hopeful." Joie gave Carole a quick hug. "I like the way it looks on you. I have to go."

"Think about what I said."

With a wave, she grabbed her jacket and headed down the outside staircase. Joie glanced at her watch. It was almost noon. One thing about a minor crisis, it passed the time. Wyatt was bound to be finished with her screenplay. However—she checked her phone—he hadn't called or texted.

What was the holdup? Was it so bad that he was afraid to break the bad news?

"Hey, beautiful. Want a lift?"

Joie slowly turned. An old, faded red truck with the passenger side window rolled down, slowly drove along beside her. She didn't have to look inside to identify the driver. She would have known that voice anywhere.

Joie stopped and so did the truck.

"That depends." She leaned against the door. "Where are you headed?"

Wyatt grinned. "I hear there's a spot west of town where the kids go to make out. I thought if I could convince a certain woman to go with me, I might check it out." He lifted a brown wicker basket. "I have fried chicken?"

"Why didn't you say so?"

Joie was in the cab in a heartbeat. Margie's famous chicken plus the chance to neck with Wyatt in the great outdoors? Anticipation of the dual treat almost made her forget about the screenplay. Almost.

Wyatt turned right at the town's only stop light and headed toward Planter's Landing. Its reputation as *the* place to park if you wanted some action was well earned. On Saturday night, the spot was crowded with teenagers and their borrowed cars. Joie doubted they would have much trouble finding a spot on a weekday afternoon.

"I won't enjoy the food, or you, unless you tell me."

Wyatt rested his arm on the back of the bench seat, his fingers close enough to play with the ends of her hair.

"Tell you what?"

"The screenplay?" Joie grabbed his hand, gripping it in her lap. "What did you think?"

"I have one question before I answer."

"Go ahead."

"There is a certain format to writing a screenplay. How did you learn it?"

"Did I get it right?"

Joie had found the structure of the process came surprisingly easy. But perhaps she was mistaken.

"It was perfect."

She beamed. "I watched a YouTube video."

Wyatt sputtered, coughing several times before he began to laugh. "YouTube? Really?"

"What's wrong with that?"

"Not a thing." He told her of his recent use of the website. "It's amazing what you can find."

"Tell me what you thought, Wyatt. And don't hold anything back. I can take it." Her fingers tightened on his, but to his credit, he barely winced.

"Let me stop the truck."

Pulling to a stop at the edge of Planter's Landing, he unbuckled his seatbelt before turning toward her. Joie couldn't read his expression. Was that good or bad?

"I was leery when I started it. I had no idea you wanted to write the screenplay for *Left of Mayfield*."

Joie shrugged. "It's my baby."

"But not all authors are equipped to adapt their work. Most of the time it is best to leave it to someone who knows what they're doing."

"It was that bad?"

Joie had tried to prepare herself for this possibility. If Wyatt hated her writing, so be it. But it turned out the truth was harder to swallow than the idea of it.

"You wrote a beautiful book, Joie. You can be proud of that."

"I am." She tried to smile. "I *wanted* to write a good screenplay."

"You did."

"What? Wait." Joie's head whipped around so quickly, she swore something popped. At that moment, she didn't give a damn. "You liked my screenplay?"

"I loved your screenplay. You made the words sing, Joie."

"Why didn't you say so?"

With a scream, Joie launched herself at Wyatt, but something held her back.

"Safety first," Wyatt chuckled, unbuckling her seatbelt. Then sat back and waited. A second later, Joie was in his arms, peppering his face with kisses.

"Thank you, thank you, thank you," she said between kisses.

"You did the work. You deserve the glory." Wyatt felt around, searching for the lever. A second later, the seat popped back, giving them plenty of room for two bodies behind the steering wheel. "But I don't mind sharing in your excitement."

Wyatt cupped his hand behind Joie's head, pulling her lips to his. His arm anchored her to him, his long legs stretching out until her body blanketed his. His back was braced against the door, giving him the leverage to deepen the kiss and enjoy the silkiness of her hair, the curve of her back, and enticing the slope of her butt.

"You've done this before," Joie sighed when he lifted his head. Wanting to savor every bit of him, she ran her tongue over her lips so his taste would linger.

"Kissed a woman?" Wyatt's smile brushed over her cheek. "A time or two."

"I meant, you've done this," she motioned to how they were perfectly aligned. "In a truck. With a woman. You didn't fumble once."

"Maybe once or twice. But it's been a long time. I had forgotten the simple joy of making out. I wish I could tell those teenagers at the high school how lucky they are. They are in such a hurry to move on to the next step, they don't take the time to enjoy their innocence."

"A few of them do. I was twenty my first time."

"In a hayloft." Wyatt smoothed her hair from her face.

"Yes. Which reminds me, you didn't share your first time."

"It was nice."

That was an evasion if she ever heard one. Joie wasn't letting him get away with it.

"Nice? Sorry, I need more than nice."

Wyatt sighed, his blue eyes resigned. "I was fifteen, and she wasn't much older. The first time wasn't all sky rockets in flight. Though at the time, I was damn proud of myself. In retrospect, I had more fun than she did."

"I didn't have an orgasm my first time. Or my second. Or my third. It takes time for most women to understand their bodies. Men don't have that problem." Joie smiled sympathetically. "I don't think many of your sex worry about their partners. Your girl was lucky to have you."

"You're giving more credit than I deserve. I was selfish. I assumed that because I enjoyed it, so did she. It took time, and experience, for me to realize it didn't work that way."

"Thank you for your due diligence." Joie gave him a kiss that started sweet, but quickly heated up. "I have no complaints."

"None?" Wyatt cupped her breast, the pad of his thumb finding her nipple. "No requests? Nothing you would like that I haven't done? Or something I should do differently?"

"I'm good," she moaned. "*So* good. There is only one thing I want."

"Anything."

"A kiss," she whispered, brushing her lips against his.

"So little?" Wyatt moved his leg between hers. Her gasp had him sending her a knowing smile. "I said anything. Use your imagination."

"There is one thing. Maybe two. Or three."

"Now you're getting the idea. Where should I start?"

For the next hour, Wyatt made her requests come true. Over and over again. Her wishes were another matter. Joie couldn't tell Wyatt that she wanted more than this. Sex was wonderful. Amazing. She broke the rules. She knew it wasn't fair. She knew he wasn't at fault. But she couldn't help the way she felt. She wanted more. She wanted forever.

Good luck with that. Between them, they had a lifetime of hang-ups. Joie had been blessed with a vivid, fertile imagination. But as she lay in Wyatt's arms, even *she* couldn't picture a happy ending.

CHAPTER SEVENTEEN

"SHE WANTS TO write the screenplay? Since when? Why didn't her agent mention this when we were negotiating terms?"

Caleb Landis was on the phone in his Beverly Hills home, but his voice and his personality made it seem like he was a mere five feet away. Wyatt was used to the way his father boomed out a sentence—especially when he was making a point. It made lesser men quake. However, Caleb had raised his sons to respect their father, not fear him.

Wyatt waited calmly until his father was finished winding himself up, then proceeded to calm him down.

"She wrote the screenplay six months ago. Before anyone was after the screen rights. I don't think she planned on letting it see the light of day."

"Then why now?"

Wyatt chose his words carefully. The old man didn't have his wife's ability to sniff out a potential romance, but he was close. Wyatt still had hopes of getting out of Monroe before his parents blew his affair with Joie into something it wasn't. They were anxious for him to find happiness. He didn't want Joie dragged into their inappropriate, if well-meaning, machinations.

"Joie and I have developed a nice rapport." Wyatt liked the way that sounded. Friendly and innocent. "She trusted that I would give her an honest critique."

"And?"

"I emailed you a copy. What do you think?"

"I haven't had time to read it. Besides, no one has a better nose for a good script than you. You got that from your mother."

And his father. However, Caleb Landis always gave his wife credit for their sons' achievements. She was the college graduate. She was the one with the breeding and brains. He was a bull. Determined and unstoppable. Caleb had taken five hundred dollars and turned it into a Hollywood dynasty. Laughingly, he called Callie the beauty to his beast.

Wyatt knew better. Caleb Landis may have started out a roughneck full of sharp edges and little education. But he had made himself over. He was a man comfortable dining with royalty and heads of state. Though he preferred beer, he knew how to pick out a superior bottle of wine. Most of his rough edges had been smoothed down. With time and the love of Callie Flynn.

An important part of the original Caleb remained. His business savvy. He would listen to what Wyatt had to say. Then he would read the script, use what Wyatt had told him combined with his sharp mind. Caleb trusted his son's instincts. But he was where he was—at the top—because he trusted himself first.

"It's good, Dad. With a little polish, it could be great."

"That's it?" Caleb snorted. "I expected more."

"You've read the book. What else is there to say?"

"There's nothing you want to tell me? Your father, not your business partner?"

Wyatt recognized a trap. He didn't try to maneuver around it. Instead, he faced it head on.

"There's nothing to say. Except, the weather has turned cold, and I'll be home soon."

"By yourself?"

He had to give his father points for perseverance.

"Naturally. You know me. I prefer it that way."

"You didn't used to," Caleb sighed. "I'll read the script this afternoon. If what you say is true, our lawyers will draw up a separate contract. I assume Ms. Trent is ready to sign?"

"You'll have to ask her. After she and her agent look it over."

"Agents," Caleb scoffed. "What good are they? It would be so much easier to do business one on one. Ms. Trent sent me a very nice email. Friendly. Then her agent jumped in. Leeches."

"Mom has an agent. As do Colt and Garrett and Nate. Face it, Dad. We are the odd men out."

208

"The world is filled with necessary evils." It was as close as Caleb would get to admitting that agents were an important part of the Hollywood process.

"I have to go, Dad." Mrs. Pringle, Margie's neighbor, needed him to trim her hedges. He had explained that he had never done that before, but she was willing to take a chance on him.

"Call your mother." Caleb ended every conversation the same way.

"I will. Bye. I love you."

"I love you too, son. Take care."

Instead of putting his phone away, Wyatt called up his YouTube app. Under search, he typed, *how to trim a hedge*. There were endless possibilities, but he recognized a name that he had used before. The guy was direct and to the point in his instructions. And the videos were short.

As he grabbed the gloves and protective goggles which had recently become a part of his daily life, Wyatt made a mental note. As soon as he was back in Los Angeles, he was going to buy stock in YouTube.

"IT'S A MODERN day miracle."

Joie wondered if everything that came out of Tracy's mouth was an outrageous overstatement. True, the students had a new sense of purpose. And their numbers had multiplied. In fact, the day after Colton Landis made his inspiring appearance via Skype, Tracy had been inundated with teenagers who had suddenly found the theater their calling.

The recording of Colton went viral within hours, and every kid within shouting distance of the school district wanted to be present in case it happened again. Wyatt had assured everyone that it wouldn't. This had been a one-time deal. Which made the students lucky enough to be there when it happened, instant celebrities.

And by the looks of them, they were enjoying every second.

"A month ago, I was begging for bodies to fill the parts. Now I'm turning them away."

"Enjoy it," Joie told her. "The bloom on the rose will fade fast. These kids have the attention span of a gnat. But," she added when Tracy's face fell, "if this is a successful production, you won't need the lure of the sexiest man alive."

Tracy nodded. "It would be nice if Colton surprised us by showing up on opening night."

Tracy's students weren't the only ones with stars in their eyes. Rather than deal with the teacher's fantastical delusions, Joie decided that was her cue to leave. There was nothing she could say beyond one word.

"No."

"But—"

Joie didn't turn, staying her course toward the exit.

"No!" she shouted just before the door shut behind her.

"You could wait until you hear my question."

"Wyatt." Joie jumped at the sound of his voice. "Where did you come from?"

"According to my mother, I grew inside her womb." Wyatt lifted Joie's chin, giving him access to her lips. The kiss wasn't long, but it was memorable. *All* his kisses were. "I found her explanation hard to swallow."

"How old were you?"

Without a flicker of his blue eyes, Wyatt deadpanned, "Twenty-two."

"Jackass," Joie laughed, taking his hand as they walked to the parking lot. "Are your brothers as bad as you are?"

"Worse." He helped her into her car.

"I feel for your mother."

"She gets that a lot." Making certain she was buckled in, Wyatt met her gaze. Joie couldn't help it. His eyes got her every time.

"Why the sigh?"

"You are just so damn pretty."

"Would it do me any good to argue?" His crooked smile told her that he wasn't as annoyed as he wanted her to think.

"Facts are facts, Landis. You're pretty. What is there to argue about?"

His sigh came from the gut, loud and resigned.

"Drive safe. I'll meet you at your place."

"Sex?"

"You're insatiable. Thank God." Wyatt brushed his hand over her hair. It was such a sweet, affectionate gesture—one she was coming to crave. "Sex is a definite yes. But after we work on your script."

Joie waited until Wyatt was in his truck, then pulled out of the lot. He had told her that her screenplay was good. That it sang. However, every gem needed polishing. Rather than be offended, Joie was thrilled. She had worked with the same editor since her first book. She knew how important another set of eyes and a fresh perspective could be to a story. She couldn't wait to hear Wyatt's suggestions.

And then? Sex. Sounded like the perfect evening.

IT WASN'T EASY loving someone who didn't want your love. It was a new experience for Joie. All of it. She had never been in love before. Crushing on a boy didn't count. Except when you were sixteen and thought the world would end if he didn't ask you out.

Love. Real, adult, heart in your hand love was a whole different feeling. And the longer she lived with it, the less she liked it. No, Joie was not a fan. How could she be? Words were her life. She was a verbal, expressive person. They were three little words, yet suppressing them was giving her stomach problems.

"I'm happy to say you are healthy as a horse," Dr. Jennette Pascoe told her after a thorough exam. "I will send your blood to the lab for the usual tests, but I don't anticipate any problems."

"You don't think I have acid reflux?"

"No."

"Gastrointestinal—"

"No, Joie. Your stomach? Your intestines? Fine and fine."

"That's good." Frowning, Joie gently poked her belly. "The symptoms just started. Since I was scheduled for my yearly exam, I didn't make a special appointment.

"This began within the last week?"

"Yes. The severity fluctuates. Last night, around three in the morning, I would have sworn there was something going on in there. It felt like an army was breakdancing."

"What did you eat before going to bed?"

"Besides the side of beef and basket of habanero peppers? Not a thing."

Recognizing sarcasm when she heard it, Jennette scribbled on Joie's chart. "No late night snacks. Anything worrying you? Trouble with your writing?"

"That couldn't be better."

"How about your personal life?" Joie couldn't look her in the eyes. "Ah," she nodded sagely. "Trouble in *Landisland?*"

"I love living in a small town." Joie frowned. "Until I don't. Everyone knows everything. Maybe *that* is what's wrong with my stomach. Nosey neighbors."

"It has its drawbacks," Jennette agreed. "And a few perks."

"Mostly perks," Joie conceded. "As for Wyatt? What could be wrong? We are two adults enjoying each other's company."

"Okay." Jennette wrote something else before putting down Joie's chart. "Would you like to start on some form of prescribed birth control?"

"I haven't been on the pill since college." Joie thought about it then decided to spare her body the influx of unnecessary hormones. "I'll stick with condoms."

"And a spermicide?"

"Yes."

"Good girl. I wish I could tell you the number of *oops* pregnancies I've dealt with because women and men think condoms are one hundred percent effective."

"Trust me, Wyatt is extra careful." Joie hoped that hadn't sounded snarky. She was just as careful. But he was extra, extra cautious.

"From what I've read about his marriage, that's understandable."

"What have you read?" The second the words were out of her mouth, Joie wanted them back.

"It's just gossip," Jennette said. "Speculation. From what I've read, Wyatt is a very private person. He keeps his personal business to himself. But I can tell you what the gossip says."

Joie shook her head. "Forget I asked."

"I knew you would say that." Jennette walked Joie to the waiting area. "One piece of advice?"

Advice could be a bitter little pill to swallow. Especially when her emotions concerning Wyatt were so topsy-turvy. However, Joie respected Jennette—as her doctor and her friend. Besides, it couldn't hurt to get someone else's perspective.

"Tell me what you think."

"I believe that your health is directly related to your state of mind. I believe those late night stomach problems will disappear if you clear the air with Wyatt."

"Clear the air."

Joie sighed. That was an interesting way of putting it. The air wasn't murky. At least from Wyatt's perspective. His position had been cut and dried from day one. Friendship. Sex. No sleepovers. And a goodbye without notice. How much clearer could their situation be?

Joie was the one who had created the problem. A big fat one. And no matter how she tried, she couldn't think of a solution that had a happy ending.

"It isn't that cut and dried."

"Then dump him," Jennette said without emotion—a doctor giving her patient medical advice.

"Yikes. That is a bit drastic." Though if Joie were honest, the solution—no matter how drastic—had crossed her mind.

"Stress can take a toll. I don't like that you are having problems sleeping. I could prescribe something to relax you. Maybe a mild sedative."

Joie shook her head, then slipped on her jacket. "Aspirin is my drug of choice. And only as a last resort. I only mentioned my late night discomfort because that's what you do when you visit your doctor. Now that I know that I'm going to live, it will probably go away on its own."

"I hope so."

Joie walked to her car and slid behind the wheel. It was a relief to find out that there was nothing wrong. But that didn't solve her problem. Her problem was Wyatt. And he would go away—soon. Unfortunately, in this case, she didn't think out of sight would equal out of mind.

"WE SHOULD GO dancing."

"You and I?" Joie asked Carole as she flipped from television station to television station.

Hundreds of channels and nothing to watch. They were winging the entertainment selection for this week's Wednesday get-together. After her third trip around the dial, Joie decided it had been a bad plan.

"You and Wyatt and me and Dex. Saturday is live music night at that place over in Junction Creek."

Joie shot Carole an amazed look. "You want to drive thirty miles to a place that serves warm beer and stale peanuts so we can shuffle around a sticky dance floor? Remember the last time we went there? I don't know what smelled worse. The unisex bathroom or the men who were responsible for stinking it up."

"It wasn't that bad." Carole laughed when Joie raised her eyebrows. "Hey, I dated one of the few *non*-stinky men for over two months. Besides, this time, when one of them asks, you can use Wyatt as a genuine excuse not to dance. For a woman with your imagination, you could have come up with something more creative."

"In a situation like that, honesty trumps creativity," Joie reasoned.

Carole shook her head. "All you said was, *I don't want to.*"

"It was the truth. Besides, you danced enough for both of us. You were about to jump on the bar before I pulled you out of there. The men might have enjoyed the show, but their wives and girlfriends would have rioted. You were already getting the stink eye. Reenacting *Coyote Ugly* would have blown the top off the place."

Carole didn't look the least bit repentant. "Tequila loosens my inhibitions."

Grabbing a handful of popcorn, Joie laughed. "What inhibitions?"

"I have a few," Carole said. "However, after a few shots, I tend to forget that fact."

"Which is why you bring me along as a chaperone. Not that you appreciated my efforts."

"I did." She took the bowl from Joie. "The next morning. After the tequila had worn off. Dex will watch out for me this time. So what do you say?"

Joie stared at the TV. "Why the hell not." Right about now, even Junction Creek sounded good.

"Excellent."

Carole commandeered the remote, stopping when she came across a showing of *Casablanca*. It had already started, but that didn't matter. Carole was a Bogie junkie. And this one she knew by heart. Fine with the choice, Joie settled back, munching on another handful of popcorn.

Since they knew the movie so well, Joie didn't feel obliged to remain silent. The classic lines were already embedded in their memory.

"What is Dex up to tonight?"

"Beats me. For an open book, that man has the disconcerting ability to keep a secret. Not often. But when he puts his mind to it, I can't budge him."

Joie frowned. "You sound concerned."

"No." Carole stretched out the word. "Perplexed bordering on confused. Something is going on. I hope it's a nice surprise. I don't think it is."

"Does it have anything to do with this?" Joie tapped the cast on Carole's arm.

"Why wouldn't he say so? *My* home was sabotaged. *My* arm was broken. *My* car was keyed. If Dex has information, he damn well better—"

"Wait," Joie interrupted. "What about your car?"

"Didn't I tell you? God, so much crap has been happening, I'm losing track."

Joie rubbed Carole's shoulder. "Tell me."

"This morning when I went to get into my car, I found the word bitch carved into the driver's side door. Officer Petry informed me that technically what happened to me isn't called keying. That happens when a key is dragged in one continuous line. I was a victim of straight-up vandalism."

It was Joie's turn to worry. Carole was rattled. And who could blame her? Things were adding up to a nasty total.

"Officer Petry is an insensitive ass. Who cares what the technical term is? I want to know what he is going to do."

"File it." The attempt at humor fell flat. "I spoke with Drew Harper again, but I have to wonder what he can do? What can anyone do? Unless this person is caught red-handed, this could go on forever until…" Carole's voice trailed off.

"Don't even think it."

Joie didn't want to believe that anyone could hurt Carole. But they already had. Last time, luck and pepper spray had prevented further damage. Next time? She shuddered. None of it made any sense.

"It feels oddly random." Carole shot her a look that said, *are you kidding me?* "Random is not the word. Scattered," Joie decided. "Broken water pipes. Then the attack. Nothing for over a week. Now your car?"

"Are you suggesting the psycho has ADD?"

Attention Deficit Disorder might be stretching it. "More like a child who is lashing out."

"A child?" Carole tapped her cast. "That was a big boy with a bat, Joie. Not a temperamental toddler."

"I've known a few so-called adults who were pretty immature." Joie cleared away their empty dishes. "It was just an observation. I should leave the analyzing to the experts."

"Your instincts are as good as anything we have right now." Carole joined her in the kitchen. "But who? I've racked my brain, and all I've gotten is a headache."

"There is always—"

"No," Carole sighed, running her hand across her face. "I don't want to talk about it anymore. Not tonight."

"Okay. Shall we rejoin Rick and Elsa?"

"He and Louis are about to walk off into the fog."

"Really?" Joie glanced at the television. "I missed most of the movie."

"No worries. It will be on again. And again." Carole used the remote, making the screen go black. "How was your yearly checkup?"

Joie had mentioned her trip to the doctor. But not how it had ended. Lately, Wyatt seemed to invade all her conversations. God, was she becoming one of *those* women who couldn't find anything to talk about but man troubles?

"Don't be ridiculous," Carole scoffed when Joie asked. "We talk about our men. It's what women do."

"And men? Do they talk about us?"

"Probably." They exchanged glances, laughing. "It's a mystery what men talk about when they are alone. But we must slip in there somewhere between football and baseball season. Right?"

"Sure," Joie said with little conviction, sending them into another bout of laughter. "Dex might not talk about you, but you're always on his mind."

"What about Wyatt?"

"What about him?" Joie closed the dishwasher. "Does he think about me? Sure. When his dick gets hard, I'm a convenient solution."

"Ouch." Carole frowned. "Where did that come from?"

"I didn't mean it." If she did, it was only a small amount of the time. Half at most.

"Is he getting itchy to head back to Los Angeles?"

"I don't know. Maybe? Wyatt seems content to roll along the way things are. And that would be fine. Except…"

"Except you love him. And he doesn't belong here."

"No. And I'm resigned to that." Joie didn't miss Carole's raised eyebrows. "I *am*. I'm the small-town girl. He's the big-city boy."

"Sounds like something from a book. But not yours. You have more imagination than to paint your characters into that kind of corner."

"If this were a book, I would give myself a backbone." Frustrated, Joie dumped the uneaten popcorn into the garbage, slamming the cupboard door when she was finished. "Wyatt is entitled to his secrets. But I've told him everything. Is it too much to expect him to share a little?"

"He was burned. Badly. Or at least, that's what I've read."

"You too?" Was Joie the only person in town who hadn't checked out Wyatt's life with the help of online gossip? "You know most of that stuff is inaccurate crap. Right?"

"But *so* entertaining." Seeing that Joie wasn't in the mood to make light of it, Carole sighed. "Honey, when you've lost your sense of humor, I know there's a problem. Do you want me to tell you what I know?"

"Absolutely not."

"Have you asked Wyatt?"

"Until the past few days, it hasn't bothered me. Much. Not enough to risk rocking the status quo boat. I get sex with a funny, interesting man." Joie flopped onto the sofa. "If I ask questions, that will make Wyatt uncomfortable."

"So instead, you are the one with an upset stomach."

"True." Unseeing, Joie stared at the ceiling. "Did I mention the sex? Great. Mind-blowing. Otherworldly sex. Why should I risk that to satisfy my intimacy issues?"

"Because intimacy makes sex better," Carole reasoned. "And what the hell is otherworldly sex? Do you float above the bed like ghosts?"

"There are moments when that is how it feels." Closing her eyes, Joie smiled. "The floating. Not the ghosts."

"Talk. To. Him."

Joie peeked out of one eye. "What do I say?"

Carole slung her good arm around Joie's shoulders "You'll think of something. You always do."

CHAPTER EIGHTEEN

WYATT DIDN'T UNDERSTAND women.

It wasn't an original thought. Before cavemen were capable of uttering the words—or forming the thoughts—there must have been an equivalent idea pinging through their pea-sized brains. Venus. Mars. Whatever your thing. It amounted to the same idea.

Women were different. And hats off to the man who deluded himself into believing he had decoded the puzzle. Let him be happy for a little while. Because Wyatt knew without a doubt, the guy was wrong. Women were the eternal mystery.

"I don't want to cuddle." Joie pushed him away and rolled from the bed.

"Is something wrong?"

"What do you think?"

How was he supposed to answer that? At the best of times, it was a minefield a man would be wise to avoid. Right now? The blood was just beginning to reroute to his brain after a very satisfying round of sex. To top it off, Joie stood naked in the middle of the room. The sight of her made the odds of rational thought slim to none.

"I think I have no idea what happened between a fantastic orgasm and now. Talk to me, Joie. I can't read your mind."

"I want to fight. I want to yell and vent and, yes, I want you to read my mind." Suddenly, the steam she had built up seemed to escape in one long sigh. "But that would give me temporary relief. The problem would still exist."

Hopefully, Wyatt patted the empty side of the bed. But Joie shook her head and slipped on a thick, fluffy robe.

"We can talk right here," he called out as she left the room.

"I need tea. Hot tea. And bring me a pair of socks when you come."

Resigned, Wyatt pulled on his jeans. He had asked. But, as tempting as the cozy bed was, he didn't want to stay there without Joie. Nor did he want to let whatever was bothering her fester. She wanted to talk. He was ready to listen.

Joie had the water on to boil, and two cups sat on the counter.

"Would you rather have coffee?"

Until a few weeks ago, Joie hadn't owned a coffeemaker. She liked to get the occasional cup when she was out but never made it for herself. Wyatt liked coffee. Lots of it. He still wasn't sure how he felt about her buying the expensive machine just for him. On the surface, it wasn't a big deal. But it represented several things. Joie's knowledge of his likes and dislikes. She had started keeping his favorite cookies. His hand hovered near the panda bear-shaped jar that sat on the counter. How many times had he taken one without a second thought?

"It's a cookie, Wyatt. Not a commitment."

Great. Now she could read his mind? Bypassing the jar, he handed her a pair of fuzzy socks.

"I don't want anything." Even to his ears, he sounded oddly petulant. He took a seat at the table and added, "But thank you."

Joie poured the steaming water into her cup. As she dunked the tea bag, she raised her eyes to his.

"I have no secrets. None. Not from you."

The clouds began to clear. He didn't need for her to explain. They were together every day. Lunch. Dinner. Sometimes they would meet for breakfast. They took walks around town. Joie showed him the sights. There were times they would sit in his truck, listening to the classic rock station while they simply held hands.

If they didn't have sex, it was an unusual end to the evening. But he never stayed. And she never asked him to. She never asked why. Until now. The strange part was that he wanted to tell her. The urge to unburden himself wasn't new. The need to lighten his load had always been there.

As much as he wanted to talk, it had been easy to keep it to himself because he didn't want to hurt the ones he loved. The last thing he had wanted was to see the pain his words would cause his family. His mother and father in particular.

Joie was the first person he felt he could tell the truth. But every time he began, he thought of all the reasons not to.

"It's ugly, Joie." She wasn't. Joie was light. Sweet. Kind. She shouldn't be saddled with his crap. "You can't unhear something. I can tell you that from bitter experience."

Forgetting the tea, Joie took his hand and led him to the sofa. Instead of taking the seat next to him, she climbed onto his lap.

"Words are powerful weapons. They have started revolutions. Ended wars. Good can be done with them as well as bad." She smoothed a soothing hand over his brow. "Let me take some of your pain away, Wyatt. I'm strong. I can handle it."

"It's a long story."

Joie wrapped her arms around him. "I'm not going anywhere."

"Your feet are bare." Holding her close, Wyatt walked across the room to retrieve her socks. He set her on the counter, slipping one onto each foot.

"I can walk," Joie chuckled as he carried her back to the sofa. "Detour to the hall, please."

Without hesitation, he did as she asked. "I like having you in my arms."

"And I like being in them. Here we are. Can you open the closet or do you need to put me down?"

Wyatt scoffed at the idea. Shifting her weight to one arm, he opened the door. "What do you need?"

"The blanket on the top shelf. Lovely. Now, back to the sofa."

When they were settled, this time, side by side, Joie arranged the blanket over them and took his hand.

"I don't know where to start."

Joie rubbed her cheek against his shoulder. "I know it's a cliché, but how about starting at the beginning?"

"I met Stephanie at a party."

"Glitzy and glamorous?"

Wyatt nodded. "It seems there is always a party in Hollywood. Usually to raise money. A friend of a friend was throwing this one. What does it say that I can't remember the friend? Or the charity?"

"It says that like any human, time dims our memories. How many parties do you attend in a year?"

Wyatt smiled, kissing her hair. Joie was ready to champion him without any of the facts.

"Too many."

"So stop worrying about it. I imagine Stephanie was beautiful? I would be disappointed if you said no." She squeezed his hand, encouraging him to continue.

"Beautiful. But not unusually so."

Stephanie had been like so many other women he met on a daily basis. Picture perfect. Ready for their close-up. Wyatt enjoyed looking. And sometimes touching. But he never felt more than a passing affection.

"You had sex with a beautiful, available woman." Joie somehow made a snort come off as sarcastic. "Shame on you."

"I was bored." Joie's words helped, but he wasn't letting himself off the hook. "And horny. She was good in bed. So I went back for a second helping. Over the period of a month, we had sex four times."

"I would bet the royalties from my next book that Stephanie initiated each encounter."

"Your money is safe."

It was always the same. Stephanie would just happen to be at the same party or restaurant. Wyatt wasn't a fool. He knew it wasn't a coincidence. But as he had said, the sex was good. And he was a man who appreciated the initiative.

"The last time was in the bathroom at a very famous Beverly Hills restaurant."

When he mentioned the name, Joie whistled. "Women's or men's room?"

"Men's. Stephanie followed me in."

"Hussy."

"I could have said no."

"Why didn't you?"

That was a question Wyatt had asked himself a thousand times. Make it a thousand and one.

"The novelty appealed to me. Add on a couple of whiskeys—neat—and I let her have her way."

"Oh, boy."

"I know," Wyatt nodded. "I don't deserve an ounce of sympathy. I knew it was the last time. And I think she did too. We had never dated. Never shared a meal or exchanged more than a few heated words."

"I could walk into the middle of this movie, and I would still know what was coming."

"Then you're smarter than I was. Three months later, Stephanie showed up at my office. She claimed she was pregnant."

To his credit, Wyatt didn't take her word for it. He always used a condom. Always. But nothing was foolproof. He insisted that she see a doctor of his choice. And submit to in-vitro DNA testing. Both were positive. Stephanie was carrying his child.

"How did you feel?"

"Resolved. By then I could tell that Stephanie was not mother of the year material. She spoke of the baby as a thing. An asset. She made no bones about it. She wanted to be Mrs. Wyatt Landis. Our child was her ticket."

"You wanted to be a father."

Wyatt felt a chill. "How do you know?"

Joie snuggled closer, sharing her warmth, and support. "I can hear it in your voice."

"It didn't take long. I had the best parents in the world. I knew they would make great grandparents. I married Stephanie out of necessity. But I loved our unborn baby."

As though sensing that he was coming to the hard part, Joie didn't speak, letting him tell it in his own way and time.

"I made certain Stephanie ate well and tried my damnedest to keep her away from tobacco and alcohol. I cut back on my hours at work, getting home every night for dinner. However, domestic bliss had never been her goal. She wanted excitement. Wild parties and wilder friends. Short of locking her in a room with a twenty-four-hour guard, I couldn't keep her at home."

"Is that when she lost the baby? While she was partying?"

Wyatt felt his heart rate increase. Sweat broke out on his upper lip, and his breathing became shallow. Remembering what had happened was bad enough. He lived with it every day. It haunted his dreams. But this was the first time he had ever spoken the words. His throat tightened. His mouth grew dry. With effort, he finally said it aloud.

"Stephanie didn't lose our baby. She had an abortion."

Joie gasped, her hand tightening on his. "After you married her? After you had given her what she wanted?"

"Yes."

"Why?" Joie raised her head. Tears filled her eyes. "She must have been crazy."

Wyatt cupped Joie's face using his thumbs to brush the moisture as it rolled down her cheeks. He had never cried for his lost child. Not because he didn't want to. He couldn't. The tears would not come. His mother had mourned the loss of her first grandchild, but she believed it to be nature's will, not the whim of her unbalanced daughter-in-law.

Joie's tears were the first shed knowing the truth. Wyatt felt his eyes sting. For the first time, he felt close to joining her.

"Stephanie—" Wyatt took an unsteady breath. "She was bipolar. I had no idea—it came out after her death. There was prescribed medicine she should have been taking, but more often than not, she didn't. I found two full bottles of her pills in the bottom drawer of her dresser."

"Maybe she stopped taking them because she was worried they would harm the baby."

It was said with such hope that Wyatt hugged Joie close, giving her comfort.

"The prescriptions were dated months before I met Stephanie. She hadn't taken them for some time, Joie. There were times when I thought she seemed off. Different. Too up. But I didn't think there was a medical explanation." Wyatt's free hand tightened around the blanket, turning his knuckles white. "I should have paid attention."

"Stephanie chose to go off her meds, Wyatt. She chose not to tell you about her condition. You can't blame yourself. None of it is your fault."

"She was carrying my child, Joie. It was up to me to keep them safe." Wyatt blamed himself for failing to do so. And he always would.

"There was no way to anticipate what she would do. You said it yourself, you couldn't watch her every second of every day."

Wyatt nodded. That much was true. "I believed she would take care of the baby. It was her leverage. It was the reason I married her. It was the only reason I would stay married to her."

"You planned on divorcing her after she gave birth." Joie made it a statement, not a question.

"Yes. I had my lawyer draw up the papers at the same time he did the prenuptial agreement. Getting her to sign the prenup was a breeze. I imagine she thought once she had a ring on her finger and my child, she was set for life."

And she would have been. At least financially. Wyatt would not have left her high and dry. In exchange for a no-contest divorce and full custody of their child, Stephanie would have been well compensated. *Very* well compensated.

"Stephanie wasn't stupid. I'm sure it didn't take her long to figure out that I was committed to our child—not to her."

"She wanted to hurt you."

"And she knew exactly how to do that." Wyatt took a ragged breath. "Stephanie aborted the baby shortly after her second checkup. She was almost six months along."

"I— Oh, Wyatt." Joie's distress vibrated through her body. "I don't know what to say. I can't wrap my head around what she did to you. To your child."

"Stephanie didn't tell me right away. She saved it for when she could get the most impact. My mother had organized a baby shower. We were on the way to it when she dropped her bombshell."

They were living in Beverly Hills, only a few blocks from his parents' house. Stephanie had waited until Wyatt was helping her from the car. She said it in such a matter-of-fact manner he thought he had misheard. Or that she was pulling a cruel, sick joke. But one look into her eyes and he knew she was telling him the truth.

Stephanie had deliberately ended her pregnancy.

"I will never forget her expression. Triumph. She had gained her ultimate victory."

It was all he could do not to strangle her. Wyatt had wanted to take her life as easily as she had taken the life of their unborn child. Somehow, he pulled back. To this day, Wyatt didn't know how he held himself together long enough to drive Stephanie home then call his parents. He made up an excuse. Something about Stephanie not feeling well.

The next thing he remembered was waking up in a hotel room with a whopping hangover. Three days had passed."

"You drank away three days?"

"I vaguely recall making a stop at a liquor store. There were six empty bourbon bottles littering the floor, so it must have happened. After that? Who knows? At least I had the sense to lock myself away where I couldn't hurt anyone."

Wyatt had showered. Downed a handful of aspirin. And driven home. Stephanie greeted him at the door, crocodile tears rolling down her perfectly made-up face. She actually tried to backtrack and claim that she had lost the baby.

"How did she plan on pulling that off?"

Wyatt rubbed his cheek against Joie's hair, the scent of wild roses filling his nose. Without realizing what was happening, he began to relax—just a bit.

"There was no plan. It was pure desperation. Stephanie knew it was over. Along with our child, she had put an end to the lifestyle she had craved. At that point, she would have said—or done anything."

Wyatt wouldn't have returned to the house, but he needed a change of clothes. Calmly, he packed a suitcase. He would have his assistant clear out the rest of his things later that day. He never planned on setting foot here again. Grabbing his laptop and a few things from his office, he left without looking at Stephanie.

"I told her she would be hearing from my lawyer. That was the first time she threatened to kill herself. If I didn't stay, she would slit her wrists. I told her to be my guest." Wyatt closed his eyes at the memory. "Not my finest hour."

"I would have handed the bitch the razor."

"No, you wouldn't have."

"Probably not," Joie conceded. "But I don't blame you for walking away."

"I didn't care what she did. I just wanted her out of my life."

Unfortunately, that proved easier said than done. No amount of money would induce Stephanie to sign the divorce papers. And she promised that if Wyatt filed on his own, she would go to the tabloids. Wyatt hadn't been moved. She could make up any story she wanted. He didn't care. But when she threatened to tell the world what had really happened to their child, he agreed to stay married to her.

"I had told my family that Stephanie miscarried. It wasn't easy to lie, but the truth would have devastated my parents. We didn't live together. Or socialize. But for the next two and half years, she remained my wife."

"Was it difficult?"

"I buried myself in work. Now and then, news of Stephanie's wild escapades would reach me. Usually via a *caring* friend or malicious business rival. I didn't care. She couldn't do anything more to hurt me."

Joie nodded, then frowned. "Your family must have questioned why you didn't divorce her."

"They did. But I refused to talk about it. They assumed it was because I felt guilty over Stephanie losing the baby."

Wyatt constantly worried that Stephanie would break her silence. On the night she died, she had called him threatening to do just that. She told him if he didn't move home and make their marriage a real one, she would go to his parents and tell them the truth.

"The next time my phone rang it was the police telling me there had been an accident. The roads were slick with rain. Stephanie was driving too fast, losing control of her car on Mulholland Drive. At least that's what the police determined after their investigation."

"You don't think it was an accident?"

"I have no idea."

Wyatt's belief fluctuated depending on his mood. It would have been just like Stephanie to take her own life in such a dramatic fashion. Then again, it was possible that the crash was deliberate, but she planned on living. When her publicist leaked hospital bed pictures, the internet would have blown up.

Or perhaps it had been an accident. Wyatt would never know.

"My family believes that I mourned her death."

"You've never set them straight?" He shook his head. "Wyatt, don't you think it's time? If they knew the truth. About Stephanie and the baby, you could grieve properly."

What the hell was she suggesting? "I grieve for my child every day." Wyatt tried to pull away, but Joie held tight.

"I can't begin to understand what you've been through. But I know what it is like to lose someone. When my father died, my mother and I grieved separately. It would have been easier if we had found a way to do it together."

"I can't, Joie."

"Why not?"

"Because it would kill me to cause them that kind of pain. Losing their grandchild was hard enough. But knowing it shouldn't have happened? She would have been five years old this year."

"She?"

"I found out the sex when they did the DNA test. Her name was Amanda Callie Landis."

Gently, Joie wiped at his cheek. Lifting his hand, Wyatt frowned when he felt the moisture.

"It's okay," Joie crooned, pulling him close. "Cry for Amanda Callie. I won't let you go."

The pain flooded his body until Wyatt thought he would explode. But somehow, Joie's soothing touch and soft words held him together. He didn't know how long he cried. Once the tears started, they wouldn't stop.

Wyatt cried for his little girl. For the years he had missed and for all the things he would never see her do. Her first steps. Her first words. Holding her hand as he walked her to school. Holding her close the first time a boy broke her heart. Watching her get married. Holding her child in his arms.

He would never know how that felt. He would never know his Amanda Callie.

JOIE HELD WYATT as he slept. She kept watch over him. When he stirred, she would quiet him with a touch or a few softly whispered words. He was exhausted—body and soul. All she wanted to do was keep him safe.

No, that wasn't true. She wanted to go back and punish the woman who had inflicted this pain on him. Joie had never considered herself to be a vengeful person. But until now, she never had reason to be. The man she loved was hurting. He was a good man. Thoughtful and caring. She knew without a doubt that he would have been a wonderful father to his precious little girl.

Goddamn, Stephanie. Joie hoped the bitch was roasting in hell.

Wyatt stirred. He mumbled something unintelligible, a frown marring his brow.

"Shh," Joie crooned. "Sleep, my love. Sleep."

He settled again, sighing when Joie stroked his hair. As she calmed Wyatt, she calmed herself. He didn't need her anger. He had plenty of his own. Joie hoped that she had helped. Telling her everything that had happened hadn't been easy for him, but she knew the power of words. Holding them inside for so long had eaten away at him. Wyatt blamed himself for things he couldn't have foreseen or controlled.

She hoped that he would begin to understand that Stephanie had been ill. Her actions had not been those of a reasonable, logical person. He needed to let go of his guilt. If she had helped him take a small step in that direction, that was what mattered.

Closing her eyes, Joie let her body relax and her mind clear. Wyatt was a good man. Better than he gave himself credit for. Her last thought as she drifted off was that he needed to look around at all the good he had done here in Monroe. The people he had helped and befriended. He didn't need the money. Only a good man would have given so much of his time when it wasn't necessary.

"They have come to love you." Half-asleep, Joie brushed her lips over the top of his head. She whispered the words she couldn't bring herself to say when he was awake. "I love you, Wyatt."

I LOVE YOU, Wyatt.

The words settled over him like a sweet spring breeze. He had no doubt who said them. *Joie.* Consciously, he would never admit how much he longed to hear her say them. But in his sleep, he could bask in the moment—treasure their meaning.

With a start, Wyatt's eyes flew open. Jesus. Where was he? He breathed in once. Then again. He knew that scent. Joie. He had fallen asleep in her arms.

It all came flooding back. Telling her everything. Her reaction. Her comforting words. Her soothing touch. Wyatt waited for the crushing guilt to descend. But instead, he felt lighter. Almost free. The ache still lingered. He doubted it would ever leave as long as he remembered the loss of his baby girl.

However, he had slept with Joie—without the dreams. The healing had begun without his knowledge. Little by little. This town. The people. Joie. It had been the perfect combination for his broken spirit.

Last night hadn't completed the process. But it had started the final chapter. For the first time, Wyatt could see a light at the end of the long, dark tunnel. And that light was Joie.

Standing, Wyatt picked her up in his arms.

"Are we moving?" Joie asked with a sleepy sigh.

"I'm taking you to bed. Your sofa is nice, but it isn't conducive to a good night's sleep."

"I sleep there all the time."

"You are shorter than I am."

"Mmm." She smiled, nuzzling his neck. "I like it that way. There is so much more of you to touch. And lick. And kiss." Joie emphasized her point by doing all three to his neck, his jaw, and finally his mouth.

"You are mighty frisky for someone who is half asleep."

"You're doing all the work. All I have to do is lie back and enjoy."

Wyatt chuckled—something he wouldn't have thought possible while he was telling Joie his story. He tipped her chin, giving him access to initiate a long, slow kiss. Keeping his lips on hers, he let her slip to the ground.

"I like it better in your arms," Joie complained.

"Let me help you off with your robe. Now jump into bed."

With a resigned sigh, Joie did as he asked. Lying on her back, her eyes widened. "What are you doing?"

"Taking off my clothes." Wyatt draped his jeans over the nearby chair before sliding under the covers.

"But it's late." Joie twisted to get a look at the clock. "Quarter after four. You never stay this late."

Wyatt opened the end table drawer, taking out a condom. "Want me to go?"

"No, thank you." Eager, Joie reached for the packet.

"May I stay for breakfast?"

He saw her eyes light up. "Yes, please."

Drawing her into his arms, Wyatt covered her smile with his own. He didn't know what tomorrow would bring. But for now, he was exactly where he needed to be.

CHAPTER NINETEEN

JOIE PAUSED OUTSIDE of Carole's shop to breathe in the brisk morning air. She hadn't taken her usual walk around town, deciding she would rather spend the time with Wyatt. Having him with her when she woke was a novelty she didn't think would ever wear off. He would be leaving town soon. She wanted to enjoy as much time with him as she could.

A touch of melancholy threatened her good mood, but Joie ruthlessly pushed it aside. She wasn't going to let the thought of Wyatt leaving Monroe dim her good mood. Between the sex, the cozy shower for two, and a breakfast cooked by a drop-dead gorgeous man, she wasn't going to let anything get her down.

"Carole," Joie called out as she entered the building.

The smell of clean wool greeted her. The skeins lined one wall in a rainbow of colors. On top of the wool was a touch of cinnamon. The special potpourri was Carole's own recipe. It was such a hit with customers that she had started making extra to sell here in the shop and online.

There was no one around. Nothing unusual about that. But the absolute quiet of the room gave Joie a sense of unease. There was always something going on in the shop—even if it were just the sound of the radio coming from the workroom.

"Carole? Are you here?" Again, nothing. "Twila?" Joie didn't think the woman who worked part-time was scheduled for today, but she called out to her just in case.

Joie was about to poke her head in the storage room when she heard a loud thump from above. That was strange. Carole never left the front door unlocked when she went upstairs. It was a big no-no to leave the shop—and her valuable merchandise unattended.

A shiver of unease ran down Joie's spine. Cautiously, she approached the stairs. She considered calling Wyatt, but she hated to bother him over nothing. *Better safe than sorry*, a voice in her head

234

called out. If this were a movie, she would be yelling at the heroine not to go up there.

This isn't a movie, Joie reminded herself. She reached for her phone. *And you are not an idiot.* The decision on whether to wait for back-up was quickly taken out of her hands as a scream rang out. Joie hit the stairs at a run. Luckily, she had Wyatt on speed dial.

"ANY CHANCE YOU'LL have time to swing by my place today? The water in my toilet won't stop running. You did such a fine job on my hedge, I know you can fix the problem in no time."

Wyatt had barely stepped into the *Monarch Café* when Mrs. Pringle called out to him. He was so used to it by now that he didn't blink an eye. Though what trimming a hedge had to do with her constantly running toilet water, Wyatt didn't know. However, it seemed to be the common notion around Monroe. If he could do one thing, it only followed that he could do anything.

It wasn't true, but the confidence of the townsfolk gave his ego a nice boost.

"I'll try to stop by, Mrs. Pringle. But I can't promise you anything."

"You let people take advantage," she told him with a wag of her finger.

"Yes, ma'am."

"And she's the biggest culprit of the bunch." Dex laughed as Wyatt took a seat at the counter. "I don't know why you do it."

Wyatt shrugged. "It feels good to be useful."

How many times had he said that over the past month? Mostly to himself. Wyatt knew his time in Monroe was coming to an end. Yet he kept hanging on. Just today he had lined up three new jobs— four if he counted Mrs. Pringle. It was time for him to hang up his handyman tools and head back to Los Angeles. Soon.

Joie was the problem. Or was she the solution? Wyatt couldn't imagine leaving her—especially after last night. He knew that

Monroe was her home. She made it clear that she had put down roots and never planned to leave. Especially to follow a man.

The irony of the situation wasn't lost on him. Wyatt had vowed never to marry again. If he had stayed in Los Angeles, he was certain that keeping that vow wouldn't have been a problem. It took a woman from a small town in Nevada to get him thinking that maybe his longing for a wife and family hadn't died with his baby girl. Had Joie taught him to dream again only to dash them?

"I need some advice," Dex said as he poured Wyatt a cup of coffee.

"Join the club," Wyatt muttered under his breath.

"Did you say something?"

"Nothing important." Wyatt took a sip of coffee. "What's the problem?"

"I think I know who attacked Carole. Or at least who was behind it."

"That's great. Tell the police so they can bring the creep in." When Dex hesitated, Wyatt frowned. "You said you *think* you know who it is? Is that why you haven't said anything? I know it would be rough to accuse an innocent person, Dex. But this is serious."

"I'm almost positive it's my ex-girlfriend. Sharon Lincoln. We dated about a year ago. She has an organic farm over in Prosper. I bought some of her heirloom tomatoes for the restaurant and decided to ask her out. A week earlier, I had made up my mind to forget about Carole and get on with my life. I don't have to tell you how that turned out."

"What makes you think Sharon is guilty?"

"She started texting me a few days ago." Dex took out his phone and handed it to Wyatt. "It's crazy. She thinks we belong together. She was waiting for me to come to my senses—her words—when she heard that Carole and I were engaged. She didn't take the news very well."

"Jesus, Dex." Wyatt looked up from reading the texts. "That's putting it mildly. Did you tell Carole?"

236

"I didn't know how."

"At least tell me you showed these to the police."

"No." Before Wyatt could explode, Dex added, "But I sent them to your friend. Drew Harper is checking out my theory. He said he would call me today with an update."

"Drew is the right man to call. But you have to tell Carole, Dex. If only so she can protect herself. What if Sharon shows up out of the blue? Carole could end up with a lot worse than a broken arm."

"Shit. I was so worried about Carole's reaction I didn't think about that. I'll go over and talk to her right away."

Just then, Wyatt's phone rang. He smiled when he saw it was Joie.

"Good morning. Again."

"I need you at Carole's. Now!"

Wyatt didn't hesitate. He grabbed Dex's arm and headed for the door.

"Is Carole all right? Are you?"

"I'm outside her apartment. I heard a scream, Wyatt. The door is locked, and nobody is answering."

"I'm just across the street with Dex. Hold tight."

Wyatt said a silent prayer of thanks when they found the street clear of traffic. They cut diagonally across at a full run.

"I have a key, and I'm going in. So hurry."

"No. Damn it, Joie. Do not go in by yourself." Wyatt could see the door to Carole's shop. "We're almost there."

"Too late, the door is open. Holy crap."

"Is Carole okay?" Dex barreled ahead of him into the shop. Not waiting for an answer, he was across the room in a few strides. Wyatt was right behind him.

"Joie?" Wyatt called out as they raced up the stairs. "Joie! Say something."

"Carole is fine. But whoever it is that she coldcocked is going to have a massive headache."

237

Wyatt hadn't breathed since he had left the diner. Seeing Joie unharmed, the air rushed into his lungs. He pulled her close, burying his face in her hair.

"I told you not to open the door."

"And I didn't listen." Her voice was steady, but she clung to him for dear life. Feeling how her body trembled, Wyatt tightened his embrace.

"Where is Carole?" Dex demanded.

Joie pointed toward the bedroom just as Carole stepped into view.

"Here I am." She rushed to Dex. Her clothes were ripped, and her hair looked like it had been combed with an eggbeater. But she moved under her own power and other than a scratch on her cheek, there were no visible signs of injury.

"Are you hurt?" Dex ran a thumb over her cheek. When she winced, so did he.

"A few scrapes and bruises. Your girlfriend isn't as lucky."

"My— Son of a bitch. Sharon did this?"

"Then you do know her." Carole tried to push him away, but Dex held on. "She claims you've been screwing her behind my back."

Dex breathed in. "And you believed her?"

"No," Carole conceded. She jabbed him in the chest with the finger on her non-casted hand. "But look at this place. She's a psycho bitch. Why didn't you warn me?"

"That seems to be the question of the day."

"While you two figure it out, I'll make sure Dex's ex isn't pulling a Glenn Close in *Fatal Attraction*."

"She isn't dead," Carole called out. "Unfortunately."

"Wyatt wants to make sure she doesn't pop up and do any more damage." Joie dialed the police. "I wonder if Officer Petry will believe us now."

THE ROOM WAS a shambles. Sharon had done a number on Carole's apartment. Even with the extra help, cleaning it up turned out to be an all-day job.

"Tell us what happened."

Carole exchanged glances with Joie. There were five volunteers armed with cleaning supplies working away at the room. There would have been more, but only so many bodies fit in the small space. Carole understood, when she agreed to the help, payment would be a detailed recounting of her run-in with Sharon Lincoln. Three days later, it was still all the town could talk about.

"I might as well get the story out there," Carole had told Joie the day before. "That way I won't have to tell it over and over again."

Joie agreed. The group assembled represented a nice cross-section of the town. They would tell their friends, who would tell their friends. By tomorrow, if someone hadn't heard all the details, she wasn't interested. And Joie knew from experience there wasn't a soul in Monroe who didn't like to be abreast of all the gossip. They respected a person's privacy—up to a point.

The story wouldn't travel beyond the town limits, but in their small circle, it would make the rounds like wildfire.

"I opened the store as I always do," Carole began. "Nothing seemed amiss."

"The door was locked?" Tilly Brent, the town's only lawyer, asked. "How did she get in?"

"She broke into the apartment by the side entrance." Carole pointed to the door. The window had a piece of cardboard taped over where the glass had been. "I'm grateful she didn't get into the shop."

The women nodded, murmuring what a tragedy it would have been if all of Carole's beautiful creations had been ruined.

"I heard a sound—like something breaking. I know it was foolish to come up here alone; I didn't stop to think."

Joie had already let Carole have it on that score. So many things could have gone wrong. But it hadn't. So she had let Carole off with a verbal chastising. Followed by a few tears of relief and a big hug.

"What I found when I opened the apartment door stunned me." Carole swept her good arm dramatically around the room. "I couldn't believe my eyes. Look at the walls. I don't know what she used to make those holes."

"A sledgehammer?" Betty Fielding checked out the damage. She worked at the hardware store and knew a thing or two about such matters.

"The police didn't find one. Though by the looks of her hands, I think her fists are a possibility."

Joie rolled her eyes. Carole had a captive audience, and she was milking the moment for all it was worth. There had been nothing wrong with Sharon Lincoln's fists. The holes had been made using a chair—the pieces were at the police station bagged as evidence.

"I couldn't see anyone in here, but I swear I heard her heavy, out of control breathing."

"Where was she?" Betty asked, eyes wide.

"In the bedroom. I found her hacking at the mattress with a nail file." Carole nodded when the women gasped. "I know. She used *my* nail file. I don't know what her plan was, but she came to this fight unarmed."

"Isn't that a good thing?" Joie asked. She shuddered to think what might have happened otherwise.

"For me?" Carole nodded. "Hell yes. The second she saw me she fell to her knees and let out an ear-piercing scream."

"That must have been what you heard," Tilly said to Joie.

"It certainly got my attention." She could smile *now.* "Luckily, Carole had everything under control by the time the cavalry arrived."

"What did you do?" Tilly demanded.

"The second she started jabbering about Dex, I clocked her with my good fist." Carole demonstrated the motion. "The woman went out like a light. Glass jaw."

That elicited a round of whoops for Carole's pugilistic skills.

"She was still out cold by the time the police arrived. Though Wyatt had tied her hands behind her back, just to be sure she didn't wake up and cause more damage."

"Wyatt Landis can tie me up anytime he wants."

"Seriously?" Tilly rounded on Betty. "You do realize that we heard you. Me, Carole. Three members of the PTA. *And* Wyatt's girlfriend. Honestly."

Looking thoroughly browbeaten, Betty blushed. Joie patted Betty's shoulder. Tilly could be a bit of a bully sometimes.

"Don't worry about it, Betty. Wyatt is a lovely bit of eye candy. Isn't he, Tilly?" Joie's look reminded Tilly that she had been seen on more than one occasion ogling a shirtless Wyatt.

"He is," Tilly agreed quickly, having the good grace to look embarrassed. "There is nothing wrong with a healthy fantasy life, I always say."

Joie winked at Betty, giving her another squeeze.

"Any more questions before we get to work?"

"I have one." Bernice Markum raised her hand. You had to love a polite first-grade teacher.

Carole smiled. "Go ahead, Bernice."

"Why? I mean, she was responsible for everything, right?" The pretty brunette looked around with a puzzled expression. "Your broken arm. The broken pipes. That nasty word that was carved onto the door of your car. Why would she think any of that would make Dex drop you for her?"

"Crazy never makes sense." Joie couldn't help but think of Stephanie and the pain she caused Wyatt. Sometimes there was no logical explanation.

"Amen to that," Carole sighed. "Sharon claims things got out of control. She asked her boyfriend to *scare* me." She tapped her cast. "Ya, right. She had no idea he would get hopped up on cocaine and take it too far."

"Do you believe her?"

"I don't," Joie said to Betty.

"I agree. Sharon did everything else. She snuck up here while I was busy with a customer and sabotaged the pipes. The car was easy. When Dex didn't answer her whacked-out texts, she decided to take out her frustrations by trashing my apartment. Like Joie said. Crazy never makes sense."

CHAPTER TWENTY

FIXING THE WINDOW in Carole's door was the last of Wyatt's handyman jobs. It wasn't official. It wasn't a headline in the *Monroe Cryer*. No one gossiped about it over coffee at the *Monarch Café*. But he knew it. And though they hadn't discussed it, so did Joie.

"You do excellent work. You could make a fortune at this in Los Angeles."

Wyatt took the tube of caulking from Dex, running a thin line around the new pane of glass.

"I already have a fortune."

"Hey, that's right." Chuckling, Dex shook his head. "I keep forgetting who you are when you're in the real world."

Stepping back to admire his work, Wyatt wiped his hands on a rag. "Monroe isn't the real world?"

"It is," Dex said. "Only more idyllic."

Wyatt couldn't argue with that. Monroe, its people, and the easy lifestyle had played a big part in lifting his spirits and healing his soul. As for his heart? When he arrived, he would have sworn it was dead. Now it beat with a vengeance. And ached when he thought about a life without Joie.

"Word on the street is you'll be heading out tomorrow or the next day. Friday at the latest."

"How the hell—? Word on the street should mind its own business."

"You *are* our business, son." Dex slung a friendly arm over Wyatt's shoulders. "Have been since the day you ran your truck into one of our trees. That won't change when you're back in Los Angeles making fancy deals."

"That's comforting," Wyatt said it with a trace of sarcasm, but the truth was, he liked the idea that there would always be a place for him here.

Wyatt packed up his tools. He had acquired quite a collection—enough to do anyone proud. They wouldn't get packed away to gather dust. He planned on giving them a place of honor in the trunk of his Bentley. Right by his Gucci workout bag and Louis Vuitton briefcase.

He jumped into the cab of his truck and started the engine. Running his hand over the steering wheel, he was surprised at how attached he had become to the old bucket of bolts. The plan had always been to sell it as soon as he returned home. But now? Well, he had a big-ass garage that sat empty most of the time.

Wyatt didn't give a damn how incongruous the truck would look sitting next to his three-hundred-thousand-dollar luxury sedan.

It was clouding up. He had gotten used to clear blue skies. And air that didn't come with a warning advisory. One more thing he was going to miss. The list was getting longer. But they were all things he could live without.

He pulled to a stop outside of Joie's house. A second later, as though she had been waiting for him, she appeared on the porch. Her dark hair was twisted into a messy knot that he found incredibly sexy. Feet bare, her toenails were painted a bright shade of crimson. That was new. Wyatt planned on kissing every toe as he explored her handiwork.

Joie's smile made him a little lightheaded. Could he live without Joie? Yes. Did he want to? No. But he might not have a choice.

However, right here? Right now? She was his. And he wasn't going to waste a second.

"Did you get Carole's window fixed?"

"Yes."

Wyatt advanced with a purposeful stride, his eyes locked with hers. He could tell the instant Joie understood his intent. Her gaze heated with anticipation. God, he loved that she could read him so easily. And that she wanted him as much as he wanted her.

Without warning, Joie jumped into his arms, her legs wrapping around him. Wyatt caught her easily—happily.

"Did you have a good day?" Joie punctuated her words with a sweet barrage of kisses.

"Yes." Catching her chin in his hand, he deepened the kiss, making them both breathless. "And it is about to get even better."

Wide-eyed, but hardly innocent, Joie batted her lashes. "How?"

Holding her close, Wyatt walked into the house. He kicked the door shut and headed for the stairs, taking them two at a time.

"Do you want me to tell you—in detail?"

Her soft laughter sent a shot of need through him. Her lips were close to his ear, close enough for him to feel her warm breath when she whispered, "Surprise me."

Wyatt grinned. "My pleasure."

THE PLEASURE HAD been mutual. Though Joie didn't know how she could match Wyatt's capacity for giving. And giving. And giving. Multiple times. Over and over again. She was going to miss this. The sex—obviously. But the moments after were just as precious. More so. The quiet followed by conversations about nothing—and everything.

Joie knew that she would be lonely when Wyatt was gone. Lonelier than ever before. But she wouldn't go back and change a thing. How did the song go? *If I had known my heart would break, I would've loved you anyway.*

"What are you thinking about?"

You don't want to know. So Joie saved them both the uncomfortable conversation.

"They are calling for snow tomorrow afternoon. You should get an early start."

Joie waited for Wyatt's denial. When it didn't come, she couldn't decide if she were grateful for his honesty or angry that she was right. Either way, she had her answer without asking the question. He planned on leaving. Tomorrow.

"I don't want to go."

That helped—not a lot. But she would take what she could get.

"It's time." Joie lay on Wyatt's chest, her chin resting on her hand. His eyes were closed, giving her the chance to take in every detail one last time. "I've signed the contracts. We smoothed out the screenplay. It has been lovely, Wyatt."

"I can't ask you to go with me."

"And I can't ask you to stay."

His eyes slowly opened. So damn blue. That shade—like nothing she had ever seen—had become her favorite.

"Why not?"

Was he joking? The answer was too obvious for words. But it seemed he wanted her to say them.

"In Los Angeles, you are a huge fish in a very large pond. What can Monroe give you when you already have the world?"

"You."

Without the slightest intention, the man could break her heart into a million bits. Then with one smile, patch it together again.

"I'll be here whenever you feel like dropping in."

The bright blue of his eyes dimmed. "I don't know if that's enough."

"Neither do I." Determined not to cry, Joie kissed his shoulder. "I guess we'll find out."

Covering her lips, Wyatt rolled her onto her back. The kiss felt desperate as though they were holding on by their fingertips to something determined to slip away.

One more time, Joie thought as she welcomed him with her body and her heart. If this were the last time, she wanted him to remember her with passion and joy—not with tears. Never with tears.

WYATT'S EXIT FROM Monroe was much less dramatic than his entrance. There were no flashing ambulance lights or emergency rooms. But there was Joie. Who knew when they met in such a dramatic fashion that she would come to mean the world? Or that driving away would feel like the biggest mistake he would ever make?

Yet here he was, ready to say goodbye.

"Drive carefully." Joie wiped the first snowflake from his shoulder. "Once it starts, the storm can hit fast."

"I'll be halfway to Los Angeles before it amounts to anything."

Christ, had it come to this? Wyatt cupped Joie's cheek with his hand. *Had they gone from talking about anything to awkwardly discussing the weather? Well, fuck that.*

"I will be back." He dropped his forehead onto hers.

"I know."

"Say it like you believe me."

"Wyatt…"

"What?"

Joie sighed. When she looked at him, her eyes weren't sad. They were wary. For some reason, Wyatt would have preferred sad.

"Don't make any promises."

"You think I'm lying?" Wyatt couldn't believe what he was hearing.

"No." She took his hand, her fingers linking with his. "Today it's the truth. But tomorrow? A week from now?" Joie shrugged. "Time can turn the truth into a lie."

"Fine. No promises." He pulled her into his arms. His lips brushed hers. "Try to make a lie out of this."

It was a kiss like no other they had shared. If he couldn't convince her with words, he had one other method at his disposal. Their bodies spoke the truth even when they couldn't say the words.

Wyatt lifted his head, his eyes staring into hers. He held her a few moments longer, then stepped back. With one last gesture, a brief caress of her cheek, he jumped into the truck. Driving away was the hardest thing he had ever done. But one thing kept him going. He *would* be back. And that was the absolute truth.

"IS HE GONE?" Carole took the seat opposite her.

Joie nodded. There was no solace for her. Not in her writing or her home. Wyatt was everywhere. In every room. In her every thought. Short of a cloying, sugary, romance novel with a surprisingly tragic ending, Joie couldn't think of a single word to put on her computer. And the last thing she wanted was a hardcopy of her bittersweet relationship with Wyatt Landis. Though she had the perfect title. *How to Break Your Heart in Just Over a Month*. Maybe not perfect. But it said it all.

With a shake of her head, Carole handed Joie a cup of tea, freshly brewed by a concerned Dex.

"Thanks."

Joie stared out the window of the *Monarch Café*. Not even her town was a safe haven. She had made the mistake of imprinting every inch with Wyatt. Now she had to live with it. Perhaps in a month or two, the memories would be a comfort. However, not today.

"Oh, get over yourself."

"Excuse me?"

"The tragic, poor me sigh. The hangdog expression. I told Dex not to bother with the tea and sympathy. You brought this on yourself."

"Remind me to put out the word that I'm looking for a new best friend," Joie muttered into her tea.

"I am the best friend you will ever have." Carole crossed her arms, refusing to bend. "How many times did you berate me for the way I handled my Dex situation?"

"Three hundred and six."

"That's awfully specific." Carole almost laughed. But she was on a mission, and that meant no mercy. "Did you tell Wyatt that you love him?"

"No."

"Idiot."

"He didn't say it either."

"And if he were here, I would say the same thing."

"Maybe he doesn't." Joie sipped the hot liquid, then met Carole's gaze. "He said he was coming back. But…"

"He loves you, Joie. He won't be able to stay away."

"Maybe."

"Did you tell him that if he asked, you would go with him?"

"This is my home. Wyatt respected that. I wouldn't have gone with him."

It wasn't exactly a lie. Nor was it entirely the truth. Joie still believed it was a mistake for a woman to follow a man. To give up her dreams for his. But damn it, this was different. Her dreams weren't dependent on a location. Have laptop, will travel. Monroe would always be here. It would always be in her heart. But the lion's share of that organ belonged to Wyatt.

Joie sighed. Was she an idiot?

"You will not believe the news."

Mayor Barbara Osweiler burst through the door in a swirl of energy and snowflakes. The predicted storm had arrived with a vengeance. By the looks of things, they would have well over a foot by morning.

"Coffee, Mayor?" Already knowing the answer, Dex poured a cup, adding a large dollop of cream.

"You are a lifesaver, Dex." Mayor Osweiler removed her fur-trimmed gloves and cupped the mug in her hands.

"Well?" Larry demanded. "What's this unbelievable news?"

The old man had his usual seat at the counter. But unlike most afternoons, he was flanked on both sides by other customers. Rather than keep people at home, the storm had brought them out en masse. That Wednesday at two thirty, the *Monarch Café* was standing room only.

"I still can't believe it." It was a rare occasion when the mayor was at a loss for words, but this appeared to be one of them. The mayor took a piece of paper from her coat pocket. "Look."

Since Carole was the closest, Barbara handed it to her. After a few moments, Carole raised her head, her eyes wide. Silently, she handed the paper to Joie.

"What?" Frowning, Joie scanned the document. "Is this the deed to Brad's land?"

The mayor nodded. "The land we wanted to rent for the Founder's Day celebration. But it no longer belongs to Brad Makepeace. The new owner is…" she paused for dramatic effect. "The. City. Of. Monroe."

That got the café buzzing. As she read the document, Joie's fingers tightened on the paper, turning her knuckles white.

"You go right ahead and tear it if you need to," the mayor said, patting her shoulder. "That's a copy."

"How did it happen?" Larry voiced the question on everyone's mind. "The town couldn't afford to buy it. Not at the price Makepeace must have asked."

"Do you want to tell them, Joie?"

Joie looked at the grinning Mayor Osweiler. She took a steadying breath. "Wyatt Landis."

"Wyatt Landis!" The mayor repeated with enthusiasm. "Can you believe it? That wonderful man bought the land then signed it over to all of us."

The noise rose from a buzz to a din. Everyone spoke at once; the excitement level practically rattling the café's windows.

"The papers were delivered to my office about an hour ago." Mayor Osweiler took the empty seat next to Carole. "Naturally, I didn't want to spread the word until I verified the information. While I was trying not to hyperventilate, my secretary phoned Wyatt's lawyer. The darling man—Wyatt, not the lawyer—had put this in motion almost two weeks ago. He used his connections to expedite all the formalities."

"I can't believe Brad agreed to sell." Carole looked as bemused as everyone else. "It must have cost a fortune."

"We'll never know. The amount has been redacted." The mayor carefully loosened Joie's grip, then took the paper, smoothing it out on the table. "See? There's a black line whenever the price is listed." She sighed with pleasure. "That dear boy. What could have motivated him to give us such an extravagant gift?"

It wasn't necessary for Joie to look around. She could feel all eyes on her. She met Carole's gaze, knowing what was coming.

"Idiot."

This time, Joie had to agree.

"Where are you going?" Carole asked as she grabbed her coat.

Joie was about to do something that at one time would have been unthinkable.

"I need some man advice. From my mother."

CHAPTER TWENTY-ONE

HIS OFFICE HADN'T changed. The décor was as tasteful as always. Browns, tans, and the occasional touch of green. It was soothing. Classic. Professional. And he realized, boring as hell. No, his office hadn't changed. But Wyatt had.

"You want to redecorate?"

By the look on his assistant's face, the news was not welcome. Derrick had overseen a complete remodel just over a year ago. But it had taken another six months of searching for the perfect accent pieces before he proclaimed the project finished.

There were those who thought Derrick was a bit of a control freak—especially Wyatt's brothers. The office was run with brutal efficiency. His attention to details made him invaluable. Derrick never hesitated to carry out Wyatt's orders. Until now.

"That's right. I want something warmer. With color."

"What kind of *color*?"

"I don't know." Wyatt looked around. "Figure it out. If you need help, call Mom. I like what she likes."

Derrick's eyes widened in horror. "As much as I admire your mother, I believe I can manage on my own."

Out of respect, and the desire to keep as much drama out of his office as possible, Wyatt refrained from laughing. But he couldn't help but smile as Derrick huffed out of the office. His first day back and already things were hopping.

There was a stack of contracts on his right and unread scripts on his left. Though he had kept up with his email and Derrick sorted through the business end, it seemed his inbox was always overflowing. There was so much to do and normally, that wouldn't be a problem. But his mind wasn't here. It was still in Monroe—with Joie.

The drive to Los Angeles had been uneventful, leaving him plenty of time to plot his next move. He didn't plan on giving Joie enough time to brood. Or fall back into a life without him in it.

What was technology for? Hundreds of miles separated them, but that didn't mean he couldn't speak to Joie every day. He could see her beautiful face whenever he wanted. She thought he would forget her the second he was back to his old life? Wyatt would prove her wrong. Over and over again.

It had been over twenty-four hours since that last kiss, and he could still feel her in his arms—still taste her on his lips. It wasn't desperate if he called her now. Wyatt mulled it over for a second. Nope, he decided. Not desperate at all. He was reaching the phone when his office door burst open

"There you are."

Colt never bothered to knock. It was a trait from their childhood. One that taught his brothers that a smart man locked his bedroom door unless he wanted to be caught in the middle of something embarrassing. It had been annoying when they were kids. Now, it simply made Wyatt laugh. In a flash, his brother skirted the desk, giving him a hearty hug.

"How did you get by Derrick?" Wyatt's assistant guarded his door with the devotion of a rabid Doberman.

"He wasn't there—much to my delight. Never mind that. Let me get a look at you."

Colt stood back. His blue eyes, so much like Wyatt's, scanned him from top to bottom. "You look good, Wyatt. Damn good." He nodded. "Yup."

"Yup? What does that mean?"

"It means I can't wait to meet your Joie. She has to be the reason you look so relaxed and rested." When Wyatt didn't correct him, Colt let out a whoop. "I knew it. When is she getting here?"

"She isn't."

"Please tell me you didn't fuck it up already."

"I did not." Wyatt didn't appreciate his brother taking sides against him when he didn't have the facts. As confusing as they might be.

"Joie likes it in Monroe."

"You didn't say I love you."

Wyatt groaned. Little brothers were a major pain in the ass—especially when they were right.

"Suddenly you're the expert?"

Crossing his arms over his chest, Colt sent him a smug smile. "Who do you think said it first? Me or Sable?"

"With your ego? You." Wyatt gave him a friendly shove, but put enough muscle behind it to send Colt sprawling onto the leather sofa. "You assume everyone loves you. Why should Sable be any different?"

"Because she matters more than anyone." Colt turned serious. "I knew Sable was the one for me long before she did. I wasn't sure how she felt, Wyatt. But I am now. I tell her every day. And it feels damn good when I hear it back."

"I told Joie that I was coming back." Wyatt hated that Colt had put him on the defensive. Everything had made perfect sense when he said it in his head. When he said it to someone else? Not so much.

"There was a blizzard yesterday."

"How do you know that?"

"Monroe, Nevada has been on my radar for some time. That tends to happen when my brother takes up residence there. When I heard about the snowstorm, I thought you might not make it out."

"It had just started when I left. The snow chased me for almost a hundred miles. And before you say it, this isn't *Seven Brides for Seven Brothers*, Colton. Joie isn't stuck in the mountains until the spring thaw."

"I like that movie," Colt grinned.

"Asshole."

"Maybe. But my woman is snug as a bug in our rug—so to speak. Where is yours?"

His woman. Wyatt liked that. Joie *was* his woman. And he planned on keeping it that way.

"I was about to find out." Wyatt picked up his phone. "Before you interrupted."

"Dial, man, dial." Colt headed for the door. "Mom expects you for dinner."

"I'll be there."

"And Wyatt?"

"What?" Wyatt said impatiently.

"Don't screw it up." Colt grinned when he saw Wyatt's eyes narrow. His brother knew from experience when he had pushed far enough. With a wave, Colt made his exit.

Don't screw it up. Don't screw it up.

Colt's words bounced through his brain as he pulled up Joie's number. Damn little brothers. He had spent his life contending with three of them. And the youngest of the bunch was the worst.

Wyatt waited, frowning when it went to voicemail. Joie was probably writing. It wasn't as though he expected her to sit around waiting for his call. Disappointed, he set aside his phone and got to work. It was no big deal. He would try her later.

WYATT PULLED HIS Bentley to a stop in the driveway of his parents' Beverly Hills home. Instead of heading in, he sat in the car, staring at his phone. Four calls. Four trips to voicemail. And no response from Joie. It was frustrating. And a little concerning. *More* than a little.

Common sense told him nothing was wrong. Joie was a big girl. She could take care of herself. Had done so every day of her adult life—long before they met. However, the memory of Dex's crazed ex-girlfriend kept floating through his subconscious. Bad things happened to good people. It was a nasty fact of life. Better that he looked like an overanxious fool than take any chances.

Picking up his phone, he hit speed dial.

"Wyatt! Long time no talk."

"Hello, Carole."

Wyatt felt his tension begin to ease. If Joie were lying in the hospital, her best friend wouldn't sound so chipper.

"We miss you already. That snowstorm did a number on the mayor's roof. And I can't tell you how many people have lamented that they couldn't call you to shovel their driveway."

"It looks like I got out of town just in time."

Carole laughed. "Amen, brother. Not that I object to hearing your dulcet tones. But to what do I owe the pleasure of your call?

"Joie isn't answering her phone."

"That's funny. I spoke to her this morning. No. I take that back. It was last night. The first snowstorm of the season always gets me a bit discombobulated."

"Then you haven't seen her today?"

"You're really worried." Carole chuckled. Wyatt ground his teeth. "That is so sweet. Seriously sweet. I was worried about you, Landis."

"Worried about what?"

"I thought I might have read your feelings wrong. But it hasn't been forty-eight hours, and you're chomping at the Joie bit. You do love her, don't you?"

"Carole…" Wyatt wasn't going there with Joie's best friend.

"I guarantee you will speak to her this evening."

"Guaranteed?"

"If I were a betting woman, I would stake my supply of hand-loomed Irish wool on it."

"I guess that's the best I can ask for."

"Hell, yes," Carole's voice rose an octave. "That wool cost an arm and a leg. And Wyatt?"

"Yes?"

"Don't you dare break her heart."

Wyatt took a deep breath. "What if she breaks mine?"

"*That* I can live with. But she won't."

Those few words lifted his spirits more than he would have thought possible.

"Take care, Carole. And tell Dex I said hello."

As Wyatt climbed out of his car, he checked his messages one more time. Nothing had changed in the last five minutes. No word from Joie. If Carole didn't make good on her promise, he was getting in his truck and heading east.

"There he is."

The second Wyatt stepped through the door, he was lifted off the ground. The arms that held him felt like thick bands of steel. In the past, he wouldn't have stood a chance of breaking their grip. But he had bulked up a bit since the last time his brother had ambushed him.

Wyatt had the element of surprise on his side. In a blink, he reversed positions, locking his arms around his stuntman brother.

"What the hell?" Nate wasn't used to having the tables turned on him. "Where did you learn that move?"

"From you." Wyatt laughed, turning the wrestling hold into a hug. "But this is the first time I had the muscle to pull it off."

"It's good to have you back, Wyatt." Nate was the younger brother, but he topped Wyatt by a good three inches. "What the hell have you been up to?"

Wyatt waited patiently while Nate measured his bicep with his hand.

"Are you finished?"

"Maybe." Nate pushed at Wyatt's midsection. "Impressive."

"Jesus." Wyatt slapped Nate's hand away. "I wasn't exactly flabby."

"No." As Colt had earlier, Nate circled him, checking out the differences. "You were lean. Like a runner. You're going to need to get your suit let out. It's a little tight on your arms and around the back."

Wyatt had noticed that when he dressed that morning. He would have Derrick make him an appointment with his tailor.

"Wyatt!"

"Hello, Sable."

With her short dark hair, high cheekbones, and slender figure, Colt's fiancée looked like a supermodel. But under her designer clothes, she had the badass skills of a superhero. She was the only person—man or woman—who Wyatt had ever seen knock Nate on his ass in a fair fight. For that reason alone, he would have loved her. The fact that she made Colt happy cemented the deal.

"You look rested. And happy." Sable said as they hugged, her dark eyes filled with understanding. Though Wyatt had sworn Colt to secrecy about Joie, this was the woman his brother loved. Naturally she knew everything Colt knew. As it should be. "We've missed you."

"Speak for yourself."

"There is my favorite pain in the ass director," Wyatt grinned, hugging Garrett. He and Nate were twins, but not identical. However, they had shared a womb. There were times when they seemed to think as one.

"You need to get this suit tailored, Wyatt. Did you get fat while on vacation?"

Almost as one.

"It's all muscle," Sable observed. When Wyatt raised his eyebrows, she shrugged. "I could tell when you hugged me."

"Let's drop the subject. Please." He turned to Garrett. "Where's Jade?"

"She'll be along. She had a late meeting at the center."

Jade Marlow ran a place for abused women to get together and talk. She knew from bitter experience how important it was to find support from those who knew what others had been through—and survived.

"And Paige?" Wyatt inquired about Nate's fiancée.

"Out by the pool with Beauty. That puppy won't pass water without jumping in. I was on my way to change into my trunks when you arrived."

"Damn it."

The exclamation came from the kitchen.

258

"Was that Lorena?" Rather than wait for an answer, Wyatt went to see for himself. The others followed behind.

The longtime Landis cook stood by the sink, her hands resting on her ample hips. Lorena Secord had been with his parents longer than he had. She was more a member of the family than an employee. And her food could make the angels sing.

"Is there a problem, beautiful?"

"Hello, my dear boy." Lorena patted his cheek—a sign of affection he had treasured since he was a little boy. Distracted, she looked at the water-filled sink.

"It's clogged." Frustrated, Lorena stomped her foot. "Your mother wants tonight to be perfect. How can I do anything when my sink doesn't drain, and there isn't a plumber within twenty miles who is available until tomorrow morning?"

"What's so special about tonight?"

"How should I know?" Lorena threw up her hands. "I'm the cook, not the social secretary."

Wyatt sent Garrett a questioning look. His brother sent one back that said, *hell if I know what's going on.*

"Colt. Go get the tools from the trunk of my car." Wyatt took off his jacket and rolled up his sleeves. "Don't worry, Lorena. I'm certain it's nothing serious. Let me take a look."

"Excuse me?" Nate exclaimed. "Is this the same guy who can't clean the lint trap in a clothes dryer?"

"I can," Wyatt informed him as he took a towel and laid it under the sink. "I choose not to. I prefer to send my laundry out."

"I would love to stick around and watch you flood Mom's kitchen, but I see enough muck and mayhem when I'm filming a stunt. Paige in a bikini holds much more appeal. Good luck, Wyatt." Nate's laughter trailed behind him.

"This thing weighs a ton," Colt panted as he returned with Wyatt's tool box. With a dramatic flourish, he hoisted it onto the counter. "Here you go, Josephine."

Wyatt simply stared.

"You know," Cole urged. "Josephine? The plumber? Come on. Those old TV commercials?"

"Colt. My love. My darling." Sable rubbed his back. "I've told you. If a joke has to be explained, chances are it isn't funny in the first place."

"You're good for him," Garrett told Sable. "Before you, women always laughed at Colt's jokes. That's why he thinks he's stand-up comedian material."

"I'm funny," Colt grumbled.

"Yes," Sable nodded with a straight face. "But only in bed."

Colt grinned. "You weren't laughing this morning when I—"

Sable slapped a hand over his mouth. "Don't you dare!"

Kissing her palm, Colt pulled her to him, whispering something for her ears only. Whatever he said elicited a laugh and a blush.

Ignoring his little brother's antics, Garrett turned to Wyatt, shaking his head in amazement. "Where did you get that?"

Wyatt patted the red box. "I had a productive month."

"I can't wait to hear about it. Come on, kid. Enough of the canoodling." Garrett grabbed Colt around the neck. "Let's go play some pool. But Sable has to sit this one out. I'm tired of getting schooled every time she picks up a cue."

"Party pooper." Sable gave Wyatt a quick peck on the cheek before trailing after Colt and Garrett. "Good luck."

"Are you certain you want to do this?" Lorena looked skeptical.

"Have you ever known me to screw up?" When Lorena would have answered, Wyatt quickly added, "Since I became an adult."

With a resigned sigh, Lorena untied her apron. "I trust you, darling boy. But I have a soft spot for this place. I would rather not watch. If you need me, I'll be in the garden."

"Do we have a bucket?" he asked before she left.

"In the pantry."

His family's confidence was underwhelming, but Wyatt didn't let it bother him. He had never been Mr. Fixit. They would find out soon enough that he had the skills to back up his words.

In no time, Wyatt removed the elbow joint and had the clog removed. The dirty sink water was in the bucket, ready to be thrown out and with a few efficient turns of his wrench, the pipe was tightly back in place.

"Not bad if I do say so myself." Wyatt slid from beneath the sink. Taking the towel, he dried up the last bit of moisture. "And they didn't think I could do it."

"I never doubted you for a second."

Wyatt froze. The easy thing would have been to shoot to his feet, probably knock his head against the cabinet in the process. Instead, he calmly stood.

"Joie?"

He wasn't hearing things. Or hallucinating. There she stood. In his mother's kitchen.

"Nice suit." Joie held up his jacket. "I've never seen you in your real world clothes. You look—right."

That was how she wanted to play it? Cool and calm? Okay. He could do that.

"Nice dress."

Joie's lips twitched. And Wyatt knew everything was going to be all right.

"You've seen me in a dress."

"Never one like that." He circled her—slowly—taking in the way the dark blue sheath molded her body like a second skin. Some might call the hemline demure because it ended just above her knees. But the slit in the back that traveled halfway up her thighs blew demure to hell. "Sweetheart, that is one serious fashion statement."

Eyes twinkling, her gaze followed his every move. "What does it say?"

Wyatt stopped behind her, his hand going to her waist. Leaning close, he whispered, "Bend me over and fuck my brains out?"

Joie gasped. He knew that sound. She liked his suggestion. He kissed the side of her neck. This time, she rewarded him with a quiet moan.

"This is a bad idea."

Wyatt pulled her closer until her back was flush against him. "How long has it been since I touched you?"

"Forever." Joie took his hand and brought it to her lips. "But we can't do this here."

"You're right. Let's go."

Joie tripped when he tried to maneuver her toward the front door, her high heels catching on the tile floor. Without breaking stride, Wyatt swept her into his arms.

"Stop," she laughed. "What will your mother say if we disappear?"

"Have you met her?"

Joie nodded. "We spent a lovely afternoon together. I need to get her lemonade recipe."

Wyatt kissed her. When he lifted his head, he licked his lips. "It is damn fine lemonade." Changing direction, he walked through the kitchen. "Is Mom outside?"

"Yes. Wyatt. Put me down." Joie pushed at his shoulder, but he kept walking.

The French doors that led to the patio were ajar, making it easy for Wyatt to push through. There he found his family enjoying the mild evening. Flowers bloomed in every corner, a riot of color that rivaled his mother's pretty flowing dress.

"Wyatt!"

Callie Flynn. Screen goddess. Respected actress. Even in bare feet and no makeup, she was the most beautiful woman Joie had ever seen. She rushed across the patio to greet her oldest son as though it was an everyday occurrence for him to walk in with a woman in his arms.

"Hello, gorgeous."

Wyatt held Joie with one arm, hugging his mother with the other. He kissed Callie's cheek.

"I see you found Joie."

"Is it possible to die of embarrassment?" Joie murmured, closing her eyes.

"Do you mind if we skip dinner?"

"Of course not." Callie patted Joie's hand. "We don't mind, do we, darling?"

"Not at all."

"Oh my God. Is that your father?"

"You haven't met?" Wyatt asked matter-of-factly. "Dad, this is Joie. Joie, my father, Caleb Landis."

"Nice to meet you." Caleb nodded. "Drive carefully, Wyatt. And bring Joie here for lunch tomorrow. We'll get acquainted."

"Will do. Good night, everybody."

With a happy sigh, Callie watched her oldest leave. Knowing it would be there, she reached for Caleb's hand.

"Did you see him?"

Caleb brought her hand to his lips. "I did."

"He looks like Wyatt again." Callie rested her head on her husband's shoulder. "With an added verve."

"Love will do that to a man."

"And a woman. I like her." She turned her famous grey eyes toward Caleb. "Wyatt's Joie. She'll be good for him."

"Already planning the wedding?" After over thirty years, Caleb knew his wife well.

"No." Callie grinned when she saw his expression. "Surprised?"

"A little. You didn't hesitate with our other sons."

"Wyatt suffered through the big wedding with Stephanie."

Caleb shuddered at the memory. "We all did."

"Something tells me that this time, he will want something small and private. And Joie will agree."

"Because?"

Tears filled Callie's eyes. After so long. After so much pain. Wyatt had the one thing she always wished for him and all her boys.

"Because she loves him."

CHAPTER TWENTY-TWO

"WHAT JUST HAPPENED?"

"I carried you to my car."

Wyatt had placed her in the passenger seat, made certain she was buckled in, then drove off. Where they were going Joie had no idea. Their destination wasn't a high priority at the moment.

"While your family watched." Joie could feel the heat bloom on her cheeks. "I will never be able to look your mother in the eye again."

"If my mother had a problem with what I did—or with you—she would have said so."

"But—"

"Relax. You have been given the Callie Landis seal of approval."

"How do you know?"

"Experience."

"She approved of Jade, Paige, and Sable."

"Yes," Wyatt nodded.

"But not Stephanie." It wasn't a question.

"My mother saw through Stephanie in a heartbeat. But there was a baby involved. We were all stuck."

Wyatt turned, starting up a hill. The sign read Mulholland Drive.

"Wyatt—"

"I'm taking you to my house. I bought it a year and a half ago."

"Good."

After Stephanie had died. That was all Joie needed to know. She didn't want to be with him in *their* house. It would have felt wrong.

"Start talking, Joie."

"What would you like to know?"

"This time of night, with these roads, it takes about thirty minutes to reach my house. The second we walk in the door talking will be off the table for the next twelve hours or so."

"What about dirty talk?"

"I stand corrected." Wyatt shot her a heated look. "I'll start. I left you in Monroe yesterday morning…"

Without missing a beat, Joie picked up the story. "By the afternoon, the snow was coming down in earnest. I didn't feel like being alone so I went to the *Monarch Café*. Half the town had the same idea."

Joie told Wyatt about Mayor Osweiler's dramatic entrance and the stir that was caused by his gift to the town.

"Please tell me that isn't the reason you're here."

"It is not," she assured him. "But it was outrageously generous, Wyatt. There was talk of erecting a statue in your honor. Someone threw out the suggestion that you should be portrayed bare-chested and holding a hammer. I have no idea what they decided."

"What made you decide to come?"

"My mother." Seeing his expression, Joie smiled. "You aren't the only one surprised. When it comes to men, she has given plenty of advice. But I have never asked. Mom was born wearing rose-colored glasses. They have never slipped. Not once. Until now."

"She told you *not* follow me to Los Angeles?"

"*Don't be a fool, Joie.*" Joie used her mother's sing-song voice. "*If he comes back, you'll know he's serious. Wait. What do you have to lose?*"

"I was coming back, Joie. Soon."

"I know."

"Not that I'm complaining." Wyatt took her hand, kissing the palm. "I wouldn't wish you any place but here. Tell me why you didn't take your mother's advice?"

"Because I knew exactly what I had to lose."

"Tell me."

"Time. I don't want to miss a second, Wyatt." Joie took a deep breath, ready to say the words.

"I love you, Joie."

"Damn it, Wyatt. That's what I was going to say."

"Should I apologize for stealing your thunder?"

Wyatt grinned. Even in the dim glow of the streetlights, Joie could see the twinkle in his beautiful blue eyes. She had pictured the moment differently. More romance and less laughter. She found that she liked this version better.

"I love you."

Joie heard the hitch in Wyatt's breathing. "Say it again."

"I love you, Wyatt Landis."

"Perfect timing."

Wyatt pulled into the garage, parking next to the old pickup truck.

"You're keeping it?" For some reason, the knowledge sent a jolt of pleasure through her.

"That truck is priceless." Opening her door, Wyatt lifted her into his arms. "It led me to you."

Joie wound her arms around Wyatt's neck. She hadn't given up a thing to follow Wyatt. She had taken a leap of faith—and gained everything.

EPILOGUE

CHAMPAGNE-FILLED GLASSES sat on the living room table surrounded by a large rose-filled vase. In the center sat six gold statues. Tonight the Landis clan had set a record for the most Academy Awards ever won by a single family.

"Seven counting Nate's." Caleb toasted his son.

A week earlier, Nate had received the first ever Academy Award for Excellence in Stunt Work. The entire family had been there when his name was called.

"I didn't win for *Left of Mayfield*. However, since Wyatt produced *The Last Bank Job,* it was still a family affair."

"You earned that award all on your own," Wyatt said, hugging his brother. "I'm proud of you."

"I agree with Wyatt," Paige kissed her husband. "You deserved it. I still shudder when I think of you hanging off that moving train."

"I was never in any danger."

Wyatt laughed. *Bullshit*. Nate was the best stuntman out there. However, there was always an element of danger in what he did. Paige knew it. It was something she was willing to live with because she loved him.

"Now it's my turn." Nate raised his glass. "To Joie. The woman who wrote *Left of Mayfield*. And congratulations on your Oscar for Best Adapted Screenplay."

"I second that." Wyatt clinked his glass against Joie's. Before he drank, he gave her a lingering kiss.

Joie's had been the first of their wins tonight. That was followed by Best Actress for Callie. Colton won for Best Actor. Garrett took the award for Best Director. Then *Left of Mayfield* won the big one. Best Picture. As producers, Wyatt and his father had accepted the honor. But it had been a family affair from start to finish.

They had left behind the after parties and endless interviews, gathering where they always came together—Callie and Caleb's home. It was where they raised their family with love and laughter. And watched with joy as it grew. Four sons. Four smart, caring, beautiful women who made them happy.

Wyatt looked around at his brothers. As boys, they had shared everything. It was only right that they were together, sharing this evening. He was a lucky man. He felt Joie take his hand. No. Not lucky. He looked at her smiling face and felt the familiar twinge near his heart. He was blessed.

"I need some air."

"That sounds good."

They left the rest of the family and made their way to the patio. Wyatt frowned. He hadn't realized it had gotten so chilly. He removed his jacket and draped it over Joie's shoulders.

"Such a gentleman."

"When the mood strikes." He smiled, brushing her mouth with the pad of his thumb.

Joie had abandoned her high heels the second they walked in the door. She had removed the pins that held up her hair, letting the long dark tresses fall down her back. But that didn't stop her from looking like she had just stepped off the cover of a magazine.

"I'm glad you picked the yellow dress."

"I could tell it was your favorite."

As soon as the Academy Award nominations were announced, designers had lined up for the privilege of dressing Joie for the occasion. She had narrowed her choices down to her three favorites, then asked for Wyatt's opinion. He had told her that he liked them all. But she knew him well. He preferred when she wore color. And yellow fit her perfectly. Bright and sunny.

"Men have it easy. A tux is a tux is a tux."

"Meaning it's the man who makes the tuxedo. And my man outshined everyone else."

"Don't tell Colt that. His ego couldn't take it."

Joie laughed. She wrapped her arms around him, resting her head on his chest.

"How are you feeling?"

"Great." She took his hand and placed it on her still flat stomach. "My mother claims she was sick for nine months straight. Your mom told me she sailed through all three of her pregnancies without a nauseous moment. So far, I'm with Callie."

Sometimes Wyatt was afraid he would wake and find that none of this was real. Joie was his wife. And pregnant with his child.

Wyatt and Joie had been married right here in his parents' backyard. It had been a quiet, intimate ceremony—just as Callie predicted. Not long after, Joie had broached the subject of children. She had done so cautiously, not wanting to hurt him with the reminder of what he had lost.

However, Wyatt hadn't hesitated. He wanted a family. A family with Joie. Deciding to let Mother Nature take her course, they had stopped using birth control. With that relaxed attitude, they were able to simply enjoy each other without any pressure.

A month ago, Joie announced that she was pregnant. Their first child would be born in October. The month in which they had first met. To Wyatt, it felt like perfect symmetry.

Wyatt ran his hand over Joie's belly and his growing child. He knew this happened every day. For him, it was a miracle. The baby he had lost would always be in his heart. The little girl that he would never know. But he believed she would understand that he had enough love for *all* of his children.

"Did you ever dream we would end up here?" Joie rested her hand over his. She met his gaze, all her love right there for him to see.

"I thought I would never find this." His kiss was tender, holding a promise for tomorrow. Forever. "Thank you, Joie. For being my best friend. For loving me—faults and all. And for teaching me to dream again."

COMING IN DECEMBER

DREAMING OF A WHITE CHRISTMAS
HOLLYWOOD LEGENDS BOOK FIVE

Caleb and Callie's story

COMING IN AUGUST
FLOWERS ON THE WALL
(Hart of Rock and Roll Book One)

PROLOGUE

COUNTING FLOWERS ON the wall. That don't bother me at all. Playing solitaire 'til dawn. With a deck of fifty-one.

He hated the song. It was the music that nightmares were set to. When the first familiar note pounded through the broken down trailer, he knew what it meant. Their fragile peace was at an end.

Smokin' cigarettes and watching Captain Kangaroo. Now, don't tell me. I've nothin' to do.

When he was younger—still innocent enough to believe that this time would be different—he would cover his head with his pillow and pretend the music hadn't started. He didn't have to worry about his sister. At least he knew she would be fine. She was practically a baby and blessedly, the monster left her alone.

He was the one it sought out. *He* was the one who felt its wrath.

Was it a joke that the walls of his tiny room were covered daisies? The faded wallpaper made his skin crawl. Taking it down wasn't an option. He had tried. The scars in his hand had been his punishment. Or—as the monster put it—his reward for being such a clever little boy.

Counting flowers on the wall. That don't bother me at all.

"I need my little boy." The voice was sing-songy, and though the words were slurred, they were unmistakable.

The bedroom door slammed open.

"There he is." The monster grabbed his arm, jerking him out of bed. His breath was foul. Sour from cheap whiskey and stale cigarettes. "Come keep daddy company."

"I have school tomorrow."

He knew the slap was coming. Not across the face. Teachers noticed when he showed up for class with a swollen lip. The monster knew better. He aimed low where they would be covered by long sleeved shirts or blue jeans.

"What good is school? Don't I teach you everything you need to know? How to pour a drink. How to light my stogie?" The monster took his cigar from his mouth, blowing on the end until it glowed red. "How to put it out?"

The hot tip hovered near his face. Closing his eyes, he waited for the pain.

"Nope. I'm not done with it yet" The monster threw him through the door, his teeth holding the cigar as he unbuckled his belt. Eyes narrowing, his slowly slid the leather from the loops around his waist, then slapped it against his hand.

"Why?" Asking never helped. The answer didn't hurt as much as the belt. But it was close.

"Why?" the monster jeered, slowly advancing. "Because I can."

AFTER THE RAIN
(One Pass Away Book One)

PROLOGUE

LOGAN. LOGAN. LOGAN.

Logan Price closed his eyes, taking it all in.

"Hear that, kid?" Starting quarterback Gaige Benson slapped him on the back. "Two games under your belt and you're a star. Now let's go out there and add super to the front of it."

The announcer for the team set them in motion down the tunnel with his familiar introduction.

"And now, let's hear it for your division champion *SEATTLE KNIGHTS*."

The roar of the crowd. There was nothing like it. A packed stadium. Fans chanting his name. Few people would ever experience what it was like to take the field in a professional football game.

Logan Price had been working for this his entire life. He could still remember in exact detail the first game he ever saw. Too small to climb onto the stool in his father's bar by himself, his old man had lifted him onto the seat.

Stay and be quiet.

Not an easy order to follow for an active, inquisitive little boy. One look at the game and for once, Logan had no problem following his father's command. The old TV transported him to a foreign world filled with bright lights and shiny helmeted warriors. Logan didn't know what he was watching. He did know he wanted to be one of those men.

A Sunday afternoon in rural Oklahoma. *Lefty's Pub* was filled with after-church drinkers who figured they had done their duty to God and family. The rest of the day was their time. A beer. Or two. Or six. Cronies who understood a man's need to unwind before the start of another workweek.

And football.

If the Friday night high school game was their true religion, the Sunday afternoon games were a close second. As Oklahoma boys, they hated anything Texas. The men of Denville gathered every week to root for whichever team was playing the Dallas Cowboys.

No matter how the games ended. Whether the crowd was happy or disgruntled. It meant more drinking. Hours later, husbands, boyfriends, and sons would stumble out, pile into beat-up trucks, and weave their way home to frustrated wives, girlfriends, and mothers.

As he grew older, Logan's view changed. He moved from the stool to behind the bar. And he promised himself one thing. He would never become one of those men. He wouldn't spend the week at a job he hated. His home wouldn't be a semi-wide trailer filled with hand-me-down furniture and a wife to whom he couldn't face going home.

His Sundays were going to be spent playing football, not watching it.

"Ready to take down this vaunted Arizona defense?" Gaige yelled at him, butting helmets.

Vaunted. Good word, Logan thought. His QB liked to use what his granny called highfalutin talk. Must have been that Ivy League education. He knew that Gaige Benson didn't grow up with a silver spoon in his mouth. He came from the mean streets of Brooklyn. He had the scars to prove it.

Like Logan, Gaige had vowed to get out of the life into which he was born. In the process, he polished himself up like a new penny. He took advantage of his full-ride scholarship to Yale. He didn't spend all his time on the football field. Fancy vocabulary. Fancy clothes. Fancy women. They were all part of the package Gaige purposefully fashioned for himself.

Seventeen years after clawing his way out of the tenement that he grew up in, very little of that borough-rat remained. Until game time. No one was tougher than Gaige Benson. Three-time league MVP. Considered one of the best ever to play the game. No one stood in his way when he was playing the game. He had the scars to prove it.

"Gather round."

Knights head coach Harry Coleman gathered the team close. He had to yell over the crowd, but he had the voice to do it. Booming was putting it mildly. The first time Logan heard it, he stood right beside the man. The ringing in his ears didn't go away for three days.

"Divisional game. If I have to say any more than that, you shouldn't be out here. Go kick some ass."

The defense took the field to start the game. Arizona had a rookie quarterback drafted in the second round from a small college in the Midwest. The only reason he was out there was because the regular starter suffered a concussion in last week's game and the regular backup had food poisoning. Thrown into action at the last minute, Logan swore he could see the guy's hands shaking before he took the first snap. When the ball went sailing between his legs, Logan shook his head.

The moment was too big for some people. For Logan, it wasn't big enough. He aimed for the biggest stage of all. The Super Bowl. It wasn't a matter of *if* he would get there, but when.

"Three and out." Gaige grinned, pulling on his helmet. "Come on, kid. Let's go show them how it's done."

Logan ran onto the field. *Kid.* He shook his head, grinning. From the first day of training camp, Gaige had hung that moniker on him. Ironic since he was almost twenty-five, a good two years older than most of the other rookies. However, he supposed when someone had been in the league as long as Gaige, all the new guys seemed like kids.

"We're starting on the ground," Gaige instructed them in the huddle. "Sweep out left. Basic. Got it?"

Lining up as he had a thousand other times, Logan checked the defense. He knew he was fast. One of the fastest in the game. What set him apart was his anticipation. He had the uncanny ability to read the guy covering him. He knew when to fake left or when to fake right. Stutter step or flat out, in your face, catch me if you can.

His speed got him out of Denville, Oklahoma. His brains and determination got him to the NFL.

The sounds of the game were as familiar to Logan as the back of his own hand. The call from scrimmage. Each quarterback had his own unique cadence. Gaige was a master of mixing his up. Study him all you want. Good luck figuring it out. His teammates knew. A signal just before they broke the huddle.

Pay attention, you were golden. Slack off even once? Gaige could ream a guy out with the best of them. And he had no problem doing it in the middle of the game.

An entire YouTube channel had been devoted to Gaige and his rants. They were as legendary as the man himself. With a ball in his hand, he was cool as ice. The rest of the time, watch out.

No one would ever accuse Logan of lacking focus. Today was no exception. They were driving down the field. First and ten from the Arizona twenty-yard line. He already had three carries of thirty-five yards. It was going to be a good day.

"Ready to take it in?" Gaige asked.

"Always."

"Then show them what you've got."

A quick snap later, Gaige handed the ball to Logan. The offensive line created a seam. Not a big one. Just big enough. Using the push of his powerful legs, Logan surged through. One more step. They wouldn't catch him. No one could.

Like everything connected with the game, Logan heard the snap of the bone with total clarity. The agony that surged through his body was so intense he almost passed out. In the next few minutes, he was going to wish he had.

"Get back." Logan heard Gaige through the haze of pain. "Goddamn it. Move the hell off."

The three-hundred-and-fifty-pound linebacker didn't get off by standing. He rolled. Crushing Logan's broken leg as he went. He would never know if the move had been deliberate. Now, it was the last thing on his mind. He only cared about two things. How bad was the injury and when would he be able to play again.

"Hold on, kid." Gaige took his hand. "They're bringing the stretcher."

The team doctor checked his eyes. Logan knew he was asked some questions. What they were and how he answered, he would never remember. By the time they carted him off the field, Logan knew the break was bad.

"Gaige." Logan reached for him.

"I'm here, kid."

"Is it over?"

"The game?" Gaige walked with him, his head bent toward Logan. "No. But I promise we're going to win the bastard."

They loaded him onto the open cart. They had him secured and the vehicle rolled away before Logan had his answer. He wasn't wondering about the game. It was his career.

To no one in particular, he whispered the question again.

"Is it over?"

AFTER ALL THESE YEARS
(One Pass Away Book Two)

PROLOGUE

SEAN McBRIDE WOKE up with a smile on his face. It happened a lot lately. And he thoroughly approved.

He stretched his long, athletic body. Some mornings every inch of him ached. Such was the life of a professional football player. Everything was about preparing for the game. Focus. Concentration. The goal was to be ready for game day.

He had to hold it together for sixty minutes. Pull out a win any way possible. Sacrifice his body to the football Gods and pray he walked away healthy enough to do it all again next week.

Sean dreaded the day after the game. The adrenaline had long ago worn off and he felt all of his thirty years. There were degrees of bad. Sometimes he shuffled to the shower, the aches and pains palpable, but mercifully bearable.

Then there were the bad days. After a day of three-hundred-pound defensive backs using him as their own personal punching bag, he didn't get out of bed—he crawled.

Bruised from top to bottom, his joints creaked and his muscles protested like screeching banshees. Those were the times he wondered why he did it. He could have been a doctor. Or a lawyer. He could have taken his father's advice and gone into the family business. No seventeen-year-old with dreams of glory in the NFL wanted to think about becoming a butcher. But damn. Cutting meat sounded good on those mornings.

This was a good Monday. His body felt lithe—limber. The bruises were there. That was part of his life. However, yesterday had been one of those rare games when every moment fell into place.

From the kickoff to the final whistle, the outcome of the game was never in question.

Sean caught every ball thrown his way. He evaded the defense. Fast as the wind. Three touchdowns. One hundred and eighty-two total yards. A damn good day for any wide receiver. He would have had more if Coach Coleman hadn't taken him out of the game in the fourth quarter. With a big lead, there was no reason to risk injury when he wasn't needed.

The after-game celebration moved from the locker room to one of the team's favorite hangouts. Naturally the atmosphere was raucous. Cautiously so.

The Knights were having a stellar season. Ten wins, two losses. Sean and his friends had enough games under their belts to understand how quickly that could turn. Injuries tended to come in bunches. So far, they were healthy. However, that was bound to change. The hope was to get to the playoffs with all their major players on the roster.

After the game, they had a few drinks. Three was Sean's limit these days. A few years ago it was a different story. He would have closed the place down after a win. He and his bed partner of the moment would have moved on to someone's apartment, partying until dawn before going back to her place and fucking like demented rabbits. Then he would go home alone and catch a few hours sleep until it was time to grab a quick shower before heading to the Knights' headquarters to review film from the game.

Those days were over. Sean wasn't a kid anymore, high on his own press clippings and more testosterone than brains. Not that he had settled down completely. He could still party with the best of them. However, he chose his moments—ones that never took place during the season.

Women were another matter. Sean liked sex. Always had. If there were a God, he always would. While his bed partners weren't as varied, they were almost as frequent.

Sean knew players who abstained a few days before the game, saving their *juice*. He wasn't one of them. Sean had plenty of juice, thank you very much. Sex was necessary for a happy and healthy mind. For *his* happy and healthy mind.

A big plus to having sex at night was sex the next morning. It was one of his favorite things. A partner, warm and willing.

The perfect way to start the day.

Speaking of which. Smiling, Sean turned over. His hand reached out, expecting to find a soft, sweet woman. Instead, he found cold sheets. Sitting up, he looked around the room. Like the bed, empty. The bathroom door was open and the light off.

Not bothering to cover up, Sean jumped out of bed. Buck naked, he searched the house. She wasn't in the kitchen. Why would she be? She didn't cook, not even coffee. She was on a first-name basis with half the baristas in Seattle.

Was that it? Would she be back soon with two cups of steaming black caffeine and his favorite muffins? Sean was talking himself into that scenario when he saw the note.

He picked up the paper that had been propped against the lamp by the front door.

Sean.

Thank you for the past few weeks. After years of building it up in my mind, I was worried that it couldn't live up to my expectations. I should have known better. It was everything I had hoped for—and more.

We didn't make any promises. No strings were attached that need to be broken. After all these years, you can finally breathe easy. It's over. We are now friends without the expectation of benefits.

When we see each other, it will be as if it, we, never happened.

Sean read the note. Then read it again.

What the fuck? What was in those drinks?

Sean searched his memory for some kind of clue. The bar. His teammates. Then she was there. They laughed. Everything was smooth and easy. They seemed to be developing a rhythm. In his mind, they were together. Not a man and a woman—a couple.

It sounded good to him. He would have sworn she felt the same. He didn't want another woman. He wanted her. In his arms. In his life.

No expectations? Hell. He woke up with plenty of them, only to find out he was alone. Alone in bed. Alone. Period.

Sean scrubbed a hand over his face. He remembered the way she tasted. The way she melted into his arms. The curves of her luscious body pressed against his. Her sighs. His belief he would never get enough of her.

Crumpling the note into a ball, Sean tossed it across the room. Suddenly he felt every ache. His legs felt like lead. Slowly, he shuffled toward the bathroom. He needed a shower. Long and hot. Determined not to look at the bed, Sean's peripheral vision wouldn't let him off the hook that easily. It captured everything. The rumpled sheet. The pillow still holding the imprint of her head. A slash of red on the floor.

Frowning, Sean picked up the scrap of silk. So small he wondered why she had bothered. The image of her standing in nothing but her heels and the panties popped into his head. Unconsciously, his body tightened with desire.

Right, that was why.

Sean ran the smooth material over his cheek, feeling it catch on his morning stubble. He breathed deeply. He smelled vanilla and spice. Her essence. He would never forget it. As long as he lived, he would be able to close his eyes and conjure up her scent. Her taste.

His eyes popped open. *Friends? Nothing more? Bullshit!*

Keeping the panties in his hand, Sean headed for the shower. This wasn't over. Not by a long shot. It was just the beginning.

AFTER THE FIRE
(One Pass Away Book Three)

PROLOGUE

SHE HAD ONCE asked him if he believed in a higher power.

God? Buddha? Fairies dancing around a blazing fire late at night? Something. Anything bigger than us.

Gaige Benson hadn't known what to say. Not then. But as he stood in the empty open-air stadium—the stars lighting the evening sky—he knew the answer.

Football was his religion. The field he played on and the building surrounding it, his cathedral. If a higher power had a hand in it, then his answer was yes.

He believed.

Walking to the center of the field, Gaige took it all in. He found football at the age of thirteen. A boy who saw his future mapped out. Working in a factory. Drinking away his salary. Divorce. Doling out child support without maintaining a relationship with his children. A weekend father, who half the time didn't bother to show up.

The first time Gaige picked up a football, he felt a connection. The first time he threw it, it wobbled with the grace of a drunk leaving his favorite watering hole on a Saturday night. But it didn't matter. He threw the ball again. And again. Until he taught himself to make it spin in a perfect spiral.

At the time, Gaige didn't know his talent could be useful. Where he came from, Brooklyn kids didn't dream of bigger or better. Most of them didn't dream at all. Gaige was no different.

One day he was passing a playground when a football landed at his feet. The boys on the field yelled for him to toss it back. Without thinking, Gaige sent it sailing, a perfect strike. Then kept walking. He was wary of the man who ran after him. Strangers were the enemy—according to his father. They either wanted money or accused you of something you hadn't done.

Gaige took everything his father said with a big grain of salt. Don Benson didn't have a dime to his name. Why would anyone expect to get money from him? And if a man accused his father of something, chances were he was guilty.

But Gaige was a cautious boy. He fought when necessary and ran when he had no choice. The man trying to get his attention was big. His dark complexion didn't worry Gaige. In his experience, a man was either good or bad. The color of his skin had nothing to do with it.

It turned out that this man wasn't simply good. He was the best thing that ever happened to Gaige.

Terrance Aldridge coached the local Pop Warner football team. A boy with an arm like Gaige's shouldn't let his talent go to waste. Gaige listened. Play football? On a field? With other boys? Was such a thing possible? He didn't know if it were a scam—nor did he care. If there were the slightest chance, he would take it.

The only obstacle was getting a parent's permission. Terrance gave him the papers to be signed, telling Gaige to have his folks call him if they had any questions. Gaige didn't laugh aloud, but he wanted to. His mother never asked questions. Unless they were directed at his father. Wynona Benson hadn't made a move in fifteen years unless she received permission first.

His father was another matter. His word was law. Don Benson could do no wrong. If he drank too much and staggered home two days late, it was his right. If he backhanded his wife—just because—whose business was it? He earned the money. He made the rules. End of discussion.

Gaige hadn't asked his father because he knew what the answer would be. No! Not because he thought there was anything wrong with football. He watched it every Sunday—after laying down a bet that he never won. No, he wouldn't let Gaige play because he was a mean bastard who wanted everyone to be as miserable as he was.

Gaige got around it easily enough. He forged his father's signature. It wasn't the first time and it wouldn't be the last. There was no reason to think anyone would find out. His parents didn't care how he spent his days as long as the police didn't come knocking on the door.

He could steal. Lie. Cheat. Hell, his father wouldn't bat an eye at murder. *Do what you want as long as you don't get caught.* The mantra at the Benson house.

Gaige had no intention of his father finding out. He tried out for the team and made it. The money for equipment was another matter. Gaige didn't steal. Or cheat. Lying was a necessary evil. He would have done almost anything to play but it looked like his first and only dream would die before it had a chance.

Luckily, Terrance was able to dip into a discretionary fund to help boys like Gaige. It rankled to take charity. Especially when the other boys on the team had families to pay their way.

"Don't let it stop you, Gaige," Terrance told him. "Remember. And one day, when you have the means, pay it forward, son."

Twenty-five years later, Gaige hadn't forgotten that kindness and generosity. When he saw someone in need, he did something about it. Over the years, the *Gaige Benson Foundation* paid out millions of dollars to charities and individuals. He had filled the board with people he trusted and could count on to distribute the funds judiciously and without prejudice. The first man he had recruited was the man to whom Gaige owed everything—Terrance Aldridge. Friend. Father figure. Teacher.

"Hey, Gaige." Logan Price called out from high in the stands. "You coming? The guys are waiting to go to dinner."

"Five minutes."

Closing his eyes, Gaige breathed in the air. February in Texas. Tomorrow he would play in his first—and last Super Bowl. Win or lose, he was hanging up his cleats. He was thirty-eight years old. He had more money than he would ever need. He had won every award from Rookie of the Year to league MVP—four times.

This season he put everything on the line to get here—including the possibility that he had lost the only woman he had ever loved.

Gaige Benson was known for his razor-sharp focus. Any distractions off the field were left there as soon as the first whistle blew. It wouldn't be any different tomorrow. Nothing would get in the way.

His gaze drifted to the section where she would be sitting. If she showed up. Gaige planned on going out a winner. But what about the day after? Or the day after that? His future stretched out in front of him. He had plans in place. There were hundreds of options for him to consider.

Do you believe in a higher power?

Her voice and that question had haunted Gaige for almost sixteen years. If there were a God, he prayed the woman he loved would find it in her heart to forgive him. He had a lot of years left. He didn't want to spend them alone.

In his lifetime, Gaige Benson had dreamt of only two things. Playing football. And loving Violet Reed.

DREAMING WITH A BROKEN HEART
(Hollywood Legends Book One

PROLOGUE

THE ROOM WAS dark. Too dark for Garrett's liking. A little stuffy, a slight antiseptic smell with an overlay of sex. That's what you got from a cheap motel and furtive lovemaking. Odors and memories you'd just as soon forget.

The sounds from behind the closed bathroom door indicated his partner was trying to remove all traces of their recent activities. It shouldn't hurt. This wasn't the first time, and damn his weak resolve, it wouldn't be the last.

If he smoked, he would have something to do with his hands. Watching his father struggle with lung cancer put the fear of God in him and his brothers at an early age. All four of them had their vices; smoking wasn't one of them.

Get up. Get dressed. For once, be the first to leave. Even if he could find the balls to walk out on her, he couldn't leave her alone at this time of night. In this part of town.

God, it was like a furnace in here. Despite having the AC wall unit on high, Garrett knew it must be hotter in here than outside. The sheet riding low on his hips was too much. Damn modesty. The room was too dark to see anything; if she didn't like seeing his naked body, she could turn away. Garrett whipped off the coarse cotton material at the same moment the bathroom door opened.

"You don't have to go," Garrett said to the shadowed figure.

"Yes, I do."

She always made sure the light was off. Her silhouette showed a tall woman, thin. Too thin. Even by L.A. standards. She was gaining weight — slowly. Garrett could attest to that. He knew it was a struggle. One she fought every day.

Garrett felt the anger drain from his body — his heart melt. Her demands were not capricious whims. They weren't her attempt to gain the upper hand. Her goal was not to manipulate. She had her reasons. They were real. Legitimate.

"It's still early."

Garrett kept his voice low and even. Shouting didn't help. She never fought back. Retreat. That was her coping mechanism. The last time he blew up it was two weeks before she would take his calls.

"I…" she cleared her voice. "His flight gets in at midnight."

"Don't be there."

"You know how he gets."

Garrett knew all right. She was devoted to a man who treated her like crap, forgot her existence ninety percent of the time, yet expected her to be there when he decided to come home. His fists clenched the mattress. It was the only thing preventing him from grabbing her, begging her to stay. *For once, pick me.*

"I don't know when I can see you again."

I don't know if I ever want to see you again. Garrett thought the words. He would never verbalize them. She was his drug of choice. Weeks passed. The need for her grew. Outwardly, his life looked smooth as glass. Inside, the itch grew.

Garrett became an expert at compartmentalizing. His work never suffered. His family never suspected. No one had the slightest clue about what was raging inside of him. *She* knew. Because she shared his unbreakable habit. Enablers. That's what they were. It was sick. Sometimes, like tonight, he hated himself. He wished he could hate her. Then, maybe, he could walk away.

"I'll be out of town for the next month."

Garrett wished he could see her face. Was she sorry he'd be gone? Relieved? Would she miss him half as much as he was going to miss her?

"Take care."

Garrett waited a second, letting the motel room door close behind her. Jumping up, rushing to the window, he pulled back the thin, dingy curtain. He never walked her to the taxi. Even the minutest chance of them being seen was too much.

The ritual of watching until she was safely inside the vehicle, seat belt on, doors locked, was something he never ignored. Nothing bad would happen to her when he was around. It was when he wasn't there that trouble found her. One more frustration. It wasn't his place to protect her. Knowing that drove him crazy.

Garrett grabbed his jeans from a nearby chair, pulling them on. Unlike her, he wouldn't clean up before he left. He would carry the smell of her with him — let it fill the interior of his car. Tomorrow he would pretend it was still there.

Damn it. Enough. He deserved more than this. They both did. One month. When he got back, one way or another, things were going to change.

DREAMING WITH MY EYES WIDE OPEN
(Hollywood Legends Book Two)

PROLOGUE

NATE LANDIS NEVER thought much about the way he looked.

Women seemed to like his face. That was genetics. He was the son of Hollywood royalty. Alone, they turned heads. Together, they dazzled. It made sense that they would pass some of that on.

Nate took it in stride. He was strong. Healthy. His body was trained to do what he wanted it to do, under what could only be called extreme situations. He ate right, worked hard, and played harder.

At some point, his lifestyle would catch up with him. Age would take care of that. Right now, he was in his prime. If he wanted to scale a mountain, that's what he did. Jump from a plane? A piece of cake. Race car driving. Deep sea diving. You name it; Nate was the first one in line.

When he was three years old, his mother called him her little daredevil. Fearless, she swore he gave her wrinkles for worrying what he would get into next. Nate would always laugh, peering closely at Callie Flynn's flawless complexion. What wrinkles? In her fifties, she was, and would always be, one of the movie industry's great beauties. Nothing he or his brothers did could alter that.

As Nate stepped to the edge of the cliff, he didn't think about the two-hundred-foot drop. He'd jumped from higher than this. It was what he did. And he did it better than anyone else. For some reason, today he thought about his mother.

Callie never discouraged him from pursuing danger, even though Nate knew she wished he had chosen a safer way to make a living. She didn't say so, but he knew she worried about his safety. It didn't stop him — he seldom thought about it. Until today. As he waited for the director to signal the camera was rolling, for the first time Nate let himself worry about his mother's reaction if something happened to him.

He shook off the morbid thought. Now wasn't the time. He needed to focus. Ninety-nine percent of the time, if something went wrong, it was due to a loss of focus. Nate took a deep breath. He cleared his mind. Three flashes of light. That was his signal. He squared his shoulders, coiled his body. And jumped.

Nate Landis was a stuntman. Some might say it was his calling. If a director needed it done big and done right, that person called him. Nate loved his job.

He let his body relax as he sailed through the air. The count in his head was precise. If he pulled the ripcord too soon, the shot would be ruined. Too late, he risked ending up a pile of broken bones.

Nate planned every stunt. He worked out the timing, the logistics, and the angles. He never let anyone perform a stunt unless he tested it. Over and over again. He refused to rush. Anxious directors. Bottom-line producers. Some tried to push him into cutting corners.

Few things made Nate lose his temper. His brother Garrett claimed Nate had the longest, slowest burning fuse in history. But he had his hot buttons. Endangering himself and his crew was one of them. Last year, a director, trying to save time, ran a stunt when Nate was away from the set. Poorly conceived and executed, two stuntmen went to the hospital with second-degree burns.

Todd Winesap went to the hospital with a broken jaw and a tarnished reputation.

It took a lot to make Nate mad. But watch out when it happened.

Nate ran the count through his head. Eight, nine, ten. He gave the cord a firm, steady pull. Smooth as glass, the chute opened. Even so, he traveled at a high speed. The parachute was safety measure number one. Number two was the large, air-filled target waiting below.

Having done this stunt hundreds of times, Nate knew what to expect and how it should feel. And he knew when something was wrong.

The air bag, that Nate had personally supervised the placement of, wasn't where it was supposed to be. He didn't have the time to wonder how that had happened. If he didn't act fast, he wouldn't be around to beat the shit out of the asshole responsible.

Grabbing the guide strings, Nate pulled a hard right with all his considerable strength — and prayed.

DREAMING OF YOUR LOVE
(Hollywood Legends Book Three

PROLOGUE

LIGHTS FLASHED FROM every direction. It blinded and dazzled all at once.

Screams drowned out every other sound. This was Los Angeles. Busy streets in every direction. Jet patterns overhead. The excited—in some cases rabid—fans that surrounded the roped-off red carpet made it seem like nothing existed but them and the bright lights.

It shouldn't have been a pleasant experience. Alighting from the over-the-top luxury of a Rolls Royce into chaos and mayhem? No normal human being would willingly seek out such an experience.

However, Colton Landis was not a normal human being. He was an actor.

Colt turned his world-famous megawatt smile on the crowd, eliciting another deafening burst of heartfelt screams.

"We need to get inside, Colt. The movie starts in ten minutes."

"Relax, Deb."

Colt's publicist had been with him for five years. Deb Kline knew how to spin a press release like nobody else. They saw eye to eye on most things. Except how much he should expose himself to his fans. If she had her way, he would zip from point A to point B as quickly as humanly possible.

In this case, point A was the limo, and point B was Grauman's Chinese Theater.

"I'll relax when you are safely inside. Have you forgotten Dallas already?"

"Dallas was an anomaly."

Colt continued to wave and smile. Deb wanted him to curb his accessibility. She had always been cautious, but after a fan somehow breached security during a press conference to announce his next movie, she was particularly leery of events like this one.

"Colt."

"Don't go over there, Colt."

Deb knew the second Colt observed the waving autograph books, her words fell on deaf ears. He believed in giving his fans what they wanted. It was one of the things that made Colton Landis a huge movie star. He genuinely loved his fans. He loved meeting them, speaking with them, having his picture taken with them. Most of her clients searched for any reason to avoid these moments. Not Colt. He didn't have a public persona and a private one. What you saw was what you got—twenty-four hours a day, seven days a week.

Colt made her job as a publicist a dream. Keeping him safe was a nightmare.

He refused to have a bodyguard. Part of it was ego—and he had plenty of that. Many of his parts portrayed him as a big, macho, tough guy. How would it look if he had a bigger, more macho, tough guy constantly shadowing him? Not great for his reputation. He would look weak. And in Hollywood, perception was everything.

It was a valid argument. Not so valid? Colt believed that, for the most part, his fans were harmless. Not that he was a naïve Pollyanna. There was no need for Deb to point out the entertainment world's tragic examples of the heinous acts obsessive fans could commit.

Colt lived the life. He grew up watching his superstar mother traverse that fine line between making herself accessible to fans and maintaining some much-needed privacy.

However, he didn't have a family to consider. No wife. No children. His life was his own. A bodyguard would mean he was giving in. Turning his life over to fear instead of embracing every single moment of his fairytale existence.

"Ten minutes."

Deb didn't know if Colt heard her over the screams. Nor did she care. She was getting him into that theater if it meant grabbing his ear and dragging him along like an errant five-year-old. And wouldn't that make a great picture in *People* magazine? Okay. No ears. *Ugh. This man was going to make her old before her time.*

Colt held a woman's phone at arm's length, including himself in a selfie of her and her three friends.

"I love you, Colton."

Colt couldn't single out the speaker. The cry came from every direction. He waved and called out, "I love you, too."

He signed a few more autographs, moving along the line. Deb was right. He needed to get inside. It wasn't fair to keep everyone waiting. Ten more, he promised himself. It killed him to see the expressions on the faces of the fans who were left out.

"Thanks. See you soon," Colt called out to the crowd.

Handing her signed book to a dreamy-eyed woman, Colt gave the crowd a final wave.

"Ready?" Deb tried to maintain the *stern teacher* expression she had spent twenty years cultivating.

Colt had a way of making her professional mask slip. Thank goodness she was old enough to be his youngish grandmother. While his charm was undeniable, her age and experience allowed her to put the sexual pull that radiated around him into perspective.

Until he turned his smile on her. Full blast.

"Am I that big of a pain in the ass?"

There it was. That naughty twinkle in his deep blue eyes that made the world swoon. On screen, it was irresistible. Paired with dark hair and a tall, muscular frame, was it any wonder the camera loved him?

Reluctantly, Deb returned his smile.

Colt was her client. He was also her friend. She knew he wasn't trying to be difficult. He was being himself. For a man who was adored by millions, catered to on a daily basis, and could buy and sell two or three third-world nations without raising a sweat, Colton

294

Landis was surprisingly down to Earth. And hard-headed. And opinionated.

On top of that? On occasions such as this one, a major pain in the ass.

Still, if she were honest, there wasn't a single thing about him that she would change. As movie stars went—hell, as human beings went—Colton Landis was a joy to be around. Not that she would ever tell him that. The last thing he needed was another person extolling his endless virtues. Colt hated that kind of treatment. One of the reasons they worked so well together was because Deb didn't kowtow.

Deb was about to hit him with one of the nifty sarcastic one-liners he loved, when a scream came from the crowd. Not a *we love you* cry, but one of terror. Before she could react, Deb saw a man jump over the velvet rope. He carried a knife.

Colt pushed her to the side, effectively putting himself between her and the attacker. *He isn't after me*, Deb wanted to protest. But everything happened so fast, she didn't have time.

In the blink of an eye, the man raised the knife and stabbed Colt.

IF I LOVED YOU
(Harper Falls Book One

PROLOGUE

IT WAS SOMETHING out of a fairy tale.

Thousands of flickering lights dazzled her senses, almost as much as the tall, wickedly handsome man who so expertly danced her onto the shadowed balcony. The music that filtered from the nearby ballroom only added to the already magical atmosphere.

Women dreamed their whole lives of a moment like this — a prelude to a happily-ever-after ending. Ever so briefly, she let herself drift into that fantasy as if she was one of those women. For a moment, she let herself pretend that her childhood had been filled with the kind of whimsicality that allowed those fantasies to carry over into adulthood.

But no, she wasn't a romantic, hopeless or otherwise. She didn't want a prince to sweep her into his arms and carry her away on his faithful steed. She was more than capable of rescuing herself. She preferred it that way.

The stars were in the sky, not in her eyes.

"I'm glad you asked me to dance," her partner whispered, pulling her closer.

Suddenly, she was nervous. The champagne she downed earlier had completely worn off. No more floating on a cloud of false courage. If she was going to do this, she was going to have to do it on her own.

"Jack," she said. Damn, it was hard to sound seductive when your voice squeaked. "Jack." That was better, lower, and slightly husky. She'd read somewhere that guys liked husky voices.

"Rose."

"Yes?"

"Nothing, I just thought we were saying each other's names." He put his lips next to her ear. "I like the way you say mine."

"Jack." Good Lord, she had to stop repeating his name. "I need a favor, Jack. A big one." Or should she say, she hoped he *had* a big one. Rose groaned to herself. At least she hadn't said that aloud.

"I'll help if I can."

"You're the only one who *can* help." She took another deep breath. "I need you to take me home and screw my brains out."

www.ingramcontent.com/pod-product-compliance
Lightning Source LLC
Chambersburg PA
CBHW070830250626
47159CB00003B/720